EX-WIVES

Sandra Howard

WINDSOR
PARAGON

First published 2012
by Simon & Schuster UK Ltd
This Large Print edition published 2013
by AudioGO Ltd
by arrangement with
Simon & Schuster Ltd

Hardcover   ISBN: 978 1 4713 2795 7
Softcover   ISBN: 978 1 4713 2796 4

British Library Cataloguing in Publication Data available

Printed and bound in Great Britain by
MPG Books Group Limited

In memory of my sister, Carma.

ACKNOWLEDGEMENTS

Huge thanks to James Davenport and João-Paulo Ferreira for their colourful and extremely knowledgeable help with all matters South American; to Clare Woolfenden for her generous guidance and insights into the finer points of the advertising profession, and thank you, as well, to Maurice Saatchi for suggesting my reading on the subject.

I am enormously indebted to Richard Quest and Jimmy Mulville for giving of their precious time, inviting me 'back screen' and initiating me into the world of television—it was a treat—and to John Sullivan for his help in this and many other ways. My heartfelt thanks, too, to William Weston for his immensely expert suggestions over twentieth-century paintings; his gallery in Albemarle Street W1 is a delight to visit. Thanks equally to Geoffrey Boot for his highly qualified thoughts on flying hazards and single-engine planes, to Judge Nigel Van der Bijl for his wise guidance on the difficult and sensitive business of detecting illegal substances in transit; to Steve Delabecque for his specialist help in the areas of surveillance and policing, and John Wolfe for his invaluable medical expertise. Any mistakes are entirely my own.

I borrowed from a crack-cocaine trial in Sir Ivan Lawrence's excellent book, *My Life of Crime*, and I lifted the flavour of one or two passages in Mark Johnson's vibrant account of his recovery from the blackest depths of drug addiction. His book, *Wasted,* is a punchy, moving read.

Finally, I can never say enough thanks to the team at Simon & Schuster, above all my inspirational editor, Suzanne Baboneau, who steers me gently from the wilder shores; to my indomitable agent, Michael Sissons, always such a steadying hand, and to Michael, Sholto, Nick and Larissa, my loving, long-suffering family, who put up with constant questions and come up with all the answers.

Quatrain

What is this day with two suns in the sky?
Day unlike other days,
With a great voice giving it to the planet,
'Here it is, enamoured beings, your day!'

Jalal-ud-din Rumi, Persian, 1207–73

Part I

Part I

CHAPTER 1

Kate Nichols had no religious conviction. She wished she did. To have the comfort of a profound binding faith, belief in the afterlife, the soul and God's will would lift away some of the weight. Doubts were dark and unsettling, a walk on life's shadier side of the street.

She remembered a sunlit walk in Hyde Park, sitting on a bench for a moment and feeling the deliciously sensual heat of a strong spring sun. A young mother and small boy had stopped in front of her; the boy seemed to have something wrong with his shoe.

The girl had squatted down beside him and told him to put his sole on her knee.

'Do trainers have souls as well then, Mummy?' He looked at her quizzically while she fiddled with the Velcro strap.

'God is in everything,' she answered, stifling a small yawn. His faith was being formed very early, Kate had decided. She wondered if he'd ever come to feel doubt.

Would certainty give strength? Would it be healing to imagine Harry's soul, the very essence and heart of him, free of his drowned body, clear of that shattered, submerged plane and soaring? Didn't there have to be something more?

'God rest his soul,' people said, which, when you thought about it, suggested the spirit buried with the body, marrow for the bleached dry bones. Kate let out a thin, tight sigh in her seat beside the freshly lit sitting-room fire. Harry had drowned and

3

that was that. He was dead and gone.

'Katie, love, you must buck up a bit. It really is time.'

She swung round to face her mother, Rachel, who was spread out on the sofa, writing Christmas thank you letters on her lap. She rested her pen and had that inevitable look on her face, a sort of caring, exasperated warmth, patience-wearing-thin anxiety that Kate could do without.

'Can't you ease up on me, Mum, and stop acting like a nervous nurse on a psychiatric ward? And who says I'm not "bucking up"?'

It was a morning lull on Boxing Day, perfect thinking time—and a blessed moment of peace since they were staying with her sister, Sadie, who had three children under five. Sadie was feeding the baby, her other two were being remarkably quiet. Rupert, her husband, was outside in the crisp Hampshire air, clearing any leaves that had dared to stray onto his groomed front gravel. Sadie's family was absorbed.

The sweet soothing loneliness of her London flat suddenly seemed very beguiling and Kate fought an impulse to cut and run, go home a day early. She sighed again, more pointedly, imagining the fuss they'd make, the heavy pressure to stay, and had to meet her mother's eyes.

They were stunning, piercingly blue, those eyes, they would have stopped a lion in its tracks, turned back the seas; no one could escape their gaze. Rachel always knew what was going on in her daughter's head, she was uncannily clued-in.

Her look was sympathetic, though, must-stick-it-out support. 'I know it's hard, darling, not to think and brood, Christmas is that sort of time. The

4

anguish of last year was inexpressible, but it is almost fourteen months now and you can't go on like this, barricading the world out like a recluse.'

Kate refrained from saying she didn't particularly see why not and contented herself with an unresponsive stare.

'It's one thing being sweet with the children—and with Ru,' her mother added, with a twitch round the lips. They both thought Sadie's husband was a bit of a prat. 'But all this clinging to grief is indulgent and it's not fair to Sadie. She has such a full load, us staying, all the non-stop meals, Ru's parents yesterday as well . . .'

'Don't be boring, Mum. You do most of the cooking anyway.'

'It's not only the meals. Rupert is a demanding man as you well know, and just think of not being able to hand back those three little darlings—she's up to her eyes . . .'

Rachel tailed off with a pale, apologetic smile. It was a sensitive area. 'Well, I've said my piece. Better finish these wretched letters. But, Katie darling,' she eyed her daughter. 'You're thirty-three and beautiful, which no mother should say; couldn't you just make a bit more of an effort and start going out now? See a few films and have friends round?' It was rhetorical, no answer needed, and Rachel had already picked up her pen.

Kate stared at her mother's bent head and mentally took a step backwards. There could have been a baby. She and Harry had just begun trying for one after two years with no ties. Two years of paradise, travelling, picture viewing, free as the air they'd flown in—Harry had been an art dealer and had his own plane. An experienced pilot,

5

knowledgeable, passionate about art, his enthusiasms had been irrepressible and irresistible. He'd been on the trail of a painting that fateful day last November, an unrecorded gem and a rare find. The owner lived on the island of Alderney and Harry had taken off in high excitement in his little Piper single-engine plane.

No one could understand. Even her mother who couldn't be closer, like a second skin, whose awareness was as acute as a bat's hearing, even she hadn't truly absorbed it. Kate didn't need compassion, her grief was natural and normal. It was guilt she clung to with the tenacity of a guard dog and she had no intention of letting go. She needed it, intense, harrowing, gut-crushing, suffocating. People tried to reason with her, her sister, mother, father, pleading and begging her to think sanely, but Kate felt sane enough, quite rational. And if she chose to feed and nurture her guilt, plump it up like a fatted goose, then that was her decision.

Harry had begged her to come with him on the trip to Alderney. Did an advertising pitch come before that? Where was her spontaneity? Others could have stood in. She should have been beside him in that plane and she hadn't gone, it was as starkly simple as that. And now she had to live out her life in that knowledge, the overpowering ever-present feeling that she had no right to be alive.

Harry had piled on the pressure. 'It's an undiscovered Lowry, Katie, closeted away in Alderney! A private owner, an elderly woman who says her father met Lowry at a Manchester Academy meeting just after the war and bought the painting then. I feel really sorry for her. She was

6

widowed almost as soon as they'd retired there, apparently, and then the recession did for her savings so she's had a struggle. She needs to sell.

'You must come, darling!' Harry's eyes behind his glasses had shone with persuasive enthusiasm. 'Don't be dutiful, we'll be knee-deep in Pampers before long. Your agency lot will understand. They'll manage without you—but I won't!'

The hand through the thick, unruly hair, the endearing frown lines . . . Oh, shit, shit, she couldn't squeeze out another tear. 'Cry Me a River'—she had cried an ocean and still failed to drown.

Her mother sealed an envelope carefully and looked up. 'Ben will be here any minute and I know he's going to ask you to come to a party with us. Don't put up a wall. I really would like you to go along with it, this once. Mark Simpson's giving it, the television presenter, but it's a private party at his house, nothing too threatening or tedious . . .'

Rachel was distracted by a kerfuffle on the other side of the door, a small body pushing against it with a steady chorus of staccato wails. The door yielded all of a sudden to reveal two-year-old Amelia, in thick pink tights and a duckling-strewn smock, hugging a doll, struggling to keep her balance and so taken aback she quite forgot to cry.

Only for a moment. Making an ascending wail like an aeroplane taking off and bumping the doll along behind her by its arm, she stumbled over Sadie's chic rugs and stripped boards to fling herself at her grandmother.

'Joseph's pulled out all her hair, Nana. I hate him,' Amelia wailed, holding the doll aloft for inspection. It did have some sizable patches of baldness, Kate could see.

'I'm sure we can stick it back, love, don't fret. We just need to find the tufts and some glue.' Rachel set aside her writing kit and gathered up Amelia's pudgy little hand. She gave Kate a wry, weary glance as if to say, 'Who's the lucky one then?' and went with her granddaughter to the door.

Kate hugged her moment of privacy, although Amelia had looked so edible and huggable that she longed to be scrunching her up instead, drinking in the Comfort-washed, Marmite-toast smell of her and kissing that hot, teary little face.

She could well imagine the kind of party her mother had been pressing about. It would be splashy and brash, whether in a private house or not, full of people in love with their own images, especially Mark Simpson, the host. And Ben must have asked if he could bring her, which, in her present belligerent mood, made Kate squirm.

Ben was well liked, well connected, he and Rachel had a huge bunch of friends and were asked to every first night, party and charity do going. They went to very few of them. Their relationship was unusually strong, even intense, and Kate knew how much they loved to be on their own. They were going to this party, though, and she felt the weight of persuasion bearing down. Nothing for it, she would have to go too.

Kate's parents had been divorced for six years. Rachel was in her fifties, still turning heads with her slender good looks and arresting eyes; she had a fierce intelligence. Men had been chasing ever since the break-up, but she'd looked at no one until Ben. He had been newly a widower. Only a few months previously his wife had died of a lingering brain tumour.

From the first moment Kate was aware of him, the very dawn of the involvement, the relationship had seemed to gallop away like a racehorse loose on the Downs. A year on, Rachel still had a lightness of step and gave private, whimsical little smiles; she was in love with Ben not in any skittish, kittenish way, she cared deeply.

He was coming for lunch, expected in minutes, and Kate couldn't miss her mother's high, the blaze of energy and compressed anticipation—after only a few days apart over Christmas. Her wool dress was carefully chosen too, the hazy deep-mauve colour of distant hills that emphasized her slim figure and fairness. She and Sadie were the blondes of the family, Kate had her father's dark hair.

Rachel glowed in Ben's company, but she was hiding tension. No one else would have noticed, but Kate understood her so well and couldn't help connecting it with Ben. She hadn't got his measure. He was impressive. She liked him, a lot; liked his thickset frame that had a natural grace, his warm eyes and the dark, greying hair like her father's. And it said something too that, even with the whisper of disquiet she felt, a disconcerting sense of something out of kilter, she could still relax in his company and enjoy his quick wit. Ben was everything her brother-in-law, Rupert, was not.

It was so hard to make out. Kate felt a slow burn of concern that she knew wasn't just out of loyalty to her father. At times her mother seemed almost scared. Asking a mild question about Ben's import business once, her reply had been obliquely guarded, more like a government minister than someone brimming over with a new love.

Ben had been a brigadier in the army and

9

resigned over issues with Iraq. It had caused quite a media stir. Kate had asked about the financial leg-up he'd had, starting afresh in a new business career. She'd been curious about his backer, Spencer Morgan, an influential, larger-than-life billionaire, and had simply queried whether Morgan interfered or gave Ben free rein. Why had her mother needed to be evasive about that?

It had made Kate more watchful. She'd seen Rachel give nervous starts when the phone went, glances to see Ben's reaction; sometimes when they were out in the street together, her mother gave backward looks. She often clicked off hurriedly from calls, and coming into the room just before Christmas, Kate had heard her mutter, 'Katie's here.' Rachel had quickly supplanted the strained, troubled look on her face with a smile and gone on to talk smoothly about the presents she'd chosen for Rupert's parents. She'd wanted to make clear that she had no intention of saying more. But why not? They'd always shared confidences. Kate had felt free to talk about anything that came up, silly fears, secret prejudices, deviant sex, nothing had ever felt taboo. As a teenager she'd told her mother all about losing her virginity.

She sighed. It was easy to be warm about Ben, yet Rachel must sense her thimble-full of reserve; it was like being slightly dishonest over a new dress, impossible to hide what she really felt from someone quite so close.

She ought to be helping with lunch. Kate rose slowly and saw through the window that Rupert was still outside, well wrapped up in a waxy Barbour jacket and Burberry-check scarf and rather aimlessly inspecting a pair of shiny new pruning loppers. She happened to catch Ben's car turning in at the gate and watched as Rupert carefully balanced the loppers on a stone ball statue to be ready to help unload. His pink face shone with pleasure and pride, standing in front of the glossy-white front door of his fine commuter-belt house.

It was on the edge of a manicured village near Basingstoke: early Victorian, stuccoed, and painted buttermilk yellow. The redbrick garden wall was rather stern and tall, although it had a softer face in summer when a scampering Albertine rose was in riotous flower. Sadie had a horse that she stabled with a neighbouring farmer. She loved riding. Perhaps the horse was her release and chance to fly.

Kate didn't dislike Rupert. He was puffed-up and pedantic, yet a hard-working banker nevertheless—in mergers and acquisitions, working for a solid Canadian bank. He was just yawningly boring, a conformist, an assiduous socializer, a man to make your eyelids droop. Sadie, to her sister's surprise, seemed contentedly slotted into the mould.

Everyone came into the hall to say hello to Ben, he was fresh blood, an excitement. He wore a broad encompassing smile as he and Rupert came in with a rush of cold air. Setting down a couple of clinking carriers, Ben gave Sadie's cheek a kiss. 'Hi, all, this is quite a welcome party! And Katie's here, too! It's great to see you.'

Rachel had come up beside him and he put his arm round her. 'Hello, darling, such stunning daughters,' he said, giving her a kiss and a squeeze. 'What a trio you are.'

His arm was possessive and protective and

11

Rachel was leaning into the hug. His mature masculine good looks and a tangible sense of their love caused Kate to feel snagging splinters of jealousy as well as concern. She felt hollow, overcome with a gouging ache of need and yearning—for lost intimacies, closeness and physicality.

'Come along, all, let's go on through,' Rupert said bossily, making a move. 'I'm sure Ben's ready for a drink—time for some Boxing Day fizz.'

'You must have these,' Ben said, reaching into a carrier. 'They're still cold.'

He pressed two handsome bottles of champagne into Rupert's uncomplaining hands, glancing towards the kitchen as he did to where a tray of glasses was ready on the table. Ben went in to collect it, carrying it into the sitting room, more host than guest. He had an air of firm authority, a patriarch, an officer with his troops. There was nothing in his manner to give the slightest clue to Kate's mystifying little qualms.

*   *   *

Sadie set down an enormous Le Creuset dish on a laminated table mat, one of a set whose racehorses seemed improbably proportioned. She looked frazzled, her pretty, bobbed fair hair clinging damply. 'It's only beef casserole, not turkey at least,' she confessed, with a coyly confident smile. It was out of the freezer, but one of Sadie's specials; Rachel was off the cooking hook.

There was nothing coy about Rupert as he poured red wine with a wine-waiter's flourish. 'I think you'll find this quite soft and pleasant,' he remarked in his bufferish way. 'It's an Australian Cabernet Franc.' His boyish face had a pink sheen after its morning outdoors and was looking just a little bit plumper, post Christmas.

Kate sipped the wine and thought it on the sharp side, although Ben made all the right good-guest noises. 'Mmmm. Interesting, excellent—may I look at the bottle?'

She caught his eye. She wanted to bring things round to his business, but was keen to pitch it just right. 'Can you shut up shop over Christmas, Ben,' she asked lightly, 'or is it difficult with an import company? I mean with things like bananas, say, that can't be frozen. It must be easier if it's coffee or Brazil nuts.' Kate knew he imported food products from South America. 'I'm very clueless about it all,' she added with a little covering laugh, anxious not to seem over-inquisitive.

'I can certainly take a proper break,' he said with a smile. 'Actually our most hectic time is in the run-up to Christmas, and the December demand for our big seller, acai, went satisfyingly through the roof this year.'

'Gosh, I've never heard of acai,' Rupert chipped in. 'What is it?'

'It's the berries of the acai palm, which is unique to the Amazonian basin. They're a gorgeous deep-magenta colour and easily transported; we ship it in as a frozen pulp. You'll find it in health drinks like smoothies and even in hair products now,' Ben said. 'Acai is one of these so-called superfoods, high-fibre, a powerful antioxidant, packed with vitamins, immensely good for you.'

'Unlike certain other exports from that part of the world then,' Sadie said, with a laugh.

13

Watching Ben, very tuned in, Kate thought she saw a shadow come into his face. It was only a butterfly flutter and not really a furtive or guilty look. Still worrying, though, and she suspected he'd seen her noticing it.

'Sadie was into all that scene, back in our youth,' she said, 'doing stuff in the clubs of Rye. She was the wilful one, this wonderful earth mother who's so happily settled—Ru's done a good taming job!'

'Should I be hearing all this?' Rachel said tritely and uncharacteristically. Her eyes had flitted to Ben with a quick, troubled, quizzical look as well. It was also a look of connection that had the comfort of intimacy, and Kate felt confused, mistrustful of her own judgement. She had an unhappy sense of being deliberately excluded.

The rest of lunch was rather hurried along. The baby, Rose, started yelling and Amelia had a fit of loud attention-demanding tears.

Aside from Sadie who had the baby to feed, everyone opted for a walk. Rupert bundled up four-year-old Joseph and Amelia as if for Siberia and they set off at a slow pace, their breath steaming in the frosty air.

Kate turned back early to give Sadie a hand. She stood beside her sister at the sink, drying pans and bowls emerging out of murky soapy water, gazing out of the kitchen window and feeling no need to talk. The sun was low, the pale light fading, a crisp stillness settling on the garden. It would be a wintry scene in the morning, everything covered in Christmas-card glitter, she thought.

She had Ben on her mind, his business, the imports from the Amazon, and a newspaper article suddenly came to her, a piece about cocaine

14

trafficking in Colombia; it just popped in like a clever idea in the night. Her hands felt clammy. Sadie's druggie quip must have prompted it; Kate probably wouldn't have read or remembered the piece, but for the photograph of a remarkably handsome man, and the caption, 'Colombian Defence Minister, charged.' He'd had responsibility for cracking down on corruption and had collaborated with the criminal barons.

It was just an association of ideas. Ben had been out in Colombia in his military career. Rachel had only recently become guarded about Ben, she'd talked proudly about his time in the army, early on. He'd been in the Intelligence Corps and sent to Colombia to train local units about human rights, she'd said, some government assistance scheme. She'd wryly described how the unit being trained hadn't quite seen the point of it all . . .

'Katie, you're miles away! Give me the towel, we're pretty much done here.'

'Sadie, can we talk? I'm a bit worried about Mum. She seems tense. She's keeping it well hidden, but I've sensed it quite strongly in the last few weeks. She zipped right up when I asked the simplest thing about Ben's business the other day, which seemed odd, really unlike her. I mean, just suppose he's into some dodgy deal or other, something not quite a hundred per cent on the level? It's not impossible . . .'

It sounded far-fetched even as she said it. Kate longed to retract her words.

'Are you out of your tiny mind?' Sadie snorted, not mincing hers. 'He was a brigadier, for God's sake, he resigned over Iraq for all sorts of principled reasons; he was a real hero in most

15

circles with that rave press. And the idea of Mum as adoring as a puppy, swept off her feet by a criminal con man! I mean she'd win *University Challenge* single-handed on a bad night, she knows what's what. Let's get real round here.'

Sadie stabbed at a rubber towel-holder with a corner of Kate's tea towel. 'Ben found a bigwig backer, upright as billionaires come, and they started a business. Mum's happy and in love, end of story. Come on, hon, ease up a bit. Isn't it great something's actually going right for a change?'

That wasn't, Kate thought, her sister's most sensitive remark.

Sadie knew it and looked abashed. 'Sorry! Put it down to tiredness. I'm just feeling so *swamped*! My help has only gone and broken her ankle; she's not back till next week and she's hardly going to be much use even then. Think it's okay if I leave the children with her of a night? We've got dinners and things coming up . . .'

She gave an uncertain, cautious smile, suddenly on the defensive, and had such a worn-out set to her shoulders that Kate gave her a spontaneous hug.

'Now who's being neurotic! The girl can hop about and change a nappy, can't she? She's not ill. It'll be fine. Why don't you go and grab a quick kip now, while you have a chance? I'll do them some tea when they're back.'

'Thanks, I am rather dead on my feet.' Sadie smiled. 'Quite a role reversal,' she said, her weary smile widening into a grin, 'you, worrying about Mum's boyfriend—a real sign of the times!'

*   *   *

16

Kate stared at the fading embers in the grate. The fireplace was set a foot or so up the chimney breast, a smart, square opening that she could see would appeal to Rupert's obsessive sense of orderliness. He meticulously cleared out the ash every morning and filled up a chic basket with small neat logs.

The fire needed reviving, but her mind was on Ben. Earlier that evening he'd helped take out the tea-things and stayed in the kitchen, leaning companionably against a worktop while she saw to the tray and decanted the Christmas cake into a tin. They'd chatted, but it had been a one-way conversation, Ben in the driving seat.

That was a couple of hours ago. Kate was alone in the sitting room and still going over everything he'd said, word for word.

He'd talked about Harry in a way that hadn't, at first, jarred. 'It isn't easy, is it, Katie, being around people all day? There's a rather beautiful line in a book I'm reading that just made me think of you. "When wretchedness falls upon us one summer's day like snow, all we wish for is to be forgotten." 'It was describing the views of Thomas Browne who must have known a thing or two about mortality. Doctors in the seventeenth century saw so much death and raging disease. He wrote about the best of men gone without trace, the iniquity of oblivion.'

That had been sensitively put and if only Ben had stopped there. 'After the war,' he continued, watching her steadily, 'servicemen often spoke of feeling shame at having survived. Why them and not me kind of thing, although they obviously knew they had no option but to, well, soldier on!'

That had been more annoying and touched a raw

nerve. Why couldn't people leave her alone? Why couldn't she feel whatever she wanted? 'Which is really by way of saying,' Ben had carried on disarmingly, 'that your mother and I do want you to come to this party with us . . . I hope you will.'

She had stared at him in a non-committal way and said nothing. 'Think of it as a stoic test,' he said, smiling. 'Or perhaps more to the point, how much Harry would have wanted you to lead a full, happy life without him and not simply be "soldiering on". And I know this will sound particularly fanciful, but imagine Harry's own crippling guilt, had he known about yours! He would have felt unbearably upset, twice as badly as you do, don't you see?'

'No,' Kate scowled. 'I don't, you're talking in riddles. I haven't a clue what you mean.'

'Well, Harry pushed very hard for you to go with him that day, as I understand. It was selfish and demanding, typical male behaviour. But think of his wretchedness now, if he knew how much you were suffering and bearing all the blame.' She had kept up her stare, icy and tense, her stomach clenched. 'You were just doing your job, Katie, trying not to let people down.'

Rachel had called to him then, as if on cue, and, with a sheepish shrug of his shoulders, a light look of contrition, Ben had hurried out of the room.

Kate stared at the dying embers in the grate. It hadn't been selfishness, just typical spontaneous enthusiasm, Harry's need for her to share in the excitement. Why hadn't she been irresponsible for once in her life, dropped everything and gone?

She tried to shake off her mood, energetically stoking and blowing at the near-dead fire as if

18

purposeful industry might be a useful distraction, and had just about coaxed out a feeble flicker when Rupert came in.

'I've been dispatched to see how you're doing, Katie,' he said cheerily, despite giving the weak flame his baleful eye. 'How about a nice little G and T? I'm having one.'

Squatting back on her heels she beamed her warmest smile. 'Thanks, Ru, but I promised Joseph a story when he's all tucked up. Love a drink later.'

Joseph was scrubbed and in striped pyjamas, but far from tucked-up. He was roaring round his room with its navy-elephant frieze being a vroom-vrooming aeroplane with his arms outstretched. Kate caught him and tickled him until he begged her to stop. Sadie wasn't there to complain it was getting him over-excited.

Kate read him a Doctor Seuss story, one of her own old childhood books. She'd kept them all, shelves of them in the house near Rye where her father, Aidan, still lived—where he was wretchedly battling it out with cancer.

She was leaving for Rye next morning to be with him, although not staying over New Year's Eve. He hadn't wanted her there, seeing the new year in with him, when it was certain to be his last. Kate felt desperate about it, but grateful too. He had Hannah, who was his nurse and more, and the emotional strain would have been hard to bear.

The party her mother and Ben were pushing for was on New Year's Eve. It left her no out, Kate knew she had to go. Mark Simpson, giving the party, was a television newscaster and she imagined it full of self-important celebrities who certainly had no interest in her. Nor she in them. Her father

19

would understand that and privately sympathise, but he'd also press her to go; he would talk about climbing aboard life's zippy old merry-go-round again and having another ride.

Joseph was fidgeting. Kate held the book so he could see the pages. He knew the story and its speedy, catchy rhythm always drew him in.

"'Then NEW troubles came! From *above*! And *below*! A Skritz at my neck! And a Skrink at my toe—'"

'What's a Skritz, what's a Skrink, Auntie Kate?'

'Well . . . fuzzy little troubles—'

'They're not fuzzy. This one's got wings like flies and this one's like a blue lizard.'

He was young to be into lizards, surely. It must be the holidays in the Algarve. He was fixing her with eager, inquisitive blue eyes, a shade lighter, but definitely his grandmother's. Kate hoped he would have some of Aidan's genes as well. Her father had always looked beyond accepted horizons and led an untrammelled life. As a small child, waving him off to distant trouble spots, Kate had pictured him as the good cowboy, riding out under a fiery sun to do down evil men.

He'd been an explorer in his youth, a television war reporter with all the horrors and dangers of that job, continued to work overseas and more recently turned to writing. Tears were close, but she switched back to Joseph with a smile. 'You're quite right, they're not fuzzy at all; I was the fuzzy one. Now we'd better be quick and finish the story or Mummy will be in for goodnight kisses and telling us off.'

His eyes were heavy by the last page. Rupert came in and stood looking down fondly, Sadie too.

Kate left them and went on down. Ben was in the hall near the front door, half turned away, head lowered, talking into his mobile. It was obviously a very private call. He seemed alert to the possibility of interruptions, lifting his head, looking round at times, and saw her on the stairs. He gave a smile, acknowledging her, then faced away again, muttering and concentrating on the phone. He'd snapped it off by the time Kate reached the bottom of the stairs.

Rachel was cooking supper. A tempting smell of baking cheese was coming from the kitchen, ham and leeks au gratin. 'Hardly up to the minute,' she said, as Kate came in. 'I should throw away all my old cookbooks and start again.'

'You're an ace cook, Mum,' Kate replied vaguely, wondering about Ben's call.

It had probably been business, something tricky that had cropped up. On Boxing Day evening? When he'd said at lunch he could take a proper break? God, she thought angrily, it could be a relative with emotional problems, a chat with one of his adult sons. She should loosen up, listen to Sadie and just be glad that their mother loved him and something was going right for a change.

CHAPTER 2

Kate left for Rye the next morning. She was impatient to be off but tried not to show it, hugging everyone goodbye. It was over two hours' drive and she was having lunch on the way with a friend, Donna Blane, who lived on Romney Marsh, just up

21

the coast from Rye. It was a good chance to see her.

Donna lived alone, buried in the remote patchwork of windswept fields that made up the Marsh, but she had her animals: Labradors, Jacob sheep, a donkey, two tabby feral Marsh cats, peacocks, hens and a parrot. They would see off any marauders. She was a singular woman; original, difficult, loyal and, above all, a uniquely talented artist. Kate seldom saw her, but knew she could always turn to her in any crisis.

Donna painted the low-lying marshlands with such evocative genius you could almost smell the salt-spray gusting in from the shingled coastline, feel whipped by the wind flailing the tall reeds. Flat fields dotted with sheep, silent dark dykes, eight-hundred-year-old churches, her pictures lived and breathed the lonely beauty of that rich earth wilderness. They uniquely captured the sense of an enchanted isolated place, free from the hub and rub of everyday life, solitary and compelling.

It was windy on the motorways and on Romney Marsh; as Kate negotiated the maze of lanes winding across the desolate landscape, the wind had the force of a battering ram. It practically whirled the Fiat off into the fields. Kate felt emotionally exhilarated by its winter rage, although the bitter cold was reaching into her bones. She had the heater on max, was wearing a fleece, thick tights under her jeans, yet her fingers were still white and numb. They often were—something Harry had never understood.

Donna had been Harry's friend. He'd met her through a local art-world contact and immediately seen her quality. They'd had a great rapport, but she wouldn't be talked into having an exhibition, nor would she part with any paintings.

'I will have a show one day, Harry,' she said. 'And I do want to give you a painting, too—you know the one—just as long as you keep coming to see me. You lift my spirits up higher than the Marsh skies.'

Kate stopped the car abruptly. Fourteen months and it could still crumple her like a blast of machine-gun fire. The memories were branded, still lividly in focus. She could see the ashen-faced policeman at the door of her flat, clear as the fields outside the car. See him stepping into her small hall with his eyes full of compassion.

'I'm afraid I have very bad news. There's been an accident . . .'

He sat stiffly on a ladder-back chair in the sitting room, delivering his fatal message. 'The weather closing in with such speed . . . Exceptionally strong turbulence, gale-force crosswinds . . . Always a difficult approach . . .' She had begun to shiver uncontrollably and a blanket was found. She remembered him holding out a mug of sweet tea while she sat in a traumatised state.

Her mother had arrived and fired torturing questions in a voice of steel. What about Air Traffic Control? Why hadn't they turned Harry back to Biggin Hill? Was the weather really to blame or was it engine failure? The Piper PA 28 was a single-engine plane. He had 400 hours' flying experience, private aircraft flew into Alderney regularly. Kate could still see every pained line on that poor policeman's face as Rachel demanded answers with an unsparing, determined look in her eyes.

The Air Accident Investigation Branch would produce a comprehensive report, he assured her

23

wretchedly. He had talked of legalities, the need for Kate to identify the body. Harry's fished-out bloated remains, she had thought with cold clarity, cocooned in her silent trance. She was beyond emotion.

The tears came three days later, a savage shattering attack that had sent her hurtling like a tiny craft displaced by a great whale. People had been with her constantly, and feeling desperate to be alone she'd slipped the collar of their minding, crept out of her flat like an adulterer and into the car. It was a capsule of privacy, the wheels going wherever they chose, and it was where her internal sea wall had finally crumbled and all the pent-up agony was released. Kate had howled like a starving wolf in the snow, cries of raw grief that became steadily more hysterical. The tears were blinding; she couldn't see to drive and the car had been swerving dangerously, weaving about like a stumbling drunk in the road.

A police car had flagged her down and steered it into the kerb. How had they got her home? Those hours were a complete blank. Waking up in a drugged state and in her nightclothes she could remember nothing of them.

*　　　*　　　*

Donna was outside opening the gate to a large gravel yard, the animals alerting her to Kate's arrival. The house, beyond another gate, set back in a softly structured garden, was substantial, part seventeenth century with an imposing Dutch-looking coving that curved up handsomely clear of the roof. It would have been a wool-trader's house,

24

Donna said. Romney Marsh was sheep country and much of the trade in those days had been with Holland.

'I thought we'd have lunch outside,' she said, as they went indoors.

'It's December, for Christ's sake! You're not serious?'

'Yes, I am, you wait and see. It'll be fine.'

Kate followed her to the kitchen, chilled to the marrow from the drive, and discovered Donna meant it. Glass doors led out to an exotically planted patio that was far from a brochure conservatory. One side was entirely open to the garden and she could see the table was already laid.

The patio had a glass roof, a heater and proved to be a wind-free haven, an oasis of pale trapped sun. They had home-baked bread, hot soup and local sausages, and life soon returned to Kate's bloodless fingers. The peacocks were totally tame, coming up close for company then lying at full stretch out on the lawn with their majestic tails spread behind.

'What a privilege,' Kate sighed, gazing out, stroking the fat tabby cat on her knee. She felt released, nothing was expected of her, she could speak or stay silent as she chose. Donna was the sort of woman who would never take away the pills or the pistol. No one dictated to her and she lived by her own rules.

'So what's up?' Donna asked. 'Just Harry and worry about your father?'

'That, yes, but it's actually more Ben, if I'm honest. He's so much on my mind.'

'You don't like him? He's not right for your mother?'

'No, it's not that. The opposite really, I'm almost too impressed with him, worrying he's too good to be true. Like that scene in the Woody Allen film when the woman turns back at the altar, just because the guy is too perfect by half! But I do have a weird sense of some kind of undercurrent swirling around, Donna. Mum seems secretly on edge and I hate not knowing what's going on.'

'You can't be in on everything. She might have good reason not to involve you.'

'If she's not too bloody love-struck to see straight,' Kate snapped, taking out her frustration on a friend.

Donna let it drop and talked about her brother, who lived in Madrid with his Spanish wife, and who'd just been over for Christmas without her. 'She couldn't miss the parties,' Donna laughed. 'Talk about opposites. John's a dry, brainy old stick, yet he's happy as Larry in the tailspin of her social whirl.'

The sun had gone down, the chill air stealthily invading and staking a claim. 'Any new paintings?' Kate asked, nervous of seeing them. She was passionate about Donna's art, but it brought Harry too close. The screw never stopped turning, there were no potions or plasters to stem a bleeding heart.

Donna's studio was cold, north-facing and chaotic. Encrusted easels, paint tubes spewing through table slats, jars choked with brushes, canvases crazily stacked.

An unfinished painting on the easel was of thunderclouds, dark as a nun's habit, hanging low over a churning sea. It was a powerful depiction of doom, Kate decided, ignoring the hinted-at

26

sunlight, the needle-thin arrows of brilliant light, and seeing her own lonely agony in the blackness with a juddering shock of recognition.

'Time I was off to Rye,' she said.

Donna handed over a bubble-wrapped painting she had ready by the door. 'This is yours now,' she said, with a shrug.

Kate could see what it was through the wrapping and couldn't summon up any proper thanks or enthusiasm. The painting had been for Harry. It was unwanted baggage, painful to have at home, and they stared at each other, both well aware of the problem.

Walking with her to the car, Donna gave another shrug. 'Give it away, stamp on it, do what you like—I just don't want it here any more reminding me I never gave it in time.' She grinned suddenly, which lightened her weathered, high-boned face like flooding sun; she looked instantly more beautiful. 'Come and see me again,' she said, 'whenever you need.'

Her honey-coloured hair was fading, drawn back with tortoiseshell combs. Was she in her fifties, sixties? Kate felt a sense of connection and she wondered about Donna's past. She never spoke about emotional upheavals or partings, but she must have suffered some great sadness. She seemed to understand intimately the parameters of loss.

*　　　*　　　*

Kate drove away with the painting on the back seat, there in the driving-mirror and challenging her, as if daring her to reject it like a hurt, angry lover. It was one Harry had particularly loved, hauntingly

27

seductive with a vastness of sky and a boy running wild in the wilderness, shirt tails flying. It had a feeling of delirious abandon; Harry had called it 'the release of a soul'.

The road to Rye wound through more flat, deserted stretches of marshland where the dark shapes of smugglers must have once loomed in the mists. Night was falling and in the gloomy isolation Kate had an eerie sense of history brought near.

Reaching Rye's lit streets she saw the cafes and dives where she and Sadie had danced—Sadie trying ecstasy and coke, she sticking to tame puffs on a spliff. She carried on down the well-known lanes with a crescent of silvery moon directing her eye like a pen-torch to the familiar old haunts and hideouts of a country childhood; the frogspawn brook for tadpole-collecting, the copse where they had signed their names in pricked-finger blood and formed secret societies.

Rachel had her work cut out, looking after the two of them single-handed while their father was away for long stretches. She'd fitted in a job, though, translating German and French books, novels mainly, into English. She was trilingual; her parents had left her in a Swiss boarding school while they managed two hotels in the mountains. Skiers in winter, walkers in summer, it was non-stop. They'd had no time for their lonely only daughter.

Kate remembered seeing her father on the news, the relief of his returns, haggard, travel-worn, shaking with exhaustion, but his face with a big wide grin on it. His hair had been thick and dark in those days, he'd had a strong jaw, a fast-growing beard; she could still remember its stubbly feel,

28

rough as a cheese grater, at times, when he gave her a goodnight kiss.

When he was home and he and Rachel stayed in London overnight, Mrs Brooks would move in. She was a substantial woman; floorboards groaned, sofas sank low, but her meringues floated off the plate and she had a similarly soft-centred heart.

Mrs Brooks was widowed now, living in a terraced pebble-dash cottage by the sea, whiskery, stained, old and childless. Kate went to call on her as often as she could and thought she seemed a happier woman, lighter-spirited since Mr Brooks's demise, lighter in every way.

Her husband, Sidney, had been an evil little man. Kate's hatred of him was cemented in, it could never be erased. He had cupped her thirteen-year-old's breasts one murky, dark evening, pushing her into the shadows of a deserted alley and pinning her to a cold, rough wall with the weight of his body while he fumbled with his flies.

His greedy, fat, pale fingers working her hand, mouth hanging slackly, his wheezing through his nobbly, hairy nose, and the smell of him; it had been like stale pee and mouse droppings. His swollen pink cock, his pressing weight, the muttered threats, 'Go on, go on, or yer fucking head gets bashed to the wall . . .'

Kate had squirmed, struggled, tried to resist, but only with the spurt of stickiness had she managed to wriggle free. She'd raced to street-lit safety, gasping, too scared to scream and finally reached the sanctuary of the library where she was supposed to have been waiting for her mother to come and collect her.

The librarian was preoccupied, helping a woman

on crutches. Kate had studied a row of toddlers' pop-up books, keeping her back turned; she'd felt shivery and bruised all over, her skin crawling with a sense of recoil. The feeling of uncleanness and urge to scrub her hands raw had been acute. She'd told no one about it, thinking of Mrs Brooks; it had just seemed better that way.

Twenty years on nothing had faded. At the time however Kate had overcome it well, simply shut it out and slotted Sidney Brooks into a box labelled disgust and derision.

Mrs Brooks had deserved more than that vile little runt making disgusting demands—insensible to her needs, she felt sure. He was pint-sized and the thought of him balanced on top of his wife like the upper round of a cottage loaf . . . Had Mrs Brooks gritted her teeth and thought of tea and chips, sunny days on Camber Sands? Poor woman.

*　　*　　*

Kate parked in front of her father's garage and lifted out her bag. Her anticipation was high, yet her chest was tight. Aidan was frailer every time she came, wasting away; she dreaded seeing fresh decline, his life painfully accelerating to its untimely end. The doctors gave him three or four months. He was only sixty, but calm and brave. Kate fought the lump in her throat.

Returning home always brought back a whole package of childhood memories and emotions. She looked up at the old house feeling fierce affection. It was a converted pair of nineteenth-century cottages, weatherboard and brick, settled and at ease with itself. The garden, as far as she could tell

30

in the dark, was still in good shape, looked after by Aidan's kind-hearted neighbours. They cut the grass for him and planted vegetables that Hannah, who lived in, cooked to healthy perfection.

Kate turned her key and went in. Hannah was in the hall, waiting. 'He's been impatient to see you,' she said in a low voice, 'but I think he might be having a little sleep . . .'

Kate nodded. The words wouldn't come, her heart was thudding, straining to get out. She turned the handle cautiously and opened the sitting-room door.

He was in his favourite old armchair—looking lost in it, like a skinny-necked boy in the wrong collar-size. A mahogany standard lamp beside him was pooling light onto his bald patch. He'd always been so strong and active with his fine dark hair, thick eyebrows and striding gait; Kate remembered her childhood awe at the way people used to stare after him, recognizing him from television, she realized later. Now he was a shadow, a whisper of his former self.

The mahogany lamp with its parchment shade was an old friend. Years ago, before the divorce and after a run of teenage parties, the sitting room had had a makeover with gutsy, new, tweedy loose covers fitted and a smart ottoman introduced. Now the fabrics were frayed with age and the room looked more its old self again.

Aidan's Jack Russell terrier, Millie, was in her basket at his feet, rumbling with ascending speed like an approaching tube train. She shot across the room, a bullet on short little legs, yapping hysterically before grudgingly, quivering with suspicion, accepting that Kate was family and to be

31

spared.

'Hi, Dad.' He was blinking, coming round from the rude awakening.

'Katie, darling, you're here! Come and give me a kiss.' He stood up and held out his arms, but there was so little of him to hug. She had to turn away to hide a prickle of tears.

'Pull up that chair,' he said, 'and let's hear all. Hannah will bring us some tea—or do you want a drink? It is six . . .'

'Tea's what I need. You are coping, Dad, you and Hannah? I do wish you'd try this new Sutent. Can't you even do it for us?' It was a kidney cancer drug that might buy him a few more weeks, but he was being typically stubborn, suspicious of side effects, sticking out his firm jaw and digging in. He decided, he called the shots.

Hannah brought in a tray with tea and home-baked scones, setting it down on the sofa table and leaving without a word. She was soft-footed about the house, a slight, pale auburn-haired woman in her forties, always unobtrusive, almost subservient in a way; Kate wondered if she'd ever been harshly treated or had lived in fear.

Hannah was in love with Aidan, that was obvious, but she gave no other clues; it was impossible to know what went on inside. She could deflect questions with skill. She was Yorkshire-born and had trained as a nurse in London, but Kate had discovered little else. She'd tried quizzing her father about Hannah many times, but he resolutely pulled down a blackout blind. He hadn't, for whatever reason, wanted her going there.

Aidan's own emotional feelings were opaque. Kate remembered his original upbeat call about

32

Hannah's arrival; he'd described her as a pleasant, competent woman who would be living in as a sort of housekeeper. 'She's fine about being here alone when I'm away, Katie. And Millie's come round to her, can you believe? Hallelujah to that!'

Passing the Millie test would have been the clincher, Kate thought. She was a monstrous little dog; the postmen had insisted on the letterbox being moved to the garden gate.

The teapot was under a crocheted tea cosy that she could remember Aidan bringing back from the Balkans. She went to the sofa table and poured two cups. Hannah had arrived before his cancer was diagnosed and the fact that she was a nurse had later seemed almost divinely ordained. If only her skills had not been needed, but they were invaluable now.

'Have a scone, Dad,' she said. 'It's a while yet till supper.' However much he ate, though, never seemed to make any difference.

'No thanks.' He rested a hand on Kate's arm as she brought over his tea. 'You managed Christmas okay, with everyone constantly around? I can vividly recall being in Bosnia with a camera crew always with me when all I wanted was to be alone. God, it was a wretched hell; picking our way through the burned, ransacked remains of villages, bodies everywhere . . .' He seemed to relive it all for a moment, but then snapped back with an abrupt change of mood. 'Rupert was on his best witty form, I take it? Sharp as a chef's blade as usual?'

'He's not that bad, Dad, don't be too hard on him. But he was rather into his new Christmas gardening tools . . .'

'And how was Mum?' Kate detected a small

tremor in his voice. It was a routine question, but her father needed to ask it, to talk about her; his tension was palpable and she felt taken aback, concerned to have picked it up.

'Fine, Dad, she was nagging about going to parties—which I could do without!'

Kate suspected he wanted to ask more, even about Ben, but couldn't trust himself. Her parents' break-up had come as a wretched surprise. Their relationship had seemed close and positive, no hint of boredom or sourness, no heavy atmosphere. She and Sadie had been in their twenties at the time and the sadness and shock of the divorce had left them reeling; as nonplussed and shaken as a wife discovering an affair. How could they not have known?

Seeing her father's newly laid-bare emotion, Kate felt bemused all over again. The break-up had happened just as she was starting a new job in advertising, and, preoccupied and busy, she'd simply accepted her parents' platitudes, the veil they'd cast over what had gone wrong. Now, though, with her mother seeming almost fearful at times, and closing other doors as well, Kate felt actively worried. She wanted at least to try and make sense of the split.

It was unfair to press Aidan and intrude, but when she thought of the finite time left she needed to know what lay behind it all. 'Dad,' she said, 'I feel guilty as sin, springing this on you, but what really happened with you and Mum? I don't believe you just ran out of steam, which is all she ever says; you're not those sorts of people.'

He stared at her so long and unseeingly that Kate felt ashamed. She had no business stirring up

34

still waters like a child poking around with a stick. The past was the past, old sores and better not re-infected. 'Sorry, Dad, forget I spoke. It's none of my business.'

'No, it's okay. And you're right, it wasn't exactly like that . . . but I take all the blame.'

'Isn't any break-up always a bit of a two-way thing?'

'Maybe so . . .' Aidan took a sip of tea then raised himself in his chair, more parentally authoritative. 'Look, love, if Mum hasn't talked about it, then that's as it should be.' He hesitated. 'Isn't it?' His eyes were heavy with strain and illness; he wanted Kate's support.

'You have a say, too,' she urged. 'It's only up to Mum as far as her side goes.' She felt out of her depth all the same, and could see that her probing was causing him pain. However frustrating, she had to cool it. 'Okay, Dad, I've got the message, I'll shut up for now.'

Rachel had never given a hint of any emotional side to the break-up. They'd gossiped about other failed marriages, friends of her parents, people who'd fought it out in the press, written diatribes. Someone had slashed all her husband's suits, another woman had hurled orange paint at a Porsche. At times Kate had tried to find out more of what had happened closer to home, but with singular lack of success.

'Why were you the one to leave, Mum?' she'd once asked. 'Why did Dad stay home?'

'It just seemed best. I could work in the British Library, see London friends . . .'

That had sounded reasonable enough at the time, but thinking about it now, Kate could see how neatly her mother had sidestepped all personal questions. Disingenuousness was unlike her, yet she'd explained away the sad demise of a long marriage with meaningless equivocations. It caused a small surge of pique. She and Sadie had hardly still been in white socks . . .

Feelings of disillusion, even of shipwreck were creeping in. Closeness to her mother meant everything and Kate needed it to be an impregnable structure, not something as flimsy as a Japanese screen. She hated to feel any uncertainty, ambiguity versus truth. Her father was dying . . . So little of life felt on sure ground.

He was looking distant and his keenness to take the blame for the rift was bemusing. Had there been another woman? Was she being very harsh on her mother, jumping to conclusions? Had Rachel simply been covering up for him?

'More questions, Dad!' Kate ventured. 'I know I shouldn't ask, but are you and Hannah very close?'

Not a flicker of readable expression crossed his face. 'I don't know what I'd do without her. She's wonderful, such a good, patient nurse . . . Now, love, why don't you go and see what's happening about supper? Hannah might like us to come quite soon.'

Kate rose stiffly, feeling deeply thwarted. She didn't want elliptical answers and circumventions, just a few facts. She went to the door fighting a sense of derailment.

She looked back with a forced smile and Aidan held her eyes. 'Um, before you go, darling, I do want a quick private talk. Just between us and kept secret.'

'Of course, you know you can trust me.' She went

36

back to the chair beside him.

'I haven't got long now, as we know, and Hannah's going to need somewhere to live. I'm not talking money, I'll take care of that. It's more . . . about her safekeeping. Will you find her a quiet private place, Katie? Better not involve Sadie or Mum.'

'That's the least I can do, Dad; I'll see she's safe and settled. I do understand.' But she didn't. Kate felt no further on. Hannah remained a great enigma, her past life shrouded in obscurity.

*   *   *

On her last evening Kate and her father were alone, having supper. Across the table Aidan was in his own little reverie and she tried to imagine what it must be like for him.

'Dad,' she said, making him jump, 'I'm only half committed to this New Year's Eve party tomorrow night and I'd so much rather be here with you. I really don't want to go.' Her thoughts had been for her father, but silly selfish dread of the party came into it too, all the determined celebrating, everyone kissing on the stroke of twelve . . .

Aidan pushed away his plate of chicken casserole. 'I don't want that, Katie, as you know very well. A New Year's Eve bash may seem like an anathema to you, but you do need to make more of an effort now. Don't bolt the door on the future and deny me my dreams. Let me enjoy imagining the grandchildren I'd love to have known.'

'Well, that's very sensitive, I must say, that really sorts me out . . .' Sarcasm didn't come easy and she felt wretched. How could she give in to such

37

juvenile touchiness? Her own little irks were less than dust motes, pathetic puffs of nothingness beside the crushing finality of his cancer.

Aidan promised he'd be fine. He'd be working on the memoir he was writing, part poetry, mostly about his war experiences, but in no shape yet, he said, for her to read.

Kate clenched her fists under the table. She talked about being back at work and the agency's pitch for an important new account. 'I'm involved in it, Dad, and may have to be in the office this weekend with all the last-minute panics, but I could come on Sunday.'

'I'd love that, but just if it works out. And about the party Mark Simpson's giving tomorrow night, do go with an open mind. The television crowd really aren't that bad.'

Kate tried not to feel irritated. 'Time for bed,' she said with a smile, 'I have my instructions. But I have a small favour to ask first, Dad. There's something I need to show you.'

She went out to the car for Donna's painting and returned, tearing off the chilled bubble wrap before propping the picture up against one of the kitchen chairs.

He studied it, leaning back for more perspective, and she could see him surrendering to its insistent joy. 'What a rare talent Donna has,' he said. 'It has such force. It's a glorious shout for freedom and it makes me feel there really is a God up there after all.'

'Can you give it houseroom, Dad? It was meant for Harry and I don't want it at home.'

He looked at her impatiently. 'Katie, that picture is a New Master. Put it on your wall, sell something

38

if you're out of space. You're clinging to all those pictures from the gallery, why is this one any different?'

'It's just very poignant. Donna loved Harry too. *She* understands; she didn't want it either.'

'That's all the more reason to accept it with pride.'

'I don't want it at home, Dad.'

'I'll have it here if you insist, while I'm still around, but I hope you change your mind. And don't go giving it to Sadie and Rupert; he's only into horse prints and it would be a crime.' Kate smiled, aware that he'd avoided bringing Rachel into it.

She felt less tetchy and tense now, despite being lectured, calmer all round. She locked up, turned out the lights and they went upstairs to bed.

Even emotionally spent and her mind suffering from overload, she slept deeply and without dreams. The love she felt for her father sustained and carried her far.

Next morning he came outside with her to say goodbye. They had a stroll in the garden and he pointed up to a high branch in the large oak tree. 'See the tawny owl?' Kate could just make out its small distinctive form, hunched and still. 'I've spotted another one, too. Fingers crossed for a little tawny owl family in the spring.'

Kate drove back to London crossing more than her fingers and praying that her father would live to see that day.

CHAPTER 3

'We'll come and pick you up, love—be silly to take two cars. Say, around nine?'

'Fine, Mum, any time,' Kate muttered, resenting being denied the independence of her own car. She paced the sitting room with the phone, feeling thwarted and peeved.

'We won't stay long, just to see in the New Year,' Rachel said apologetically, hardly failing to pick up the tensions vibrating the line. 'I can't think what to wear.' She laughed. 'Ben says that off the box Mark Simpson is into shirt tails and stubble, but he hasn't met Mark's wife and I've never seen any pictures of her in the press.'

'Surely you know all these television people from Dad's day,' Kate remarked. 'You were in that world.'

'It was a while ago now,' Rachel replied patiently. 'People move on.'

It had been an unfair dig, Kate thought, since her mother had asked after Aidan before anything else, sounding strained, talking about the new drugs that might give him extra months. Her concern had been deep and genuine, uncluttered with bitterness, whatever the truth of the past.

Kate felt newly obsessed about the past. It seemed completely inaccessible, roped up, tidied away under a tarpaulin. She'd thought of nothing else on the way back from Rye. Closeness to her mother had carried her through a terrible year; it had been a bridge over the chasm. Now, as well, clutching her phone in the darkening room, Kate felt a deep sense of loneliness begin to envelop her, reflective and silver-grey, as pervasive as the gathering dusk outside.

She tried to shake off her mood and make more of an effort. 'How does Ben know Mark Simpson?' she asked in a brighter voice.

'They met at a charity dinner and hit it off,' Rachel said with emphasis, implying that if television newscasters could see Ben's point on a single meeting, then why did Kate seem to be holding back? 'They play tennis too, now,' she added, over-egging it.

But Kate did see Ben's point, which was the odd and frustrating thing about it.

'I'll wear my L.K. Bennett black dress,' she said, feeling more humble, 'and I've had my hair cut for tonight. They squeezed me in even on New Year's Eve! Not much off—when I think of the fuss Harry used to make!' Fatuous remark, she bit her lip.

'It's a good length, just below your shoulders, darling, it suits your face. See you later, then. And . . . try to enjoy the party and have a little fun.'

Some hope of that. Kate wondered about the dress. Was it too short and bare-shouldered— falsely flaunting her wares? But signs of availability didn't come entirely from clothes.

She stayed in the sitting room holding the silent phone, gazing out at the wintry early dark. Her flat in West London was on the first floor and overlooked a communal garden; it was large and light with high ceilings and splendid sash windows. The paintings in the room were magnificent. Kate took strength from them, she felt them in her veins. She loved the Hockney, the William Scott with its crystal clarity, the soothing Ivon Hitchens, the

41

Miró, which she could hardly believe she owned. It had an awesome, arresting precision, a power almost like a religious revelation with the shivers it brought to her spine.

She had an unrecorded oil sketch by Toulouse-Lautrec as well, that Harry had tracked down on the Isle of Man. It was of an English cabaret artiste of the time called Lucy, who he believed had retired there. Harry thought Lautrec might have given her the sketch after seeing her perform.

The gallery, the flat, Harry's plane, everything had been mortgaged up to the hilt. Insurance policies had helped and Kate had her job. She'd sold the plane, the gallery and much of the stock, yet managed to hang on to her favourite paintings. They were vivid and robust, illuminating, sensual, friends and therapists—all she needed to keep her sane. All she had now, without Harry.

*　　　　*　　　　*

Rachel and Ben arrived late, nearer ten than nine. Kate went down as soon as the bell rang to find them waiting on the outside steps. An Arctic wind was funnelling down the street and it had been raining for days; a dank smell of leaf-mould lifting off nearby gardens clung to the very masonry. Rachel gave her a kiss and was so effusively apologetic about their lateness it was hard not to wonder what they'd just been doing.

'Hope I can find this place,' Ben said cheerfully, as they set off in his gun-grey Prius. 'It's near Primrose Hill. I dropped Mark home once and it's such a muddle of streets round there.' He glanced in the mirror. 'You're looking stunning, Katie. Not too cross with us for being late?'

'No, of course not, it'll have hardly got going. We've a long night ahead.' She sensibly kept her thoughts—the less time spent at a garish, loud, pointless party the better—to herself.

They found the Simpsons' house easily. A heavy music beat was thumping out into the street and the house was lit up like a Halloween pumpkin, hard to miss. It looked just pre-war with a white front porch like an American deck and a typically crabby London front garden, overhung and slippery with moss.

The garden was floodlit and Kate felt exposed, walking up the path with a mean wind-driven drizzle spiking her face. The front door was open, she could see the crush in the hall, people at the windows where no curtains were drawn or blinds pulled down. A few smokers were out on the porch, men in black sweaters and girls with goosebump cleavage who leaned on the rail, staring disinterestedly, as she came up the couple of steps with Rachel and Ben. But then they weren't television celebrities.

Mark Simpson was just inside the door, welcoming late arrivals. He was in shirt tails, but there was no sign of any designer stubble. Kate found him curiously sexless, but he did it for millions of viewers, she knew.

'Hey, Ben,' he called out, 'good to see you! And these two beautiful girls, lucky man! Grab some champagne, the bar's just through to the left. The food will be coming up soon, too. Oh, and you haven't met Maureen, my wife,' he said, suddenly remembering the silent woman at his side; he made introducing her seem like an optional afterthought.

Maureen had short greying hair, was wearing no make-up and was in a drab figure-disguising olive dress. She managed a wan smile and Kate wondered if she minded such casual treatment. She was definitely the hen to Mark's peacock, uncompromisingly plain. A little mascara, colour in her bloodless cheeks and a few highlights might have helped. Instead she looked a picture of misery at her own party and Kate felt a bond of sympathy.

She moved on with Rachel and Ben into the body of the crush, suppressing a small self-pitying sigh. A pleasant-faced man holding two glasses of champagne greeted Ben, who responded warmly. 'This is Roger Grieve,' he said, bringing in Rachel and Kate. 'He's given me some excellent financial advice with the business!'

'I'm glad to hear it.' Rachel smiled.

'Very routine stuff, just over his employees' pensions,' Roger answered, being jogged, trying to avoid spillage from the glasses. 'I'm a bit out of my depth here,' he said, with an engaging self-deprecating grin, 'it's more my wife, Maggie's scene. She's a producer, for radio. I'd better get back to her with these drinks. Hope to see you later, perhaps.'

Rachel turned to smile at Ben. 'I remember you saying how well you got on with Roger Grieve,' she said, when he was out of earshot. 'Nice man.' Kate thought so too. He'd seemed genuinely modest and with a look of integrity—if such a look was possible. And with a rather endearing sort of clean-cut formality about him too, slight self-consciousness in his jeans, as though he'd be more at home in a suit than the 'glamour-casual' dress code of the evening. Ben, by contrast, despite his upright bearing and

44

presence, had an easy adaptability that didn't fit Kate's preconceptions of the army top brass. He melded naturally into any group, however disparate their worlds.

She was pleased to have met someone that she and Ben both warmed to; it made her feel more positive about him, even hopeful of a few other likeable people around. Not for long, though. Rachel elbowed her. 'Oh Lord, groan, groan . . . we could do without him!'

A bulky television newsman was pushing towards them, obviously remembering Ben as a resigning brigadier. The man was revoltingly drunk and the film of moisture on his lardy face gave a look of sweating butter. Kate felt he needed to watch it with his health. He started quizzing Ben in a desultory way before his eyes moved lazily onto Rachel.

'And here's my favourite lady, the beautiful Rachel!' he drawled. He leaned towards her to plant a slobbery drunken kiss, stumbled, and splashed whisky all over her silvery silk dress. Kate didn't fancy being next in line and decided it was time to cut loose.

She saw a door further down the hall, opposite the bar, and made her way towards it, wistfully hoping to find some corner to lose herself in or, at worst, a chatting group to tag onto who might not even notice she was there. She thought about Ben. People rated him, she knew. He hadn't slagged off the government when he was in the news, he'd dealt with the press well. He had friends in the media, business, politics, Rachel talked about them at times, and he had his publicity-seeking backer who gave huge parties to which all London's glitterati

45

came.

Kate reached the door and, still thinking about Ben, collided with a man coming out. He held onto her, steadying her, and their eyes met. 'I'm really sorry,' she said, flustered, 'I was in a daze.'

'No, my fault, no question.' He was still holding onto her and his hands were warm on her bare arms. He had interesting eyes—dove-grey, Kate couldn't help noticing before he gave her a shock by bursting out laughing. 'This is very funny. I was just coming to look for you and you fall right into my arms!'

'But I don't understand, you don't know me. You were looking for me?' She felt sure they hadn't met, then wondered perhaps if he did look quite familiar.

'I saw you from the window,' he said, which was no answer and only made her more curious. 'Let's have a drink and find somewhere to sit down—it's a long shot I know, in this scrum, but I feel lucky.'

Kate smiled and they went into the room where she'd been going. She stiffened slightly when he took hold of her hand, although he somehow managed to convey it was all about being ready to nab a place to sit down. She was sure now that she didn't know him; he was probably an actor or something, which would explain it. She wached so little television.

With no waiter or free chairs anywhere, he had to accept defeat. 'I'm not doing very well,' he said, adding confidently then with a grin, 'banking on my luck, though, it's going to come good.' He let go of the hand he'd reached for and picked up her left one instead. 'Married? Divorced? Husband coming on later? We must find a nice quiet corner, there's

46

so much I want to ask.'

'You don't seem to be holding back as it is. And you may not get any answers.'

'Oh, but I must! They're very relevant questions.'

'Relevant to what?' Kate asked gracelessly, ineffectually trying to ease out her hand from his.

'To midnight for one thing,' he said, 'to my chances of a kiss.' Kate felt stumped for a suitably sharp retort. She could see over his shoulder, which gave her mixed feelings, a redhead in a blue-sequinned sheath making a beeline in their direction. 'I'm Richard Marshall,' he said, only to be interrupted, when presumably about to ask Kate her name, by the blue-sheath girl making more headway.

'Richard, Richard,' she came bouncing up to them with a bubbly smile on her face. 'Where've you been all these weeks and out of my life? Obviously some lush, sexy hotspot, you jammy bastard—that's a great tan.'

'Hi Cheryl.' He pecked her cheek. 'It was a hard-graft trip, no fun, I promise. And, well, just right now,' he leaned into Kate's side in an inclusive way, 'we're doing a little negotiating, a tiny scrap of business . . .'

It was friendly enough, more plea than put-down. Cheryl didn't seem to care about not being introduced—which would have presented him with a slight problem—but she did give Kate a rather hard glance. 'Say no more, it'll keep,' she piped. 'Catch you later.' And swivelling on her stilettos, she plunged back into the throng.

'She was very good-natured,' Kate said, 'considering your blatant dishonesty.'

'What was dishonest about it? I told her the

absolute truth.'

'A little business?' She couldn't carry on; a great drama was unfolding right in front of them and her attention was irresistibly drawn.

Two sizeable women, tightly wedged into a small, chocolate leather sofa, had begun swapping insults and obscenities of such ferocious speed, invention and venom that even Kate, in the advertising business, heard a few new words.

One of the women suddenly heaved up out of the sofa, not an easy manoeuvre, and the other immediately followed. They stood eyeballingly close, hurling ever more molten abuse, trembling with fury and looking dangerously about to tear out hair and drive in red talons. The entire room had died to a fascinated hush.

It became mesmerized when the two women suddenly kissed each other dramatically on the mouth. Hefty bejewelled arms were flung free of enveloping garments, well-cushioned bodies pressed ardently close and the couple became a single misshapen mass like a Henry Moore sculpture. It was a monumental embrace.

'They do it all the time,' Richard whispered, grabbing Kate's hand and pulling her down with him onto the sofa. As they sank into it, he said, with grinning satisfaction, 'Told you my luck would change. I just hope they've clocked us, though, and don't sit down again . . .'

Kate felt uncertain how to react. She looked round the room. It was smallish, a study or den, and thinning out fast, people were going to dance or in search of food. Even the passionate women were edging towards the door. Richard was fingering her wedding ring in a rather vague way, not letting go of her hand.

She was relieved when a waiter came in with a tray of drinks, which solved the immediate problem. Releasing her hand, Richard jumped up to wave him over.

'You're a hero,' he said, taking two glasses of champagne. 'I don't suppose you could rustle up any food? Risotto or something, whatever's going . . .' He gave a winning smile and Kate saw him fish out a note that found its way into a pocket in the young waiter's shiny black trousers. Richard was certainly covering all the bases.

He settled back and handed her a glass, brushing at her fingers as he did. 'I'd love to know your name. And this husband of yours . . . is he around? In bed with the flu? Off the scene altogether?'

'I'd rather not answer those questions,' she said mildly, with an apologetic smile. Explaining about Harry felt too sympathy-seeking and revealing.

'Okay, understood, but won't you tell me your name? You came in with Ben Townsend and I know you're not his daughter. Are you a friend of the interesting woman who's always with him these days? She's stunning-looking.'

'She's my mother, Rachel, and I'm Kate Nichols. How do you know Ben?' she asked, feeling intensely curious.

'I don't actually, just a bit about him. And that's only really because I'm interested in his business backer, Spencer Morgan,' Richard went on quickly to explain. His hesitation over knowing anything about Ben seemed odd. 'Morgan fascinates me,' he carried on, picking up on her surprise. 'He turns companies round faster than revolving doors and people flock to invest with him.' Richard left it

49

there, rather abruptly, giving a sort of enough-of-all-that headshake and moving on with a smile. 'So it's Kate, is it? Katie to me, it sounds much friendlier and more you.'

'That's a bit hard on all the friendly Kates around.'

'Ah, but I'm talking about this Kate.' He studied her face. 'You know, of course, you're beautiful, especially your eyes. It's impossible to tell whether they are green or gold. I could spend a lifetime trying to decide.'

She let that pass. 'Your face is familiar,' she countered. 'Are you someone important in television I should know about?

'I'm a lowly television reporter. I make documentaries and do the occasional bit of presenting.' That was sure to be an understatement, Kate felt, and he was a well-known personality whom she should have known. He was smiling, probably tuned into her thoughts, and went on, 'I was a financial journalist for years, which I enjoyed, but it was much less money. I needed to branch out.'

'Are you working on a documentary right now?' she asked, thinking a financial background must explain his interest in Ben's backer.

'Yes, all about cocaine, from source to snort, that sort of thing. I'm just back from South America, actually, filming the early stages, hanging out with cocaine farmers in the Bolivian jungle. They're paid to grow pineapples and bananas, but they carry on trading the coca leaves, which is a nice little earner and lighter to shift. They don't get rich, of course—the big guys screw them, and they have parties in their primitive jungle homes instead of buying a

50

truck or saving for a rainy day.'

The gauche young waiter was back, looking shyly pleased with his success. 'It's Thai chicken and risotto in the bowls,' he said, 'and some afters.' He'd brought walnut bread, slices of apricot tart and bottles of water and claret. Richard took over the tray, saying it was a triumph and he'd go far, and the young man blushed like a girl.

Sharing the warm food and wine Kate felt the die was cast. They were settled in together and she might as well relax. Richard talked about the women street-sellers in La Paz, Bolivia's capital. They wore long *pollera* skirts, he said, round bowler hats and carried impossibly laden panniers on their backs.

Kate enjoyed his company—and the wood-pigeon eyes he kept trained on her—but she soon felt it was time she explained about Harry. It seemed only fair to give Richard the chance to move on and find someone more suitable to kiss.

'You're ravishing, Katie, I can't take my eyes off you,' he said, with a warm grin, giving her just the opening. 'Can I know more about you?'

He was waiting, expectant; she had to say something. Why was she hesitating? She should be telling him about her situation, encouraging him to go, explaining.

Richard cleared away the plates, refilled their glasses and took hold of her hand again. 'So why are you, Katie, here on your own, warding off admiring men?' He was fingering the back of her hand. 'Am I allowed to know?' He looked serious now, not teasing or amused.

'I only came because my mother nagged on,' she said, feeling self-conscious since he'd dropped his

51

smile. 'My husband was killed in a plane crash just over a year ago and I'm always being told I have to make more of an effort and put myself about. But you can't force these things, I'm fine with life as it is. Still, tonight I am being dutiful.'

He touched her face. 'What a terrible thing. You can't have been married very long. Was he on business? Was it a scheduled flight, a private plane? Can you talk about it?'

'He was flying himself, he had his own plane. No one was with him, no one else died. It was work; he was on a trip to the Channel Islands, just coming in to land.'

'Thank God you weren't with him. How did it happen?'

'Bad weather conditions. He was an experienced pilot, it was a sudden freak storm.'

'Not many people have their own plane . . .'

'Flying was a great passion of his—and it was a very small plane, a single-engine Piper. Harry was an art dealer. His parents had died when he was young, he'd inherited a bit of money, and he had an acute eye for paintings. He'd soon set up in a gallery.'

'Were his parents in an accident too?'

'Yes, they were in Greece, staying at a hotel that caught fire. They were amateur archaeologists. They'd recently sold the family business and were away on a dig, enjoying their new-found freedom. Harry and his brother were in their teens and at boarding school. Sorry if I'm putting a bit of a damper on things, bringing all this up. I mean,' Kate eyed him, 'given your declared plans for midnight . . .' She bunched up her lips in a closed-mouth grimace then carried on more seriously, 'I

52

had to explain. But I'm sure you can see now that I'm really not your ideal date for tonight and it's time you moved on. I won't mind at all. You've looked after me wonderfully. It's been fun.'

Kate felt awkward, realizing suddenly that by spelling it out she was actually making it quite hard for him to leave. Richard was grinning again. If he felt cornered he was certainly hiding it well. 'Nice try, but you're not getting rid of me that easily,' he said emphatically. 'I'd sooner settle for adjusting my plans.' He reached for his glass, looking smugly pleased at having put the lid on that particular idea.

She wondered about him, coming to the party on his own apparently, and attaching himself to her. He was older than she was, early forties, possibly, and hard to read. He might have an unravelling relationship, be in a state of flux, in a row with his wife, he could be divorced, anything; he must have some sort of emotional hinterland.

'What an unlucky family,' Richard said reflectively, breaking into her thoughts. 'Your husband was called Harry?'

'Yes, Harry Winfield, which was my married name. I use my own at work and its simpler to keep to that now.'

'Was he young too? How long had you been married?'

'Two years—and yes, he was a bit younger than me,' Kate answered abruptly, wanting him to leave it there.

He seemed to absorb that and he sipped his wine, distracted by some thought of his own. She glanced at him. His face showed his age, yet in a sexily channelled way, with folds either side of his mouth and a pronounced frown line between his

53

brows. His forehead was half covered by a fall of brown hair, and it was a telegenic face, she could see. She imagined he'd have quite a following. Had he been a bit miffed that she hadn't recognized him and been more forthcoming? He hadn't given that impression, though—even after hearing that she'd just had a year of evenings in.

Kate felt flattered and her curiosity was growing. At moments he looked ground down, as though some quite serious nagging anxiety lay hidden behind his grey, intensely luminous eyes. It was a look, she thought, that she'd seen in her father's eyes, only days ago. Was it guilt, remorse, heartache? Some sort of deep emotion anyway.

Richard squeezed her hand suddenly, giving her a slight start. 'Come on, Katie! I'm sure you haven't danced in all these months. Shall we have a turn on the floor?'

She didn't answer. He was attractive, interesting, but it was a party thing, a passing moment. He would have his life, whatever its complications, and she had no wish to be a bit of froth, a television personality's evening doodle. That wasn't, to be honest, the reason for her silence. It was the thought of shuffling round a packed floor, dancing close with his body pressed, making her feel weirdly unsettled. Richard seemed to understand her need for caution, though. He gave another of his warm smiles.

The disco was somewhere at the back of the house, belting out loud rhythmless pop, and he wrinkled his nose. 'Actually, shall we sit this one out? It sounds more for my teenage kids.'

'Tell me about them,' she said, glad of his sensitivity—and the useful intelligence.

54

'Not now, it doesn't feel quite the time, but what about lunch tomorrow? It's kind of a non-day, New Year's Day, and I could bore you with them then.'

'Can I let you know in the morning? I'm not sure what's happening yet.'

'Sure. But I hope we can! Do you have a job? Are you back at work Tuesday?'

'Yes. I'm in advertising.' Kate stared at him feeling muddled-headed, wishing she hadn't postponed a decision on lunch. 'It was because of my job that I wasn't with Harry that day,' she found herself saying. 'We had an important pitch, a big new account, but he had wanted me to come . . .' To her acute embarrassment her eyes filmed over and she fished about in her bag for a tissue, feeling far too emotionally vulnerable for her own good.

Richard rose and stretched out his hands. It was an authoritative gesture, firm and managing. He was used to weeping women, she suspected, recovering and letting him pull her to her feet.

He gave her a quick paternal hug and she felt comforted, grateful for it, guiltily wishing it had lasted longer. Distant strains of Duffy were coming from the disco and he said briskly, 'This one sounds a bit more like it. Let's go and have that dance!'

The disco was a dining room and conservatory by day, he said. It had transmogrified into a silky black tent for the party, with winking stars and criss-crossing laser darts. They stood in the doorway, looking round. Two huge television sets installed in diagonal corners looked like flat-faced bruisers, about to spar in the ring. An entertainment spectacular flickered on their squat electronic faces that cut to the crowds lining the Thames. It was about ten minutes to midnight and then the great

55

firework display would begin. The sound was down on the televisions, but Kate imagined it would be pumped up with the first boom of Big Ben.

Rachel and Ben were just leaving the floor and came over to say hello. Kate thought how glowing her mother looked from her dance. She introduced Richard, feeling an unreasonable twinge of irritation when he immediately fell prey to Rachel's arresting gaze. She had a sophisticated ability to have people eating out of her palm and he was no exception.

'We were just coming to find you, love,' Rachel said. 'We might nip off soon after midnight, but don't feel you need come. There's a fleet of taxis standing by—ask the efficient-looking woman by the door.'

'Cool, Mum, but I expect I'll grab a lift. Don't wait, if I'm not around.'

'I can run you home,' Richard said. 'I have my car and I'm reasonably sober.'

'About the only person here who is,' Ben laughed. 'But we're keeping you from the floor . . .'

They wished each other a Happy New Year and Rachel hugged her goodbye. Her mother's warmth, her special smell, the familiar Guerlain scent, were compelling bonds. They brought back memories; her mother always there for her—through childhood illnesses, exams, boyfriends. Love freely given and nothing sought in return.

Ben had come beside her, ready to leave, and Rachel smiled. 'Speak in the morning if we don't catch up later?'

'Sure, any time.' Kate looked on after them, as they disappeared up the dark hall, feeling confused.

'Anything wrong?' Richard asked, taking her

56

hand and leading her onto the floor.

'No, tiny tensions with my mother, that's all.'

They danced to Nina Simone, 'The Look of Love', constantly interrupted by people greeting Richard on the floor. He seemed well in, well liked. Kate was pleased that he cut short any pauses for chats, smiling, but firm. And glad of his height; she was quite tall, taller than Sadie and her mother, and wearing heels tonight, but he still had the edge. He held her close, his hand lightly pressing on her back and his cheek came to rest on hers. She didn't draw back, his nearness was reassuring and she was enjoying the dance.

With the first boom of the midnight countdown everyone crowded onto the floor. 'Shall we go?' Richard murmured in her ear.

'I'd be grateful,' she said, dreading all the jollity and kissing, feeling jostled by the thronging crush. She couldn't cope and just wanted to be somewhere quiet to think of her father. She ached with love for him. Nothing felt more poignant than to know that he would never see in another New Year, that he might not live to see the spring or the baby tawny owl he hoped for. She prayed he was asleep.

They'd made it out into the hall just as midnight struck. Richard held her hands in the dark hall and leaned to touch lips. 'Here's to a better year,' he said, with smiling eyes. 'The last one wasn't that great for me either.'

Kate didn't ask why. She smiled back at him vaguely. She didn't want to talk about the last year or the one ahead.

He took her in his arms and kissed her passionately. She was completely unprepared. She couldn't think and didn't stop it developing in all its

57

force and urgency, the meeting, searching tongues. She felt overwhelmed. Giving into it came naturally, though, while her mind wasn't functioning, and she let the passion flow, let it burn . . .

Then she broke away and stared at him in shock. He'd given no warning. Why hadn't she resisted? She felt angry with herself for such shameful loss of control and knew she should feel angrier with him.

'Don't be too cross,' he said, brushing over her lips with his fingers. 'I'm sorry. It was wrong of me. You just looked so sad . . .'

He gazed at her intently, smoothing her cheek with the back of his hand, and Kate felt a coil of need that wasn't going to go away. It was too powerful, deep in her gut, making her quiver while she felt ashamed and disloyal.

'It won't happen again,' Richard said. 'I know it's not how you want things.' He gave a little headshake, as though he needed to know that the air was cleared, and that he could confidently assume he was absolved.

'I think perhaps I should make a move,' she said, hearing her own loud heartbeat, feeling knocked off course and at a loss for the right remark. She longed for some quick, apt witticism to consign a passionate kiss to the party long grass. 'But you really needn't take me home. I'm probably in time for Ben's lift, and anyway it's early,' she grinned. 'I wouldn't dream of dragging you away.'

'You can't go yet. We haven't toasted in the New Year and I want to know why you were looking so sad. Were you thinking of Harry? Sorry if I . . .' he left off there, smiling wryly, acknowledging the unfinished sentence. 'And I'm certainly going to

58

take you home!'

'If you're really sure . . .'

'Very. We'll go soon, a quick sip of champagne, a last dance—perfect restraint on the floor . . .'

*   *   *

They said little as he drove her home in his sporty black Mercedes. Kate thought of his remark about his past year not being great. It had been a statement, though, and since she couldn't imagine refusing to have lunch the next day, that was the time to ask questions. She did feel intensely curious. He seemed confident they would be meeting up and the very inevitability of it seemed to loom like an approaching car's headlights, fuzzy in the distance, becoming clearer as they came near.

'I hope we can have lunch,' Richard said, drawing up outside her building.

'I think so, but could you still call?' She wrote out her mobile and house-phone numbers on a scrap of paper. 'We'd need to fix where to meet.'

'Oh, I'd come and pick you up,' he said, giving her his phone number. 'I know where you live now, after all.'

'Yes, true,' Kate answered, thinking how much else he knew about her as well. Apart from knowing that he had teenage children—and that she'd kissed him—she knew nothing at all. Was she about to have lunch with a married man? She wished she was better armed.

CHAPTER 4

Kate despaired of having any sleep at all. Five o'clock in the morning already. The clock was like an unkind photograph, it kept drawing her eye and she felt deeply frustrated and hard done by. After a year of sleepless nights it seemed like a bad habit was returning and she wanted to be looking her best if she was to have lunch with Richard, not a washed-out wreck in the harsh light of day, a baggy-eyed anticlimax.

Richard was constantly in her mind. She had to see him again, married or not, even after a sleepless night with whole rucksacks under her eyes.

It hadn't helped her wakefulness, looking him up online the moment she was home. He'd certainly played himself down; Kate blushed to think how stand-offish she must have seemed, saying coolly that his face was familiar. Apart from his documentaries he'd chaired a series of half-hour financial discussions on television, done a *Panorama* programme on banking; one of his documentaries—on hidden poverty—had won an award. He was a big wheel.

A short biography had described Richard's early days on newspapers, his coups as a financial journalist and transition to television; it mentioned two children and confirmed he was married. Kate had scrolled on, looking for photographs of his wife, but he seemed, oddly, always pictured on his own. She finally found an unclear black and white photograph of 'Mr and Mrs Richard Marshall' arriving at some function. His wife was wearing a handsomely braided flowing shift, her hair was up, making it hard to tell the colour, and she was glancing away. Her face in profile had a slightly fleshy look, not as Kate would have imagined. She sighed. It seemed too much to hope that it was an out of date biography and his wife was off the scene.

One lunch: it would be easier to get over Richard when she was back at work and hectic, Kate told herself. And he might even shed some light on her concerns about Ben. A slim hope, but it would justify seeing him again, knowing now that he was married. She burrowed deeper under the duvet, trying to decide what to wear, until she had a sense of everything blurring and the wings of drowsiness beginning to lift her away.

*   *   *

The persistent ringing was like a dawn reveille. Kate pulled herself out of a deep sleep and reached for the phone. She looked at the clock. Half-past eleven, how could she have slept so late? It must be Richard, which threw her into an instant spin; she felt unsure how to handle it, what to say.

It was her mother calling, which caused every ounce of adrenaline to drain. 'I was asleep, Mum! We were at a party till late, remember?'

'Sorry, darling, I was only checking in to say Happy New Year . . .'

She sounded forlornly anxious, so out of character that Kate felt quite cut up. 'And to you, Mum,' she said, 'and to Ben.' She thought of her father; the room seemed to tip on its side like a trick of the camera, nothing felt in its rightful place, only the lump in her throat. 'Then I think of Dad . . .'

'You mustn't. More than anything he wants your New Year to be happy, surely you can see that? Are you coming for lunch? Possibly even a nip round the sales?' Kate sensed her mother coping with her own emotions, making an effort to sound positive and cheerful. 'Last night wasn't too bad, was it?' she carried on. 'Richard Marshall seemed to be looking after you well.'

'Yes, he was good, a nice man. I'm not sure about lunch, Mum—just have to get my head round the day. I couldn't sleep, but then I really zonked out!'

'Give us a call when you're ready, we won't eat before two.'

Kate returned the phone, annoyed at the silly evasion. She got up and fidgeted about, putting off getting dressed, knowing she was waiting on Richard's call. It was pathetic; she should forget about it, have a bath, get more of a grip.

She shook in some bath essence and sank back in the softened water. It was cradling, relaxing and she gave into indulgent thoughts about Richard, enjoyable things he'd said, the warmth in his teasing eyes. He'd caught her unawares and unnerved her with his kiss, but where was her control? She should never have responded, certainly not as passionately. It had felt genuine and emotional somehow, though, almost as if she were a raft or a live-saving rope, from the way he'd clung. Kate felt bemused.

Her nipples hardened in the scented water; they were perked and firm. She looked down at them feeling pulls of desire. Her body was a sex-free zone, white, sun-starved, thinner for all the wretchedness of the past year. She thought of seeing him again, the kiss progressing, and her hand began to wander, yielding to the shivery pulls.

The phone went. Not her mobile which was almost within reach, but the landline and it was ringing on and on. Kate leapt out of the bath and ran as naked as a streaker, leaving wet footprints on the honeycomb carpet as if it was dew-covered grass.

'God, sorry, I must have woken you,' Richard said, 'We're still on for lunch, I hope. Shall I come about one? I thought I might cook some brunch at home. Any restaurants that are open will be full of putty-faced slobs wallowing in their hangovers—under-staffed as well and stinking of stale garlic.'

Kate laughed. 'They won't want you doing their PR.' She hesitated, but only for a second. 'Come and have a drink here first,' she said. 'I'll make some Buck's Fizz.'

'Thanks, I'd like that.'

Kate decided on skinny jeans and a cream crew-neck sweater. She dressed and put on a little make-up before calling back her mother and saying that she'd just firmed up to have lunch with a friend after all. Playing it close didn't come easy and she bit on her lip, but she didn't want her mother making a meal out of a one-off casual date.

Rachel suggested an early evening movie, which seemed like a good idea; a handy excuse should one be needed, if, for any reason, lunch became strung out.

Calling her father, Kate tried to sound cheerful and find the right note. 'You okay, Dad? I hope you and Hannah had a nice boozy time with a decent bottle of wine . . .'

'You sound lifted, Katie. The party wasn't that bad after all? Tell me about it.'

'Not much to say, Dad. A guy called Richard Marshall looked after me. I quite liked him.'

'He makes good documentaries; I'm impressed with what I've seen of his work. Did he say what his next one's about?'

'Yes, cocaine. He'd just been in South America, the Bolivian jungle.'

She told him a bit about the party, the passionate women, her poor opinion of Mark Simpson, the host. Aidan laughed. 'You're alone amongst millions there, but I do rather agree. Mark's a bit two-dimensional and keen on himself. Thanks for the call, darling.'

He knew better than to ask if she was seeing Richard again. He understood.

It was twenty to one already and Richard was back in her mind. She made a quick call to Sadie, promising to babysit on Thursday night. Rupert's City dinners were big in her sister's life, important to his job and Sadie had been angling for her to stand in, with that moan about the help's broken ankle. Kate felt virtuous; it was a slog out to Basingstoke.

She went into the kitchen to see to the drink. It was a narrow room with sleek pewter units and a granite worktop. She had breakfast most mornings looking out at the communal garden. The champagne was in the fridge. Kate had slipped out of bed at three in the morning, wakeful, worrying whether to suggest the drink, and had put it in then, along with a carton of orange juice.

The carton, she noticed, about to open it, was long past its sell-by date. She remembered a couple

64

of oranges in the fruit bowl and squeezed them, yielding only a very little juice. It would just have to be an alcoholic Bucks Fizz.

The buzzer sounded. Kate froze, she couldn't believe how hard her heart was thudding. She wished she felt more confident and prepared. In the hall she pressed the door-release button and told him to come to the first floor, then stared at herself in the hall mirror, moistening her lips. Madness, feeling this way: it was pointless, it wouldn't do. She could hear Richard sprinting up the main stairs and bent over to give her hair a good toss.

She opened the door, giving an involuntary smile. 'Hi! Come on in.' He looked tired. There were dark weary shadows under his eyes and she wanted to smooth his brow and ease away the lines. He was wearing rust-coloured jeans, a white shirt and a charcoal sweater, no coat.

'You look lovely, Katie, very rested,' he said, coming in.

'Hardly! It was a late night—by my standards at least.' She closed the door behind him. 'Come and sit down and have a drink. Did you go back to the party?' she asked, prompted by his look of tiredness.

'Certainly not! What do you think? I was awake all night, as it happens. I was thinking about you.'

'That's an unusually corny line, coming from a journalist . . .'

'But true.' He grinned and his face shed its exhausted greyness, gaining colour and warmth like a chameleon. She wanted him to kiss her cheek and expected him to, but he kept his distance.

'You go on in and I'll bring the fizz,' she said at the sitting-room door. Going into the kitchen, she

65

turned to see Richard was behind her.

'Let me open that.' He took charge of the champagne 'I wasn't joking, you know. You did keep me awake last night. This is vintage,' he remarked, twisting the cork, waiting while the champagne almost overflowed. 'Far too good for a mix.'

'Have it neat, it would solve my problems, I only had two oranges.' She held up a little glass jug that she'd found in a cupboard, its contents clear to see. 'I could tell you had things on your mind last night, by the way. I refuse to be blamed for keeping you awake!'

'Were you that aware of me then, Katie?'

'Not especially. I'm just stating facts.'

Taking him into the sitting room, Richard stood staring and she enjoyed the look of amazement on his face. 'I should have known, with an art-dealer husband, you'd have a few paintings,' he said, 'but I'm stunned. I mean, is that a Miró? And a Hockney! Some other time maybe, I'd love a run-down on the others, they must have interesting histories. This is a great room too, fabulous space, terrifically bright and lived-in.'

'You mean my untidy desk and all the books,' Kate asked, dwelling on the implications of 'some other time'.

She poured a finger of juice into the glasses and Richard topped them up. 'And the rug with its zigzag geometry,' he said, 'sassy colours.'

He clinked glasses and took a sip. 'This is seriously good champagne. We might have to take it with us, be criminal to waste a single drop.'

'It's from Ben. He gave me a case. And one of the half-bottles for my evenings in.'

'Generous. Shall I tell you one of the things keeping me awake last night? Will you keep an open mind?'

'Depends on what it is,' she said, as they moved over to the sofa.

'It's about Ben actually. I worried what you might have felt when I asked about him.'

'Go on. Should I have been suspicious?' Kate smiled, wondering what was coming.

'I didn't want you getting the wrong idea, thinking I just wanted to pry. I mean, once I'd confessed to an interest in his backer . . .'

'Is that why you came looking for me? To quiz me about Ben and Spencer Morgan?'

'Well, yes, actually.' That hurt. But what had she thought—that he'd seen her through a misted-up window, a reluctant-faced woman in the black coat she'd worn at her husband's funeral, and had an attack of calf love? That she could have caused sparks in his eyes at that filtered distance?

'But when we collided like that,' Richard said, 'I was done for. I couldn't get a handle on it. I forgot all about sniffing around, doing a bit of investigating; I couldn't have given a fuck about Ben Townsend or Spencer Morgan, I wanted nothing more than to be with you—which I know you'll say is another corny line, but it's also one that happens to be true.'

She took him head-on. 'Are you telling me all this because you really want to keep a lead into Ben?'

'Not exactly.' Richard's eyes were soft and, despite her tension, Kate felt a dangerous physical pull. She ached for him to take her hand. 'It's about getting off on the right foot,' he said. 'My need to try and explain that if we ever do talk about him, even if I asked a question or two, you'd know you could shut me up and that it was as unimportant as the brand of toothpaste I use. And I say *ever*, because I'd love to see more of you, Katie. I know you don't want pressure. I understand. I know what I'd have to settle for.'

'How's your drink?' she asked, smiling, feeling adrift in a sea of emotions.

'That's a nicely inscrutable answer. I think it's time we were off to Chelsea! But it is just brunch, I'm afraid, and not in a wonderful, glamorous space like this—certainly no Mirós around.'

Kate picked up the thick winter jacket she'd put ready on a chair and Richard helped her on with it. 'Great coat,' he said. It was the russets and burnt-oranges of a New England fall, a fiery blend. Her instinct had been for brightness in the wake of Harry, to her mother and Sadie's surprise. She'd needed the warmth of colour to defrost the diamonds of ice within.

'I do have a few questions of my own,' she said, sharpening up. 'I mean, what exactly do you want to discover about Ben or his backer? And am I about to have lunch with a married man?' She felt a slight fraud, asking that, and hurried on. 'Apart from the fact that you have teenage children, I don't know a thing about you.'

'Trouble is, I really don't know what I hope to find out. It's only a private hunch of mine, but even by billionaire standards, Spencer Morgan is distinctly opaque. I don't trust him. And as to your second question . . . The answer's no. Well, almost no. My divorce is through next week. I'll be a free man then—although it'll make little difference . . .'

'Now who's being inscrutable?' she said, checking for her keys as they went out.

Richard's black Mercedes convertible was parked right outside and he saw her into the passenger seat. 'Cool machine,' Kate said. 'I didn't really take it in last night.'

'It's a ten-year-old SLK. My wife, ex-wife, kept the Volvo and I had an irresponsible rush of blood, getting this. I went on-line to *Desperate Sellers*, feeling like a real mid-life crisis case!'

'What's your wife's name? Was it all friendly and straightforward?'

'It hasn't been bitter, no fighting, just . . . very complicated. Her name is Eleanor.'

Richard rounded the World's End bend in Chelsea into New King's Road and turned almost immediately down a side street, Thornby Terrace. He parked outside a four-storey Victorian end-of-terrace house with a low stuccoed wall, a small patch of front paving and no porch. The knocker and letterbox on the juniper-green door needed a polish and the paint was slightly cracked. The façade of number 6, Kate felt, was in need of a little TLC.

'It's more cheered up inside,' Richard said, reading her mind. 'I only have the ground and first floor.' He unlocked the door, cursing at a fluffy white cat lazing on the step who took off with a hostile backward scowl. 'Thinks she owns the place, that wretched creature; she pisses in my back garden. We're at war, but she has the piss hand. She belongs to two young gays who live in the upper half—they have a separate entrance up an outside staircase round the back.'

He pushed open his front door and took Kate

69

into a hall that was the brighter and more welcoming for being generously opened up by a large square arch. The walls were freshly painted in a light neutral tone. A rectangular white table just inside the arch and, laid for two, seemed to be multi-purpose, hall, dining and kitchen table combined. The kitchen ran along the front wall with the sink under the window, looking onto the quiet street.

Richard relieved her of the half-empty champagne bottle she was carrying, put it down on the table and helped her out of her coat. 'I was a bit strapped with the divorce,' he said, talking over his shoulder as he hung it in an understairs cupboard, 'but there's just room here for the kids when they want to stay—they do now and then, it's nearer the action than Barnes, where their mother lives. Polly, my daughter, has a habit of bringing a gang of friends, though, which I could do without.' He smiled.

'How old is she?' Kate asked, meeting his eyes.

'Sixteen, and my son, Ed, is eighteen. Polly's the problem; she's wilful, into boys and weed. She thinks I've behaved badly, which hurts. But then I guess I have.'

Kate was impatient to know more, why he was divorcing, what had gone wrong. She looked around, sensing Richard was interested to know her first impressions. The chairs belonging to the glossy white table had bright sienna-orange cushions, and at the far end of the room a squashy, grey leather sofa, facing a large flatscreen television set into the opposite wall, had cushions in similarly strong autumnal tones. She looked back at him. 'I chose my coat well for this room.'

'I like that thought,' he said, pouring the champagne. He handed her a glass. 'Have some of your own booze. We'll move onto wine soon. You settle in while I see to the food.'

She wandered to the far end of the room where a pair of glass doors looked out onto a small, square walled garden, the scene of Richard's battles with the cat. The walls were white-painted brick, trellised and profusely climbed by a glossy evergreen, star jasmine, she thought. In one corner, rising out of a scattering of conventional shrubs, was a banana tree, to her surprise, which seemed to be thriving happily in London's sheltered warmth.

She thought of Harry. He had been out of her mind, displaced, and guilt about it coursed through her veins, overtaking her like a blush. She tried to focus on Harry's features, she couldn't let him fade. She remembered her first sight of him. They'd met quite by chance. She'd gone alone to a Turner exhibition at Tate Britain and been absorbed in one of the classical dream paintings, wondering at its explosion of softness, when a man beside her started speaking. 'Mystical, isn't it?'

She'd assumed he was talking to her and turned. His eyes were still on the painting, but he soon made more direct contact and they'd continued round the exhibition together. His knowledgeable flow and unstoppable enthusiasm had been captivating. Kate was only too glad to accept when he suggested a cup of coffee and, six months later, his offer of marriage.

Richard came to stand beside her. They both gazed out at the garden, rather in the way she and Harry had done at that first meeting; it was a little unnerving. Being in Richard's house was too, hard to believe after her resentful determination not to enjoy that party.

'Come and talk to me while I cook the eggs,' he said.

They went back to the kitchen end of the room, where Kate stood watching while he scrambled the eggs. Then he lifted a dish out of the oven, full of crispy American-style bacon, grilled tomatoes and hash browns. The aroma was potent. 'That looks and smells delicious,' Kate said. 'I'm surprised your wife let go of you.'

They were both hungry and Kate drank wine, which she seldom did at lunchtime. It was a mellow claret and was untying knots, working on her like a massage. 'I'm being a real glutton—where did you find fresh baked bread on New Year's Day?'

'I was up early. I had you on my mind, remember—but the bread's out of the freezer.'

'You've told me a little about Polly, what about your son?'

'Ed's more easy-going. He plays the guitar; he's good, it's his thing, although of course his classical style is hardly in the Segovia league. He has A levels this summer, swotting away for them, poor sod. They're both at day schools in Hammersmith.'

'Does he get his musical talent from you?' Nina Simone was playing. It was a natural choice after their dance, which she was glad about, but it gave no clue to his tastes.

'No, not from me,' Richard answered shortly. 'I had to put that song on . . .' he reached to put his hand over hers, but in a paternal, smiling-about-the-CD, sort of way. It seemed small progress, the way she was feeling. Comforting and protective, her hand felt like a bird in a warm nest, but she wanted something more.

He sat back. 'You know, I so nearly didn't go last night. Funny thing, fate.'

'Why? Not in the partying mood? Was it to do with your feelings about moving out and the divorce?'

'Connected, certainly. It's not easy walking out on your wife and family, not something you do lightly. The guilt doesn't go away.'

She was just going to ask if he wanted to talk about it, what had gone wrong, when the phone rang. It was a discordant splintering sound, breaking into the intimate mood. Richard sighed. 'Has to be family,' he said, 'friends call my mobile. I'd better get it.'

He pushed back his chair and went to the phone, though it was well within reach. He seemed tense; Kate had seen a muscle pulse in his temple. Was 'family' a precautionary euphemism and he anticipated a call from a girl?

'Hi, Poll, what's up?' Richard muttered, with the phone pressed tight to his ear. It was clearly a family call, yet he seemed embarrassed all the same, leaning back against a worktop, looking at Kate regretfully, as if to say they hadn't needed this intrusion and he minded inflicting it. Little he could do about it, though, without appearing secretive, which she thought he was at pains not to be.

He rubbed his eyes while his daughter talked, his face sagging, drawn and grey again. 'No,' he said suddenly, in a tone that meant business. 'You can manage fine without me.'

Kate was surprised by his firmness—his drained look of stress too, and reaction to Polly's problems.

'Did Mum have her lunchtime pills?' Richard

73

demanded. 'Did you see her take them?'

He listened, frowning. 'Try and keep a better eye, Poll. It's important. Put me onto Grandma. I'd better have a word.'

Glancing at Kate, his face softened then he concentrated on his daughter again, who seemed to take issue with that plan. 'All right, all right,' he said impatiently. 'I'll leave Grandma for now. And this fuss about Beth, why should she mind a metronome? You can play CDs, plug up your ears—do something healthy like go for a walk . . .'

Kate could imagine the teenage response to that and Richard smiled in her direction.

'Yeah, yeah, I get the drift, Poll,' he said. He listened a while further then broke in firmly. 'No, you can't, not just now. I'm not alone. I'll call Grandma in a bit, see what I can do. Hang on in there, Poll, it's not that bad.'

He came back to the table. 'Sorry about that. She's bored out of her mind—angling to come here with her friend. Thank God they're back at school this week.'

Kate could still see the strain in his eyes and she rested her hand on his arm, fingering the wool of his sleeve. It was an unconscious gesture and she was only aware of doing it when Richard glanced down. She eased away her hand. 'I couldn't help hearing your side of things. Do go if you think you should, if it would help with any problems. I'd more than understand. I should be off soon anyway.'

'No, don't go yet, and I certainly don't need to; Polly's only trying it on.' He was looking at her with an intense expression, impossible to read, but causing Kate an acute attack of need. Couldn't he lean closer, kiss her, *do* something?

74

'Why did you leave, if that's not being too inquisitive?' she asked calmly. 'Did you have a great bust-up?' The thought of that caused a keen wave of jealousy. Surely he wouldn't have 'drifted apart' any more than her parents had done. It must have been a powerful relationship. 'Did either of you have affairs?' she added, annoyed with herself for continuing to press him but hoping for any lead.

He sighed. 'It's nothing that simple. Eleanor's bipolar—which is a more user-friendly word, but it doesn't make her any less manic or depressive. The problems are the same. Rodent operators still catch rats, refuse collectors still empty dustbins.'

Kate felt slightly shocked by the analogies, but he'd spoken in a matter-of-fact way, not sardonically. 'I don't know much about bipolar,' she confessed, 'except that it can be very serious. I can't imagine living with anyone in a really depressive condition, I can't even bear people round me being the slightest bit down. How did you manage? It must have been extra hard when the children were young.'

'It was doable, just, while I was on the FT, but not when I went into television.'

'Because you were away so much? Did you have to get live-in help?'

'Eleanor's mother moved in.'

'And that had its own set of problems?' Kate imagined the intrusion on intimacy.

'Some.' Richard looked wry. 'It made life possible. I could work, earn money, travel. No, my mother-in-law was the one with problems, she thought the attacks were actually worse with me around. Eleanor hadn't been bipolar as a child; she'd had a bad patch at university, but her mother

75

had never truly seen full-blown manic phases in action. I was naturally held to blame. She considered me the trigger in every case.' He ran his fingers through his hair with an appealing smile.

'What brought you to the point of leaving?' Kate asked.

'My mother-in-law paved the way. It was partly a need to have Eleanor to herself, I suspect, but she was convinced things were better when I was away on trips, out of the house. She even said it might be best if I left altogether, so that Eleanor could concentrate more on her work—she's a professional musician, a lead violinist. I knew my mother-in-law was wrong and it's not like that, but it was my out and I grabbed it, guilty as I feel!'

'But you shouldn't, you have a life to lead . . .'

'If only. Eleanor's mood swings have increased since I left. She's volatile, reckless, wrapped in cotton wool, unable to let in the world. You can't get into her head and reason. The manic phases can make her immensely fired-up and productive: she goes into a frenzy of playing, practising her fiddle till her fingers are raw. But more often the extremes of mood can be a destructive disaster. Ed and Polly have lived with it and know the ropes, except that with things no better since I left, they hold it against me like mad. I'm an ogre to Polly, she thinks all men are monsters and I cap the lot. They're young adults, but I've let them down—Eleanor too, of course.'

'Would you still have feelings for her, I mean, if it wasn't for the illness?' Kate stood up and took plates to a worktop. She didn't dare turn to look at him.

Richard came over; he took the cheese dish from

76

her hands and put it in the fridge. 'Let me make some coffee first,' he said. 'Then I'll answer that question if you want.'

It was good strong coffee. Kate had it black and sipped it slowly, aware of Richard watching her. 'I was twenty-five when we got married,' he said. 'Eleanor was talented, excitable, obsessed with her career. I knew it would be a challenge and that I had a rival in the violin, but she wasn't a depressive in those days and I was young enough to think I'd get a look in. Typical cocksure male, you'd say, but I tried. I was there for her, making everything smooth and good. She never noticed; it was like I was wallpaper. Some men might thrive on that and get a masochistic kick out of it, but I needed more. Look at me, Katie. This is tedious stuff, haven't you had enough?'

'No. You haven't actually answered what I asked.'

'It's a difficult question. Feelings, love; they come in many shapes and sizes. They're really powerful, you can go on loving and hurting, obsessively jealous, living on crumbs or nothing at all, but I'd failed with Eleanor in months. I felt selfishly sorry for myself—and never more so than when she became depressive. It took the innards out of me. Now it's all about sadness and guilt, and a suffocating sense of duty. Divorcing doesn't entirely free me, you see, and the frustration is immense.'

Kate sensed that his instincts were to preserve a façade and he didn't often open up. He must feel she was a safe person to unload on, an uncomplicated neutral friend. The thought brought her low. 'You can't possibly go on shouldering all the responsibility,' she said. 'It isn't all yours any more.'

'It affects my children. Eleanor's life may be at risk. I hope this won't hurt, but losing Harry after so short a time means your memories are unblemished, they're all about love. How can anyone else match that?'

Kate looked at him, bemused; his voice had an edge. 'It's not like that,' she muttered, realizing with an internal shiver, the shock of honesty, that she didn't think of Harry in terms of love. Richard was holding her eyes, expecting her to go on and she explained, 'I feel guilty to be alive, I think of little else. And I'm constantly being told to think of the future, not the past.' She smiled, glad to have found a suitable form of words, a shield for the truth. 'I should be going now,' she said.

'Can I see you again, Katie? It's my birthday on Thursday. Can we have dinner? Will you help me celebrate?'

She had just called Sadie that very morning.'I don't think I can let my sister down. Her husband has a big dinner in the City and I promised to babysit. They have three children under five!' Kate longed to say that any other night would be fine. 'I'd have loved to otherwise . . .'

'Perhaps I could come and keep you company?'

'Feel free to retract that! Sadie, my sister, lives near Basingstoke *and* it's your birthday, after all. How old are you going to be?'

'Twelve years older than you. Not quite old enough to be your father.'

'You don't know how old I am.'

'Yes, I do. Are you putting me off coming?'

'I'd think it amazing of you, beyond any call of

duty. Are you really up for it?'

'I've never wanted to change a nappy more.'

CHAPTER 5

It was a dark, depressing morning. The clouds were like a lid pressing down on the city. Hurrying along Tottenham Court Road from the tube station Kate thought everything looked uniformly cheerless and grey; the office blocks, shops, pavements, the rubbish bags waiting collection, the pale, inscrutable faces of people returning to work. London was in monochrome.

She cut down a rear alley, past depots and back doors where a couple of men were having a breather from loading, leaning against a wall with their smokes.

They watched her progress. 'Want a puff?' one called, cupping his cigarette.

'I'll pass on that,' she tossed back, feeling intensely alive in the grey morning gloom, enjoying Soho's seedy, grimy streets, hugging a sense of elation that felt wickedly high enough to be a crime.

Her agency, Impetus, was smallish, a hundred or so thrusting achievers, yet it had carved a creative niche for itself and was growing fast. Kate loved her job, despite all the buck-passing and balls-ups, bullshitting and back-biting that went on. The quick, witty creativity of the business gave her a buzz. She went in through the revolving, glass entry doors, feeling a warm nugget of anticipation.

The reception had space and a cool allure; black sofas, silver walls and a wide screen that soundlessly rolled out their best ads all day to engage waiting visitors. The pinkly lit ground-floor coffee shop was busy, giving off tantalizing wafts of fresh-brewed coffee that Kate resisted. She touched in and took the stairs to her second-floor office.

Dan, her would-be office suitor, was in early as usual. He was a group account director, one rung above her, and his zone was usefully distant from hers. He waved and blew a kiss as she scurried past, which jarred. Everything about him did. Dan always seemed just off-key and missing the point. He was sure to wing over an email before she'd even logged on, and wander over any minute for a companionable moan about work. He had his frustrations with the creatives right now; they constantly rubbed up the *Dreamer* client the wrong way, who was a real pain, the cause of great agro, and had diverted from the agreed script for the *Maximan Briefs* campaign as well, taking it, as Dan had complained with labouring emphasis, way off brief . . .

Kate thought the *Maximan* script was pretty much rubbish, new direction or not. Dan handled that account, though, and he cared. She regretted making her feelings quite as caustically known. The ads—shot in a luxury hotel in Mauritius—showed a hunky man on a balcony, taking the air in his poncy briefs. It was the casting she minded, the man looked too much the male model; not enough sex appeal, not a mature, interesting character. She was picturing Richard's face, every crevice of it, feeling hopelessly aware of him, almost airborne with butterfly nerves. Surely he'd call soon?

Dan drifted over for his chat. He stood a little distant, like a doctor at the end of a bed, cracking

80

his knuckles and giving off nose-tickling whiffs of pine aftershave. He asked after her Christmas, how she'd managed, and his very solicitousness grated like a clash of steel. She invariably felt a heel about it, though, and found herself agreeing to come for a drink at the pub at the end of the day.

Her inbox was loaded. Kate worked on FMCG, Fast Moving Consumer Goods, principally on a new shampoo called *Karess*. The client, Jack Clark, urgently needed a call. Ad agencies packed up between Christmas and New Year whereas Jack, from the avalanche of emails in her inbox, had been slogging it out in Slough since Boxing Day. It was important to get a meeting in the diary, as the TV ads were scheduled, the scripts ready to present . . .

Kate called him before she did anything else. 'Hi, Jack, good Christmas? We're looking to next Tuesday for the animatics—then you and I can carry on over lunch . . .'

He sounded immensely relieved to make contact. She warmed to Jack, however much he would agonize over every hair on the girl's *Karess*-shampooed head and insist on the hideous puce plastic container being up front in every frame. He would worry if the sales quadrupled overnight, if the commercials broke every record. Kate wondered if he ever relaxed enough even to smile at a pretty girl in the street.

Her mobile rang and for the second day in a row she had to hide her disappointment from her mother. 'You busy?' Rachel asked. 'Sorry to call at work, but I was hoping we can have supper one night this week. I know it can't be Thursday, Sadie's filled me in! You are a saint to be helping her out, but it'll be a long night and I'm glad you'll have company. You did enjoy the lunch with Richard, didn't you?'

'Yes, Mum, as I told you last night. I quite like him and, more to the point, he knows where I'm coming from and is happy not to get involved. I expect he'll drop out of the babysitting, though. I don't think he'd quite bargained on Basingstoke.'

Kate had needed to confess to her mother about having lunch. She'd also called Sadie just to make sure they were okay with the plan for Thursday night and had known it would get back to Rachel. Was Richard really likely to drop out? Probably. She wasn't truly convinced that he was the type to content himself with a platonic relationship; it didn't fit the spec—not if that kiss was anything to go by. He'd given conflicting signals over lunch, though, and she had no idea where she stood.

'Supper would be great, Mum,' Kate said, feeling sudden desolation while trying to sound positive, upbeat and bright. 'You did mean just us? Does Ben have things on? Which night's best for you?'

'How's Friday? Ben has an army dinner. And yes, only us, I'd love a cosy chat.'

'Cool. But let me do the cooking, so you come to me for once.' Unsure what her mother wanted to talk about, Kate felt home ground had advantages. Then she remembered a work problem and had to retract her offer. 'Sorry, Mum, can it be with you? I'll have to stay late on Friday—and probably go in Saturday as well. We're pitching for a new account on Monday and the creatives always come up with the best ideas at the eleventh hour.'

Kate clicked off. Something was up. She and her mother often had supper, although less frequently since Rachel had moved into Ben's large, high-ceilinged flat in Pimlico. Was she about to be told they were getting married? Kate expected that any day. Why then did she feel so full of tense anticipation and on edge? Was it fear of how she'd feel if her expectation was confirmed? Why was she uncertain about Ben? Her clever mother clearly had no doubts.

She checked her phone, no missed call. Richard was going to have to be in touch before Thursday, if only to pull out. Now she had to set to and plough through the day.

*   *   *

The Robin Hood wasn't full. Dan and Kate had a sticky, wobbling table all to themselves, which was a first; the entire agency usually decamped to the Hood. It must have something to do with the excesses of New Year's Eve. The few people up at the bar were looking round like a sparse audience in a theatre, wishing for some reassuring signs of life—or that they hadn't come.

It was seven o'clock in the evening. Kate stared past Dan to the polished-wood pulls, the over-ornamented gilt mirror behind the bar. She felt morose, sunk in a mire of anticlimax. Her rosy earlier elation had entirely drained. She debated, sipping a glass of acid white wine, how soon she could decently leave—ten minutes, fifteen? They'd talked about work, done the easy bit, but she would have to say something, find the energy . . .

'Kate, you're moping. Life has to go on!' Clichés came easily to Dan. 'I want to put a proposition to you,' he said, 'no strings, but it would make my day if you said yes.'

83

She smiled, with effort. 'Tell me more. No promises.'

'It's *Tosca* at Covent Garden in three weeks' time. I've got tickets. Will you come?'

It threw her, not at all what she'd expected. Dan's walnut eyes were earnestly trained on her, his close-cropped hair standing upright with electricity, like a mass of mini antennae.

She was always saying no. It wasn't as if he was a turn-off for others and rated a tosser at the agency; he had his fans. She'd once overheard two PAs discussing him in the toilets, talking loudly through a partition wall. 'Want to know the arsehole I really fancy?'

'Dan Green—hardly *difficile* . . .'

She stared across the table at the object of a PA's heart flutters. 'Thanks, Dan,' she said, with another game smile, 'it's a terrific invitation, but you must take someone more in the market. I'm really not the greatest date, as you know.'

'I live in hope! But don't get me wrong, Kate, this isn't a come-on, I know the scene and all that. I'd just like your company, that's all.'

It was an opera she loved. It would be easier if Richard had called. But he hadn't and, as Dan had said, life had to go on.

'It's wonderfully generous, very glamorous, Covent Garden no less—and as long as you know it's out of the goodness of your heart and I'm not up for a thing, Dan . . .' She couldn't lay it on the line more than that. It still felt a mistake, something she would live to regret; she could imagine her sinking heart on the night.

Her mobile rang and every head in the half-empty pub seemed to turn. The volume was on

84

max, she couldn't bear to miss a call. Not Richard's best effort, where was his sense of timing? Had he called even five minutes earlier she might have resisted accepting a date with Dan.

She cradled the phone tightly. 'Hi!' she said. 'Dreadful reception, I can hardly hear you,' which was a lie. 'Hang on, I'm just going outside.' Bored drinkers watched her every movement as she stumbled over a chair leg and hurried out. 'I was in a pub,' she said breathlessly. 'Better now.'

'Sorry to drag you out. I thought you wouldn't want a call in the working day.'

'Any time's great. I'm glad you've called. Thanks again for lunch. Listen, you mustn't feel stuck with the babysitting, I mean it is Basingstoke! And won't you want to see your children on your birthday? Or go out with friends?'

'It's the first day of term, so I'm taking them to dinner on Saturday. I am keen to see you.'

'How were things at home—you went there after dropping me?'

'Yes, I had to really. Eleanor had locked herself into her room and wouldn't communicate. In the end I left supper outside her door, sent everyone to bed and came home. But let's not talk about any of that. Can we plan Thursday? It might be a bit tricky to call tomorrow. I'm filming all day, you see, up at five, back late—hoping for some action with the border police and sniffer dogs at Dover. A nice little haul of cocaine would fit the bill! I'll come to the agency, shall I, if your sister wants us there early, pick you up straight from work?'

'I hate to bring you into Soho—'

'Don't be silly. We'll talk Thursday if not before. I loved seeing you yesterday.'

He wouldn't call tomorrow, that was clear. Had he been drawing back a bit? Hard to tell—but anyway, where the hell would he be drawing back from?

Kate returned to the pub, apologized fulsomely to Dan and ruthlessly used the call to get away. She'd forgotten all about an aunt and cousin coming up for the sales, she gushed, really had to rush, expected at her mother's . . . It was easy to lie through her teeth to Dan; she'd been doing it for months, thinking up excuses, turning down every one of his offers.

It wasn't so easy to put Richard out of her mind. She thought of him arriving at her flat—impossible to believe it was only yesterday—and how shattered he'd looked at first sight. Inside the flat, though, the lines of exhaustion had melted away; it had been almost as if a soft, potent intimacy existed between them when a look could say so much. But they weren't intimate: not lovers. A kiss on New Year's Eve counted for nothing.

*   *   *

Home with her paintings, her soup and poached eggs, Kate considered her loss of sanity. Richard must have friends, girls he took out, that he brought back to his bedroom at 6 Thornby Terrace, friends at work like Cheryl at the party in her blue sequinned sheath. He was a free man with a bachelor pad, attractive, telegenic, he would have girls after him, no question.

Going to the bathroom upstairs in his house, Kate had looked round. The children seemed to have two narrow front rooms, the main first-floor

86

room divided up. Richard's bedroom was at the back.

She wondered again what he wanted from her. He'd been sensitive and sympathetic, hearing about Harry, she'd appreciated that. Did he just want the company of an attractive female, someone safe, unpushy and presentable who wouldn't over-complicate his life and make demands? Was he anxious not to be tied down, trying to find fill-ins and avoid too many man-hunting females? She'd settle for anything, Kate thought, going into the kitchen with her tray. Sex would make it more difficult, after all.

Who would have imagined that thirty-six hours after meeting him—in quite the wrong state of mind—she would feel hopelessly smitten? The litmus test was the hurt she knew would be coming, inevitably.

What about Harry? How could anyone ever take his place? The guilt would always be there, time wouldn't wear that down.

Richard was twelve years older than she was, mired in problems, with teenage children, still deeply committed to his family. If only Dan was less of a turn-off, or if only she'd met a nice, unexceptional young man at that party, someone suitably adoring who had nothing better to do with his life than to worship at her feet.

CHAPTER 6

Kate had seen the sense of leaving for Basingstoke straight from work, but wished she could be home having a shower. Cleaning up at the office wasn't the same. She was tinkering around in the washroom putting on make-up and inevitably being watched. It was obvious she had a date.

'A new man in your life at last?' Mary queried, coming alongside, smiling at Kate in the mirror. 'Don't tell me Dan has actually won through?' Mary was a copy writer and newly married. Kate liked her, but was annoyed that Dan's painful attentions seemed common knowledge.

'No, hand on heart, not Dan. And no one "in my life" exactly, Mary, just a guy who's keeping me company and being a friend—though I wish he'd be a bit more!'

'So I see . . .'

Kate had only just returned to her desk when Susie on Reception called. 'Richard Marshall for you—lucky sod,' she added, under her breath. 'Says he's fine to wait.'

'I'll be right there.' Kate felt a rush of blood to her cheeks. She shut everything down, assembled her various carriers, remembered the smoked salmon in the office fridge, put on a little more lip gloss and collected her black coat.

Coming out of the lift she felt her cheeks burning all over again. Richard was talking to Impetus's CEO, Jeremy Finch, laughing politely at some Finchie bon mot. They must know each other, she thought.

'Hello, Kate,' Richard said, meeting her eyes. 'All set?' He took over the carrier bags and offered his arm. 'Good to see you, Jeremy.' Leaving the building together, Kate felt her stock might be on the rise.

* * *

Setting off in stodgy traffic, they made slow progress. The wind was relentless, the rain turning to sleet; Kate was glad Richard was driving.

'Tell me about your day,' he said, giving her a quick glance. 'If you had any dramas and crises they don't show.'

Kate described the tedium of the *Maximan* client. 'The guy I work with, Dan, takes him so seriously, never dares humour him. He was in to see some revised scripts and we struggled through the usual client neuroses, then things went a bit belly-up when a copywriter yawned and said he had his best ideas mid-shag. It didn't help when one of the others, a girl, said he should be grateful for the pulling powers of *Maximan Briefs*.

'But I want to hear about your day at the docks,' Kate carried on. 'You were hoping for some action, some big haul. Did the customs have any useful coups?'

'They sure did. It was great for the programme—like those wildlife films that capture some amazing sighting, crocodiles mating or something. The customs found a kilo of cocaine in a Fiesta while our camera was trained, street value of about forty thousand pounds. It was a couple from Bradford with a small child who was clutching her lunchbox for dear life. When customs opened it the stuff was done up to look like a packet of sandwiches.'

'I suppose they were arrested and the child will be taken into care,' Kate said. 'It's sad.'

She felt taut with nerves as they drove on. 'You looked to be having quite a chat with Jeremy Finch, our head honcho. Had you met him before?'

'Only from firing questions at him as a financial hack when I'm sure he had gritted teeth! But we're both members of the Soho Club. You must come and have a drink there.'

They had reached the motorway; Richard drove fast. Kate arranged her hand in easy reach, but his didn't stray from the steering wheel. He played CDs, Nelly Furtado then Alison Krauss who was new to her, as she confessed.

'She's hotter in America,' Richard said, keeping his eyes on the road. 'I first heard her in Tennessee.'

'Do you enjoy all the travelling?'

'Not any more, I'm going to need to do less of it or I'll go mad.' Kate glanced at him, but he didn't turn. He had a good profile, too good, she felt it in every notch of her spine. What was going to happen? It was his birthday evening, after all.

'Almost there,' she said. Hayley, the hobbling help, and her boyfriend were holding the fort since Rupert's dinner in the City had started early. Hayley lived locally with her mother, and in times of greater mobility would have stayed the night. Sadie was right, though, a girl on crutches wasn't ideal: nappy changes, Amelia's moods—tantrums were not unknown. Did Richard really know what he was letting himself in for?

He parked tidily beside a small rusty Peugeot near the front door. Hayley let them in, leaning

90

heavily on one of her crutches as if testing its strength with her soft plumpness. She suddenly thunked across the hall with surprising speed and yelled up from the bottom of the stairs, 'Back in your bed, young Joseph, do you 'car!' Kate could see him at the top, fiddling with the latch on the slatted gate. 'Your aunt's 'ere now, you've seen 'er—and 'er friend. Back in that bed at once!'

She turned round, pink in the face, and gave an impatient glance towards the kitchen. Her boyfriend had come to the door. He had acne and a little triangle of ginger beard and wore a leather jacket of the same colour. Hayley's coat was over his arm.

'That's me friend, Wayne,' she said, rather as though talking about her dog. 'We'll be going then. Rose was fed early and Amelia's done 'er screams. She's gone off now.' Hayley sniffed and struggled into her coat, clearly thinking it was all right for some.

Richard held the door for them. 'She seemed to think we had the long straw,' he said, when they were gone, 'but she just might be wrong—here's a young man who's not tucked up in his bed . . .' Kate followed his eyes and saw Joseph creeping down the stairs; he was well up to opening the stair gate.

He came running across the hall in his pyjamas. 'Can I have a story, Aunt Katie? Can he read me one too?' He took hold of her hand, pulling on it, and looked up at Richard.

Kate knelt down to Joseph's level. 'This is Richard, not "he"—and one story only and that's your lot.' She gave him a hug. 'It is very late.'

Richard squatted down, too. 'Hello, Joseph! Good to meet you. Do you want a shoulder-ride back up?' Joseph studied him, then nodded cautiously. 'Remember to duck at the top, though. Sorry about the story, I'll read you one next time I come.'

Once they got him to bed he listened sleepily to Kate reading *Bob the Builder*. Richard listened as well, leaning against the door frame while she sat on the bed, feeling self-conscious, turning once or twice to smile.

They looked in on Amelia whose golden curls were spread wide on her pink-striped pillow. Her chubby cheeks were flushed and a faint nasal snore was escaping.

Rose, the baby, was sleeping peacefully. 'Baby alarm on?' Richard whispered, as they stood looking down at the cot. 'She's a beautiful child. They all are.' Kate felt the weight of her empty womb and left him to go to the door.

Downstairs in the kitchen, unpacking the much-travelled food, she was pleased to see Sadie's promised casserole in the fridge with a Post-it note saying, *'Please eat!'*

'You've had a long wait for a birthday drink,' she said, as Richard came in with a cooler bag from the car, 'and you're forty-five if I've worked that out right. Quite a milestone.'

'I'd rather not think of it that way,' he said dryly. He unzipped the bag and took out a bottle of champagne. 'This isn't up to Ben's standard, but it's cold at least, and I've brought a very small tin of caviar. Or do you hate the stuff?'

'It's the ultimate treat. But Rupert's left us some champagne, he was very insistent.' Richard continued to peel the foil off his own bottle and Kate returned Rupert's bottle to the fridge.

92

He opened cupboards, looking for glasses, and she did nothing to help. She felt rooted, her chest thudding. She couldn't bear to be in this faux-intimate situation; she wanted the real thing, touch, contact, kisses. She felt both connected and at arm's length, as close and separate as railway lines. Richard seemed unreachably remote.

'That cupboard for glasses,' she said, forcing herself into line. 'I'll do some chopped egg for the caviar in a minute, but the fire will need reviving, I'm sure. Bring the bottle and come with me so I can drink a birthday toast—and give you my extremely small present.'

Richard seemed not to be expecting one. 'That's not allowed, not the point.'

Kate wondered what was as she stuffed firelighters under the dead logs. She also wondered about the long evening ahead. How would they cope? So much was unspoken between them. Richard seemed to have decided to be avuncular and friendly, to assume that was what she wanted and stick to it like a leech. If only he had a clue how obsessed she'd become, how acute her need; he'd been filling her head, driving her to distraction, ever since New Year's Eve.

'It'll be at least midnight before they're back,' Kate laughed. 'What a way to spend your birthday. You'll be bored out of your mind. We'd better see what music and films they have, although whether Rupert's tastes are quite what you'd choose . . .'

'I'd far rather just sit and talk and look at you, make our own entertainment.'

He said it without emphasis, pouring the fizz and handing her a glass. 'Anyway,' Kate smiled, taking it, 'right now it's Happy Birthday!' She leaned

93

forward and touched glasses; it was a chance to kiss him, but she felt inhibited.

'This is a real non-event,' she said, handing over the present, which was in a shiny, silver *Happy Birthday* carrier she'd found, festooned with black sports cars. 'The bag's the best thing about it.'

Richard went to sit in an armchair by the fire and peered in at the contents of Kate's gift, his glass on the slate hearth beside him. He became completely absorbed, inspecting the various bulb packets she had given him like a commuter, home from his evening train. Only the Labrador and slippers were missing.

No other person, she thought, watching him, could have expended as much time and energy on the choosing of a small present as she had. But what did you give a man you'd kissed passionately, yet hardly knew, for his forty-fifth birthday? Harry's birthday had been in May, often coinciding with Whitsun; they'd gone on sightseeing trips and she'd bought him presents of clothes.

Richard looked up. 'It says the narcissi are richly scented and the tulips in the picture look dark and glossy like aubergines!' His smile was warm, his hair thick and clean, his legs were stretched out in his black jeans, his shirt open-neck and showing some chest hair. 'Lilies, too. Will you help me plant them, Katie? Instruction as part of the present—perhaps even this weekend?'

'You've missed a packet, I think,' she said, using it as an excuse to come and sit on the chair arm.

He smiled up. 'Can there be more?'

'You won't thank me for that one—it's lion-dung pellets, ammunition for your feline war. Cats are territorial, or so the website says, and if they

94

imagine a lion about the place they think twice about leaving their mark. I'm sure it's all a great con and the garden will stink to high heaven—but only time and a hot summer will tell!'

Richard thanked her with a squeeze of her hand and that was it. The fire was alight but with no cheery crackle and flames, and he knelt down to jiggle it with a poker. Kate felt a fool, staying perched on the arm of his chair, and she stood up, dejected and crushed.

'I'll go and do the bits for the caviar,' she muttered, talking to his back, and almost ran out of the room, across the wide hall, in her thwarted frustration.

The kitchen was the hub of the house with a small playroom leading off it and a pair of double doors to the dining room. Kate saw a bowl of hyacinths on a dining-room window sill and transferred them to the kitchen table. They had an overpowering scent. She laid two places, found napkins, set out wine glasses. Perhaps music would help. No sound from the baby alarm, that was something at least.

*   *   *

They made inroads into the champagne—and the caviar. It was a sumptuous feast in front of the revived fire. Sitting on a rug at Richard's feet, Kate spread fingers of crisp toast with caviar, chopped parsley, egg and onion, which she handed up to him. She leaned back on her heels, savouring the exquisite salty fishiness; keeping it on her tongue, feeling bonded by taste buds alone. It was pure indulgence. She couldn't quite imagine a similar

95

scene with Harry; he would have been sneaking looks at an art catalogue, not giving himself to the romance of a gloriously exotic food.

She knelt on the rug until pins and needles set in, then went to sit in her opposite chair feeling a little morose. Why hadn't Richard chosen the sofa? Why didn't he come and sit on her chair arm, top-up her glass, brush over her fingers with a sexy touch? Where was his easy connecting banter of the party? What had changed?

Kate stood up. She pulled her wrap-over print dress more tightly to her, telling herself to get with it. Richard was behaving properly, sensibly, and she was being a dope. It was time to go and see to the supper, yet she couldn't bring herself to leave. She offered to refill Richard's glass, but he shook his head.

'Mustn't forget I'm driving,' he said with an open friendly smile, then he reached into the basket for another log to throw on the fire. It was impossible to know his feelings.

Supper could wait. Kate sat down again. 'Why are you so interested in Ben and Spencer Morgan?' It came out rather too suddenly and sharply, but she was desperate to provoke some verbal interaction if nothing else.

'You're sounding very fierce, Katie. It's just my curiosity. I only mentioned it because I was anxious you shouldn't get the wrong idea. I hate to think you might have been worrying about it.'

'Well, I have. Tell me what you think is going on. I know you have your suspicions about Spencer, but does that affect Ben? I mean, it could cause problems for his business, couldn't it, since Spencer helped set him up?'

96

'Look, Katie, I'd love to talk about it all, but you're close to Ben, he's almost family; it would be only natural if you passed things on.' She saw the force of that, but would Richard think differently if he knew she sensed something not quite right that was causing her mother tension?

'Let's leave it for now,' he urged. 'I know nothing much, it's just that Morgan's speed of acquisition has something of the Madoff's about it, that's all.'

Kate felt loath to leave the subject altogether. 'Mum wants me to have supper tomorrow with her, just us. I suspect she might tell me that she and Ben are getting married.'

'How would you feel about that?'

'Fine, obviously. I'm sure she knows what she's doing.' Richard didn't raise an eyebrow or press her further, which, given that hardly ringing endorsement, wouldn't have come as a surprise.

'Seeing them together on New Year's Eve,' he said, 'they did seem very bound up.' He looked at Kate with gentle eyes. 'It must be such an emotional time for you, with your father's illness, desperate. I don't mean to say that your sadness over that could make you less keen on Ben being in your mother's life, just that it might not seem the ideal time. I'm very sorry about your father. I heard it was cancer and terminal.'

Kate felt sure she'd never mentioned Aidan to him. 'How do you even know who my father is?' she asked.

'I have met him. It was a while back and obviously made an impression on me. He might not remember.'

'Oh, I'm sure he would,' Kate said, making the television connection which she should have done before. 'But how did you know he was my father?'

'From you, your name. I remembered seeing old press photographs and your mother was with him, Mr and Mrs Aidan Nichols. He was an exceptional war correspondent, brave, hugely respected—but you know all that, of course.'

'It's renal cancer and he hasn't got long, three or four months. It's eating my heart out. He's only sixty. He was very much in my thoughts on New Year's Eve . . .' She remembered talking to her father about Richard on New Year's Day. Typical of Aidan, not letting on he actually knew him; he'd never have forgotten meeting him, she was sure.

Richard looked at her from his prim distance by the fireplace. 'My father died at fifty-six,' he said. 'A massive heart attack. It happened with no warning at all, no early tremors or breathlessness. I arrived minutes after he'd died. I know the strain of what you're going through, nothing's worse, but in my case that terrible suddenness meant I had no chance to be with him and feel I'd said goodbye. Treasure your time with your father, for all the pain.'

'I'm so sorry,' Kate said. She stared across at Richard, feeling an emotional swell. She felt her heart couldn't handle a sorrow on top of her own, yet she wanted to reach out and absorb a share of his more distant grief. She pictured him driving at dangerous speeds, arriving just too late . . . The sense of loss must linger, attached, creeping into his thoughts, whatever the passage of time. She had his eye and added helplessly, 'I wish there was something to say.'

'It was years ago, it's a softer sadness now.'

'Shall we have supper?' Kate smiled. 'It only

needs heating up, nothing for you to do. Stay by the fire. Perhaps you'd find a not too bad film if you hunt through all those DVDs.'

'Can we skip the film? I'll come and open the wine. Rupert would have done it an hour ago, I'm sure, and let it breathe. Perhaps we should look at the children too. Let me do that.'

Was he trying to show her up? Kate tipped a few new potatoes into a saucepan, washed and hygienic, straight from the packet, feeling riled. The evening's tensions were getting to her. She slammed the pan on to boil, put the casserole in the top Aga oven and tried to get in control.

'Three sleeping children,' Richard reported, coming back downstairs, 'all fine.'

She held up a screw-top jar of spinach soup. 'I made this last night or there's smoked salmon, but they've both had a day at the office. And then it's Sadie's casserole. Hardly the birthday dinner of your dreams; you should be fine-dining somewhere smart.'

Richard said he was where he wanted to be. He stopped the soup overboiling, heated the defrosted French bread, put butter in a dish. He poured the wine and held a glass to Kate's lips as she washed spinach. It was the closest they'd come to an intimate moment, but she couldn't keep sipping forever. They simply sat down on opposite sides of the kitchen table, smiled and got on with the meal.

Kate asked after his daughter, Polly. 'She's in with an older crowd who lead her on, I think,' Richard said. 'The worst sort of influence. I do what I can to rein her in, but it's hard, long distance, and with little backup. It doesn't help my guilt about leaving, but she'd have found ways to go

99

clubbing, even if I was around, I expect. Polly's bright, she's good at excuses, runs rings round her mother and grandmother.'

'My sister was wild in her teens. When my parents stayed overnight in London and we had a babysitter Sadie used to climb out of her bedroom window onto a flat roof, jump off into the arms of a boyfriend and go clubbing—even at fourteen!'

'And you stayed dutifully at home?'

'I had to cover for her, didn't I?' Kate snapped, minding his grin. She was terrible at being teased. The incident in an alley with Sidney Brooks had made her less keen on sneaking out at night. It preyed on her mind; she should probably have reported him, although it had seemed too painful to face up to at the time.

'This has to do for pudding,' she said, bringing a mini birthday cake out of its box. 'Shall we have it with coffee?' The kitchen was full of heady aromas and she had drunk quite a lot of Richard's claret. She needed physical contact, she could barely stand the strain.

'You went to all this trouble, Katie: presents, cake, candles, flowers . . .'

Richard stretched out his hand and allowed the back of it to touch her fingers round the stem of the glass. 'You're bewitching, Katie. I could sit here all night, looking at you. And the stillness and quiet is amazing. You forget, living in London, about perfect quiet.'

'I think you just spoke too soon,' she said, as a few snuffles reached them down the baby alarm. They swelled into jerky wails, like a faulty CD, and soon into a constant fury. 'I'd better go,' Kate sighed, rising to her feet. 'You stay.' Rose was about to wake the whole house.

Rose's cot was still in an alcove dressing area of Sadie and Rupert's bedroom. Kate walked up and down with her, making cooing noises that she realized Richard must be hearing in the kitchen. She felt like declaring passionate love for him down the baby monitor.

The rhythm of walking or the cooing settled Rose. She became warm and heavy against Kate's chest, a comforting bundle to hold. Had she had a dream, a teething twinge? Kate tucked her back in, tiptoed away and stood listening in her sister's bedroom, fingers crossed.

The room had a faintly acrid smell, the scent of intimacy, and she wondered about her own bedroom. Did anything of Harry linger on? Was he in the very fabric—his DNA, the sweat of his crotch? How would it feel, inviting another man into the bed that still had Harry's groove?

She didn't feel ready to return downstairs and sat at Sadie's kidney-shaped dressing table hunting out a lipgloss from a tray of jumbled make-up. She dabbed some on her lips, staring at her own face: miserable wide-set eyes, wide mouth as well, with lips that often began to tremble. They had when she'd been upset about a client's carping once and Dan had said it was *adorable*. God, Dan. Her lips were trembling now. Kate fought the tears. How could she have become so instantly obsessed?

Perhaps Richard was right and it was just a very emotional time. But he didn't know his own part in the avenues of her emotion, the extremes of her aching need; she wanted to have physical contact, more than a single kiss. He'd decided, obviously, to skip any involvement and treat her as a widowed

101

friend and she could do nothing about it. But a soft glint of connection still appeared now and then in his dove-grey eyes like a capricious sun. He knew and admired her father . . . She gave a deep sigh; why did everything feel so poignantly charged?

Her hand trailed the banister as she went downstairs and her head was bowed. Richard had talked about them having a drink at his club, but could she go on seeing him on his terms? She looked up. He was at the bottom of the stairs, watching her make her way down. 'You took a while,' he said. 'I could hear Rose had stopped crying. Are you all right?'

Kate was one step up from the bottom, her eyes level with his forehead and, sensing in his oddly strained tone some evident tension, she lifted her hand to brush back his hair and smooth his frown. 'You looked worried,' she said, a little embarrassed as her hand went to his brow, but it had been a spontaneous gesture.

Richard grabbed her wrist in a tight grasp and pulled away her arm. 'Don't do that,' he said, his fingers digging in all the harder, sparks flying in his eyes.

'Do what?' She scowled back, feeling a powerful rise of anger too, catching the heat of his electric charge.

'Just don't,' he said, still gripping her wrist, glancing away. 'I can't handle it.'

She came off the step and stood facing him. 'Can't handle what?'

'Tender fucking touches,' he muttered. 'Do you need it spelled out?'

'Yes, actually—is a little consideration such a hanging offence?'

'Are you being deliberately obtuse? Can't you see this isn't working? I can't cope.'

She felt chilled. Was that it, the brush-off, the romance that never was? But to react in that extreme way, to have such a pressure-cooker eruption, give off waves of electricity—and when he was ending something that hadn't even begun . . . Kate didn't know how to communicate her confusion; she was the one who couldn't cope. She stood facing him feeling about to snap, as taut with the strain as a loaded fishing line. But he wasn't spooling her in and she said tightly, 'I don't understand what you're saying. And you're hurting my wrist.'

Richard let go of her. He dropped his arm down stiffly by his side, stretching and clenching the fingers. 'Sorry,' he muttered. 'Not consciously, I didn't realize.'

'Any more than I did.'

He stared. His eyes were haunting, the fingers of both hands clenched. 'You do understand,' he said. 'How can you not? It's obvious, all too clear. You need time, you were in a new marriage, you've lost a young, glamorous husband, you're not ready for a relationship, but I'm burning up. I know this is very abrupt and I'm handling it badly, but I can't see you anymore, not like this. It's carving me up, making me unsafe. Better to end it now.'

They were still standing close and she held his stare. He was right. She'd known perfectly well what he was saying, just finding it impossible to accept. 'I thought I could do it, Katie, anything to be with you, but it's not in me, hard as I've tried. I can't do it your way, and that's it.'

'But you could some other way?'

'Don't play games.'

'You think I would?'

She didn't flinch when Richard wrenched her dress open. She stood motionless, feeling extraordinary confidence, as though the baton of power was being transferred. It was in her hands, she could run with it and win. She wanted the kiss in all its force; wanted the heat of his breath, the roughness, the feel of his mouth on her neck, her shoulders and exposed breasts. She arched backwards in his arms, in thrall to the intoxicating sensations, the feel of his brushing hair and buried head.

They sank to the floor, on to the cold, hard hall tiles. Kate's hands were mapping the hard stretch of Richard's back as she clung and raised her body off the floor to meet his mouth, back on hers. She was tasting wine on his breath, sharing the heat and damp of his exertion. She had no sense of time, place or the hardness of the tiles. The moment was now. Richard was in all her senses.

The crunch of tyres on the gravel drive reached her distantly, but the sound was soon jaggedly sharp. Richard wasn't hearing it. 'Shit, shit, it's them,' she hissed in his ear, yanking free and clutching her dress, bra, scrabbling up her shoes. 'Say I'm having a pee,' she yelled, dashing chaotically across the hall, 'say anything—say how do you do!'

Kate locked the door of the downstairs loo and leaned back against it, panting. Richard hadn't met Rupert and Sadie, but she knew he'd manage; she just hoped it would be with his shirt buttoned up and tucked in.

It sounded all right. She could hear he was doing

brilliantly and adored him all the more. 'We had a great time with Joseph, such a bright child . . . Yes, one sleepy cry from Rose and that was it! And the casserole was terrific . . .'

Kate called through the door, dragging on her hair with a musty clothes brush. 'Hi, you two—you made good time! Just having a going-home pee . . .'

She couldn't do up her dress. One of the ties securing the cross-over was missing, torn off probably, somewhere out on the hall tiles, drawing the eye, telling a story like a dropped handkerchief. Did she go out trying to keep the two sides wrapped over with tight-folded arms? How could she even pick up her bag or anything she was handed?

Feeling in a complete panic she flushed the chain, playing for time and looked round frantically for inspiration. The washbasin was set into a dressing top with mini-soaps, hand lotions, ornamental boxes; very pukka and suitable for all the dinner parties Sadie and Rupert gave. Kate lifted the lid of a little porcelain box and discovered a whole covey of safety pins inside, a 'sow' pin with a row of little piglet ones dangling. She shook a couple loose, looped up the single tie, fastened her cross-over dress and came out looking, she hoped, as confidently composed as a girl in an ad for sweet-breath pills.

'How was the dinner? Long speeches?' she asked.

'Certainly long,' said Sadie. 'We left the moment we could, promise! I was so worried.'

'Well, you took long enough saying goodbye,' Rupert snorted. 'I can never get her away, she's impossible.'

'We wouldn't have minded, Ru,' Kate assured

him. 'You really needn't have rushed.'

Rupert discouraged any more lingering, he was a banker in need of his bed. 'So good of you coming, hugely appreciated,' he said briskly, seeing them out with unseemly haste. They could hear him locking and bolting the door behind them and he'd switched off the outside light even before they were in the car.

'That was close,' Richard said, pulling Kate tight to his side as he drove away. 'We called it "getting off at Edge Hill" in my distant youth—the last railway stop before Liverpool Lime Street Station.'

'We weren't quite as close as that.'

'Not far off . . .'

Clear of the village he pulled into the side and kissed her long and hard. Kate sat back up, a little shaken. Caution and nerves had begun circling like clamouring seagulls. 'We should get back,' she muttered, dropping her head onto his shoulder, quivering with the feel of his soft fondling of her hair. She battled against the clamour and crowding caution.

'And when we do—am I coming in? Or do you not want me to?'

Kate was silent. She wanted him to, overpoweringly, her body was wet with need. 'I'm frightened,' she said, unable to explain of what or why. It was fear of the future, her feelings. She lifted her hand to his face. 'Not tonight. I need adjustment time really. Can you understand?'

'How could I not, Katie? But you're seeing your mother tomorrow night and I want to see you . . .'

'Yes, and I'll be late leaving work, too. We're on a big new pitch. I'd planned to have supper with my mother at my flat, but I'm going to her now. She lives with Ben in Pimlico.'

'You mean you'd wanted it to be on home ground? There was a tiny bit of tension between you, wasn't there, on New Year's Eve? Is it to do with Ben?'

'I just feel ever so slightly excluded: silly of me really, petty.' Kate's instinct was still to keep her concerns about Ben to herself.

'Do you have a good reason to feel it or is it just a hunch? It's a natural instinct, though, not wanting to lose your mother, especially after all you've been through. Let her do the talking. Sorry, I've no business giving lectures like that. But I do have a little proposition to put.'

'Oh, yes?' Kate said, hearing the change in his tone. She touched his cheek. 'Go on.'

'Suppose,' he said, 'after supper you came on to Thornby Terrace? It's no distance from Pimlico, it's almost on your way home. I could run you back if you wanted, but I'd much rather you stayed the night. Will you think about it—if everything feels right?'

Sensitive restraint only went so far, she thought with a private smile, her mind darting to overnight bags and her mother getting ideas. 'It won't be early,' she said. 'What with working late as well, close on midnight, I expect.'

'I think I can manage that. I've been marking time all week and learning a great deal about the virtues of patience and endurance.'

CHAPTER 7

Kate despaired. Her mother was cooking, Richard waiting . . . It was already half-past nine. For Impetus to win the account for a new bedtime drink, *Sleepyhead*, would be a huge feather in their cap, but the creative team were pissing around endlessly and thinking backwards. You couldn't take milky drinks forward, they said lazily, and seemed stuck on the theme of a girl smiling seraphically in her sleep with the slogan, '*Sweet Dreams, Sleepyhead.*' Kate thought it was dire. They were time-wasting, singing the jingle from an old ad, '*Sleep sweeter, Bournvita,*' in impossibly high or low voices; someone's dad had worked on the original campaign.

She would have to lean on Dan, Kate decided, or it would be midnight, the rate they were going, and Ben would be home from his dinner before she'd even arrived.

'My mother wanted me for supper tonight, Dan, something she needs to talk about that seems important. Any chance I could nip off now?'

'Sure, Kate, quite understand.' His face took on a look of deep concern. 'I'm counting on you for tomorrow, though; no peace for the wicked, eh!' Dan knew how to make her cringe, she thought, promising faithfully to be in on time. He never failed.

She gave her mother a quick ring in his hearing to confirm her excuse then grabbed her coat and bag, struggling to contain feelings of blazing need. She would take a taxi and call Richard on the way, she thought, aching for time to leap on.

He'd phoned at lunchtime and she'd had to face the embarrassment of explaining that she wasn't on the pill. 'You see, Harry and I,' she'd spluttered, 'we'd started trying for a baby just before he died, and after that I'd had no reason . . .' Richard had shut her up, making it clear that he wasn't in the least bothered, but she'd hated the underlining of what they were about—last night's unfinished business. And condoms, Kate felt, did have their sordid side.

Calling him from the cab took care of any lingering bashfulness. 'Only just leaving now—and we're carrying on tomorrow,' she said breathlessly, thinking with a rush of blood about leaving from Chelsea in the morning. 'I hope not Sunday as well.'

'So do I! We're planting bulbs, among other things—part of the present, remember?'

'Depending on the weather, of course,' Kate said, trying to row back a little. He was making assumptions about the rest of the weekend and she mustn't do the same. 'I have to go, we're almost there. See you later, I'll be as quick as I can. Sure you want to stay awake?'

She paid off the cab in a great fluster. Dan had had to repeat a question three times that afternoon; whole new strategies had passed her by . . . Kate refused to believe Richard could really be as emotionally involved as he'd sounded. He was passionate and persuasive, but wasn't that all part of winning through? He was hardly divorced. And he was out of her league, a television personality— and with sex appeal. He could have the pick of the bunch. It would be little more than a weekend fling and she was bound to be hurt.

109

Kate climbed the stairs to Ben's flat thinking about the repercussions, the commitment and pain she'd feel whether it became an extended fling with Richard or not. She imagined clinging on when he'd started to ease off, making recriminations and demands. Wouldn't it be better not to let it develop—or at least not fall into bed at the first opportunity as she was inevitably going to do? And it would have been cooler not to arrive with an overnight bag. Better to have held off a while longer and been firmer about going home. But she was incapable of not being with him. Her need was extreme.

Supper with her mother, though, came first. No looking at her watch and seeming jumpy. Kate wondered whether her mother had a particular reason for wanting an evening together. Rachel hid her tension superbly well, but she *was* feeling it. Was she about to announce that she was marrying Ben? Surely, though, whatever was troubling her couldn't be something as simple as how Kate might react to the news? She and Ben were living together and obviously in love; she could hardly imagine her daughter losing much sleep if they decided to seal the deal. Surprising really, that they hadn't got round to it already.

Kate felt confused and disturbed, and more inclined as well to hold back herself—however much she was burning to describe Sadie and Rupert's unfortunate timing and the particular colour of Richard's wondrously compelling eyes.

Rachel opened the door and gave her the loving spontaneous hug that Kate had needed; she felt the skin of a long day begin to leave her and the knots in her shoulders untie.

'Sorry, Mum, are you completely starving? I had to do a runner or I'd still be there!'

'Not hungry at all. It's you I'm worried about; at Sadie's till all hours last night and you've had such a long day—but you look amazingly well on it! Come and unwind. I haven't done much of a meal, though.'

Kate had thought of using an old, frayed leather briefcase of Harry's in place of a conventional hold-all, overcoming any sensitivities about it in her need not to advertise her later plans. She left the briefcase discreetly by the front door and followed her mother into the sitting room.

It was a lovely room, painted library-green with a cream textured sofa and armchairs with throws, a deep-red ottoman, a small dining table. It had height, yet intimacy too; a wall of books, twentieth-century oils, a gas coal fire in a Georgian grate and a big bowl of floppy impressionistic tulips. Rachel had a passion for spring flowers. She pressed a glass of cold Meursault into Kate's hands and told her to stay put while she went for the food. Kate sipped the excellent wine, looking round, admiring Ben's taste in an abstracted way while her mind was leaping on. She was feeling a fear of heights, strung up on an emotional high wire.

'It's only fish chowder,' Rachel said, coming back in with a heavy ovenproof dish and depositing it on a ceramic mat on the table, 'but with plenty of bits, mainly monkfish.'

'Sounds perfect—I resisted all the sushi and sandwiches at work.'

The soup was good, the wine peeling away more of the day. 'Is Ben back soon?' Kate asked, trying to hurry her mother along. 'I don't want to keep him

111

from his bed. You wouldn't believe Ru's impatience, seeing us out last night!'

'I would, I've seen it myself. But he does have to catch a God-awful early train; I used to think he might as well have done the dawn feed while he was at it and let Sadie sleep on. Ben's at an army dinner, I'll be lucky if he's back by midnight.'

That wasn't going to help with the getaway. 'Sadie and Ru were back by midnight actually,' Kate said. 'After a City dinner too. I was surprised they weren't later.'

'You still had the journey home. I was glad you weren't doing it alone. Original of Richard, coming to babysit—it reminded me a bit of those old sketches of courting couples on the sofa! How was it? Was he good company?'

'Yes, he was interesting to talk to. We had a nice peaceful time.' Playing it down was like holding her breath under water, a stream of overstatements would have to burst out of her soon. 'But, you know, Mum, it's nothing, just a party follow-up. I expect he'd like a bit of a scene, but I still feel married and in a muddle in my head, not really up for that yet. It would be in a sort of bubble, not real, superficial and short-term. Richard comes with a load of baggage too, difficult teenagers and he's still involved with his ex-wife. She's bipolar and he feels responsible.'

Why go into that sort of small print? Rachel always had that effect, though; she'd have a stony-eyed debt-collector crying like a baby on her shoulder and pouring out all his hidden fears. Richard was right to advise letting her mother do the talking.

'It sounds to me as if a little bubble might be the

112

answer,' Rachel said, looking gently amused, which was infuriating. 'Would it be such a terrible thing, though? Why not just enjoy it, make the most of his friendship and relax.'

Kate froze. She didn't want her mother spelling out the realities of life, she wanted to cling to the intensity of feeling she'd heard in Richard's voice less than an hour ago. But that had been all about his immediate needs, no real clue to his feelings. Kate knew she was laying her thoughts bare; her mother couldn't fail to see how much it mattered to her that Richard was more than a bubble and that he cared.

The phone rang and she saw Rachel stiffen; it was involuntary and obvious and she laughed lightly, smoothly making it a talking point.

'That sound always makes me jump! I'll leave it for the voicemail. Sadie and Ben always call on the mobile.' She reached out for a bowl of sliced oranges and a plate of brownies that were on a nearby side table then gave a smile. 'This is it for pud.' The distinctive smells of sweet citrus and chocolate combined potently; it was a tempting aroma and they began to talk about food.

'Coffee? I'll go and make it now,' Rachel said, getting up.

Kate followed her out. The chef's-style aluminium kitchen, with its satiny black worktops, had everything in its place. She deposited the soup dish near the draining board, feeling stupidly brought down by the talk of a bubble and the thought of Richard as a bit of fun. It was depressingly inevitable and true. Watching while her mother filled the kettle and set out fern-decorated pottery mugs, she tried to tell herself

113

that as fixated as she was on Richard, it had much to do with the emotions of the moment and she'd soon regain some perspective and see things in the round. She was looking at men again at least; she might even be the one to do the dumping in time. Some hope of that.

Rachel scooped coffee into a pot and stood staring down at it, preoccupied, even as the kettle thundered to boiling.

Back at the table, Kate thought how exquisite her mother looked in the soft yellow candlelight, absurdly beautiful for a woman in her late fifties. Her turquoise eyes dazzled, they reflected the blue of the top she was wearing. Her neck was as graceful as a heron's. She had such poise and composure; no one could have picked up on her troubled state. Ben would, though, and since Kate felt convinced he was the cause of whatever was the problem, he must know how much he was upsetting Rachel and putting her under stress. Who had been phoning after eleven at night? Why should Ben always ring on her mobile—was that so she'd know who it was?

Kate had worried about her mother over Christmas, but her father and Richard had filled her mind ever since. She felt guilty. It was difficult to ask straight out what was wrong, though, and she struggled to find a form of words.

'You did say you wanted to talk, Mum. Is it anything to do with Ben?'

She looked caught by surprise. 'Goodness, you startled me, Katie. And you're sounding so inquisitorial! But you're right, I do, only it's about you, darling, nothing to do with Ben. I wanted us to have a little time together for a change. You've

114

been unrelaxed with me lately and I wish you'd say what it's all about. Should I gather, perhaps, since you brought him up, that it's in some way connected with Ben?'

Kate felt wrong-footed. How could she possibly talk about her vague, unfounded misgivings? 'Don't think that, Mum. It's great that you're living here and happy with Ben. Sorry if I've been a bit uptight, just tiredness, I guess. The office is all go right now, a madhouse, and there's Dad as well; he's sinking fast and it does upset me to see it. I have to be at work again tomorrow, but I'll drive down and see him on Sunday. I hate to miss a chance.'

'Katie, that won't wash, you're not being straight with me. I'm not a total fool. You've been guarded and uptight and that's nothing to do with a heavy workload or Dad. Can't you try to explain what's bothering you, what it's all about, and stop holding back?'

'But that's exactly what *you've* been doing, Mum! And it's really been getting to me, if you must know.' Kate seized on the chance to move things away from Ben. 'For instance when I was with Dad the other day—maybe it was something he said, I don't know—but I suddenly realized how deeply he still cared and it brought back all those platitudes of yours about the divorce. I started minding all over again. Sadie and I did feel short-changed at the time. I brought it up with Dad actually, and asked him the truth about the rift.'

'What did he say?' Rachel demanded, with palpable tension.

'Only that he was to blame and it was for you to explain.'

'I can't, darling, not now, it would be too hard on

115

Dad. Try and understand and be patient. I will tell you in time.'

Much as Kate longed to know the emotional truths, she thought her mother must sense that the break-up wasn't foremost in her mind. Far more immediate and concerning was her instinctive feeling that there was a serious problem and intimately connected with Ben.

Rachel was looking anxiouly aware of that, but Kate needed reassurance and couldn't help ploughing on. 'I feel not trusted, Mum,' she found herself saying. 'It's almost like you think I'm unreliable, indiscreet, not fit to be told certain things.'

'Don't say that.' Rachel looked desperate. 'You're everything, Katie, you know you are. I can't go into the divorce right now. There are reasons. And I'm sure Dad would rather I didn't.'

'He almost opened up himself, so perhaps he'll tell me more next time—I hope one of you stops talking in riddles soon.'

'That's up to Dad. Don't push it, love. Please.'

Kate bit into her lip, feeling stupidly close to tears. She felt they were stalled, like horses faced with a high wall, and wished they hadn't arrived at a scratchy impasse, just when she was longing to go. It would leave a bad taste to do it right away.

Rachel looked drained of her subtle sparkle. She rubbed her eyes and taking away her hand, gave a quick glance to the door, as if longing for Ben to return and be a protective shield.

Her honeyed scent reached Kate across the table. It was an alluring smell, evocative of creamy nights, love and sensuality; she imagined Ben drinking it in. She wanted to be with Richard; it was a craving need, a driving force. She wanted the feel and heat of him, his touch; she ached to pick up her bag and be out of the door, on her way.

He would almost certainly ask whether any mention of marriage to Ben had been made, but since that seemed nowhere near the agenda, slightly to Kate's surprise, she decided to raise it herself. 'Do you and Ben think about getting married, Mum—or is that another little well-kept secret?' She hoped that hadn't sounded at all snide or provocative, she'd said it with a smile.

Rachel laughed out loud, which was certainly unexpected, and it eased the mood. 'That's the last thing on my mind! Not one of my present problems—and I do have one or two. Marriage is kind of neither here nor there, not an issue, not in our thoughts just now.' Her face became more serious and strained again. 'All I want is to see you happy and settled, darling. I think about that above everything.'

'You mustn't. I'm through Harry now, Mum, back on track. And sorry if I've been a bit sarky, I don't feel it at all.' Kate didn't; she felt loving and concerned, but she was desperate to go. She sneaked a glance at her watch. Twenty to twelve; no one could complain at that.

She stood up. 'Um, I've just seen the time, Mum, I really should be off.' It didn't feel a perfect note to end on, nothing seemed resolved. 'I'm working tomorrow after all, which I could do without! Can we call a cab?' she asked, thinking of diverting it to Richard's address. 'And I'd better have a quick pee before I go.' She wanted to comb her hair, check her face—do anything she could to herself without too obviously signposting her plans.

117

She was at the far side of the table and, squeezing past, her mother held onto her arm. 'Ben's a good person, Katie,' she said, with surprising intensity. 'No, he's more than that, he's exceptional; he has qualities that are very hard to find. Whatever's worrying you, try and believe that, and that I know what I'm doing. Trust me, love, trust us both.'

Kate was taken aback; the passion in her mother's voice was startling—and her desperate need to persuade.

Rachel was smiling, looking composed again, and she even had a humouring glint in her eye. Kate suspected that she too, wanted to part on a more cosy and teasing note. 'And after all,' she carried on, lips twitching, 'let's face it, Katie love, you haven't been entirely straight with me either . . . Where you're off to right now, for instance—it's written all over your face! You'd better hurry and make it away before Ben's back; he'll be sure to insist on taking you home, which could be a little awkward.'

Kate opened her mouth to offer some weak disingenuous explanation but seeing her mother's expression, thought the better of it.

'Just putting your advice into practice, Mum, nothing more than that . . . Can you call the cab, do you think, while I do a very quick repair job? And if I can have a squirt of that gorgeous perfume of yours, it might really help things along.'

CHAPTER 8

Kate called Richard the moment she was in the cab. 'I'm on my way, five minutes...'

'Just hurry and get here! How was your mother? Everything okay? No problems, I hope?'

'No, it was all fine.'

It wasn't fine, there were problems, but it was hardly the moment for unburdening on Richard when she couldn't think beyond her immediate compelling need. A thought flashed in, of being in a proper relationship and sharing difficult worries and fears; she put it out of her mind and listened enjoyably as Richard kept her on the line.

'Where are you? What's this cabbie doing? Taking a turn round Hyde Park or something? Tell the guy I'm ill!'

The taxi turned the corner into Richard's street and seeing him with his mobile in front of his open door, Kate's insides did a flip. The way he was leaning against the door frame, the look of him in jeans and pale denim shirt, the way he caught sight of the taxi and told her so, shoving the phone sexily into his pocket and smiling towards the cab . . . It was midnight and she was here, staying over, sleeping with him in under a week.

Richard paid the cabbie and took Harry's briefcase from her, and as they went inside Kate felt dreadfully unsure of herself, despite the unstoppable momentum since meeting him that had propelled her to this point. It wasn't the strangeness of her surroundings, she'd been to lunch here; she needed to be with him and was burning up, yet she still had a sense of being blindfold, spun round and left to find her way.

'I feel all shook up,' she said, with a stiff little laugh as Richard put down the briefcase and held her shoulders. 'It feels such a whirlwind.'

'It doesn't to me,' he said, his fingers pressing and kneading through the fabric of her coat. 'It feels the opposite, steady and right.' He took her face in his hands then traced down her neck and felt under her coat collar, discovering grooves and bones. She stood staring, feeling the irresistible pull—limp when he moved away to shoot home a bolt at the top of the door, which made a hefty, decisive clang.

'Not a bad sound!' he said, coming to stand close again. 'Locking out the world is a good feeling.' Their hands were brushing, but he wasn't taking her into his arms. Kate felt weak with longing, drained of confidence, and she was regretting her mother's perfume. It smelled overwhelming, like she was trying too hard.

Richard helped her out of her coat and threw it onto a chair. She'd taken off her daytime cardigan before leaving Pimlico, stuffed it into the briefcase, and feeling the blood rush into her cheeks as she stared at him, she imagined her chest looking blotchy, in her low black top, flushed from her jittery nerves.

'I've been in office clothes two nights running,' she smiled, 'with no chance of dressing up for you. But perhaps that's not really the point of tonight . . .'

'I have your dress-tie from last night,' Richard said. 'I saw it on the hall floor just in time and had it in my pocket all day. I feel I should really offer to

120

sew it back on. You can't wear that dress to the office again, it's not suitable. I'm not sharing it. I'd go mad with jealousy. And this top,' he said, running a light finger round the scoop of its neckline before he bent to kiss the bareness revealed, 'is just as bad.'

She shivered openly at his touch and the hammering of her heart was painful. Richard straightened up and studied her. His mouth was too close. 'Kiss me,' she said. 'You're giving me the shivers.'

He kissed her lips lightly, bringing his hands up into her hair, lifting it, running it through his fingers. 'I couldn't stand all the waiting today,' he said, bringing his cheek to hers, 'on top of the last few days. It's a whole twenty-four hours since I kissed you.'

'"Kissed" is rather genteel, considering.'

'I don't think you listen when I tell you my feelings,' his mouth was a millimetre from hers. 'Or perhaps you think I don't have any at all. I'll have to try and tell you again, the whole story, upstairs.'

'You're making it sound like a bedtime story.'

'It's a love story,' he said, pulling her hard to his body. 'And if I tell it to you many times, pour out my feelings in my little back bedroom, will you promise to listen properly this time?' He kissed her then, with crushing force, keeping her pressed so passionately tight to him that she could hear the thud of his heartbeat and feel the electrifying power of shared need. She wanted more and more.

As Richard broke away and led her firmly by the hand to the stairs, she thought about last night on the floor in Sadie's hall, being overwhelmed by the raw sexual drive and feeling a brazen new-found

121

confidence.

Tonight Kate was thinking more clearly. Sex was a given and he was seeing off any flutters of nerves, but not the indescribable ache of longing that wouldn't go away. She had to face down her imaginings and stay focused; this was a moment in time to be grabbed with both hands, but it was an interlude for Richard and nothing more. She had to remember that and keep things light.

'I'm worried about being rusty,' she said, at the foot of the stairs, in an attempt to set the tone.

'I didn't see any rust last night and I looked you all over.' He nuzzled her neck, hugging her close as they started up. 'But I'll keep a constant eye from now on—consider it my duty.' He stopped for a moment, still with his arm round her and smiling. 'Any other worries I can sort out as easily?'

'Well, I do have one silly little thing on my mind . . .'

'Let's have it then.'

'It was just so embarrassing, telling you about the pill. It felt awful, all wrong, bringing it up on the phone like that, but I had to let you know. Even if I could have picked up a prescription, it wouldn't have had time to kick in.' Kate wanted to say it was only short-term and she'd be sorted in days, but that presumed an ongoing relationship, which she was determined not to do.

He started laughing. 'What's so funny?' she demanded, quite hurt. 'I had to, didn't I? I don't see the joke.'

'Oh, Katie, what have I done to find you? You're beautiful and you're so irresistibly serious.' He was still laughing and keeping her held as they went on upstairs.

'Someone has to be practical,' she sniffed. 'Would you rather have left it to chance or "getting off at Edge Hill" or whatever you called it? Well, would you?'

'I'd almost rather that than use a condom and have to fight round a bit of rubber to make love to you. I'd hate it.' They'd reached his bedroom and Richard cupped her face. 'I want you here with me, Katie. I need you,' he kissed her lips, 'desperately. And nothing between us either . . .' He was grazing his nails down her arm and the shivers of touch found their way straight to her groin.

'But . . . What else then?'

'There's always the morning-after pill. You could pick it up tomorrow while you're at work—or even on Monday and still be in time. Let me pay for it, of course. You have about three or four days, I think, don't you, which should,' he touched lips again, 'take care of things, short-term? See us through till you're back on the pill, at least. We'll soon be sorted and fine.'

He was landing her with the responsibility and Kate felt a flash of resentful frustration at having to take care of her side of things. *He* didn't have to face asking over a chemist's counter for the wretched thing.

'Don't look at me like that, Katie. You don't really mind, do you? It means a lot to me.'

She was disarmed. She was there, with him, and as he lifted her top over her head and reached for her bra clasp, she couldn't give another second's thought to birth control.

His touch and tongue, the demanding force of his kissing, the sensuousness of his hands holding her breasts; when he lowered his head to coax up

123

her nipples in their rigid hardness she couldn't stop quivering. The things he was saying were words and thoughts she wanted to hear. Her world took on primary colours, brilliant and blinding.

As Kate unbuttoned his shirt and slid her arms round his warm bare back, a thought for the past came fleetingly and unbidden into her mind. Then when they fell on the bed together and Richard brought her to exquisite new heights, she forgot everything. She forgot all about Harry, supper with her mother with its unsettling twists and turns, she forgot the pill—or no pill—she almost forgot to breathe.

Richard had been around, he was more mature than past lovers and could sense her needs uniquely; everything felt natural and instinctive. Kate's inhibitions, if she'd ever really had any, were gone for good. The first time of sex, in her limited past experience, had been cautious and exploratory, the uncertainty of how far to give direction, whether to fake it and make a new lover feel prowess—it had always been hard to relax.

Richard's body was familiar now, after her sister's hall tiles, she knew the taste of his skin, the sense and feel and smell of him. She buried her face in the heat and damp, the prickle of his chest-hair, kissing his body with lips that felt tingling and bruised. Then she was taking him in. They had the whole night together and the door was bolted.

Life didn't work like this, out of the shadows of loneliness and finding love. Or was it all about sex? It was both, love and sex—and an uncontainable need.

* * *

They lay close; she could feel the rise and fall of Richard's breathing. Light was filtering in from the hall and he turned to gaze at her, in the semi-dark. 'Your skin,' he said, touching her cheek, 'is translucent, like a perfect pearl. I've thought about you all week, Katie, seeing you in my mind; your beguiling greeny-gold eyes, they've followed me everywhere. I've wanted you with such desperation; in this way, of course, but to reach you as well and not screw things up. I had to stop myself calling you and making you step back.' He could have put her out of her agony, Kate thought wryly, and saved her from the stupid operatic tangle she'd got herself into with Dan.

Richard's arm was round her and he shuffled to bring his face close. 'I love your smell,' he said. 'I'm not talking about this classy chic perfume, it's the intoxicating you underneath.'

'The scent is a bit overpowering! I had a squirt of my mother's before I left, then wished I hadn't.'

'I want to get you some, we'll go shopping.' Richard's fingers trailed down to a breast, to the tip of a nipple. 'I'm going to be driven mad wherever I am all day, thinking about these perfect round breasts . . .'

She brushed away his hand. 'Don't drive me mad now, I'm very comfortable. And I want to talk, hear more about your life and Ed and Polly. You're taking them out tomorrow, aren't you, to let them celebrate your birthday a bit late?'

'Yes. And I'd love you to be there, but Polly's in such a shit-awful phase. She's always judging me. I think it's best that I use the time to tell them about you, and not expose you to them quite yet; it would

125

put you off them for life! Certainly off my daughter. Will you be all right here for the evening while I'm out? I can run them home to Barnes and be back in no time.'

'No, I must go to the flat and I should sleep there tomorrow night, too. I need clean clothes and I want to go and see Dad on Sunday. What does Polly mind about? Your sex life—my predecessors?'

Richard leaned up to kiss her. 'Why don't you tell me about supper with your mother?'

'That's the most blatant change of subject!'

'I'm interested to hear. Did she say whether she and Ben are getting married?'

'They're definitely not. I was way off there. I even had to bring it up myself and she actually laughed. She said it wasn't on the radar, the least of her problems.'

Richard was warm and naked beside her, limbs involved, smelling enjoyably of sex. His eyes were gentle and Kate longed to pour out her worries about her mother. She felt in need of advice, but it was all so nebulous, pure hunch and surmise. And she felt all the more confused and subdued too, now, after her mother's moving defence of Ben.

She thought of her friend, Donna, on Romney Marsh, saying over lunch that Rachel might have good reason to keep whatever it was to herself. Richard was in the world of media and he was nothing if not quick on the uptake. He'd admitted to having a keen interest in Ben's billionaire backer, Spencer Morgan, and that probably extended to Ben.

'Did your mother go into all those problems of hers?' Richard asked.

126

Kate was resting her head on his shoulder and looked up. 'Mum was just concerned generally. We've always been really close and she seemed to think I've been a bit uptight lately and wanted to know why. I have, I know—it's just that when I was with Dad last time, I saw signs of some deep, strong feelings and I realised quite how much he still loves my mother. She's never come clean about the break-up, you see, she's always fobbed me off, and I guess it had just begun to bug me a bit all over again.'

Kate dried up. She didn't want to slip into talking about Ben, and Richard didn't need a great long family spiel.

'Did you explain that to your mother?' he queried, before adding, rather as a thought of his own, 'She'd probably sensed your slight tensions about Ben as well.' It was unnerving, but reassuring too, that he absorbed and understood so much.

'I tried,' Kate said, dealing with his question, 'but Mum still refused to open up. I'd quizzed Dad as well, but he'd only say that he had to take the blame. It's odd; something really fundamental must have happened between them, I feel sure.'

She sighed and reached up for a last kiss. 'I could do without having to work tomorrow, but we had better get some sleep now. I'll try to be back in time to plant bulbs; that was part of the present, wasn't it, I seem to remember you said?'

127

Kate was at work on time in the morning. Richard had given her a lift in. She was impressed with the creative team's late-night progress on the *Sleepyhead* pitch. They had taken the seraphically smiling sleeping girl, still in her bed, for an airborne ride in the sky and landed her on an idyllic tropical island beach. A hunky man strolls along to take her hand as she steps out of the bed in a floating nightie . . . Cut to the girl hurrying along a busy London street, bumps into same hunky man.

It was quite a distance from the prospective client's loose brief, which was exactly what she and Dan were supposed to stop the creatives doing. But a new pitch, Kate thought, needed free-range creativity, not a tight-controlled, battery-reared presentation—something to light a spark.

Dan was less relaxed about it. The new client had wanted to establish what the brand stood for—excellence, health qualities, dependability—and to create strong emotional ties with the consumer.

'Dreams, everyone has to have a dream,' one of the girls answered, when he complained to the team, cracking his knuckles. She yawned, eyeing him dreamily. 'We'll fly out a bedside table as well, with a logo mug full view beside the alarm clock.'

Kate grinned discreetly, not wanting to side against Dan; she'd been outspoken enough over *Maximan Briefs*. She wondered if anyone would notice if she disappeared for ten minutes and nipped out to a chemist. She'd had a quick online read about the morning-after pill, Levonelle One

Step. It could be taken up to three days after the event. The sooner the better, though, it seemed, but Kate thought she could wait till the end of the weekend. The surgery had a walk-in evening clinic on Mondays. She could pick up a prescription then and start taking the pill again straight away and even take another morning-after pill if need be.

Why couldn't Richard have taken care of things in the normal way? Condoms were safer, after all. She had a wistful twinge of mixed feelings, disheartened at the thought of being back on the pill; she was almost thirty-four and time had a habit of speeding up. It hadn't happened in two months of trying with Harry, which wasn't long, not much of a guideline, but mightn't it take more time still, the older she was?

Would Richard have been as passionately interested and given her the key to his front door if she'd had a child, the sort of baggage and complicated life that he had? Would he ever want another child? Kate waved that thought away impatiently. She looked round at the agency's brightest sparks who were concentrating hard in their sleekly equipped zones—getting on with the job. People were drifting out and back in again with coffee and she wandered out herself, not bothering with a coat, then sprinted downstairs, through the revolving doors and into the street to the nearest chemist.

The creative team would probably have it wrapped up by about three, she suspected, hurrying back. There should be a little daylight left for bulb planting and then the time in bed she imagined they would have before Richard ran her home. Her body was thinking along those lines; she could feel her

129

nipples, hard and smarting. Her brain was less clearly directed; her thoughts were dancing around like mischievous elves, luring her into other worlds where no such problems existed, such as whose flat or whether to give Richard a key in return when her flat had so much of Harry. A world where she was woken daily with a kiss and driven to work on weekend mornings such as today, where it was perfectly fine to travel at Richard's speed and fantasize about shared lives after only six days.

Kate bought a cafe latte at the ground-floor coffee bar, took it back up with her and had no trouble at all, joining in the discussion again. The dream theme had crystallised, everyone thought it a goer; all the account directors had given up being restraining voices and gone with the flow.

The morning disappeared. People began packing up. Dan came over with an ominously purposeful look on his face. Kate's heart sank. 'You on for a late lunch, Kate, possibly even an early film? We've earned a decent meal on the house after this lot.' He looked uptight, wanting her to say yes, too annoyingly serious by half.

Kate smiled as sweetly as she could. 'Sorry, Dan, I'm rushing away. I've promised to plant bulbs in a friend's garden.'

His face hardened. 'God, Kate, more fucking good deeds? What about getting a life and letting go of the past for a change? Isn't it about time?' He smiled unconvincingly, trying to hide his unpleasant outburst, but she could see he was fighting to rein himself in. 'It's great you're coming to *Tosca* with me, do you the world of good. You're a class act, Kate, too good to shut away!' Dan struggled to produce another fake smile then turned to go.

The opera evening was dragging Kate down like an illness; she had to get out of it, Dan would have to be told. Richard had mentioned going back briefly to the Amazon sometime soon. They were almost done in South America, apart from filming the trickiest stage of the cocaine process, he'd said—from a leaf to a line on a tabletop—when the leaves were chemically treated to become a paste.

Kate thought of Richard being away, out of the country at a time that neatly coincided with her opera evening with Dan. It would be simpler to honour the date; to try and dream up a convincing enough face-saving excuse wouldn't be easy. She could hardly tell Dan the truth, that almost overnight she'd become completely obsessed with a glamorous television personality, older than she was, but with more sex appeal in his little pinkie fingernail than the entire man-force of the agency.

She'd just seen that Dan could turn nasty when he chose. He certainly wouldn't appreciate being ditched—all the more so if he knew it was all about being on hand in case Richard should pick up the phone. It was postponing the deed, she knew, bottling out, but better on the whole, probably, to keep the peace. Dan had been patiently wooing her for months, allowing her status as a grieving widow, and she had, after all, accepted his generous invitation.

On her way back to Chelsea, Kate came out of Sloane Square tube station and started up King's Road almost at a run. With no taxis in sight she hopped on a bus, but soon jumped off again in frustration when the traffic slowed to a jam. She carried on, impatient with shoppers loaded up with carrier bags, young mums pushing buggies, people

131

talking on their mobiles. After two short nights and little of them spent sleeping, she should have felt more of a wreck, but she could have raced up to the top of a mountain if Richard was there, carried on the wings of her adrenaline. Richard called. 'How are you doing? Lunch is waiting—and so am I! Polly was here earlier. She'd been shopping in King's Road, expecting to hang around all afternoon, I think, till I took them out for dinner. I said no dice, I was very tied up and packed her off home. Ed's there so I'll go for them after taking you to your flat. It's on the way to Barnes. I'm sure Polly got the message, though, about "tied up" meaning my whole life spun on its head by a beautiful girl with soft dark hair and irresistible eyes who has a particular smile that I hope is now reserved for me alone . . .'

'I can't hear you in all this traffic,' Kate panted, hearing him very well.

She slowed down, nearing the house. Two young men, presumably the couple living upstairs, were huffing and puffing theatrically, trying to heave an immense Christmas tree over the low front wall onto the pavement. They were both slim and sinewy; one had floppy dark hair, the other was designer-bald with a moustache. Kate felt extremely self-conscious, holding Richard's door key tightly and very obviously in her hand.

They were falling about laughing, clutching each other and making little progress with the tree. They calmed down as she approached, looking interested.

The one with the floppy hair made the running. 'We saw you leave this morning and we said, "She looks nice!" I'm Mark, by the way, but everyone

132

calls me Madge, and this is Justin. We live upstairs.'

Kate smiled, feeling awkward. 'I've met your cat,' she said. 'Did you really have that huge tree up in your flat?'

'Yes, aren't we mad? It was Justin's idea. "Let's go to Norway," he said, "choose the real thing and have it shipped." But we didn't expect it to be quite this big! We had to bend it back on itself like a limbo dancer. It made a sort of lovely bower, though.'

'If you need any help taking it anywhere, I'm sure Richard would . . .'

'No, no, we're fine! Lovely to meet you, um?'

'Kate.'

'Be happy, Kate,' Madge beamed. 'See you around.'

Kate was relieved to turn her key and go inside. 'I just met the boys,' she said, as Richard took her coat and gave her the sort of hug more appropriate to someone given up for lost, found wandering in the desert, than an advertising executive returning from a few hours in a Soho office on a Saturday.

'I saw. I thought I'd leave you to it.'

She looked over his shoulder to the all-purpose white table. 'What's this amazing spread? Are you feeding a crowd of friends?' She extracted herself. 'Something smelling wonderful in the oven, all these cheeses and that exotic-looking salad, fancy bread—what are you trying to do to me?'

'It was too late for more than a picnic. I hope it'll do.'

She was hungry and they did justice to it all. Richard asked after her morning and she went into the ins and outs of the flying bedside table, feeling unprofessional since ad campaigns were jealously

133

guarded secrets. 'I did a load of email and marked time,' he said. 'I think we both could have been better employed.'

'Tell me more about you,' Kate said. 'You were asking all the questions on New Year's Eve—and at Sadie's. What about your time pre-Eleanor? Did you work on a provincial paper? I want to know it all.'

'You can have a quick potted run-down—no time for more.'

Over a bottle of ice-cold Montrachet he talked about reading economics at LSE, the month he'd spent as a DJ in America's Midwest, his time bumming around India living rough. Listening attentively and hearing about his widowed mother, Celia, who lived in Salisbury, in the lee of the Cathedral, Kate asked, 'Does she come to London much, to see Ed and Polly?'

'Ah, that's quite a little bone of contention; she feels rather pushed out with Eleanor's mother living in the house. And with the exam stage they're both at now, it's hard to fit in lunches and visits. She'll come and see them here with me at half term. She'll love meeting you then.'

'You did say you might have to be off to the Amazon again. I hope not too soon.'

'Yes, this month, I think. It would only be for about ten days, but it's hard to say when. I might have to leap on a plane at any minute. Presenters aren't usually producers as well, you see, and although I've worked out my own deal as a sort of co-producer, I can't really call the shots on timing. Half term is early this year, though, and I do want to be back for that.'

'What happens when you're there? How long is

134

the documentary? Is it a single programme or spread over a few?'

He reached for her hand. 'You really want to hear all this?'

'I do, I'm extremely interested. I'll make the coffee while you talk.'

'It's going to be two hour-and-a-half-long programmes, the first about the various early stages of production till it's refined down to a powder, trafficked, and finally finds its way onto our streets.'

Kate couldn't help thinking back to Boxing Day, asking Ben about his business and the products he imported from South America. Her mind kept being drawn back to that chat, but it was impossible to believe that whatever Ben was involved in—something, for sure, that was causing her mother tension—could be anything illegal, let alone to do with drugs.

'And the second programme?' she asked, standing up and filling the kettle.

'That's all about the scene here, distribution to the clubs, dealers, users, drugs in prisons, stuff like that. We'll do the medical bit, statistics and facts, the hidden harm to relatives, the full destructive story.

'We've filmed the small-time farmers in their shacks in Bolivia's southern jungle,' Richard said, looking over to her. 'They sell the leaves to other small operators—for small change really, not much in it for them—and those guys see that the leaves find their way to hidden pits, mainly in the Amazonian basin. The farmers are subsidised to grow fruit and veg, but they use that as cover and go on selling leaves, blowing the money and continuing to live on a pittance. But it's all relative.

135

In the north, around La Paz, the poverty is extreme. The air in the high altitude there is incredibly thin and the nights are icy. La Paz has the highest golf course in the world, but it also has street children who sleep on top of each other for warmth.'

He carried on. 'We wanted to do it all in one hit, but getting to see an illegal product being chemically processed in hidden pits in impossible-to-find locations isn't easy. People are naturally pretty suspicious, but I think our researcher out there is close to a breakthrough. These guys like the colour of our money, but well, in cricketing terms you need to have very soft hands.'

'Tell me more,' Kate said, getting a tin of coffee out of the fridge where Richard kept it.

'We have to make these guys see that one bit of Amazonian jungle looks much like any other on camera,' he said, watching her feel her way round his kitchen. 'And that no one could possibly ever find the way again to wherever they lead us. We wouldn't even be able to get out of where they take us to without their help; we'd be lost in the steamy depths of that hellhole jungle.'

'Don't say that! Will you be safe? They could abandon you at any time.'

'Would you come looking for me, Katie?'

She brought the tin of coffee and the pot to the table and kissed his head. 'That depends. Tell me how leaves become a paste,' she said, 'and how many scoops of coffee you put in.'

'Two. The paste process is a chemistry lesson, it could take all night. The gist of it is that mashed, dampened leaves are mixed with alkali and kerosene in a plastic-lined pit, then they put in sulphuric acid. You get a sort of milky

136

coffee-coloured paste, around fifty per cent cocaine—along with other acids and residue that have to be siphoned off. You add lime or caustic soda and finally end up with a yellowish cakey glump. That's filtered again, dried and packaged before it's ready for trafficking. The big guys move in and take it to secret labs in Ecuador and Columbia for purifying into the coke base. Eventually you get cocaine hydrochloride, which is the actual powder people whiff up their noses.'

She poured two mugs of coffee. 'A quick bit of gardening after this?'

He got up and came beside her. 'It's almost dark,' he murmured, closing in for a slow-motion, old-movie-style kiss, 'and was it really ever on the agenda?'

*   *   *

Kate stroked Richard's hair. 'Remember I'm going to see my father tomorrow. Will you come for supper when I'm back?' She hesitated a moment. 'And stay over, perhaps?'

He shifted, bringing his face close so that he could look at her. 'Suppose I came with you to Rye? Would that work? Or would your father rather have you all to himself?'

'I think it would give him the greatest pleasure if you came.'

Kate knew it would. She had slight mixed feelings, though. Worry about how she'd handle Richard being with her and how Aidan would read it, however much she played it down. But he knew enough about people who had television fame, he'd hardly imagine Richard was the answer to his

137

long-term hopes for his widowed daughter. Aidan would see it as a step in the right direction at least, she thought, ashamed of her whinging of only a week ago, and how sorely her sick father's patience must have been tried.

Richard was trailing her arm with light fingernails. She felt him hard against her, passionate all over again. It was late, but he was the one with time constraints, teenage children waiting to be taken to dinner, and she wasn't going to worry overmuch on his behalf.

They were laughing hysterically and rolling together when they heard the sound of the front door. Richard stiffened, they both did, but he sprang into instant action, leaping out of bed and hauling on jeans without underpants, cursing as he buttoned his shirt.

'Hi! Anyone around? You there, Dad? Has your friend gone?'

'What are you doing here, Poll?' Richard shouted, sliding his feet into loafers and making for the stairs. 'You were going home, I seem to remember. Waiting till I came to collect you . . .'

'Sorry if I'm *intruding*,' Polly called up, sarcasm dripping from every syllable, 'but I've lost my oyster card actually. I'm really stuck, I've no money. I've been looking everywhere, then I thought it could be somewhere here.'

'That wouldn't surprise me,' Richard replied, equally sarcastically. Kate edged to the bedroom door, desperately keen to listen, while struggling to stay balanced and pull on her tights. 'I was just showing my friend where the bathroom was,' she heard him explain, ridiculously. Was that his best shot? 'She'll be down in a minute, Polly, and I'd be

138

grateful if you'd at least try and make some sort of an effort. She's been at work all day; we had a late lunch.'

'So I see. You haven't done much clearing up.'

Kate hastily straightened the duvet, put Richard's pants and socks on a chair then slipped into the bathroom, pulling the chain to back up his story. It felt almost amusing, being caught out twice in as many days. She wondered, going slowly downstairs and attempting a halfway look of composure, what on earth Richard was about, pointlessly trying to keep up such a transparent façade with an extremely streetwise, London-based sixteen year old. Polly would have seen through anything he said. But he was her father and had to do what he thought was best.

He flashed Kate a quick reassuring smile as she came towards them. 'This is Kate Nichols, Polly. I'd just been talking about the birthday dinner tonight—we were almost about to leave actually. I was going to drop Kate at her flat on the way.'

'It's good to meet you,' Kate said, taking in the girl's short, spiky dark hair, her thinness and pale skin—but most of all her kohl-ringed eyes that held a look of frighteningly cold hostility. Polly was in black leggings, lace-up ankle boots and a hooded, grey woolly zip-up; she was sitting on the table with her sexy boots on a chair, picking at the grapes in the fruit bowl. 'Hi,' she muttered, neither moving from the table nor managing even the ghost of a smile. She had a rather heart-touching frailty about her all the same; it was the pallid translucency of her skin, her bitter defiance and obvious need to fight battles all on her own.

'Will you still be going for Ed, Dad?' she asked,

139

ignoring Kate. 'Or will he get the bus now? Shall I come with you or stay here?'

'Well, I was about to take Kate home, as I said, so I'll go for him anyway. You can stay here. What's under that top? Are you dressed to go out to dinner?' Polly pulled down the zip and revealed a low-neck black sweater, just long enough to be decent with her leggings. She was so skinny that the sight of an exposed cleavage was unexpected. She looked available. Kate could imagine her drinking and flirting in clubs, acting beyond her years.

'What about you, Dad? You going like that? Won't you be cold without socks?'

Richard took it in his stride. 'You mean you don't want me to dress down? You surprise me, Poll. But I do need to put on a different shirt and jacket. Perhaps you can make Kate a cup of tea and look after her . . .' And with that, and a slightly helpless, if supportive look, he left Kate to her fate and fled upstairs.

Polly climbed down from the table and went over to the kettle. She felt its weight for enough water, pinged it on then turned to lean against the worktop, staring across at Kate.

'So you're his latest squeeze? You won't last, you know,' she said, without a flicker of expression, speaking low enough to ensure that her father wouldn't hear. 'They come and go.'

'Is that what you want to see happen?' Kate said neutrally. Trying to be saccharine-friendly, she felt, would be pointless, cause more hang-ups than help. 'You don't want your father to have a life of his own?'

'He can screw around as much as he likes. I don't care. He's had a few, a blonde in place first, then a

140

redhead, then another redhead . . .'

'Perhaps it was the same redhead in different clothes,' Kate snapped, her hand beginning to itch.

'Very funny,' Polly sneered. 'But I just thought you should get the message, if you're interested, that you're wasting your time. He loves my mother underneath, you know—whatever he might say to you. That's the truth of it. He should never have left.' A triumphant note had crept in, as though she could well sense that it was the one thing Kate most feared. Polly unhooked a mug; she looked a little too obviously pleased with herself as she extracted a teabag from a glass jar. 'I'm only trying to be helpful,' she said, going to the fridge for the milk.

'That almost certainly means you're being the opposite,' Richard said more fondly, coming downstairs in a brown soft-weave jacket and laundered jeans. 'Helpful about what, I'd like to know?'

'Never you mind, Dad!' Polly could smile when she wanted, Kate thought bitterly.

Kate hadn't seen Richard in a jacket before and with the open-neck white shirt he was wearing it suited him; he looked, with his thick lively hair and soft expression, like a more mature Rupert Brooke, she thought, reminded of a photograph she'd seen of the poet relaxing in a garden deckchair. She wanted to be out having dinner with Richard, feeling proud, not making way for Polly and anticipating a lonely evening ahead. She felt pinched and dowdy, like a plain flatmate watching the prettier one waltz out on the arm of a glamorous male, which was absurd. He was only taking out his children.

'I must be off,' she managed to say brightly while

remembering with frustration that Harry's old briefcase was still up in the bedroom. Polly would snoop around inside it for sure. Glancing to the hall, her heart lifted as she saw that Richard had thought to bring it down.

She smiled at Polly. 'Sorry I haven't got round to the tea. Perhaps you might have it?'

'Perhaps,' she answered, keeping up her blank teenage stare. 'Oh, look!' she exclaimed excitedly, making them both jump. 'There's my pass, right under the table! I knew it would turn up.'

'So did I,' Richard muttered dryly. 'Now, if you want a job while you're waiting, my girl, something useful you could do, a little clearing up would be a great help.'

He picked up the briefcase and unlatched the door. Kate couldn't wait to be out of the flat and away.

* * *

'I so much wanted you to come with us tonight,' Richard said, smoothing her cheek at a traffic light, 'but as Polly's just made clear, it wouldn't have been ideal. She's smart, she'll have picked up that it's very different with you and serious, and that's the trouble. She lets things slip at home, you see. She's bitter about me leaving and it's a hard thing to counter. I have no defence. I'm impatient for you to meet Ed, but perhaps that's best without Polly— anything is! We must fix it up very soon.'

The lights changed, his eyes were back on the road and Kate digested what he'd said in silence. It had sounded good, but she couldn't feel elated or comforted with Polly's words still turning like twin-sided daggers. She had known she was on sure ground. Polly had her reasons, but wasn't she quite likely to be right about his feelings for Eleanor? Otherwise why should Richard have minded so much if his daughter let anything slip at home? He was divorced, Eleanor must surely expect him to take up with girls.

Kate wished she could see a good photograph of his ex-wife. The one she'd found online had been indistinct and there were none in Richard's flat, not even in the drawers where she'd had a quick look. Eleanor's profile in that press picture hadn't been much of a clue. Kate formed an image of her, front on, picturing the tigerish eyes and full lips that went with a volatile nature. Asking to see photographs was getting in too deep, sure to encourage him to back away, and her instinct was not to go there. Eleanor was morose and demanding, Kate knew, but, combined with exceptional talent . . . wasn't that the sort of dominating, challenging temperament that could hold a man, whatever Richard had said at lunch on New Year's Day?

It was hopeless, getting this obsessed and fixated. Why wasn't it possible just to enjoy the sex while it lasted? Why did feelings always have to get in the way?

'You're being very silent.' Richard turned with a smile as they neared her flat. 'I think I understand why, but I wish you'd be less guarded and believe what I say.'

'You mean what you said, just now?'

'What should I do to make you feel trust, Katie? Would it help if I try to explain more about Eleanor? We'll have the car journey tomorrow, if your father doesn't mind me coming, time to talk on the way.'

'Thanks. I'd like that. But trust is a two-way thing of course; I hope you have some in me!' Kate laughed, embarrassed, worried that had sounded forced. 'Why don't you come for early breakfast before we go?' she said brightly. 'My turn to cook the bacon.'

Richard drew up outside her flat and they kissed in the car. Inside the building she stood motionless, listening as he revved up and set off for Barnes. Stupid, talking about two-way trust, making so much of it, and her feelings must have been on show for him to have said what he did.

Kate waited until the sound of his engine had died. Presumably he would see Eleanor while he was home collecting Ed, and again at the end of the evening when he returned the children. She went up to her flat and, as her front door closed, she thought of Richard shafting the bolt home. She sighed. It seemed hardly worth bothering to dry her eyes.

CHAPTER 10

Kate called her father to tell him that Richard was coming with her. 'Hope that's okay, Dad. He says he's met you in the past, but thinks you'll never remember.'

'Whatever gave him that idea? I'm delighted. I'll enjoy talking about his work. I did wonder if you might bring him after Sadie told me about his babysitting skills. She was full of the hit he made with Joseph and seemed pretty taken with him herself!'

Kate put on a washing-machine load feeling more positive, then dashed out to a late-night store for breakfast things for the next morning. Back at home she washed her hair, did her nails, dealt with a few emails and two days of post.

She was putting off thanking her mother for supper, and felt vulnerable around the subject of Richard, unclothed, stripped of any veil of pretence.

She pictured Rachel and Ben discussing him and wondered, since Richard was an investigative television journalist, and an ex-financial one, what Ben would think of her new relationship. Kate didn't see him as a man to cast slurs, but imagined that if Ben really were in some sort of tight spot, he might be tempted to make subtle asides about Richard that could influence her mother's view.

Kate picked up the phone, hoping for the voicemail, but Rachel was in. 'Just ringing to say thanks for supper,' she said, feeling brittle again, and surprised at how jealous she felt of her mother sitting cosily at home with Ben. The Polly debacle had made any idea of uncomplicated togetherness with Richard seem a distant dream.

She talked about her morning at Impetus, describing the *Sleepyhead* pitch, trying to be whimsical and amusing, but it was hard to sound entirely relaxed. They both knew there were unspoken questions, sensitivities that had surfaced last night; Kate felt the phone line was strung like a necklace with all that was being left unsaid.

How could she suggest, though, that something seemed out of line about Ben when he and her mother were so close? Rachel was presenting an

145

impregnable front, hiding her tenseness superbly. To the outside world she would seem her usual attentive, charming, unruffled self. It was immensely frustrating.

'All well with Richard?' Rachel queried lightly.

'Fine. He's coming down to Rye with me tomorrow. He and Dad have met once in the past, it seems.' She left it there, keen not to be drawn.

'Katie love, I know you're hurt and think I've been less than open, but try to have some trust. I know what I'm doing, it is for the best of motives.'

'You're asking a lot,' she muttered. They were talking in code. Rachel had known over supper that the real issue was Ben. Why else would she have had that passionate outburst about him just when Kate had been about to leave?

'She was reminded yet again of Boxing Day and the newspaper article about drugs that Sadie's little joke had summoned up. But that piece had been about the demise of the powerful Medellin and Cali cocaine cartels and the small, difficult to trace, satellite units that had replaced them. It had described sophisticated new trafficking routes—the shipping of cocaine to West Africa and on into Europe on scheduled flights, the criss-crossing of the continent and the smuggling of the drugs into Britain in unlikely containers like tea chests. The photograph of the corrupt Colombian Defence Minister that had caught Kate's eye had merely been a peg. That piece hadn't had any significance . . .'

The only remote link with Ben, that she could see, was that years ago he'd spent some time in Colombia. But Kate still couldn't seriously believe that her mother's problems—or rather

146

Ben's—could have anything to do with drugs. That was too much of a stretch.

She snapped back, hearing Rachel's voice. 'I know I'm asking a lot, but have faith in me, Katie. It's important.'

She changed the subject. 'Did Sadie reach you, by the way? She has a favour to ask—Ru wants her with him in Davos the last weekend this month. It's the annual meeting of the World Economic Forum, all those bankers holed up in a ski resort. I can do most of it, just not Saturday night. And I'd have to leave mid-afternoon. Can you help out and make it by lunchtime that day? Perhaps Richard might even come for lunch? I'd love to meet him properly.'

'I don't know. He may be away. I'll help of course,' Kate added, trying to sound more positive.

Sadie called later that evening about the weekend. 'It is very important to Ru,' she stressed, sounding earnest and unassertive. Kate thought her sister danced too much to Rupert's tune. 'He's lined up a nanny and his mother in case,' Sadie carried on, 'but I'd so much rather it was you and Mum. And Joseph keeps asking to see Richard again!'

'I doubt he'll be around,' Kate muttered edgily, suddenly losing her elated need to sing Richard's praises from the hilltops. 'He travels a lot.' She was determined to play him down and said something which was no longer strictly true. 'Harry's always in my thoughts, Sadie. Richard's no fixture anyway, he has heavy commitments, a complicated life.'

'But you're sucking it and seeing, aren't you?' Sadie suggested crudely. 'Don't fuck about, hon, there aren't that many fish in the sea and I think he's great! Can't you at least go for a swim?'

147

'I've done that. And now I might just decide to head back to shore.'

Kate felt better for being doomy and difficult with her sister and she finished her chores bathed in a sort of grim, misery-fuelled satisfaction. It came as a shock when Richard phoned—she hadn't allowed herself the thought that he would. He was passionate, impressively so, given the restaurant noise, yet still had to return his children to Barnes and see Eleanor. Kate wanted to tell him to call again from home, no matter how late, any time was wonderful. She sensed him waiting for her to say it, but the words wouldn't come.

*　　　*　　　*

She woke the next morning in a cold sweat from a dream. Her mother had been flying through the sky like Wendy in *Peter Pan*, but as Kate watched, struck dumb with horror, she started falling, spiralling towards the sea below with the strange floral skirt she was wearing lifting high in a revealing circle. Ben came running along a beach, shouting up, but the wind was raging and so loud, she couldn't possibly hear. He and Kate stood together on the shore, powerless, helpless as she plunged on down.

Kate lay still, adjusting to the fact it was just a dream. Then she sprang into action, her heart pounding: Richard would be there in an hour. She showered and dressed in a shirt dress and stretch jeans, overcome with intense anticipation. Would he sweep her up and whisk her straight off to bed? Would the marital bed be an inhibiting playground and feel indecently heartless? Richard's

148

love-making had all but blanked out Harry, he'd vanished from her screen with the speed of a click of a mouse. She was deeply worried about her mother, but why had Rachel been the one to be spiralling down into a stormy sea? Harry had wanted Kate with him that day. Why had she dreamed of her mother?

Richard rang. 'Hi!' she said, feeling an elated rush.

The smile on her face faded, its warmth drained. He sounded agonised. 'Katie, I can't come, not to Rye, not to breakfast . . . Eleanor's taken some mix of drugs or pills and she hasn't come round. Her mother just called and I can't leave them to cope alone. Ed was in a panic, Polly was screaming. I have to get there and see the ambulance comes okay, see to all the business of hospital. I'm driving there now, so I can't really talk, but I am dreadfully sorry. Can you explain to your father? Eleanor will need pumping out, I expect; the hospital will know.'

'But she will be all right?' Kate mumbled, asking God to forgive her for the terrible thought that was momentarily in her head.

'It's not the first time, we've been here before.'

He was divorced, she wanted to shout; was he going to go on carrying the load for ever?

'Call you, soon as I can,' he said, and clicked off.

Kate stared at the phone. She felt in a state of nothingness. She wandered into the kitchen where she cling-filmed cut grapefruit halves and put them in the fridge, laid uncooked bacon slices back in their plastic pack. Then she poured a bowl of muesli and sat at the breakfast bar that looked down the length of the secluded communal gardens. Her building backed onto them at one end

149

and two streets of terraced houses backed on as well, at either side, creating a contained stretch of beautifully private gardens.

Victorian railings filled any gaps, making it a glorious, safe, green playground for the children of the well-heeled residents, bankers, lawyers, writers, politicians.

On summer evenings Kate loved to walk the perimeter path overhung by mature London plane trees, the scent of Mexican orange blossom heavy on the air and the ping of tennis balls a romantic rhythmic sound coming from the court screened by evergreen foliage. But summer was months away. Would Richard still be in her life by then? Or long gone?

A couple of children came out to play, despite the early hour and threatening squally clouds. They started arguing and punching each other. Kate stared down, thinking about responsibility and her own uncontainable need. It was nearly nine, soon time to be off to Rye. Aidan would be disappointed. Her mother would ask about the day. She climbed down from her stool to make a mug of tea and while the kettle boiled, pictured Richard's face with its lines of strain growing deeper as he waited to know Eleanor's condition.

*   *   *

Kate was soon clear of the city. On the motorway the rain came in fierce bursts on the back of a wind that rocked the car. Reaching her exit she drove on minor roads through a leaden, overcast landscape with bald petrified-looking trees and water-logged fields dotted with bedraggled sheep. It was a lonely

150

drive. The countryside lacked the unique stark beauty of Romney Marsh further along the coast that she particularly loved, and she felt in need of her artist friend, Donna. Her isolated farmhouse was only a short hop from Rye and Kate considered calling in on the way home. It wasn't practical, the time too tight. She had asked Richard to come round and he might still.

'Poor man,' her father had said on the phone. 'What an albatross of a responsibility.'

But he'd gone on to say—to Kate's great shame after her frighteningly selfish first thoughts—that the bipolar condition was a serious mental illness that deserved sympathetic understanding. She took it as a rebuke anyway and, in a fit of self-blame, directed her mind to Polly.

Kate tried to make allowances for her. She wondered if Richard truly understood his daughter's needs. Polly had an unstable mother, a weak-sounding grandmother—was it any wonder she schemed and manoeuvred to lure her father back by whatever means?

Had she let slip to her mother that Richard had someone new in his life, exaggerating it, calling Kate a younger model who seemed to have quite a hold? Was Polly panicking now because of that? Did she feel to blame for her mother suddenly swallowing fistfuls of attention-seeking pills? Or, if Eleanor had done it a number of times before, was it a risk—which was hard to believe—that Polly was prepared to take?

Her vulnerability was clear to see, but, since Kate herself was problem and cause, and the last person Polly would turn to, she could be no help at all. It made her feel useless and uninvolved, nothing

151

more than a bit of window-dressing, a passenger with no destination.

She was passing the lane to the church where she and Harry had been married. A small Norman church with lichen-spotted gravestones that leaned into each other like wise old men and a path to the porch lined with a herbaceous border.

It had been a charmed wedding, a perfect late-summer's day, Joseph a toddling page, his hands firmly held by the bridesmaids, the twin daughters of Harry's brother. Kate had walked down the candle-lit aisle with flowers at the head of every pew, holding onto her father's arm, so proud and confident, foreseeing only a golden future.

Aidan had been a fit man then. Striking-looking, he'd seemed to fill the church with his powerful presence, quite stealing the limelight from Harry.

Rachel had stayed overnight at the house, everything civilized and friendly. Kate wondered if she had turned to look at her ex-husband as he came down the aisle and longed to roll back time. Ben was still married then and not on the scene.

At the reception Sadie had whispered, 'I'm pregnant again!'

'I'll catch you up soon,' the glowing bride had boasted before flying off on honeymoon to Rome. There, Harry had studied paintings by day and Kate by night. She'd felt slightly piqued and disappointed, wanting his undivided attention, dreaming of tropical islands, sensual sun and not a distracting Old-Master in sight.

*　　　*　　　*

Hannah opened the front door as Kate came up the

152

path. She was wearing a charcoal coat with big buttons, a hairy old thing that looked decades old. The coat's forbidding colour emphasised her wary-eyed pallor, but she smiled with unusual warmth. 'He's having a good day! Happy to answer the phone—which isn't always the case. I was just going to take Millie for a walk before lunch.'

The little monster had shot out past Hannah on her stubby legs as if the opened door had been a pulled trigger, and was dancing around, yapping fit to burst. She bared her yellow teeth when Kate bent low to pat her, before conceding that daughterly status gave Kate the licence to take such liberties and behaving with more canine grace.

'I worried Dad might be slightly down, not having a male visitor after all,' Kate said, straightening up and returning Hannah's unexpected smile.

'No, he's fine about it, seems very relaxed, in quite a twinkly mood really.' Hannah looked embarrassed at opening up more than usual, and muttered, retreating again, fixing on Millie's pacing, bullet-like little body. 'Well, we'll be off then. You'll manage him all right?'

Kate assured her of that. She went indoors, hung up her old sheepskin and pushed on the sitting-room door. Aidan was out of his chair, already on his feet to greet her.

'Richard just called,' he said cheerfully. 'He thought you'd have arrived by now. He says you need a hands-free phone in the car! Anyway, all is well, they've pumped out his wife; she'll be over it soon.'

'His ex-wife.'

'I told him you'd call him back. Be sure you don't

forget.' Aidan grinned.

'Sorry he couldn't come, Dad.'

'We had a good long chat—and now I have you all to myself for a whole day!'

He was holding out his arms. Kate stared at her frail father, wondering at his chirpy, lively mood. 'Oh, Dad,' she cried, running to him, crumpling, dissolving as he enveloped her. She could feel every bone in his ribcage. Hugs and closeness had such finite preciousness. She was making things worse, drawing attention, and felt terrible for not matching his mood and keeping pace with his calm bravery.

'You really care, don't you?' Aidan said, smoothing her hair, assuming her tears were for Richard. 'Is falling in love such a terrible thing? Don't fight your instincts. If it feels right, give in gladly, it's much the best!'

Kate pressed her face into his well-worn blue sweater, soft and smelling of Millie and woodsmoke, soap and antiseptic. 'It's you I love, Dad, so much.'

Her voice was muffled, buried in the wool of his jumper. She lifted her head, wiping her wet cheeks on her sleeve, and noticed that his eyes were watering too. He avoided mopping them as he settled down again in his chair—trying not to draw attention, she thought.

He gave a confident smile, full of his old charisma. 'Go and call Richard. I said you would. I think I'd just like to close my eyes for a few minutes before lunch.'

'I've tired you out.'

'Go on, Katie, he wants a call. Oh dear, here's Millie back!' He laughed, as his beloved little dog careered in and leapt right up onto his thin knees.

154

Her father's positive mood was a joy, a flash of his old strong character, a silver edge to a cloud—though what had prompted it Kate found hard to fathom.

She went up to her childhood bedroom, which was dark as dusk on that sodden, light-starved day. Her body was liquid, talking to Richard. She yearned for his kisses. The thoughts in her head were meaty, tender, raw and possessive; they softened the edges of her sadness, pushed back the worry of her mother. They were obsessive, dominating, distracting, they'd put her in a daze at work. They'd let in barely anything else in the last six days, nothing but Richard.

'My flat tonight,' she said, needing to get back to her father. 'But if Eleanor's not well . . . I'd absolutely understand.'

'She's out of danger. I'll show you how much I need you, Katie, you'll see.'

*   *   *

As soon as lunch was over and Hannah left them alone with their coffee, Aidan brought up Richard again. It was as though he sensed he was about to be grilled over his broken marriage and he was getting in first.

'Have you met Richard's children?'

'Only his daughter. She just turned up at his flat yesterday afternoon. He says they're meant to phone first, but she had an excuse of a sort.'

'You seem to have handled that okay. So what's making you so edgy?'

Kate couldn't clam up, not with her father. 'I'm worried about getting too close to him, Dad. He

155

travels a lot, he's quite a bit older and in television, too—with followers and a fan club! He's in a different league. And having children in their late teens . . . he's done the family side of things. Not to mention being very involved with his ex-wife, the problems of her illness . . .'

'Is that all?'

'No, it's not all, actually,' Kate said hotly, rising as she always did when her father was being facetious and teasing. 'I don't want to be his plaything either. Richard's had a run of girls since leaving, according to his daughter—who also thinks he still loves his ex-wife underneath.'

'And you latch on and choose to believe that? You're incorrigible, Katie. You decide black's white and then won't budge an inch; you never allow in shades of grey.'

Kate pounced on that, her heart sinking to her boots. 'So you agree then, that it's at least a shade possible I might be right?' She glared at him in morbid triumph.

Aidan laughed. 'God, I do have to watch my words! Well, for a start, you know perfectly well his daughter's mixing it. And even on the balance of probabilities, my girl, I'd say you're a hundred per cent wrong.'

'Dad!' she snorted, quietly elated in fact, after Richard's call. 'I want you to come to your chair, now,' she said, 'and get comfortable, so I can ask you a few things.'

She closed the door and pulled up a chair beside him. 'What's the truth of the divorce, Dad?' She'd had to ask outright, she was resolved, yet it felt cruel now, digging into old wounds and she added diffidently, 'I would like to know.'

Aidan made it easier. 'I should have told you last time you asked. I wanted to.'

He studied his nails for what seemed an age then looked up. 'It was a situation.' Kate tensed, not expecting that. 'We have to go back to the Bosnian war,' Aidan said. 'I'd covered it all through, remember, right to the 1995 Dayton Peace Agreement. It was horrific from the start—that was in eastern Bosnia where whole Muslim towns and villages were being ransacked and burned—and by the end I think I'd lost all reason. The suffering, the torturing and killing were inhuman. The villagers were kept in indescribable camps, the women, even girls as young as fourteen, were in separate compounds where Serb soldiers and police would come and repeatedly rape them. They were treated worse than slaves.'

Kate wondered distractedly if what he had witnessed could possibly have contributed to his cancer, weakened his immune system in some way. Could anyone really know?

'I had to force myself to keep reporting it all. Even now, when I think about it . . .' He fell silent a moment, but when Kate looked inquiring he carried on. 'I think about the siege of Mostar, most of all. Nowadays Mostar is rebuilt, a charming historic city again. Even the famously beautiful sixteenth-century bridge that took a direct hit is restored. The river is still a telling divide, though— the hostility goes on.'

'What happened, Dad? What was the *situation*?'

'It was shortly after the siege. I interviewed a woman, a Croat, who was a teacher in Mostar and who had lived through it all. Her English was good, she had control of her feelings and was even able to

157

describe the horror of seeing her husband killed by a bomb.

'We did the interview, then the cameraman was needed elsewhere in a hurry and I stayed behind to thank her. It was clear enough to her, though, that I was about to rush off, too. She looked at me so forlornly, like a fleeing refugee seeing the last boat steam away, all hope gone. Her knees seemed to give way and she sank down on a pile of filthy rubble and cried her eyes out.'

Aidan looked at his daughter. 'I hope you'll believe this, Katie, but when I put my arm round that woman, Ivana, it was simply a limp attempt to give comfort.'

'But it developed into something more?'

'Only because Ivana was so ruthlessly determined it should; I simply didn't see that in time. She seemed to take my helpless gesture as a green light to taking advantage. She turned, buried her face in my jacket and clung to me. She begged me to come back that evening and hear her story. I couldn't refuse. How much of what she told me was true, I'll never know. She said she'd entrusted her small daughter to her mother, so desperate was she to get her away from the city to their village home. Ivana described the horrors of life in the city vividly—as if I didn't know. She said shyly, slyly, how kind I was.

'It was only a few weeks since she'd lost her husband, but she wore me down, telling me how cruelly he'd mistreated her. Couldn't I understand that she needed to feel a woman again, she said?

'I resisted. I talked of my marriage, how lucky I was and told her she'd find someone else, that the war was near its end. But I'd been away weeks, I was lonely, despairing, desensitised. The violence

158

and bloodshed was dehumanising. Ivana was pressing me . . .'

Kate could see it all. She felt sad for her mother. Scenes of bomb devastation filled her mind; piled shards of glass, jagged bricks, blood-stained pavements, fetid smells, unclean water. Stray animals, mourners in black garb, black arm-bands . . .

'It became serious, did it?' she asked, feeling confused. 'You really cared for her?'

'No, no, that wasn't it at all. But I'd let down my guard, you see, and she seized on that weak moment with a tenacity I still can't believe.'

'Surely Mum could have forgiven you, Dad, and managed in time to get over it? It's all very understandable. Did she even really need to know? Or did it just go on too long?' Kate could see that hardly fitted with what he'd just said. She thought of the depth of emotion she had previously sensed in her father as well; nothing seemed to add up.

'There was never any hope of Mum not knowing,' he said grimly. 'Ivana was on the phone to her even before I was home. She was ruthlessly determined, swearing it was she I loved, that it was over between Mum and me. She appeared on our doorstep just days after I'd returned and even started following Mum, queuing behind her in supermarkets.

'I had to involve the police. Ivana was eventually required to go back home, but, God knows, the damage was done. I'd been weak and faithless and deserved all I got, but Mum suffered cruelly.'

Kate's sympathies transferred to her father. He was angry, squeezing out the pus of hateful memories, yet he had a haunted look in his eyes.

She felt overwhelmingly that his transgression had been minimal and her intelligent, civilized mother had owed him more support in the circumstances, and shouldn't have turned to lawyers and divorce. Ivana had jeopardized the trust, but need Rachel have let it be destroyed?

Kate began thinking about the timing. She had been doing her A levels about then, Sadie doing GCSEs. How could they have had no idea? It was incomprehensible.

'Mum was gradually worn down,' Aidan said, sensing her thoughts. 'One small crumb was that I'd instinctively mistrusted Ivana over birth control and taken precautions. There was no baby. And to be fair to Ivana, she only turned up on our doorstep in school hours. She loved children and had a daughter of her own.'

'But, you and Mum were divorced long after Bosnia, years after! Sadie and I were in our twenties. Surely Ivana wasn't plaguing you all that time?'

'No, only a year or so, but at some point, I suppose . . .' He dried up and left the sentence unfinished. Kate presumed he felt he'd done as asked, told the story from his side and it was for Rachel to take over from there.

'I'm sorry, Dad, making you talk about it, thinking back to the hardships and pain, as well as raking over the past. I hate to have pressed you, but thanks. I do feel I understand a bit better now.' She couldn't share her deep and abiding frustration, her instinctive sense that the story was only half told.

'I'll leave it to you how much you say to Sadie. She's very into the babies and that husband of hers.'

Aidan's face suddenly creased into a broad smile.

He looked hugely pleased with himself. 'Last Sunday, my love, you wanted to be a recluse! I tried to tell you to get a life and what do you know? I chalked up a first! You have never once, ever, even considered that there might be an upside, some positive merit in taking your old father's advice.'

CHAPTER 11

Richard was dangling out of bed, pulling half the duvet with him. Kate didn't know what was going on. He reappeared holding the neck of a dripping bottle of champagne, which he laid on the bed before leaning over again and resurfacing with a couple of glasses. He had a satisfied smile on his face. 'Happy Anniversary—it's a whole week!'

'An ice-bucket under the bed,' Kate kissed him, 'Is much more romantic than a potty. It doesn't work, though, to say "anni" when it's only a week.'

'How can someone who fucks like an angel nitpick like a pedant?'

'That's really quite blasphemous.'

'Which is another nitpick.' He was pouring the champagne, waiting for the fizz to die down. 'I've sorted out the Amazonian trip,' he said. 'I'm flying out Wednesday. I wish you could come. I'm going to hate being apart, but it'll be pretty hellish, steaming hot, and these guys will only take three of us into the rainforest, which has to be the producer, cameraman and me.'

'Don't go and get lost in the jungle. When will you be back?'

'The twenty-sixth—that's if we're not abandoned

161

to our fate . . .'

It was later than Kate had thought and the day after she was meant to go to the opera with Dan. She'd been geared to telling him that she couldn't come, but now it seemed to make better sense to leave things alone. Dan had probably talked around, he'd have hurt pride as well as being bitter if she ditched him and he'd only make trouble. He wasn't the type to do dignity.

'Is there a problem, Katie? You've gone quiet.'

'It's just that I thought you'd be away ten days and now it's over two weeks.'

'Don't tell me! But it'll wrap it all up out there and I'll have a satellite phone at least. I'd have gone fucking spare without a chance to talk. We're going to need some concentrated togetherness when I'm back. Are you owed any holiday? Can we take off somewhere?'

'Sure, that'd be terrific, except I can't be away from Dad for long.' She gave a shaky sigh, but quickly converted it into a smile. 'He enjoyed your call just before I arrived. He was in a cryptic mood all day, but a good one, I think.'

Kate took a sip of champagne. She and Richard were leaning against the bedhead, which was carved and upholstered in Chinese-yellow; the bed was Louis Quinze, Harry's inherited pride and joy— fitting for a bedroom, he'd said, with such a fine ceiling rose and cornice. The conversion of a stately Victorian villa into flats had been achieved with splendid attention to scale and period features. It had lured Harry to think rich and lush, pistachio-coloured wallpaper with a bird design, silk drapes to complement it. Now, seeing the room with fresh eyes, Kate felt faintly embarrassed. It was far from a rococo boudoir, but she could imagine Richard's girly upstairs neighbours, Madge and Justin, loving it and she wished it was a little less ornate.

'What are you thinking about?' Richard asked.

'Nothing really—just perhaps that with the *Sleepyhead* pitch and your dawn start, it's time we had some kip.' She wanted to go on talking, making the most of him, sleep felt a waste of time.

'I'll try not to wake you when I go,' he said. 'Mine's an easier day than yours, though, filming some interviews with doctors, starting on the medical stuff, which I can do falling out of bed. A load of facts and statistics on all the harm heavy coke use can do.'

'Such as?'

'Paranoia, convulsions, hallucinations, mucked-up heart rhythms and even heart attacks, kidney and liver trouble.' He grinned. 'Compulsive teeth grinding and loss of enamel—bruxism, that's called. It's a long list! We can spook up the non-smokers, too. People who've given up or never even smoked often start chain-smoking uncontrollably on coke. It enhances the high. Want to try a line and a smoke sometime?'

'Have you ever?'

'There's a question,' he laughed and kissed her forehead. '"Ever" is going back a long way. Now I suppose we had better snuck up. I'll just take out the bottle and glasses.'

In bed, in Richard's arms, feeling the brush of his underarm hair on her bare skin, she had her head in the crook of his neck and could burrow into the smell that was his own. She felt a sudden panic of loss and pressed tighter to his side, hooking a leg in between his. He squeezed it hard with his thighs.

163

She peered up at him. His features were clearly etched in the shadowy light from a street lamp, his straight longish nose, well-balanced lips. Kate touched them with her fingers. She didn't want him going away. Two weeks was far too long; feelings could change, she could lose him. She felt the ache of parting like a loss.

'Will I see you before you go?' she asked.

'I want to talk about that,' Richard said, capturing her fingers with his free hand and squeezing them tight.

Kate felt cold as ice and looked at him questioningly.

'About tomorrow night—can you take in a bag and come straight from work?' He studied her in the half light. 'And stay on at my flat after that?'

'Why not come here?' she said, relaxing again. She was comfortable about it, over any hang-ups about Harry. If anything she'd felt quite shocked that he hadn't come into her mind. No ghosts had haunted. Nothing had felt wrong about Richard being there, making love in her old marital bed.

'No, it has to be Chelsea,' he said, sounding surprisingly definite. 'This is a terrific flat, Katie, but it can't be here. I'm in Harry's space in this bed; it has memories for you and I can't help thinking of you in it with him. I feel like an interloper. I can see his shirts in that linen-press, his cuff-links, cards, small change, on top of the chest. The paintings, the John Ward, the nudes, are stunning, but you and Harry chose them to look at in bed, not me.'

Kate thought with hurt pride of the space and light in her flat, the glorious outlook, the garden she was free to use. It was her home. Harry had faded, patchily perhaps like a precious fabric in

164

sunlight, and it was the bright intense light of a new love.

'I thought you liked the flat,' she said tetchily. 'You were cool about the sitting room, you loved the pictures, you said. There's the spare room that Sadie and Ru use occasionally, we don't need to be in here.'

'Don't be so sensitive! I love the whole flat. But I was meaning move in, when I said stay on, not just talking about tomorrow night. I know my set-up in Chelsea is cramped and I'm asking a lot, but it's all mine, you see. It has nothing of Eleanor, none of her belongings, no reminders.' He had plenty of those in Barnes, Kate thought jealously, feeling in a spin. He was there often enough, a slave to her every mood swing.

'Polly and Ed only bed down at mine after a party,' Richard pressed, seeming completely serious about her moving in. 'It'll only ever be an issue if they stayed all weekend.' Eleanor was an issue, year-round. Kate seethed at the thought, but she kept silent. Her mind was racing ahead as he carried on. 'And it is a chance for me to see them away from Barnes and without their mother around.' Richard gave an apologetic smile.

'Moving in is a big step,' she said stiffly, against her every instinct. She would live anywhere with him, follow him to the ends of the earth so why not say so, throw herself at him ecstatically and grab the chance? Inbuilt reserve? Too frightened of being hurt? Her heart was clamouring to be heard, yet she felt incapable of letting it have its say.

'Wouldn't it be wiser, don't you think, taking smaller steps and not rushing things?' She leaned up with a kiss. 'It's only been a week.'

'Why? What for? I'm very clear about what I want, which is you, and what I'm doing. I want us to live together, Katie. And I am older, remember, short on time!'

Kate thought she was, too. She was back for a moment in Sadie's bedroom, holding Rose, feeling the baby's weight and warmth. She felt hollowed-out. Her maternal need was a real, physical, constant pain. 'I just think,' she repeated cautiously, 'we need to take stock and be a little less headlong.'

'We'll take lots of stock when I'm back,' Richard promised, with a cocky grin, reading her caution as positive, 'and I'm determined to make the most of these two days before I go. Try to get away early tomorrow and if you beat me to it, use your key! And then on Tuesday, when I'm having a day off, I want you to meet Ed. He has a dentist's appointment in Portland Place after school. Since it's quite near your office I thought we could have a drink or an early bite in Soho, if that's okay.'

Kate felt organized, taken over, like a new young employee being told when to clock in. She couldn't decide how she felt about it—or the wisdom of being in love with the boss.

She was awake in the small hours. Richard was leaving early and she had a testing day, but the thoughts kept coming, problems she couldn't ignore. His children wouldn't take kindly to her moving in. She could imagine how Polly would react. And what should she do about her flat? Leave it sitting there, empty, languishing and gathering dust? Did she take the paintings that she loved and wanted to live with? Would they have to be reinsured? How much stuff could she bring with her?

Kate tried to settle again and Richard reached out for her hand. 'We'll sort it,' he mumbled, half asleep. 'Have faith. We'll do whatever it takes.'

* * *

The *Sleepyhead* presentation was quite straightforward; the client and home teams began a cautious dialogue like opposing soldiers on a Christmas truce. Dan schmoozed around breaking the ice, as he would call it, saying how excited and fired-up they'd all felt, while Kate shrank from his trite phraseology. The visiting client team remained inscrutable, absorbing it all without comment.

'Here's the idea,' the creative director enthused, getting started on the meat of things. Now and then Kate found her moment to pipe up. The morning wore on.

In the late afternoon, when she was intent on clearing her emails and rushing off, Dan wandered down for one of his little chats. 'We did great,' he said, leaning against a partition with a supercilious smirk on his face. 'I hate the sitting around on our arses now, but *Sleepyhead*'s in the bag, I'd say, or I'm a fucked aunt!'

'Don't let's push our luck,' Kate warned, thinking the flying-bed dream theme was hardly a genius concept. It felt no way to lift milky drinks out of their time warp, but who knew what the client wanted? She was impatient to go. It was already too late to pick up any sexy new underwear in Oxford Street, as she'd hoped, but she wanted to make the doctor's late surgery that evening at least, for a prescription for the pill.

'We should have a slap-up lunch tomorrow, you

and I,' Dan said expansively. 'On ex's, of course, we've earned it. And you do need to get out a bit now, Kate. It is time . . .'

'Sorry, no can do, client lunch,' she shot out, with transparent relief. 'Jack Clark's coming in, remember, to see the *Karess* TV edits. It'll be heavy-duty, you know what he's like with his panicky whims. I'll have my hands full. A real smooth-up job is needed.'

Dan giggled. 'Naughty, naughty—watch what you say!'

He was such a tosser. Kate felt she'd been a limp reed over the opera, and was angry with herself and frustrated. She eyed Dan coolly while trying to be pleasant. 'Jack's chosen some restaurant over in Victoria. Can't think why when I've offered him Soho's best!'

'He'll have a shag lined up round there for sure. He'll go home at midnight to his little wifeykins and say what a useless shower we are at Impetus, how bushed he is, the hours it took him to sort us all out!'

Kate's dislike of Dan was growing more active by the day. Guilt over her coolness had made her accept his opera invitation; it had been wet, but his constant wooing was a tricky situation to handle, working as she did with him daily. She'd more or less made the decision now to honour the commitment. She felt sick and despairing about it, yet with Richard far away in the Amazon rainforest it did seem the better course.

*　　　*　　　*

Kate hadn't long arrived at the office the next

168

morning when Richard rang. 'Can we firm up about tonight?' He sounded in a hurry. Kate had a dreary pile of work to catch up on after yesterday's big pitch and with slight envy remembered he'd taken the day off; she wondered what he had on. 'How about Salt Yard,' Richard suggested, 'that tapas place in Goodge Street? It's round the corner from you, and Ed's kind of place.'

'Cool by me,' she said briskly, aware of his impatience. 'Try for the table at the back of the bar, it's the best in the house. Tapas is perfect, as I've got a client lunch.'

'Say seven? But no rush; Ed and I can settle in with a bottle of Rioja and discuss you in depth.'

'That's so mean! I'll call later, around six, and let you know how I'm doing.'

Kate got stuck in and worked hard until Jack arrived. She had coffee with him, trying to loosen him up, but it was a lost cause. As he watched the animatic for the *Karess* commercial the peaks of his pained expressions were as chartable as the Alps on an atlas in their darker shades. She hustled Jack away to lunch, preparing herself for the inevitable litany of neurotic nitpicks. They would be needless, tiny insignificant details that only a client in constant fear of his precious budget being squandered could possibly imagine mattered. Kate had decided against having the usual backup and taking a junior account manager along. She knew Jack well and thought he was best handled alone.

His choice of restaurant, Gran Paradiso in Victoria, was an Italian place, old-fashioned with white tablecloths, orchids and palms. It was quiet and discreet. Kate recognised a couple of politicians, deep in conversation.

169

'It's been going years,' Jack said, handing over his coat and scarf and taming his wisps of hair. 'My wife and I always come here when we're up to see a musical.'

She liked the idea of Jack and his wife being out for a special evening. 'It's good to have a change from all the old Soho haunts,' she enthused, annoyed at the way Dan had been determined to have her believe that Jack had a girl in that part of town.

They got down to *Karess* business over herb-crusted cod and Kate kept an anxiously straight face as befitted an account director smoothing up a client's fears.

'It's the girl's breast I'm most worried about,' Jack said, with his forehead tightly knitted. 'When her arms are up high, shampooing her hair, it juts out right over the *Karess* bottle. Couldn't it be shot sort of reversed so that she's beyond the glass ledge? The product could be in the foreground then and better displayed.'

'But it's all about creation of a mood,' Kate argued gently. 'The girl's sensual pleasure at her shampoo's caressing silkiness. And the bottle is a very strong identifiable pink after all, quite hard to miss . . .'

'Perhaps if it was a girl with a smaller breast,' Jack suggested seriously, as if there were a whole species of one-breasted females available from Casting to choose from.

'But her beautiful figure sort of harmonises with the special qualities of the shampoo, don't you think? It echoes and complements the perfect condition of her hair.'

They batted the problem to and fro politely.

Kate promised to 'see what she could do', although Jack looked little mollified. He drank less than a glass of wine, but picked up perceptibly when his slice of lemon tart arrived with a generous dollop of vanilla ice cream. He clearly enjoyed his puddings. Sipping a small espresso, Kate eyed it enviously.

The thought of meeting Richard's son that evening was making her feel even more stressed-out than Jack with his issues over the bottle-shielding breast. Perhaps that story might entertain Ed. She had no real idea what was cool with eighteen-year-old boys; her encounter with Polly had shattered her confidence and left her feeling cut to ribbons.

Ed would be more civil and well-mannered, she suspected, especially under the parental eye, but still capable of a sly left hook if his father left the table. Didn't young men generally come to their mothers' defence?

Having finished his tart Jack looked up with his worried face. Kate smiled, feeling more sympathetically mellow towards him, and said she could see it was time to go. She caught a passing waiter's eye and asked for the bill. Keying in her pin she sensed Jack was watching, waiting to have her attention.

'I was wondering,' he ventured, as she raised her head, 'whether you'd like to come out to Slough one Sunday and have lunch with my wife and family.' Kate met his anxious gaze, rather dumbfounded; it was the last thing she'd expected, once again far from the picture of Jack that Dan had tried to paint. 'Your weekends must be very lonely—I mean, having lost your husband . . .' He tailed off, going a bit pink.

'That's the kindest thought, Jack, thank you, I couldn't be more touched, but weekends aren't easy right now. I go to my father in Rye, you see, whenever I can. He has cancer and hasn't long to live.' Jack looked typically desperate, convinced he was the cause of additional pain and embarrassment, having made her talk about it. 'It is wretched, but he's very brave and we're coping,' Kate said, trying to help out. 'And on the brighter side, I have just met someone actually, and my father seems pleased about that!'

Jack's look was a little distant, although his watery blue eyes stayed resting lightly on her face. 'All the day-to-day petty worries, like the small print of commercials, pale away beside something like your father's illness,' he said, with slow deliberation, as though in agony about what to say. 'It's so important in life to keep sight of what really matters.'

'Thanks, Jack,' Kate said sincerely, as they prepared to leave, 'such kind words. I'll hold onto them. Guess I'll find plenty of those petty worries to get my head round, though now, waiting for me at the office!' She dashed away, but felt they'd parted firm friends.

Back at her desk she made good headway, and later in the afternoon called Richard to say she was on course to leave at seven.

'So you and Ed will have to discuss me to my face! How was your day? You sounded in a rush this morning.'

'I had a pile of things to do before leaving for Rye. I had lunch with your father.'

Kate was stunned. 'Why ever didn't you tell me? I'd loved to have known, I'd have had a warm glow all day.' She could hardly believe that he'd gone to all the business of arranging it, made the effort, driven down. 'Did you have some reason for keeping it dark?' she asked, feeling emotional in ways that left her floundering.

'Only that I'd felt really bad about Sunday and things can always crop up, and I didn't want to say I was going and then not.'

'How was Dad? Was it all right? He is very frail, isn't he?' Kate was still trying to assemble her thoughts. Only hours ago she'd worried what her father might read into her coming with Richard, yet now, after last night, she'd have loved to see them together, two people for whom she had powerfully emotional feelings. She felt quite cheated. Her time with both of them was finite, with her father certainly, and Richard would move on. 'What did you talk about?' she asked. 'It must have come as quite a shock, seeing him now, so weak and emaciated, after knowing him as he was.'

'It was a huge shock, sure, but very good to see him again and I think he enjoyed my visit. He's sharp as tacks, stimulating company. We had plenty to talk about.'

'Such as?'

'You, television, the world . . .'

'I can't get my head round you doing that. I'll have to talk to Dad and winkle out more about it. See you later—can't wait.'

Richard was full of surprises, Kate thought, it wasn't only his earthy charms.

CHAPTER 12

'Five A levels? That sounds like real punishment, way too much!'

'Music and art hardly count.' Richard smiled indulgently at his son. 'Ed loves them—if not the physics and maths.'

'You try sitting an art or music A level, Dad. It's a killer workload, Kate's right.'

'You know she's a serious art buff, Ed? She has some fantastic paintings: a Hockney and a Lautrec oil sketch, and a Miró, too. It's a most compelling picture, the Miró, you just have to stand and stare.' Richard sat with his arm along the back of his son's chair. He was wearing a cream open-neck shirt that looked crisply fresh against the serge-green of his jacket. Kate thought he must have been home to shower and change after Rye. 'I'm sure Kate would love you to come and see them, Ed,' he said, reaching across the table to squeeze her hand. 'Isn't that right, Katie darling?'

'Of course, but only if you'd really like to, Ed.' She withdrew her hand, embarrassed; Ed's eyes had followed his father's grasp. 'My pictures are mainly early to mid-twentieth century,' she said. 'That's what my late husband's gallery was best known for, but he had other stuff too.'

'Do you have any of the early Futurists?' Ed asked. 'I love that kind of fisticuff energy they had, that amazing sense of crazy speed. Futurism must have hit people between the eyes at the time and felt quite threatening after the staid stuff they were used to.'

174

'We had one or two at the gallery.' Kate described them, feeling a wave of relief that she and Ed had found a little common ground.

'We should order,' Richard said, reaching out with his feet under the table, to trap one of Kate's. 'Ed has to get back to his "killer workload" after all.'

His son grimaced and looked down at the menu card. He couldn't have been more different from how she'd imagined, so unlike Polly and his father, with his short fair hair that stood up in stiff tufts and stocky, sturdy frame. Ed had a benign-looking, chunky, chubby sort of face with a wide forehead and square jawline; a thickish neck and broad shoulders that his well-worn blue corduroy jacket did little to conceal. His very solidity, Kate thought, gave him an air of reliability and calm. And she liked his grimacing pressed-lips smile, which was youthfully apologetic and unconfident, yet with just the hint of a look of his father.

They were down a flight of stairs in the restaurant; all the tables had gone in the street-level bar where Spanish hams and chorizo were fresh-carved on the bar-top. The waiter had brought them a selection of cuts on a board, to nibble on while they chose.

Richard was being far too overt, it was really disconcerting. The look in his eyes was unmistakable—and in front of his son. Ed seemed equable and placid, able to handle himself, yet his mother had taken an overdose at the weekend and something must be going on inside. Kate's natural instinct was to ask after her, but it was the one thing she couldn't do. It would have been like provoking a sleeping scorpion, a stinging reminder that she

175

herself was a likely cause of Eleanor reaching for the pill bottle. Ed and Polly must feel she was creating havoc just by coming into their father's life at all.

'Lucky sod, off to the rainforest tomorrow, Dad,' Ed grouched, less shy with his father, but still with a quick, nervous half-smile at Kate. 'Have you had to have more jabs for your trip? Don't go getting yellow fever and passing it on. And what about stuff like snakebite serum? Do you have to take some with you? Can people inject it themselves?'

'I haven't got a clue—and certainly no serum in my first-aid kit. Let's hope someone has. But my last jabs still do, Ed, and those giant anaconda snakes don't fancy humans much, they say. It's the alligators, blood-sucking leeches, poisonous frogs and vampire bats I'm not too keen on, and there's a six-inch beetle I'd rather not meet, along with the fifty thousand insects—probably all carnivores! I must remember to shake out my boots every time.'

'I don't suppose you've managed to pack yet,' Kate said, thinking selfishly of the few hours she had left with Richard before he was off.

He smiled. 'Mañana for all that. I'll have time, the flight's not till around five. It's a long haul, two stops; we don't land at Iquitos till the next afternoon. It's an amazing place, Ed, a thriving city in the heart of the Peruvian Amazon, and entirely cut off by road. Not even a dirt track goes there, the rainforest is impenetrable. You can only reach Iquitos by boat or plane.'

'God, forget the vampire bats—what I'd give to come along!'

Kate could have said the same.

Richard described his day in Rye and talked

about Aidan's past television career, saying how much he'd admired his war reporting. It was a prep class, Kate thought, Richard's way of spelling out that he wasn't just playing around. But Ed would be under no illusion, he had his wits, he didn't need educating. It wasn't so much what he felt about his father's new squeeze, the more fundamental question was how deeply he minded being left to handle the whole Eleanor shooting match alone. Richard had cut loose, gone as far as divorcing. Yet Ed didn't seem to hold that against him, despite having to cope with his mother's illness and suicidal attacks, his A levels, his tricky hormonal sister . . .

Kate still couldn't quite believe she was in this scene with Richard, even thinking of moving in— that he was staring at her proudly now, with loving, lusting eyes. She fastened hers on his son.

'I hear you play the guitar beautifully, Ed,' she remarked, feeling her colour rise at coming out with such a platitude. 'Do you play in concerts or is time in too short supply?'

'Only in school ones,' Ed muttered, apparently far less keen to talk about music than art. 'I would love to see your paintings one day,' he carried on eagerly, as if anxious about his abrupt answer. Perhaps he saw the need to stay connected, suitably dutiful and able to call on his father, night or day, whenever the slightest little drama exploded in the minefields of his family home.

Kate suggested the following weekend. While she was still at her flat, she thought, while Richard was away, distant, and she was half a person, feeling less than half alive.

*   *   *

177

Talking was on hold when they got back. It wasn't until they were more composed again and settling in on the sofa, that Kate put her mind to the questions she wanted to ask. She laid her hand on Richard's where it rested on her bare thigh. 'Why did you go and see my father?'

'To tell him how much I loved his serious-minded daughter, among other things, and to gauge how that went down.'

'And how did it?'

'We both agreed you needed loosening up, but he said it would be an uphill battle.'

'So you ravage me when we're hardly in the door, splat on your multi-purpose kitchen table, and it's all part of a calculated plan? No blinds pulled down, even.'

'No lights on either.'

'Suppose Polly had suddenly turned up again or Madge and Justin clocked us coming back and popped down for a bag of sugar?'

'I see what Aidan meant.' Richard flicked at her unbuttoned shirt with a grin. 'But it was far from calculated, more like sheer desperation and provocation. I'd sat at that inhibiting little table thinking how exquisite you looked, how shy you were with Ed—and serious—how your eyes had such depth. I was overcome. So was everyone else in that place, they all had their eyes on you.' He slipped his hand inside her shirt where it felt snug and wholesomely familiar. 'Early bed,' he said, sounding in no great hurry to move, his hand felt as settled as a cat on her lap, 'and a more leisurely fuck then. I'll be more accommodating and . . . what was that weird word you used the other day?'

'Genteel?'

'That's it! More genteel.'

'I wouldn't mind a cup of coffee first and I think you're spent. You need a rest. And there's a few things I want to ask before you go away.' She was hesitant, wanting nothing to jar and spoil the mood. 'I feel in the dark about what you think is going on—I mean about Spencer Morgan,' she added in a hurry. 'And to be honest, I'm slightly worried about Mum.'

Was she right to talk up her fears? She trusted Richard, but he'd ask questions, whether or not for professional reasons, and wouldn't it sound like overreacting, talking about suppressed tension in her mother that nobody else could see? It inevitably pointed the finger at Ben and if Rachel was in deep as well, mightn't it be putting her right in it?

'You can trust me, Katie. I'll try and help.'

'It's not just my mother's clamming-up, the business over the divorce that I told you about. That does bug me, of course—it's like trying to do a sum with half the figures. I mean if Ivana screwed up the marriage, even by a slow drip, drip process of wearing down, I simply don't see why Mum can't tell me about it. We've always been really close.'

Kate knew she was avoiding getting to the nub, but she leaned against Richard's shoulder and carried on. 'I almost wish you hadn't told me that everyone in television had known about Ivana, it was quite a shattering blow. I suppose I should have guessed, the crew out in Bosnia must have known.' Kate looked up with a smile. 'I'm impressed that you closed ranks and it never came out in the press. It's lifted my image of the whole media world!'

Richard stroked her cheek. 'People felt for him.

179

But this isn't about Ivana and the divorce, is it? Why can't you tell me, Katie? You're hesitating. Am I the problem? Is it hard to explain?'

He was staring at her, waiting, and she felt scrutinised, wondering at the potent look in his luminescent eyes. 'Are you studying me for clues?' she joked awkwardly, shivering. Half her clothes were still on the kitchen floor.

'For signs of your feelings,' Richard said lightly, rubbing her arms for warmth. 'Shall we make the coffee and you tell me then?'

Kate pulled down the blind in the kitchen while Richard saw to the coffee. She picked up her clothes and put on the chilli-red cardigan that had seemed suitable for her lunch with Jack. It had cheered up her black 'client' suit—whose pencil skirt, after Richard's energetic homecoming, now had a much longer back slit.

'I'm going for something more comfy,' she said, nipping upstairs for her tracksuit bottoms and being distracted for a moment, remembering Jack's comic distress at his precious *Karess* bottle being upstaged by a breast. She'd forgotten to share the story over the tapas, but decided that it might have made her job sound frivolous. Ed seemed such a sober young man.

She rejoined Richard and unhooked a couple of mugs, still slightly self-conscious, feeling more of a visitor than a live-in lover, sharing a home.

'So tell me, Katie,' he said, 'this worry you have about your mother. It's on your mind a lot, isn't it?'

'It's hard to explain. She's wound-up, hiding tension—which she does brilliantly. She's as composed and charming as ever, on the surface, but I know her, you see. It's the silliest thing—you'll

180

wonder what on earth I'm on about.' Kate smiled, embarrassed, and went to the fridge for the milk.

'Could she be fearful about Ben having another woman?'

Kate swung round. 'God, I never thought of that! No,' she asserted, 'it's definitely nothing like that. Mum's strung up with nerves underneath, she's jumpy if Ben's phone goes, but she never looks at him suspiciously. If I was to try to put my finger on it, I'd say she's almost physically scared; she glances at Ben more for reassurance, kind of sharing the strain.'

Richard looked thoughtful and interested. 'Then it rather points to someone having it in for Ben. Blackmail, upping the anti over unpaid debts—or else Ben's mixed up in something close to the wire that your mother's become involved in as well.'

'Oh no, Ben's very pukka,' Kate said hastily. Richard was far too sharp for her. 'He's like the most decent and intelligent of army top brass, "highly regarded" as they say! I'm probably just being a silly tit over all this and Mum's worrying about one of his wholesalers cutting loose or some embarrassing faux pas!'

Richard wrapped her in his arms. 'No, I think not, you're very sensitive and perceptive. But you could be feeling just a bit over-protective or subconsciously resentful of her being so entirely taken up with Ben.'

She thought about that as he poured the coffee. 'I have felt jealous of their great intimacy at times,' she said, 'but I could see it as that and—well, it was before you!' That was letting down her emotional guard. She needed to keep some protection, a film of cellophane, a shred of reserve, for her own sanity. But Kate felt too in deep over Rachel now not to carry on and she said, more openly, 'All this is quite recent as well; I've only had a sense of Mum's nerviness in the last few weeks.'

'Why haven't you asked her about it?'

She looked at him blankly. Why hadn't she? Rachel had wanted a heart-to-heart, to ask her about her own edginess, why hadn't she pressed her mother harder?

'It's delicate,' Kate answered, gathering herself. 'It implies criticism of Ben. And Mum knew, I think, that I had unspoken questions, she even alluded to them, saying I had to trust her to know what she was doing. She's a genius at deflection too, no chancer would ever have his way! I hope you'll meet her properly soon and you'll see what I mean, how astute she is.'

'Aidan still cares about her deeply, doesn't he?' Richard said. 'We talked about a lot of things today and his feelings came through.'

That brought tears close. 'But what about Spencer Morgan?' she countered awkwardly, sipping coffee. 'Think of those hostels for the homeless he's sponsored. I know being billionaire-rich goes a long way, but his heart seems in the right place.'

'Can we finish with Ben first,' Richard said, taking his coffee to the table. 'What puzzles me is why, since you obviously have slight doubts and feelings of chariness, you still seem to come to Ben's defence. I've noticed that when we've talked about him.'

'Mum loves him, I suppose that's why. Whatever stress she's feeling doesn't seem to affect their relationship. She's on a real high when he's around, like she's twenty again.'

'Can't you be older than twenty to have highs? How about thirty-three? Or even forty-five?'

Kate made a face at him. 'Ben's easy to be around,' she said. 'He's never over-smooth or winds me up in any way—and plenty of people do—all the smart-arses in the ad world for a start! Ben's quite a class act.'

'You think your mother's in the grip of a love affair and it's clouding her judgement,' Richard said, half to himself. 'Has anything in particular stuck out about Ben?'

'That's the whole problem,' Kate said helplessly, 'it's all so nebulous. I asked something about the setting up of his business once. And about the foodstuffs he imports from the Amazon,' she added quickly, backtracking, not wanting to talk about Rachel's evasion at the time. 'Ben's big success story is acai. They're berries, very antioxidant and a staple of the Amazonian locals who eat it as a fruit mush. He says acai is really catching on over here, quite a niche market. It's used in drinks, jelly beans, hair conditioners . . .'

'How did Ben cotton onto it? Does he have links with South America?'

'He knows all about the Amazon, he's had connections with Colombia and Brazil.'

'What connections?' Richard sounded sharply interested.

'Army ones. My mother said that he was out in Colombia, in the Army Intelligence Corps, early on in his career. Apparently we used to give human rights training to Colombian counter-guerrilla units, only they proved a bit too keen on violations themselves!'

183

'And the army sent Ben to the Brazilian Amazon as well?' Richard queried. His tone was sardonic and Kate thought he was making assumptions and being too quick to judge.

'Yes, actually,' she retaliated, feeling combative. 'I happen to know they did. The army does tough training expeditions out there—or they did in Ben's day. Hardly a stroll in the park, he said. I remember him telling us once, about the group he'd had to lead, a real endurance test that involved following the Amazon River right to its source. If I'd thought of it earlier,' she glared, 'he could have given you a few tips for this trip.'

'I stand corrected.' Richard smiled, looking suitably contrite.

Kate sipped her coffee. She'd been defending Ben again, she realised, and right after Richard had commented on it. 'But what about Spencer Morgan,' she repeated, 'what have you found out so far? You must have had a lead or picked up on something iffy to have got interested. Or are you just following your own nose?'

'It did start as a pure hunch. I was curious, succumbing to my journalist's instincts,' Richard said, reaching for her hand as if needing reconnection, 'but since I've been doing a bit of my own investigating I've become convinced. I think he's a fraud. And anyone cheating the system, as I'm sure he is, would do those good works you mentioned; that's par for the course, part of the kicks. I've only scratched the surface, though, Katie, and I want to keep digging. You do see the need not to pass anything on?'

'I wouldn't dream of it, either to Mum or Ben.'

'The Morgan Group is really hard to get a handle

184

on. I'm sure though, in one or two of his companies at least, losses are being missed off annual accounts and profits inflated. That suggests insider dealing, yet on the face of it, to go by available public information, all his outfits look pristine. And there's such huge variety in what he does. He has a vast hedge fund with secrecy requirements for investors.'

'What's the significance of that?'

'Keeps his name out of the database and covers his back. He manages pension funds, has his hospitality business, hotels in places like Dubai. Casinos—I saw he's just opening another of those, a splashy new complex in Trinidad. He has an investment advisory company with its headquarters in San Francisco and subsidiary outfits everywhere—Mexico, Argentina, even one in Colombia. Yet for all his reputation and talked-up genius for tycoonery, I'm convinced the bulk of his vast wealth is a scam. An empire that trades largely in fiction, for all its grandiose claims; I can't find the data to support them, none seems to exist. He runs a jet and a fabulous yacht, from the press pictures I've seen. But if you ask me about actual dirt, that's hard. I'd still bet a fistful of dollars to a dime that his billions are dirtier than a tramp's castoff clothes.'

'Can't you go to the authorities? Wouldn't you need their help to be able to prove anything?'

'They'd have to be very sure and very brave to take him on. He'd wrap the FSA round his little finger; he's a charismatic celebrity and the Morgan Group hardly has a slithery image. Pinning him down would be like trying to catch a fish with your bare hands. You'd think you have him, but you'd

185

never get a firm enough grip.'

Kate felt out of her depth and could add nothing worthwhile. The thought of all things financial was like the engine of a car, she just wanted it to function and not let her down. 'People have to start somewhere, don't they,' she said curiously, 'whether it's inventing triangular dog biscuits or cleaning public toilets? Did Morgan start from scratch—how did he get so monumentally far?'

'I can give you a mini biog—but very mini, it's past our bedtime. He started out as a barman in some dive down the Old Kent Road. His father was a plumber. Morgan raised the necessary, bought out the owner of the bar and soon had a small string of clubs of his own. It's easy to siphon off money in the nightclub business, I'll tell you how, sometime. I'm quite sure Spencer Morgan knew how to do it. He branched out into classier joints soon enough, casinos as well. Then he moved into high finance, proper legit businesses on the face of it, like his investment funds for small investors, but he's kept some of his old, less salubrious interests like the casino opening in Trinidad.'

'Spencer's out in the Caribbean, right now,' Kate said, 'on that fabulous yacht of his. I only happen to know because Mum called me, just this morning, to say he's asked them out to join him. I think they've decided to go—perhaps a sunny little mega-yacht trip will be the relaxing tonic she needs.'

'Lucky devils,' Richard said. 'We're going to have some downtime soon, Katie, you and me. Soon as I'm back we'll make plans.'

Would being with Spencer be a tonic for Rachel? Kate doubted it and wondered if Ben could be entangled with him in some way, more than a

186

grateful recipient of his financial backing. She sensed Richard knew exactly what she was thinking, though, and shut her mind to the idea.

They turned out the lights and went upstairs. Their love-making gave her confidence, but not the thought of the next two weeks, the interminable days and nights with him gone. She had to get on with life, Kate told herself, and keep a hold on reality.

It was no good, lying wide-awake, imagining living at 6 Thornby Terrace. Her mind was running on already, planning changes she could make, small surprises for Richard's return—reversible ones if he thought they were rubbish.

Richard was awake too, in his own thoughts. Their fingers were entwined and she tugged on his hand. 'Can I drive you to the airport, or will you be going with your producer and crew?'

He turned his head and looked at her so closely that Kate felt exposed; the light from his bedside lamp seemed as revealing as a shaving mirror.

'I'd love that, but the flight's at five.' He leaned and kissed her nose. 'And you'll be at work then, chatting up clients, busy with Dan.'

'No, wrong. I've decided to have a lunchtime sickie. It's all part of loosening up.'

CHAPTER 13

'Hello, Ed, come on up to the first floor. It's the door on the right.'

Kate was glad it was a bright day. Sunlight was streaming in. Last night the weather girl had said

187

rain and sleet showers were on the way for the weekend, with high northerly winds to intensify the chill.

She went to open the door and stood waiting, glancing at her reflection in the hall mirror, listening out for Ed's footfall and tentative tap on the slightly ajar door.

'I do appreciate this,' he said, coming in looking shy and flustered, stuffing bicycle clips into the pouch of his navy hoodie with a look of apology. 'I don't want to hold you up if you want to be away to Rye.'

'You're not, I promise, I'm in plenty of time. You have locked up your bike? Nothing's safe round here for a second. Just leave it on the chair,' she said, as Ed unzipped his snug-looking top. 'Will you have some coffee or there's orange juice or tea?'

'Coffee's good, thanks. But don't make it specially, I don't really need any.'

'I do though! You go on in through there, into the sitting room, and have a look round. I'll be just two secs bringing it.'

Ed's praise and adulation of the paintings was warm and generous. Even when he was perched on the edge of a sofa, cup in hand, discussing the reviews of a new Gauguin exhibition, his eyes were still being drawn like a voyeur. He was in danger of tipping his coffee.

He looked back at Kate who'd been talking about Gauguin's talent for reinvention and said, rather inconsequentially, 'This is such a beautiful flat too, with all the fantastic wall space. It would be hard to imagine anywhere better for the paintings. It kind of does them full justice . . .'

188

He paused, as though intending to extend that thought. His hesitation was like a comma, and yet he settled for simply giving another of his shy, awkward smiles.

'I know,' Kate agreed, 'it's terrific, being able to house the paintings here. They were a great help in the long months after my husband's accident—my salvation really.'

'We had one call from Dad,' Ed said, suddenly changing tack, 'but early on. I don't suppose you've heard from him lately? I don't know how he'd get in touch easily, though, from the middle of the rainforest.'

Richard had been in constant touch. He'd called from airports, from his Iquitos hotel, from the rainforest on his crackling satellite phone. The urge to talk to Ed about him and share his news was instinctive and Kate answered enthusiastically while half aware that Ed's question was probably not exactly the crux of what he wanted to say.

'Yes, I've had a couple of calls on his satellite phone. He says the trafficker minders stink of garlic, sweat and stale piss, to use your father's words; one guy munches on garlic cloves all day long. They mutter away in Spanish, but the dialect is so heavy it's impossible to follow. He says the jungle at night is noisier than a sell-out gig beside a motorway and he lies awake scared witless with bombing insects bouncing off his mozzy net!'

She omitted Richard's passed-on thoughts, lying in his tent in the steamy heat; those were for her alone. 'They've reached the pits, the hidden place where the coca leaves are mashed into a paste, and got some good footage, I think. They are on the homeward trail now,' Kate finished. 'Oh, and they

189

saw a jaguar! They stalked it up.'

The blood rushed to her face. She'd made the intimacy and closeness of their communication all too obvious. Had his question been subtly designed?

Ed was looking questioningly at her. 'Dad said you might be moving in with him.'

'Well, yes, he has suggested it, but nothing's really decided yet.'

'I, um, hope you don't mind me asking . . . but what happens to this lovely flat and all the paintings?'

'Those things are sortable, but how would you feel about it, Ed—my moving in, I mean? I hope you'd say if it would upset you or Polly.'

It was Ed's turn to blush, which he did, furiously, rubbing his knuckles and looking agonised. 'Oh, no worries about it at all, of course, I've never seen Dad so happy . . . It's just that well, at times, you see, he is still needed at home. My mother is kind of . . . up and down. She both rejects him and relies on him, she is very dependant. If he stopped coming . . .'

'You'd be fearful of what might happen?'

Ed nodded, looking wretched. 'It's hard, I know he wants a life of his own.'

Her life came into it too, Kate thought unworthily. Didn't she figure in all this somewhere? Ed wasn't helping her fears about Eleanor's insidious pull. He was looking out for both his parents, dutifully, admirably, but she felt an expendable counter in the game.

'I know the particular difficulties,' she said, 'and my moving in wouldn't change anything in the slightest, you can be sure of that. Your father would be there like a shot if needed, as supportive and caring as ever. I'm quite certain.'

Ed thanked her profusely and she saw him to the door. He had brought her down, however blamelessly; he was a good son. Kate had a job to stop the tears coming as she said goodbye, while Ed looked relieved, as if a considerable weight had been lifted off his broad young shoulders. She heard the slam of the downstairs main door and felt a keen sense of release at being alone again and able to give in to a good self-indulgent cry. But Ed's visit had left her feeling wearily defeated and the tears never came. She was dry-eyed going to Rye.

*   *   *

Back at the office on Monday Kate had an evening drink with a few agency friends. Dan was among them, but he was less of an effort in a crowd. She'd been filling in time after work, going to the gym, and the pub made a change. She started home around eight, leaving them yattering on, and made for the tube station with her head down against the wind.

At Notting Hill Gate she came out into a sleet shower and the wind blew her umbrella inside-out. Reversing herself to right it Kate had a near collision with a yuppy young couple who looked impatiently irritated. She saw them cross the road smartly to the cinema opposite where a new vice and violence film had just opened to a wide variety of reviews. Kate ploughed on up Kensington Park Road with one hand lodged inside her bag, fingers round her mobile, though she was resigned to the unlikelihood of a call.

191

As she turned into her street her head suddenly felt bombed. All the torturing passion, her obsessive thoughts of the last days—weeks now—seemed to explode then stand still, as though in shock at themselves before spiralling off on a gust of sleet-drenched wind leaving her in a state of shivering misery.

The guilt was torment. Harry had married her, nurtured her, loved her in his young way; enthused, inspired her about art. How could she have erased him in the way she had? Managed in so short a space of time almost to forget his very existence, almost to imagine he had been simply a brief bright dream? Poor blameless, adorable Harry. That unspeakable death.

Richard didn't forget Eleanor. Whether from duty or some deep hold she retained, he kept her close, in his sights, front of mind.

Depression swept in. It sprang up and slammed Kate in the face with the force of a trodden-on garden rake. She felt like a wound-up clockwork toy car, one touch and she could go shooting off, but in which direction and how much damage might she do?

Outside her flat she could hear the house phone inside ringing insistently. She turned her key feeling too low to hurry in and answer it. It would be one of her family for sure.

'Hello,' she said, finally reaching it and suppressing a sigh.

'God, you sound flat! What's going on round there—where have you been? I've kept trying you for an hour.'

'Sorry, I just walked in.' Richard's voice was electrifying, sending powerful shockwaves; Kate reeled from them and needed a moment to adjust. 'And I'm a bit tired, I guess, and not expecting it to be you. Why are you calling on this phone? I almost didn't pick up.'

'I wanted to know where the hell you were.'

'Only at the pub, I went for a drink with friends. But what are mobiles for? Why couldn't you call on that? Not checking up on me, by any chance?'

'It's no joke—I'm stuck out here in this sweltering hellhole of humidity. And I started thinking last night that you still really love Harry underneath and always will. You've never once said what you feel about me, loud and clear, not once.'

'Could anything be more obvious?' she muttered, unable to explain. Reserve was her last defence; she lived with the conviction that Richard would move on and she'd be left, disintegrated, just a little pool on the floor.

'I can't hear a thing on this goddamn fucking phone!'

'If it's Harry you're worried about,' she yelled, 'why should you need to know where the hell I am?' She was taking off her wet trench coat, as well as hopping about using heel pressure, trying to throw off her sopping boots without undoing the zips.

'Because you'd see other people in that case, if you didn't truly care—like the client, Jack, you think is so "sweet" or that jerkish Dan character who's big in your life.'

A corner of Kate's brain told her Richard didn't entirely believe that, he just wanted to hear warm words. But he'd caught her at a bad moment and uncannily brought up Harry.

'You care "underneath" about Eleanor,' she countered. '"Truly care".'

'You can't seriously think that? I do what I have to, for Christ's sake, my suffocating duty. Don't fight me, Katie, darling, just be there for me. I need you. Can't talk more, our breather's over. I'll try and call later. I've had a thought about Morgan and Ben—and since you said you're having supper with your mother and Ben tomorrow, it might just be one worth sharing. It was thinking of them jetting off to the Caribbean that put it in mind, envying them their blast of mega-yacht luxury! I've really got to go, we're off again, trudging on through this impenetrable fucking overgrowth. Not much luxury in these parts . . .'

Kate returned the receiver with her depression advancing and retreating as in the play of a zoom lens. She had no means of contact, yet the urge to call back and tell Richard, loud and clear what he wanted to hear, was overpowering. Frightening. She had to keep Harry in focus and stay loyal.

She thought of calling Donna. Between Ed's visit, weekend work and needing every minute with her father in Rye, she'd had no chance to catch up with her artist friend.

Donna had no side to her, no agenda. She understood grief, if not obsessive guilt, and they'd talked at lunch; she knew about Kate's worries over Rachel and Ben. Most of all, though, Donna had been Harry's friend. She'd see things in the round. Kate knew she should eat first, before calling; she'd had nothing since a lean tuna sandwich at lunch and after two glasses of inferior wine in the pub she felt hazy, unsteady on her feet. It would be sensible to have something, but food could wait.

She picked up the phone. 'Bad time?' she asked urgently, the knots in her shoulders easing, finding

Donna at home. 'Are you painting? Can we talk?' She didn't wait for an answer, launching in, explaining all the clashing symbols in her head, the confusion she felt. She tried to be completely honest. 'Help me, Donna, I can't let Harry down. I'm insanely in love with Richard . . .' She felt shaken, suddenly hearing herself saying it out loud at last, excited.

'Is he in love with you?'

'He says so, more or less, he even wants me to move in, but it's so soon and it would be a threesome with his ex-wife—no, a fivesome with his resistant teenage children. The daughter, Polly, is dynamite. I'm in the blackest depression. I've got no right to be alive, let alone tell another man I love him.'

There was a silence down the line. Kate felt hysterical. She wanted absolution, permission to love, Donna's blessing. 'Say something, for God's sake. I'm desperate!'

'People in the grip of depression,' Donna said evenly, 'don't have your strong feelings. Passion is the last thing on their mind. They want the world to stop, a bridge to leap off. You're not depressed. But you are going to have to learn to compromise. Loving insanely means taking whatever crumbs are going. It's not easy, but it's a path I've been down myself. I'll tell you sometime.'

Kate had always suspected a past great love. 'But don't you understand about Harry?' she insisted. 'You more than anyone should.'

'He's dead, Kate. Do you want to kill your feelings for Richard as well? You should bring him here so I can take a look at him. I'm interested in older men.'

'You can't have him, Donna. He's thin enough pickings already . . .'

Kate returned the phone with a smile on her face. It soon faded. She imagined Donna giving herself and being left with nothing. She had no children. But she had her art, and if genius came at a price, at least she was creating something lasting and worthwhile and must feel fulfilled. Kate knew she could never have that.

She heated up some fish chowder, bought on the way home, and soaked it up with soft bread. But even comfort food couldn't assuage the depth of her loneliness.

The phone went and her mood was transformed. She could let out her feelings, tell Richard how badly she'd wanted to call back and why. Kate felt released. Her slate was wiped clean, her chalk freshly sharpened, she was bursting to write the next phase.

Her feet came back to the ground. Did Richard love her half as much? He'd owned up to an ulterior motive, a reason for seeking her out at the party—she thought of that often—and he'd brought up Spencer, even tonight when the emotion had seemed so high . . .

'You wanted to say something about Spencer and Ben,' she muttered, shrinking inside.

'That was nothing, the last thing to think about— can't you talk up a bit, Katie? I only wanted to say that if, by any chance, Ben really is in some iffy situation, then he and Morgan could be jointly involved. You might just keep that in mind if you're having supper with your mother and Ben tomorrow night. You said you were, didn't you? Can we talk about us now?'

'I had wondered about a link,' Kate said, feeling bathed in a glow of belonging again and aching for Richard's return. 'Are you on another tea break?' she asked. 'Or squelching along on a jungle track dodging the vampire bats? I can't picture you out there.'

'I'm squatting on a log, which I hope isn't a slumbering alligator, swigging a can of filthy orange fizz. My shirt's sodden, my boots are oozing mud—not a pretty sight! There's a whole lot more I want to say, but my phone's fading, curse it, and we're just about to be off again. Hey! We're making good progress and the last bit is by boat. If we reach it in time to avoid another night under canvas, I might even be back a day early.'

'Oh. When will you know?' Kate shouted. Shit, shit, bloody Dan and the opera.

'Not till we leap aboard that boat! It'll be nip and tuck, for sure. Does it matter? You haven't got *plans*, have you, by any chance?' Richard gave a rather edgy, mock-accusing laugh.

He was only half joking. Kate thought of him calling on the house phone, being hardly able to deny checking up on her. It wasn't surprising if Richard was working up a bit of jealousy, out there in the steamy heat, but in the circumstances, it was the very last thing she needed. She could imagine him arriving back in a ragged state of exhaustion and finding her off on a date.

She'd hesitated too long, had to face up to telling him, couldn't risk him making the plane. 'Well, sort of, very stupidly,' she said, in an agony of self-consciousness. 'Something that was fixed a while back, the opera—I would have chucked and got out of it ages ago, but it's difficult when someone you

197

work with is trying to be kind and nice.'

'Oh, so it's Dan, is it? What a surprise. Kind and nice! Fuck it, Katie, the creep wants to score and you know it.'

The crackling on Richard's phone started to fade. 'Of course I won't go now,' Kate shouted, although his phone had gone completely silent. 'I'll be at the airport, mad with impatience.' She felt despairing. Why hadn't she shut up and not tried to explain? Shit, what a fool. Now she had the worst of all worlds.

It was eleven, six o'clock in the Amazon rainforest; Richard had probably been walking all day, his boots were oozing mud. She couldn't have felt more wretched.

Was it too late to call Dan? She found his number and rang. Her desperation to get the call over with knew no bounds.

He saw who it was and got in first. 'Hi, Kate! What gives? To what do I owe the honour? Sorry about the racket round here, it's my local Italian joint.'

'Dan, I'm dreadfully sorry about this and I just had to let you know at once, but I can't come to the opera on Wednesday.'

'Oh? Why's that, why not?'

'It's a personal problem, very sudden, but things have just become hopelessly difficult for that night. I know how infuriating it must be for you, I couldn't be more sorry.'

'But we were in the pub this very evening and you couldn't tell me to my face?'

'I've just had a call, only just discovered. I wanted to let you know right away in case it helped, in case you had a friend you could ring or something.'

'At this hour of night?'

'A girlfriend—oh, I don't know . . .' Kate was close to tears. 'I feel so bad. You were more than kind to think of taking me out of myself—and a night at the opera, too!'

'And what do I get in return? I'd lined up a real nice night out, dinner at Annabels, a car and driver . . . Oh, well. So let's make another date, then,' he said, with an oily change of tone. 'I know these family problems happen.' His smarminess was obnoxious. 'You name the day, Kate, and I'll sort it. I'm going to give you a great time.'

Shit, it was hopeless, she hadn't thought of that. 'I'm afraid I can't do other dates, Dan. I've met someone, I'm kind of tied . . .'

'So there's a man involved, I might have guessed. He doesn't seem very good at letting you know his movements, if I may say so. Well, well, so you're done with the grieving widow scene, moving on, back in the real world. It's a rough old place, you know, my girl, rocky, always a few knocks. See you around!'

CHAPTER 14

Kate clicked off from the call to Dan with one thought in her head—how to make contact with Richard again. She was desperate to know which day he was coming and be able to meet the plane. He'd been flying from Iquitos to Lima on Wednesday, overnight to Madrid and finally arriving back Thursday afternoon. Would the flights be the same a day earlier? She could go to

Heathrow both days, Kate thought, camp at the airport all night if necessary—if that was what it took.

She went online and discovered that a number of airlines flew from Iquitos on a Tuesday and on to Europe, but not only to Madrid. The permutations were immense; Kate felt close to a flood of tears. She knew at heart that it was a silly row and soon sorted, but rationality didn't come easy in the grip of a burning love. And the call to Dan wasn't helping. He was going to make trouble, that was clear as day, and she had only herself to blame. She felt goaded by fate, a plaything of circumstance, experiencing such intense helpless frustration it was like a pillow being pressed down on her face. She needed Richard.

It suddenly came to her. He would have his mobile with him as well as the satellite phone; she could leave messages. Kate texted furiously, thumbs misfiring, tumbling over themselves, and then said it all again in a voicemail. The passion poured out of her.

'I'm yours, don't you see? There's no one else, past or present. You said, "Don't fight me," well, now I'm begging it of you. Don't put me through this agony. You must let me meet the plane.'

She imagined him reaching Iquitos in a state of exhaustion, finding a string of messages and being still far too pissed off to call.

It was late, an hour since she'd spoken to Dan. Kate washed up a saucepan, tidied up and switched off the lights. Preparing for bed, smoothing on face cream, slipping on her nightie, she was glad of the discipline of routine. Her bedroom felt an alien place. Harry had receded from it, Richard rejected it. The bed looked immaculate: lacy cushions, sad plumped-up pillows, a neat cream bedcover that Maria, her cleaner, who came on Mondays, insisted on tucking in. She must have once worked in a hospital.

Kate flung herself down and buried her face in the cotton cover that smelled laundered and spare-roomish, not bounced on by children or pets. She could scent the residue of grief and tears, though, a faint tang of bodies, her Hermes scent. All the associations played in her head and she began to sob, pummelling the bed like a spoilt child, grabbing the cushions and hurling them to the floor.

It was the release she needed. She climbed down from the bed, picked up the cushions and tossed them onto a chair. Then she pulled back the bedcover and crawled under the duvet, shivering and subdued, and lay with her knees curled up, hands by her face, loosely fisted. She sensed her muscles unknitting and soon felt sleep drawing her into its soft buxom hold.

A persistent ringing hauled her back and she was instantly awake, flinging out an arm to grab the phone.

'Don't be cross. I had to call and wake you. We're back, stinking to hell, the hotel's holding its collective nose, but I had to call—even before that first bath.'

'You've found my messages?'

'No. Oh, on my mobile. I haven't got to that yet, just too jiggered to dig it out. I'm calling on the hotel phone.'

*   *   *

Kate was early at Heathrow. Waiting by the barrier with an hour to go, the longing was impossible to contain. She couldn't read her newspaper, time dragged its heels, and, flicking impatiently between her watch and mobile, her spirits began to sag; the worry about Dan wouldn't go away. He was her boss. Any pleas for time off had to be passed by him and asking twice in the space of two weeks for trips to the airport—a concocted doctor's appointment the second time—had given him plenty of ammunition.

'This new lover does seem to have an effect on your health, Kate. Wasn't it a "migraine" the last time? I assume he's married, but you'll have to sort it better than this.'

'Really sorry, Dan, no late surgery today or tomorrow and it is urgent.'

His features settled themselves into a satisfied grimace, the smile on the face of a tiger—no, a far lesser beast than that. He'd turned from her desk, clicking his knuckles, reeking of his acrid pine aftershave and leaving Kate in no doubt of his malevolent intent. How could she have felt it a *kindness* to agree to go on a date with him?

She glanced yet again at the Arrivals board and her pulse quickened. Richard's flight showed 'Landed' and even as she watched, the board tickered and flicked to read 'Baggage in Hall'.

He came through with his two colleagues and hurried over, dropping down a bag to brush cheeks and squeeze her hand. 'Katie, this is my producer, Matt, and Darren, our genius cameraman. They've heard quite a bit about you!'

They were younger than Richard. The producer

had a clean-cut unassuming look, unexpectedly, like a helpful bank clerk, while Darren, whose hair was bright ginger, was looking the worse for the tropical sun; his wide, stubby face was so covered in freckles that they'd almost joined up and his forehead had large patches of peel.

'You must all be shattered,' Kate smiled, feeling riven with impatience. They seemed interested and appreciative, but were not being met and soon hurried away. She imagined girlfriends in offices, hard at work, not risking a bad situation with a vengeful colleague as she was.

Richard held onto her hand, watching his workmates criss-cross through the muddle of people and trolleys, then he kissed her. It was a long slow kiss in the busy terminal that took no account of the jostling crowds, the curious, the greater privacy they could have had in Kate's car in the car park. 'Almost worth losing my trust in you to find those messages.'

'Don't,' she mumbled. 'I couldn't go through that again, ever.'

*　　　*　　　*

Arriving home, Richard noticed the painting instantly. She had wondered if he would.

'You've brought the Miró here. I don't believe it!'

'I could just see it over the sofa. What do you think? It can easily come down.'

'It's sensational, I'm overwhelmed, but I want *you*, I can't think of another thing. I've never longed to be home like this before. I was going demented out there in that dripping jungle and right now,

Miró hasn't a prayer.'

In bed, in Richard's arms, the sex felt to Kate like an escape—from mistrust and uncertainties, misunderstanding, family strain. He was involved with her body. He could make her come, and come again, with the lightest touch of fingers or tongue, he could sense the arc of her need, balance it with his own. He had total control. Sex, she thought, was a positive or destructive force, the glue in the most unlikely relationships; yet without love it so easily came unstuck. The best bonding agent was when the two combined.

'We must go down and pay homage to Miró,' Richard said without stirring. 'I hope you haven't had some ghastly insurance hike, but that was some welcome home!' He kissed her. 'But no more calling by with sensational paintings, you're here to stay now, moving in. It's your home too now, Katie, and we're going to make it a great little nest.'

That wasn't, Kate felt, given her aching biological need, his most sensitive phrase. 'You haven't noticed the snowdrops from Dad's garden,' she said, 'over on the chest.'

'And whose fault is that?' Richard climbed out of bed and went to put his nose in them. 'Wonderful honey scent, I never knew they had any.'

'Some do. Dad's big on snowdrops, that one's *Galanthus Fosteri.*' Richard went on into the bathroom and she called after him. 'I've fiddled in there, too . . .'

'My God, you've put a hook on the door—and a magnificent one at that.'

'And one in the bedroom,' she said, getting up and going in after him. 'I found them in a junk shop, Art Deco originals, I think.' They were aluminium, an elegant arching design with squared-off ends.

Richard hung up his white towelling dressing gown, which was usually slung over the bathroom chair. He disappeared downstairs naked while Kate had a quick shower, and joined her when he was back, shielding a glass of wine that he held to her lips.

'We should eat,' she said, out of the shower and getting into her tracksuit. 'Sex makes me starving.' Richard put on his dressing gown, which reminded her of his punishing trip and how shattered he must be. 'How are you lasting out quite so well?' she asked, with her arms round his neck.

'The company's not so bad. But I don't want to be up long. And I don't approve of these clothes.'

'This is my pyjamas equivalent. Come on, I've got things to download. You know I was round seeing Mum and Ben last night? Well, it's interesting, you'll be amazed! And you won't have remembered about babysitting again in Basingstoke this weekend . . .' She wanted him there, desperately. 'Anyway, you'll have much better things to do.'

'Like what? Of course I've remembered. I'm even quite looking forward to it. That house is branded on my heart.'

Kate boiled water for ravioli and heated the pasta sauce she had made at her flat. She'd called in on the way to Rachel and Ben's, and stocked up Richard's fridge.

'So let's hear these interesting things,' he said, helping, taking his Italian pottery plates to the table and shaving slivers from a wedge of parmesan cheese. 'You seem quite fired up.'

'That's more to do with you.' She brought over the food. 'But it was good with Mum and Ben, cool. We had a few laughs. She's a great cook too, brilliant. I could never match up.'

'Don't be side-tracked.' Richard said.

'Well, when I was about to go Mum looked at Ben, kind of giving the nod, and he said, "Can we have dinner, Katie, just you and me? I need to talk to you in confidence." It came as quite a shock, I can tell you.'

Richard stared at her. 'But you agreed to have dinner? Seeing him soon? Whatever it's about, though, Ben will be supremely convincing, and you've said yourself what good company he is and easy to be around. You will try and guard against all that and read between the lines?'

'You might remember I'm the one who was worried in the first place,' Kate said impatiently. 'We fixed for next Thursday, but it's easily changed.'

'Did you tell them about moving in here?'

'Not yet. You might have had a change of heart or met someone on the plane.'

'No one I fancied, really—but I might take a bird to the opera when you're dining out à deux . . .' Kate mouthed two words at him.

'It's the oddest thing, this invitation of Ben's,' she said, 'I can't understand it. But it is with Mum's blessing and perhaps she'll shed some light on Saturday. Sorry about the weekend! It'll be hard pounding . . .'

'Don't look so tense, I do know what I'm in for! Sadie and Rupert are in Davos till Sunday night, your mother's in charge till we arrive, then after sizing me up and down over lunch, she's scarpering,

206

leaving us to cope with three screaming offspring and a sea of nappies.'

'You'll be blinded by her charms.'

'I'll be too much on best behaviour, a shrivelled specimen under her spotlight. I've never felt more terrified in my life.'

*   *   *

They left for Basingstoke at eleven-thirty the next morning. Kate wished she hadn't sold her mother so much to Richard and made her sound unassailably perfect—some kind of mushroom-stuffing super-mum.

But she was so much on Kate's mind. She treasured the evening she'd had with her mother, just before Richard was back. Coming on top of his call from the Iquitos hotel when he'd said out loud that he loved her, it had been the sweetest thrill, talking about him openly at supper. And Rachel had seemed somehow more intensely loving than usual, almost clinging, yet never excluding Ben—although her very intensity seemed to highlight the unresolved tension that wouldn't go away.

They were still on the outskirts of London in stodgy traffic. As they inched forward, Richard sighed then turned with a grin. 'You should ask your mother to come and see the flat. I need to get over the hump of prising you away from the glamour of W11 and making you downsize.'

'I wish I could decide what to do with my flat.'

'Why are you so against letting it?'

'I can't really, the insurance doesn't let me. I'd have to take down the paintings, store them, hang repros. Forget all the agro, it's not even worth it financially.'

Kate sensed him thinking she could bring more pictures and sell a couple, but she couldn't bear to part with any and had no feel for investing. The paintings were her long-term independence. It had come as a shock to her to discover that Harry had remortgaged everything they owned.

And it felt too soon for that sort of serious upheaval. Richard had acted on a wild impulse, pressing her to move in after a matter of days. It mightn't work out, he could easily change his mind. She imagined the build-up of strain there could be with his children.

The thought of that made Kate feel punched suddenly, her elatedness drained dry. It was self-inflicted drought, but she needed a constant storm of reassurance and none was forthcoming at that moment. She retreated into silence.

Clear of the traffic Richard drove fast and the car was swaying in violent gusts of wind; it was the windiest January on record. Cold too, but no snow, thankfully, which always blocked the lanes when it fell around Rye.

'I've been meaning to ask something,' he said, without looking at her.

She heard the hesitation in his voice and tensed. 'Oh, yes?'

'Did you ever take the morning-after pill? What did you do in the end?'

'It's a bit late to be asking that! Of course I took it—the third morning after—and I was straight back on the pill. It's been lying around in your bedroom, in case you haven't noticed. But I'm sure you've seen me take it anyway.'

'*Our* bedroom. But I have the feeling you'd

rather not be on it—isn't that right? Why don't you think about coming off?'

Kate was silenced. Was she hearing right? All her longing, resignation, the wrench of every period . . . But the way he was talking, sounding so casually considerate about it, did that suggest he'd been feeling a bit guilty about his rather chauvinistic attitude at the time? Possibly even thinking he should offer to take care of things himself?

She struggled to find the right note. 'Do you mean I should use something else?'

'Katie, darling! I do love you, you're so wondrously pompous and unbending. Next, you're going to say I've only known you a month and I can't possibly want a pregnant woman on my hands.'

'It's not even a month,' she said, sticking out her chin and looking straight ahead. She spun round to face him. 'And you can't, can you? I mean, have you thought about your own children and how they'd take it? Polly would have a fit and feel even more out of it and Eleanor might . . . make difficulties.' Kate paused, her heart batting away at fever pitch. 'It would be hugely irresponsible,' she finished lamely, feeling a dutiful fool.

'Why? You want a baby, it's written all over, and I want it to be mine. It has to be. I think I'd kill anyone else who ever came on the scene. Polly would adjust in time and she'd have no need to know for quite a long while yet. And I'll worry about Eleanor, that's my cross to bear.'

'It's the next exit. Don't miss it.'

Richard eyed her. 'You must do what feels instinctively right, Katie. You needn't tell me, maybe just surprise me one day.'

209

She wanted to go on talking, to pick at it, to know what he genuinely felt. He'd sounded surprisingly possessive. Was he seeing a baby simply as a means of keeping hold? Surely not? She thought about it backwards and forwards, it was impossible to digest. He'd tossed it out with not the slightest long-distance hint about marriage—but he had thrown his hat into the ring. She couldn't allow herself to think of the supreme joy . . . Richard was giving her space, but he was standing too far back. It was unnerving, having the decision left to her. Was he really prepared to start all over?

She felt his eyes on her and he was grinning when she turned. 'Are you ever going to tell your mother your new address?' he said, which was his way of moving things on, she thought, the subject of babies closed.

'All in good time,' Kate replied crisply. 'You want to do everything at breakneck speed.'

They were turning in at Sadie and Rupert's gate. 'Which leads me to those few days away we talked about before I left,' he said, switching off the engine and holding her eyes, 'that I want to have as soon as possible. Just a short break, I know you don't want to be away from your father long.'

'I'd have to pass it by Dan,' Kate said, which drew a predictable reaction. Dan had given her a hard enough time in the office on Friday and she could do without Richard joining in. She was owed masses of holiday, but Dan could make all the difficulties he chose.

The front door was open and Joseph was outside, jumping up and down and shouting, 'They're here, they're here!' Rachel appeared behind him and Amelia pushed past them both. She stood centre

210

stage, hugging her half-bald doll, giving Kate and Richard the benefit of her most gloweringly baleful stare.

'Inside, both of you,' Kate called. 'It's Arctic! You'll turn into little cubes of ice.' The north wind was sweeping round the drive as imperiously as an angry queen.

Richard assembled various food bags, a carrier with the doll and book he'd bought the children and their one overnight bag. It was a sure sign of living together, Kate thought, glancing to catch her mother's eye and share a smile.

Something was wrong. Rachel was chalk-white, looking almost as though in shock. No one had greater composure, she could always appear gracefully relaxed—whatever her private troubles— yet now she looked openly distressed. Kate worried that her mother might be ill. But she never let on or made a fuss if she was—and if she were really ill, wouldn't she say so and be practical? It had to be more than that.

What would Richard think? Here was her mother showing clear signs of strain after all the boasts about her being a genius at hiding her feelings whatever went on inside. That was the least consideration, Kate told herself angrily, taking hold of Amelia and Joseph's hands.

Rachel smiled, masking any obvious signs of her distress. 'I like the car, Richard. Come and have a drink by the fire,' she urged, leading on indoors. 'You might have a little enforced downtime, though. Rose is yelling and I think she has to be first sitting.'

Lunch when it came was delicious, one of Rachel's easily prepared standbys. Plaice fillets

211

baked in a little thin cream with slices of tomato and mushrooms. She had laid up in the dining room, saying it was more civilized and good training for the children, in response to her daughter's protests.

Listening while she entertained Richard with her inimitable charm, holding him in the orb of her aquamarine eyes, Kate could see well-hidden signs of the immense effort it was taking. Her mother was unquestionably under great stress. Something must have happened, and in the last twenty-four hours.

'Katie's told me some hair-raising things about your trip, Richard,' Rachel said. 'People do seem to flock to the rainforests, though, all these intrepid tourists and budding naturalists.'

'Yes, and I'm sure the wildlife adapts to a regular traipse-through, but we were doing our own uncharted thing—of necessity since we were visiting an illegal site. I could have done with being on an official trail—I did have to watch where I put my feet!'

She asked pertinent questions about his job, she commented warmly on past programmes of his. Joseph chipped in. Kate and Amelia—who had a look of sumptuous delight on her peachy little face when the sticky toffee pudding and ice cream appeared—were the more silent pair at the table.

The children asked to get down to watch their favourite Christmas DVD, *Dora the Explorer,* and after settling them in front of the television Kate could stand it no longer.

'Mum, what's wrong? You're like a sheet. You seem seriously upset about something. I'm really worried.'

She caught Rachel by surprise and a look of panic flashed into her face, as though she felt cornered. 'Bad of me to be showing it,' she said with an uncharacteristic, false little laugh. She seemed unsure how to respond. 'But it's nothing that involves the family or affects you, Katie, nothing too close to home.' She hesitated. 'Just, well, someone's been murdered, I'm afraid.'

'Just! What an extraordinary thing to say!' Kate exclaimed, taken aback. 'Who? Is it someone you know?'

'It was a man called Roger Grieve. He headed up a financial consultancy that has advised Ben on his employees' pensions once or twice. I'd only met him once, just the other day, and Ben's contact with him was quite slight, but they'd got on well, I know. He was found dead in his office yesterday and the police suspect foul play.'

Kate stared at her mother in horror. 'But Mum, you can't have forgotten? We met him together— on New Year's Eve. I remember it vividly—it was just before I crashed into Richard . . .' She felt sickened, chilled right through; that gentle, endearing, self-deprecating man. Tears pricked in her eyes.

Rachel said nothing. She stared back with a look almost of naked fear then muttered like an automaton, 'Oh, yes. New Year's Eve.'

'Can you say more about what happened?' Richard asked, reaching under the table for Kate's hand. 'Why do the police suspect murder? Was there a weapon? Was it completely obvious?'

Rachel turned her gaze. 'I don't know about a weapon. He was found by the early morning cleaners, face down, slumped over his glass-topped

213

desk. But from the front, not behind it where he sat, as though he was walking up to it, perhaps. His face was battered to a pulp and Ben was told that no crashing fall, however dramatic, could have done such violent damage. He was hit from behind, it would seem, more than once and very forcibly. It is in today's newspapers, but no one is saying more than that.'

'He must have let in a visitor,' Richard said, 'someone he trusted—at least enough to turn back to his desk.'

'I suppose so,' Rachel responded rather vaguely.

They were all silent for a moment then, whatever her private thoughts, she seemed suddenly to pull herself together, surprisingly, and produce a consummate display of elegant charm. Whether it was for Richard's benefit or to prove to herself that she could do it, Rachel certainly pulled out all the stops.

'We can't let this take us over,' she said, with a warm smile. 'I must admit that it was a terrible shock, and Ben's very upset, but it's happened, nothing can turn back the clock.'

Kate had to admire her mother's guts. Her colour returned and with it the creamy, petal-smooth look to her skin that belied her age. It was as if she'd staunched a painful cut, covered and hidden it from view and could get on with life again. Her arresting eyes sparkled with more confidence; she was back in control.

'I had a proposition to put to you both, in fact.' Rachel eyed them in turn. 'I think it'll have some appeal. You're showing us up with that tan, Richard, you see, which is quite relevant. I know you've only been back days, and my daughter, as

214

you may have discovered, is hopeless with anything spur-of-the-moment, but Ben's backer, Spencer Morgan, was asking after her the other day and he came up with an invitation.'

She turned to Kate. 'He thought you might like to spend some time with us on his yacht. I explained you were newly involved and he said, with one of those airy great hand-waves of his, "She should bring him along. Both of them must come".'

'But his yacht's in the Caribbean!'

'I know it's a long way to go, an eight-or nine-hour flight to Grenada—that's where you'd join the yacht—but you could stay on for a few days. Find somewhere on the island, go off and do your own thing. Grenada's lovely, green and hilly, and you wouldn't, anyway, want more than a weekend with the oldsters.'

Richard flashed Kate his widest grin. 'I'm with your mother on this one, Katie—who's being over-kind to this particular oldster! It's a terrific proposition. How can we possibly refuse?'

Sun and sea, time away, first-hand access to the man he was investigating . . . He couldn't hide the urging journalist's glint in his eye. Kate wondered which gave him the greater buzz: a holiday with her or homing in on Spencer Morgan.

'I do have a slight problem,' she said. 'It's not that I don't want to go . . .'

'Let's have it,' Richard laughed. 'I know you won't want to be away long, and nor can I be.'

He and Rachel were ganging up on her, but they didn't know how scabrous her boss was being now, since her call. 'It's Dan,' she explained. 'He's sure to be tricky and say it's too short notice. I had to lie through my teeth to come to the airport and meet you.'

Richard rose and pushed in his chair. 'Come on, Katie! We can sort it, you must have a holiday. I'm going to make the coffee,' he said, 'I know my way round this kitchen after all. And I'll see what Joseph and Amelia are up to as well.'

They had been quiet, watching the DVD in the television alcove off the kitchen, but even as Richard spoke, a screaming match erupted that made him smile. Rachel blanched and instinctively leaped up out of her chair. Her nerves were far from healed. Richard avoided drawing any attention to her reaction, only to say gently, 'You stay right there, I can handle it fine.'

Kate went to the door, listening while Joseph reeled off a tearful litany of complaints. She stood ready in case any backup was needed, but Richard seemed well in charge, coping masterfully.

'Remember what you wanted me to do last time I was here,' she heard him say.

'Read me a story,' Joseph wailed. 'You said you would.'

'And I will. I've brought you a book about a gingerbread man. But we are going to let Amelia listen to it, too. She was asleep that time and she and I still have to make friends and get to know each other. She may have pulled out all the DVDs, but they are easily put back and we older brothers have to live with things like that. I have a kid brother and I can remember; I was the older one too.'

CHAPTER 15

Richard read the story at the kitchen table with two small people on either side of him. Amelia was in pink dungarees and Joseph looked cute in a mini lumber-check shirt and jeans. Rose was part of the action too, solemnly surveying the world and her siblings from the superior viewpoint of her baby seat up on the table.

Kate unpacked the dishwasher with her mind on Roger Grieve. That decent unassuming man—how could anyone want him dead? She thought of her mother's reaction, the look on her face that had been more than simply shock and outrage: it had hinted at real fear. His brutal murder must have some particular significance, Kate felt, some connection with her mother's troubles, whatever they were.

Rachel was calling from the hall. 'Has anyone seen my glasses? I can never find them,' she said despairingly, coming into the kitchen. 'It drives Ben mad. I really must be off as well.'

Kate glanced around. 'Aren't they on the top of the microwave?'

'Darling, you're a genius!'

'Hardly. Come and have a quick chat before you go, Mum. Let's go into the sitting room and have a moment to ourselves while they finish the story.'

Rachel gave a half-smile, a sort of don't-start-on-me-though look, and followed her daughter across the hall. Kate went to one of the armchairs by the fireplace and Rachel sat opposite, uncomfortably upright with her glasses clutched in her hand.

'I'm a shattered wreck,' she said. 'Three under five is harder work than a week of Christmases! You'll manage fine, though, love, with Richard to help. He seems very at home here, pulling his weight, and he's good with the children, too.'

'He's been here before, of course,' Kate said, thinking of Richard's explosion of passion and being caught out on the hall floor. 'You good with him, Mum?' she asked. 'You do like him okay? I'm living with him now.'

'So I rather gathered!' Rachel said, seeming quite unsurprised by the speed of it all. 'Just keep an eye on your flat now and then, won't you? You'll know the way ahead soon enough. And Katie, darling, you must come out on the yacht; Richard was keen, to say the least, and it would do you so much good.'

She stared at her mother who was in grey flannel trousers and a mustard twinset; elegant, good-looking clothes, but no camouflage for her pale face, still drained and showing the strain. 'I will have to square it at work,' she said, turning her thoughts to the need to book flights. She suddenly decided, with an intense stab of love for Richard and a determined sense of abandon, that she might just forget to pack her pill. The proposed holiday was a whole two weeks away. Could she even wait that long?

Rachel was gazing at her, although she seemed distracted again, back in thoughts of her own. When she glanced down at her watch, Kate was instantly reminded of the dinner with Ben and how badly she needed a steer. She couldn't miss her chance.

'Can't you tell me what's going on, Mum? Why

218

does Ben want to have dinner alone with me? Why aren't you coming too? And I can't help wondering whether Roger Grieve has anything to do with all this; I feel he must be involved in some way. Was he a secret old flame of yours or something? You've been hiding tension for weeks, Mum. You're never this jittery and raw.'

'I can't tell you anything, Katie, don't ask me to. It has to come from Ben. It's a highly confidential situation. Ben will explain, though he shouldn't, he's breaking rules, but he trusts you and feels you should know. And, as I told you, I met Roger Grieve only once, that time with you, with that brief chat at Mark Simpson's party. But there will come a point, I think, when you'll understand why his death has managed to unnerve me in this way.'

Kate fixed her mother with wide, questioning eyes, feeling shivers. Rachel smiled back tenderly. 'For all that, darling, try not to let it get to you. No fretting, and that's an order, either before or after talking to Ben. You'll swing the holiday, you're owed weeks of time. Buy a couple of sexy new bikinis and some glamorous things for the sun. And don't stint! They'll be flashing their diamond navel studs on Spencer's yacht, I'm sure. He will have a very eclectic mix of people, but you'll outshine them, no question. Spencer will be all over you both, he's like that, and over-excessive luxury, but you needn't hang around for long.'

Rachel stood up. 'Must go or I'll be in shtick, Ben will be clock-watching. We have a train to catch, we're staying with friends up north.'

'Come and have coffee very soon, Mum, and see where I am living—Richard would like you to, I know. Perhaps early one Saturday morning before I leave for Dad's?'

'Please do,' Richard said, coming in with a starboard lean to accommodate Amelia's outstretched hand, 'though I dread what you'll think of Katie's reduced living quarters! And thanks for the surprise of this amazing invitation. See you in the Caribbean sun if not before.'

Kate collected Joseph, and Rose from her baby seat to say their goodbyes. She stood bouncing the baby, watching Richard help Rachel into her coat, disarmed, basking in the warmth of her blue-eyed gaze. Rachel hugged them all, lectured Kate's charges about the need to be on best behaviour and hurried out to her car.

*   *   *

Kate was in a shattered state of frazzle by the time she was grilling fish fingers two hours later with a grizzling baby attached to her hip and calling to Amelia at the kitchen table to stop stuffing her face with chocolate buttons. Using her free hand to pull out the grill she turned over the fish fingers, pushed in the pan again, jogging Rose all the while, then moved swiftly to whip away the buttons packet from Amelia, which caused screams of protest.

She dashed back to switch off the grill before the supper burned. 'I'm going for Joseph now,' she said wearily. 'Coming, love?' Amelia was clearly in no mood for a civil reply, so Kate left her to her own devices.

She found Joseph in the sitting room with Richard. 'Supper's ready,' she called from the door. They were cross-legged on one of Sadie's chic striped mats, deep in some incomprehensible-

220

sounding card game and took no notice. 'It's fish fingers,' Kate tried, before going on to say, 'but I might as well be talking to the moon.'

'I'll take two of your red energy and give you two green.' Joseph slapped down his cards.

'Red are worth ninety and green eighty,' Richard said. "Know what that means?'

Joseph looked uncertain. 'Is that like eight and nine?'

'Well done.'

'Then I win!'

Supper and mess took over, fights and screams. Bathtime, bedtime stories, kisses, and finally, amazingly, all three were tucked up, fast asleep and looking angelic.

Kate stood in front of the fire watching while Richard opened a bottle of claret. He left it on the table and came over for a kiss.

'Two children,' he murmured, without lifting his mouth from hers. 'Three is too much like fucking hard work.'

He poured the wine, handed her a glass and they sat in the armchairs on either side of the fireplace. 'I'm not sure this Davos weekend can become a regular fixture,' Richard said smiling. 'Want to know what I was thinking, seeing you with your mother, worrying yourself stiff, and again when you were slogging it out for your sister all afternoon?'

'Are you going to tell me I need to get a life?'

Richard's mobile overtook any answer he might have given; it was shrill and discordant and extinguished the luxury of the moment like a sudden downpour on a bride's big day. His set expression as he took the call told her all she needed to know.

221

He gave brief cryptic responses, keeping his phone pressed to his ear. 'Still no sign . . . ? Not a word?' He gazed at Kate with a blank expression as he listened, then rubbed his eyes and answered more sharply, 'Okay, okay, I'll come . . . Yes, I know. I am too.' He glanced at his watch. 'Be about an hour.'

Clicking off, he came to sit on the arm of Kate's chair. He tipped up her face, keeping his hand under her chin, and held her eyes. 'It's Eleanor—she's been drinking herself into the ground. Ed's been into her room and found a stash of gin bottles. Then this morning at breakfast she appeared looking the worse for wear apparently, complaining about being in need of some action and excitement in her life, then she suddenly stormed out of the house in a dressing gown. She had nothing with her, not even a bag.

'She hasn't been in touch all day. Ed chased after her, but only in time to see her climbing into a cab—typical one was going by; the house is in Castlenau, hardly the place you'd expect to find roving early morning taxis. Ed's texted me on and off, keeping me in the picture, and I've held out, hoping she'd turn up at some stage, probably with a hefty taxi bill to be paid. Poor old Ed sounds pretty desperate now, though, fed up with his lot. I do know one or two places she might have gone . . .'

Kate stared. Richard would never completely belong to her. 'I haven't got my car here,' she said. 'Sadie and Rupert aren't home till late tomorrow. I'll have a slight problem if you can't get back, I'd have to stay over and go straight into work on Monday by train. It's perfectly doable, though. Don't worry.' She smiled up at him, feeling a bleak

222

echoing cavern where her heart had happily swelled.

He pulled her up and kissed her. 'I love you, Katie. I'll be back. Lock up, of course, but can you give me a key and just skip the alarm?'

He tested the key and was gone. She turned off the oven with the pot-roasted chicken and poured Rachel's homemade wild mushroom soup back into a screw-top jar. She flicked television channels and found nothing to watch. Richard called later that evening: no sign of Eleanor yet, he'd be back as soon as he could.

In bed, with the angry wind rattling the window frames, Kate couldn't concentrate on her book and falling asleep wasn't easy on a stormy night with every creak and groan of the woodwork sounding like footsteps on the stairs. Whose footsteps? Not Richard's.

She woke with a start with her heart thundering in her chest. She listened out, stiff with panic. No sound from Rose. Kate's eyes slid nervously to the bedside clock: it was ten past five, but there was no chink of light, only silent mid-winter blackness. She reached for the light switch and froze. The bed was weighted against her, she wasn't alone.

'Fuck it, did you have to give me such a shock! Creeping in like a guilty husband—how long have you been here, for God's sake? You could have woken me.'

'Not long and I'm very cold. Can I snuggle up?'

* * *

On Wednesday night, the eve of her dinner with Ben, as mystified and unnerved as she was about it,

223

Kate was worrying almost as much about Richard and Saturday night as the dramas the next evening might hold.

When he'd crept in beside her at dawn she'd immediately asked after Eleanor. 'She's back safely? You found her? Everything's all right?'

'Yes, more or less, for the moment at least. But nothing really changes.'

Richard hadn't wanted to talk much about it understandably, huddled close at five-fifteen in the morning. Yet Kate had minded, she'd felt out of it, wanting to know every last detail, how and where he'd found Eleanor, all the stresses and tribulations and how he'd coped.

In the morning she'd slipped out of bed at the first sound of Rose's waking snuffles and left Richard to sleep on. She'd sorted out squabbles, quietened the house and got three children dressed and breakfasted. Then, when Richard had surfaced and plunged into his supportive role, dealing with lunch, screams, even nappies, there hadn't been a single moment, let alone a right one, to revisit the subject of Eleanor.

And after the long day, the handover and downloading to Sadie and Rupert, only leaving Basingstoke at ten o'clock at night, she and Richard had been worn out; they'd just wanted to get home. Her relationship with him was so new, Kate hadn't felt able to raise something he seemed not to want to talk about.

He'd had a five-thirty start on Monday morning with more filming at the docks and spent most of Monday and Tuesday nights in clubland—patiently filming vein-injecting addicts, he'd said, and sad-case party-goers doing coke in London's

224

darkest corners. Kate had considered mentioning a couple of renowned snorters in the advertising world, but felt sure he'd know them anyway. Richard had arrived home after three on both nights, though, not the time for bringing up a difficult subject. She hoped his next documentary, whose theme was undecided as yet, would involve more kindly hours and healthier interviewees.

He was cramming it all in before the Caribbean holiday, she knew, but between Eleanor and his work Kate felt hardly more than a lettuce leaf in his over-stuffed sandwich. She said as much while he was making it up to her in bed.

'But a very tasty bite . . .' Richard grinned and dipped to a breast.

She hauled him back up. 'Don't start. We should be sleeping and I want to talk about tomorrow night; what it's all about, why Ben wants to have dinner with me alone. I wish I was better armed.'

'Are you going straight from work? Shall we have a drink first? I'm around—in the office all day. We could meet somewhere like Soho House, say about seven.'

Kate thought it might be a chance to talk about Eleanor as well. 'I'd like that,' she said, with a kiss. 'Oh, and good news! Dan's just buggered off unexpectedly on a shoot for our big airline account, *Dreamer,* so I can ask the woman in HR about the holiday. I'm sure she'll okay it; she's friendly, she caught me in tears over Harry once.'

'Won't she want to know why you didn't go through Dan and it's so last-minute?'

'I can say Mum's holidaying with a friend who's only just invited me—and how inconsiderate it would have been to email Dan while he's off with

225

the models on a beach in the Bahamas. He's such a con artist, elbowing in on that commercial—it's not even one of his accounts. And with a budget airline like *Dreamer*, you'd think they'd shoot it on a beach in Spain or Goa, somewhere they fly to, but no, the whole team's going out Club on British Airways!'

'You know my views on Dan. Try thinking of it in reverse, Katie—how you'd feel if I'd just been about to take out a bird I said I felt sorry for. Dan's beneath thought, but just bear in mind that he might be a touch sore when he's back from romping between Bahamian sheets and clocking up mini-bar bills to find you've jetted off in his absence. He'll need watching. Especially when you breeze in, tanned and stunningly beautiful with that golden well-fucked glow . . .'

'Don't push your luck, the sun might give me a headache. And I'm having enough agro from Dan already. I know what to expect—and don't tell me I've only myself to blame!'

'Have I said a word?'

* * *

Soho House, named for its location, was a tall Georgian building housing a warren of bars, screening rooms, cafes and restaurants. It was a club, the meeting place of the media world and had members from the upper echelons of the advertising business as well. A friend of Kate's had once said it made him think of a Hogarth cartoon with louche drinkers and cavorting revellers to be seen dangling from every window.

Richard was up on a bar stool with a beefy bearded man in a sweaty-looking open-neck, check

226

shirt. Kate felt the familiar tug as he climbed off his stool and introduced her. His lean-boned face and soft look of connection did for her every time. Harvey Wright, the man was called, a yachting correspondent and America's Cup historian. She suspected he might be slightly underwhelmed by an engine-driven floating palace like Spencer Morgan's.

'See you around,' Richard said. He gave Harvey's broad back a parting friendly cuff and made for the only free table.

'You realise,' he remarked as they took possession of it, 'that walking into a top London restaurant on Ben's arm, even if you didn't look the sexiest, most stunning chick in the city, will be noticed. Wiltons is one of the few places with private booths—why Ben chose it, I expect—and he's well known after all. You'll be in a gossip column before you know it. I don't trust him for all sorts of reasons and certainly not with you in that dress!'

Kate had changed at the office into a figure-hugging cerise number and high-heeled black boots. 'Can we keep this serious?' she said, enjoying the convoluted compliment. She knew people were eyeing her and, Dutch confidence or not, she felt boosted. Richard was showing her off, introducing her to his world and she loved it, however psyched up she was about dinner with Ben.

Richard ordered glasses of white wine and gave Kate his full attention. Her nerves about dinner receded, but her emotional need to ask questions came to the fore. She had Richard's eyes and said tentatively, 'Can we talk about Eleanor? I know it isn't really the time, it never is, but I think it would

227

help if I knew more about her illness. I know nothing about the disorder, even how it's caused. There's so much I want to ask. Things like the difficulties of bringing up Polly and Ed—I suppose there's no chance of their inheriting it?'

Kate carried on; she was in too deep, unstopping an emotional blockage, and oblivious to the comings and goings of the club. 'I wish you'd tell me about Saturday too, what exactly happened, how you found her.'

Richard looked uncomfortable, but he managed a small smile. 'Sorry—I do find it hard to talk about,' he gave another of his familiar little shakes of the head, 'but I'll try my best. Well, for a start, bipolar can be a genetic condition, however I'm sure it isn't in Eleanor's case.

'I told you how I'd expected her to be volatile and temperamental; she was a gifted musician and it seemed all part of the aura and allure. And in the early days she'd certainly shown little sign of the full-blown psychosis that came later, apart from talking of being depressed during her A-level years and at university. Various triggers set it off. Her terrible sleep patterns were an early clue apparently, and the postnatal depression she had with Ed.

'It was downhill from then on. She'd slide into a depressive decline then gamble and spend like a lunatic and go wild sexually, serious indiscretions; then would come more black destructive depression. She took appetite-suppressant pills by the handful, crazy amounts of caffeine, amphetamines . . . I made her see a psychiatrist, a marvellous, inspirational woman who explained to me that the drinking, drugs and excess, as well as

228

the harmful effect of Eleanor's antidepressant pills—misdiagnosed by a doctor who'd failed to spot the early markers—were all clear signals of a major bipolar disorder.'

Richard rubbed at his frown lines. 'I went into a depression too, hearing she had a serious psychiatric illness. I was hardly selfless and the thought of being saddled with a lifetime of coping with all those vicious, manic mood swings . . . But we had a baby son and how could I leave a sick woman?

'I picked myself up. It was heavy-duty, though; the constant risk of overdosing, self-harm, even suicide attempts, Eleanor's manic excesses and binges—always followed by the deep depressive psychosis. It was ghastly and relentless. But no less for Eleanor herself; she says it's like she needs to get out of her very skull. She imagines destitution, chaos, innumerable crises, even that I spend hours planning her murder!'

'She can describe what goes on in her head?' Kate asked.

'Yes, occasionally. She talks about the terrible darkness: a sense of being lost in a maze on a pitch-black night, of her world going fuzzy, never finding the focus.'

'Isn't the illness containable with pills and treatment, the psychiatric help, too? And what about the human spirit, isn't there a chance she could fall for someone new and find the will to recover? Perhaps, one day,' Kate ventured, wishing it fervently, 'with the support of a new man, mightn't Eleanor find the determination, that elusive will?'

Richard smiled tiredly. 'She has had lovers; she

plays in concerts, has good patches. But the cycle goes on. One prod at her self-esteem, a single word of criticism and she's set right back again, in the grip of merciless depression. It's like an oily black slick that she can't escape. In acute attacks she needs lithium and antipsychotics combined, but her lithium levels can get too high; it's a hellish balancing act. The medical team keep any need of inpatient care to a minimum and they've been a tremendous support with Ed and Polly—who have had regular psychiatric checks and shown no symptoms, thank God.'

He leaned and brushed Kate's lips. 'Can we stop talking about it now? It drags me down and I want to concentrate on you. You must go soon and find out what this dinner with Ben is all about.'

'But tell me about Saturday. How could Eleanor have been out all that time, in only a dressing gown and without even a handbag? What had she done all day? How did you find her?'

'It's not a pretty story.' Richard broke off then, looking apologetic, being distracted by a couple of tittering girls, new arrivals at the next table, who were trying to say hello.

He gave no more than an acknowledging nod, but Kate was about to leave him and meet Ben and didn't like what she saw one bit. 'Will you stay on and have supper here?' she asked, exposing her thoughts.

'The redhead is one of my ex-brief interludes,' Richard said with an irritating grin, 'so I think not.' Her hand was on the table and he covered it with his. 'I will tell you about Saturday before you go; it might help make you understand.

'I arrived to find Eleanor's mother, Cynthia,

flapping around, Ed practising his guitar and Polly out—no one knew where. Her grandmother hadn't even asked. She hadn't agreed a return time and Ed was no help. Polly is far too young to be out clubbing on a Saturday night, I felt mad as hell. Still no sight or sound of Eleanor: so I started a ring-round of her friends. I tried a conductor she knows, a notorious old roué with liver spots who dips his stick into anything going. She had been there, arrived a little underdressed, he said. He'd paid off her taxi and they'd "chatted" all morning—a euphemism if ever there was one. She'd been quite revved up as he put it; knocked back half a bottle of gin, eaten a fridge full of food before he'd summoned a cab and given her home address.

'But she diverted it and went elsewhere?'

'No chance of her going home.' Richard's tone was bitter. 'I called another guy, a harpist called Elfyn. She had "looked in", he said rather decorously, and seemed in need of comforting. But with his aged parents for tea and her "curious attire in a dressing gown", he'd thought of a friend with a dress shop and sent her on there—having first persuaded his friend, the owner, to send any bills onto Eleanor at her home address.'

Richard sighed. 'You really want me to carry on with the full blow-by-blow?' Kate nodded. 'Well, after that I tried endless other numbers in her address book and had no joy at all. The only thing left, I decided, was to call in at a few clubs, just on the off-chance.

'No one had set eyes on Eleanor so I trailed back to Barnes at about half-past three, thoroughly fed-up, to find Polly still wasn't home. She pitched

231

up a few minutes later and when I hit the roof she screamed at me to lay off, go to hell, go fuck myself—that sort of scene. She was in a dreadful state, smelling of weed, shivering wildly—she goes out with so little on—and began to sob her heart out, streams of tears. It was hard to stay angry for long; she wouldn't stop sobbing or tell me a thing. Some boy must have ditched her and it seemed best just to let her be.

'Eleanor pitched up not long after, very drunk indeed. I paid off an extremely expensive taxi and helped her to bed, which was a struggle since she passed out on the stairs.' Richard rubbed at his eyes, shook his head and smiled. 'So there you have it, Katie, my darling, the whole long sorry saga of a particularly manic bipolar day.'

He looked at her more intently, as though temporarily out of his Eleanor morass and focused again. Kate felt subdued, confused by it all, disturbed and concerned about Polly.

He seemed to read her mind as he often did and answered that thought. 'It was hard to talk on Sunday, between head butts from Joseph and bathing the babies; I was a bit frazzled all round. I've wanted to lean on you about Polly quite badly, though, share the worry and talk it through. I know you have to go now, but I do feel very helpless about her.'

'She needs someone to confide in,' Kate said, thinking she was the last person Polly would choose. 'We'll have talking time soon. My HR lady has cleared the holiday.'

He saw her into a taxi. Her mind was already on Ben and hyped-up with nervous anticipation about the evening ahead. It was darting about like a freaked-out rabbit, not knowing which way to turn. Richard had given it too rich a diet, too much to absorb.

CHAPTER 16

Kate climbed out of her taxi in Jermyn Street to see Ben paying off the one in front that had stopped directly outside Wilton's. They went in together, he in a navy coat, she in a belted black one, hurrying in out of the dismally steady drizzle. Her fingers were numb, whether from nerves or cold, she wasn't sure.

Ben was given an effusively warm welcome as their coats were taken, the maître d' making clear to all around that he was a valued customer. 'Take Mr Townsend and his guest to table five,' he briskly instructed a waiter, who jumped to it and led the way.

'I'm not sure what it'll do to my stock, coming in with such a gorgeously beautiful toy-girl on my arm,' Ben murmured. 'Send it sky-high, I should think, from all the looks!'

Kate smiled. 'But I'm a virtual stepdaughter; you'd be in the clear,' she whispered back.

The waiter saw them to a wood-panelled booth. It was against the wall, on which was hung a quiet painting of oysters on a rough-wood table that appealed to Kate. She and Ben sat opposite each other on upholstered, green velour benches where a couple of rust-red cushions were a homely touch. They studied the splendid menu cards while being plied with bottled water and bread rolls.

233

'This is a treat,' she said, when Ben had ordered a bottle of Chablis and she had his attention. 'I've only been here once before and a fish restaurant is my ideal.'

'I can recommend the dressed crab and Dover sole.'

Kate went along with that, glad to have the business of food taken care of. She longed for Ben to cut any preamble and get started, but he was too polite and civilised. Eyeing him while he gave the order, she thought how good he looked in his dark-grey suit, pink shirt and woven silk tie, pleasingly substantial and handsomely well preserved.

He smiled across the table. 'You look like a girl in love, Katie. It's wonderful to see. And your mother's feedback is what you'll be pleased to hear! She called Richard decent, positive and strong-minded—and well able, as she put it, to keep you in line.'

'That's usually said in reverse, about women who have a much harder job of it, keeping their men in line,' Kate countered, thinking that on the face of it Ben fitted her mother's description just as well as Richard. She wished she could forget her qualms. She wanted to believe in him; Rachel's passionate insistence that Ben was more than good, he was 'exceptional', had been moving. But the least likely people could have flaws. Something was distressingly wrong and Kate felt there had to be a possibility that her clever mother simply couldn't see past her love for him.

'You will remember, won't you, Katie?' Ben said, more seriously, bringing her back. 'I'm always here if you ever need help with anything, any little wrinkles or problems . . .'

'Early days for those.' She gave a wry grin then found herself saying, to her surprise and acute embarrassment and with a deepening blush, 'Richard's bipolar ex-wife is quite a problem. Her mood swings are always a crisis and he rushes to deal with them every time. It's almost as if they were still married.'

'He has to help out, you must see that? It's good that he feels responsible. And he must be a bit guilty about divorcing her at all. What about you, Katie—you're not over your guilt about Harry either?'

She blushed again, feeling her cheeks glowing red as a brazier. 'But I am, you see,' she said honestly, 'and guilty about that now, being so completely taken up with a new love.'

'Sounds healthier. Good news you can come out to Spencer's yacht,' Ben said, sensibly changing the subject. 'He has an eclectic bunch of friends, old-school bankers, blingy girls and reed-thin top models, politicians, hangers-on—people on his payroll.' Ben smiled. 'It'll be quite an experience. Richard was a financial journalist, wasn't he, before the switch to television? That'll keep Spencer on his toes!'

Kate found it hard to read anything into such a light, throwaway remark; it was uttered without side or edge, as though Ben was a good friend of Spencer and had no issues, nothing to be guarded about.

It was impossible to relax. Kate mauled her bread roll, dropped her hands down to her lap, rubbed and kneaded them, longing for Ben to get on and say why they were there.

A waitress arrived with the crab. In her white

apron and pale, mint-green dress she looked like a young student nurse. 'It doesn't change, this place,' Ben said, when she went away, 'superb service and prices to match.' The waitress returned with a silver sauceboat of mayonnaise before finally leaving them to the privacy of the booth.

How private was it? Kate looked up nervously at decorative glass panes that filled in above the wood-panelling. Ben followed her gaze. 'I particularly asked for this table, it's the best in the house for a private conversation. I understand why you're tense, but try not to be too keyed-up.'

She gave him an empty stare. 'I want to know why you needed to have dinner alone.'

'I'm about to explain. First I have an impossible request of you, which is sure to be upsetting and cause resentment, but I'm afraid is really vital—as I know you'll come to understand.'

'What on earth do you mean?' Kate felt the clutch of a chill hand.

'You won't be able to share this, Katie, not with Richard, not with a single soul. That's as it absolutely has to be.'

She should have been prepared, the need for secrecy was fairly obvious, but not to tell Richard . . . 'Suppose,' she said, forcing herself to speak calmly, anger overtaking fear, 'I don't believe you, or I promise to honour what you ask and don't stick to it?'

'I have to take that chance. You can choose not to know, of course, which might be for the best. I'm simply giving you the option because I believe you're strong and able to bear the strain. And I feel I owe it to you. You're suspicious; you think whatever I'm involved in is below board and that

I've dragged your mother into it as well. You've lost faith, even in her, and you feel left out. But you love her, Katie, you care. I know you'll see the need for absolute secrecy.'

How could she not tell Richard? She loved him to distraction. The tension would be unbearable. And how could she trust Ben—as Richard would endlessly remind her? It would ruin the holiday on the yacht. God, what could be less important than that? She met Ben's eyes in silence, angry with herself as well.

His eyes were soft. 'Richard will come round. He's in love with you, he may fight you over it and rant, but he'll accept it in time.'

Kate pressed on her eyes with a thumb and forefinger. Ben hadn't exactly thrown down a gauntlet; he sounded genuine, yet he'd laid down terms and now he expected her to dive into a very black pool when she had no idea how deep it was or what lay beneath the surface. She had Richard's words ringing in her ears, his repeated warnings about being conned.

'Okay, Ben, I do want to hear,' she said, feeling pulled in two directions and painfully unsure she could cope. 'I'll give you my word.'

Ben rested his hand on her arm for a moment; its warmth was reassuring, making it harder to stay at one remove. 'A few months ago, last October,' he began, watching her, 'I discovered my company was being used. People working for me, being paid by me, were involved in a racket and bringing in illegal goods from South America.'

Wasn't it an easy ploy to play the role of the unwitting innocent? Kate vividly remembered the Boxing Day lunch, quizzing Ben about the products

237

he imported, Sadie's aside about drugs. It had all added to Kate's worry about her mother's tension, but she had never really seriously considered the idea of anything illegal going on.

'How did you find out?' she asked more coldly, picking at the delicious dressed crab.

'I was in the street, going to post some letters one Saturday morning and bumped into my Chief Finance Officer, a man called Andy Carter. I was surprised; he lives out of London, close to our depot in Hertford. That's our distribution point, you see; the containers come on there from Liverpool docks. Andy said it wasn't chance, that he needed to see me, which put me on my guard instantly; he could have telephoned or emailed. Then I noticed how washed-out he looked, and he was sweating too, which seemed unnatural in November. I suggested coffee at the flat, but Andy didn't want that for some reason. I thought of the garden square, which is for residents only, I had the key with me so we went there.'

'He was about to be a whistle-blower?' Kate asked, still sceptical.

'Of course, you can be a whistle-blower and in deep as well,' Ben said, smiling. 'However in this case Andy was just in it up to his neck.'

Ben broke off as the waitress came for the plates; he nodded at the hovering wine waiter who refilled their glasses then carried on. 'Before I get into the nitty-gritty and ramifications, Katie, I'd like to paint in a bit of background. It will help to know something about the port we use out in Brazil, which is remote and surrounded by rainforest; all the difficulties of transport, the lack of policing.'

'And therefore ease of smuggling drugs?' Her

238

questions were falling over themselves. Asking them, though, when Ben had hardly begun, felt like stepping too close to a whirring propeller; she didn't want to be cut to shreds too early on.

'Yes, it was drugs,' Ben said, 'cocaine. I'll get to the detail, but let me finish on the background first. Remember, at Christmas we talked about our main import, acai?' He was interrupted again. Their Dover soles arrived, neatly filleted with the ladder-like fishbone deftly removed and served with iron-rich spinach and baby new potatoes.

Ben waited until the waitress had gone then carried on seamlessly. 'Acai is a truly amazing health food and with a hugely growing market in the UK. Antioxidants and smoothies are all the rage and acai ticks all the boxes. The people who got in on it early, investing and setting up processing plants out in the rainforest, were on to a good thing! It fruits just months after planting too, in the right conditions, huge stems with literally hundreds of berries in a single bunch. We import it as a frozen puree with the stones removed—which are ground down and added to animal feed—and the port we use is Santana in Amapá State.'

Kate was listening intently as she squeezed a gauze-clad half-lemon over her fish. 'Is the port significant?' she asked.

'Yes, it does have a bearing. Amapá State is in the north-west corner of Brazil, extremely remote and rainforested as I said, only reached by boat or plane. A boat trip to the nearest city in the next-door state, Belém in Pará, for instance, takes days and can be very hairy and hazardous. And internal roads are simply broad dirt tracks—though they call them highways and drive at highway speeds—deserted and virtually unpoliced. Transport infrastructure, as in much of Brazil, is a completely unheard-of concept.'

Ben took a sip of wine. 'This is all relevant, I promise—but I wish you'd eat a little of that food!' Kate had been concentrating too hard to touch a thing. She had a few mouthfuls while Ben pushed away his plate and fingered the stem of his wine glass.

'To ship Amapá's exports, manganese, gold, chrome, rainforest products, downstream to a larger port like Belém on the south bank of the Amazon, would be uneconomical,' he continued. 'So freight leaving from Santana usually goes straight to its destination. Our container ships, for instance, don't dock again till they reach Liverpool. Santana is a free port too, with no customs, and any inspections or checks are minimal to non-existent. Crime and corruption are routine, the police shoot at will. Trade unionists report death threats, a prosecuting counsel was murdered . . .'

It was all fascinating but so far Ben had told her nothing of any significance. 'Can we get back to your Chief Finance Officer, Andy, and his part in it,' Kate said firmly. 'Why should he suddenly come and tell his boss about a serious scam? Did he say how it was done, where the drugs were hidden?'

'He told me all he could, but extracting the key facts from him was a slow, painful business. He said the cocaine was hidden in the frozen packages of acai. They are sealed plastic pouches that effectively have four layers: two outer and two inner with the fruit puree contained between the layers. The cocaine solution was in a cavity in the middle, a lethal little extra parasite package. The

240

harmless-looking doctored pouches were then frozen along with the mountain of others, loaded into the freezer containers and shipped.'

Ben carried on. 'The containers arrive over here, travel on to our depot where the hidden nuggets of frozen cocaine solution are extracted and reduced by evaporation—this is all according to Andy—and restored back into a solid saleable form. Then off it goes, freshly dried out, snowy white and tempting, to be cut into and adulterated before flooding the market and luring a whole new generation of young users into its grasp.'

Something felt wrong. He was making the trafficking of cocaine sound as simple as one, two, three. 'But,' Kate broke in, wishing above all that Richard were there, asking the thrusting central questions. She felt befuddled, grappling with the unknown and unqualified to cross-examine Ben. 'I know so little about this, yet surely, even if Santana is a free port and has corrupt police, it's a very different story back here? I mean if the customs were doing their job properly, wouldn't they insist on inspecting every shipload? Aren't there searches, inspections and sniffer dogs at this end, once a ship comes into dock?'

'Of course. Customs can X-ray suspect goods, bring in the dogs, although money becomes a factor, inevitably, even with sniffer dogs. They are highly trained, but for particular individual smells, explosives, drugs, the ink on money. And think of the quantities of containers in a shipload. Which ones do you search and defrost? Do you go through a whole shipment with a fine toothcomb, just to be sure? The stuff can't be refrozen if the authorities get it wrong. And that means you're into huge compensation costs with the poor old taxpayer landed, as ever, with the bill. Seizing a shipload can't be done on a whim or a hunch and undertaken lightly.'

'But with really sound intelligence?'

'If the smuggling is on a serious enough scale, the slight risk to whoever's masterminding the whole thing—the chance of a CFO like Andy spilling the beans and causing the loss of a single operation—will have been factored in. Any genius mind will take very good care to watch his hide. He'll keep every satellite operation circling in its own space, every link in his chain carefully uncoupled from the others. He will have ensured that the rest of his vastly lucrative criminal empire stays well out of reach of being fingered.'

Ben's expression hardened. 'Whoever is running this operation will have thought it through to the last acai berry. I'm sure the owners of the packaging plants out in Amapá State—often conglomerates and investment companies as they are in my case— know nothing of any illegal activities going on. I didn't, after all, with my business.'

'There's something awfully ironic about a marvellously healthy antioxidant fruit like acai being used to smuggle cocaine,' Kate said, managing a smile. She couldn't imagine Ben possibly giving away so much detail had it not been a truthful account—and yet wouldn't hiding behind truthfulness actually be a deviously clever ploy? 'You must have been appalled, hearing all this from your finance man,' she commented. 'Did you ask why he'd told you, though, and come running to his boss?' She was impatient for Ben to go on, but nervous, sensing something worse to come.

'Of course I had to know that. My CFO was scared that morning. It must have taken some doing, coming to break ranks as he had. Andy was banking on some form of protection, I suspect, hoping that if I went to the police his confession would be used in mitigation. He'd thought the game was up, you see; his fear was tangible, lifting off him. He said he'd felt certain, from the very pertinent questions being asked—by someone he would never have believed could remotely have reason to rumble a smuggling operation like theirs—that the net must be closing in.'

'Who was that person?'

'Roger Grieve.'

Kate felt the blood drain. 'My God!' she exclaimed. 'Does that mean you think he was silenced?' She was beginning to understand more than ever why her mother had been so unnerved. 'A man loses his life for asking a few tricky questions— it seems beyond comprehension.' Kate felt in the grip of a powerful rage, that gentle, self-effacing man brutally battered to death from behind. 'But Ben,' she demanded fiercely, 'I don't really see why, if Roger Grieve's queries were hitting home and scaring him, Andy couldn't have gone to his paymasters and told them instead of you. Wouldn't he have taken a lesser risk in fact and actually got brownie points? I mean, Roger Grieve hadn't been murdered at that stage.'

Staring at Ben, Kate was suddenly struck by a stomach-churning thought. If Andy hadn't told the string-pullers—who had? *Someone* had to have reported back and passed on the intelligence about Roger Grieve's suspicions with its grim outcome. Ben had known about them . . . Andy had told

243

him . . . She shook herself.

'His murder makes me all the more determined,' he said. 'But to answer your question: the reason Andy wouldn't have gone to the string-pullers is threefold. He wouldn't have known who they were, for a start. He'd only know the man who saw him right, the small-time ringleader within my company. As I said, I'm convinced that each individual cell of an evil operation like this lives in ignorance of the others. And Andy might have thought that I'd told Roger to sniff around, even that I'd already involved the police. He'd become scared for his life. Coming to me was his safest bet.'

Kate felt charged up with the adrenaline of fear. If Ben was telling the truth, then his life—and her mother's, by association—must be at risk as well. This couldn't all be happening. But the murder was real.

She asked another question. 'Mum told me how well you'd got on with Roger Grieve, although he'd only advised you on staff pensions a couple of times. But in that case,why would he have needed to question your CFO much at all?'

'He'd have had the odd query in the course of offering us advice. I'd worked out while Andy was telling me all this, that the operation had to be on a serious scale. Roger covered a wide arc of companies, after all, and he'd probably become suspicious in other directions. His awkward questions to Andy must have been calculated potshots, an attempt to slot in the pieces of a jigsaw and pinpoint links. Roger was a good man, he'd have felt it his duty to probe and discover all he could.'

'You said just now, "*If* I went to the police . . ."

What did you do once you knew the situation? What did you tell Andy?'

'That I'd need another meeting after I'd taken certain steps, the necessary action.'

'Which was?'

'To go to the authorities—which wasn't in doubt—but there's more to it than that.' Ben sipped his wine and gazed at Kate thoughtfully.

'But if you did go to the police,' she said, feeling awash with suspicion, 'why hasn't the cocaine been seized and arrests made? Why is the smuggling still ongoing, which is how you make it sound. Are the police planning a big raid any minute? Is that why Mum was on such a knife-edge—even on top of the shock of Roger Grieve's death?'

'Her distress is why I needed to see you alone, Katie, why I had to ask you not to say a single word to anyone, not even Richard. What I've told you so far and am about to say now, mustn't get out—not even to Sadie, who might find it impossible not to tell Rupert.'

Kate exploded. 'A man has been murdered, for God's sake! Richard's heard all the detail of that; Mum told us both over lunch. So why can't I tell him any of this? And why take the risk of trusting me?' Nothing added up, she thought, clenching her hands in her lap.

'Because your mother couldn't bear your suspicions and she feels you can handle the truth.'

'Haven't I just had the truth? I certainly hope so.' Kate badly wanted to believe in Ben. She felt on red alert, yet still embarrassed, in the face of Ben's warmth, about her accusing tone. 'I need some answers,' she said, cradling the stem of her glass as she struggled to stay aloof. 'You've only given me half the picture.'

He smiled and touched her hand. 'Don't look so white and panicky, whatever will people think!' Kate couldn't return his smile, couldn't imagine ever smiling again.

She realized then that he'd seen the waitress coming for the plates. The wine waiter topped up their glasses again. Suggestions were made about dessert. 'No thanks, no pudding,' she said automatically, but the waitress was persistently persuasive and she and Ben ended up having the day's 'special'. It turned out to be an irresistibly light froth of lemon posset—the only touch of lightness around.

'You've been asking all the right questions,' Ben said, once they were alone, 'which makes me feel better about trusting you. I really shouldn't. I've been told not to breathe a single word, not even to close family. I'm under orders not to do this . . .'

'Whose orders?'

'MI6. I had a contact there, someone to turn to—a friend from my time out in Colombia in the Intelligence Corps. MI6 had a station head in Bogota, an anti-narcotics operation, which I knew through my work. You may not be clued-in to the meaning of "a friend" in the intelligence world, Katie. I remember arriving in Bogota and being briefed by our Ambassador. I was surprised when he walked me round his garden and kept referring to information from "his friend" I'd been there only hours, yet already the threat levels of the area were being made clear.

'Anyway I turned to my friend in MI6—let's call him Jon—instead of the police. He'd become a good mate as well and we'd kept in touch. And

246

Andy's exposé had put me in an invidious position; I could imagine the police being sceptical, to put it mildly. "No suspicions at all, sir? Not a little dicky bird? Your very own business and you hadn't a cluc? Pull thc othcr onc, sir, if you don't mind me saying so . . ."'

'But your friend, Jon, believed you?' Kate asked, wondering how to find proof that he even existed. 'And presumably if you told him things like when the next shipment was due, he's been able to, or is about to, take the necessary action? He hasn't taken any, though, has he?' she said, the light suddenly dawning. 'What's going on, Ben? What is this really about?'

'Try to be patient. I will explain. I told Jon every single detail I could. Andy knew how and where the cocaine was hidden en route for Liverpool, the process of returning it to powder form at the depot, the handover to silent strangers, but he knew nothing else. He had no idea, for instance, how the drugs were originally transported from Colombia— the obvious source—through Brazil and finally to Santana Port; who sold it on, who was in overall charge. The string-puller would have seen to that, as I've explained.

'My friend, Jon, however, with his MI6 expertise and local knowledge of Colombia, could work out the route the cocaine must have taken. He's had to think outside the box over this, which is actually proving useful to MI6. Brazil isn't a well-trodden route, you see, despite its potential for much larger shipments of drugs to Europe. Colombian traffickers have a job to bring the stuff across country to suitably remote or unpoliced ports in Brazil. They used to fly it overland, transport it in

247

small planes, but a new law was passed a few years back, which allows light aircraft suspected of carrying drugs to be shot down in Brazilian airspace.

'The traffickers had to switch to boats on the Amazon after that.'

Ben paused; the pudding plates were being cleared. He ordered coffee, which came quickly with slivers of dark chocolate and soft squares of fudge, then he continued. 'Transporting drugs on the Amazon has its own problems. The riverboats have a shallow freeboard, they're always overloaded and frequently attacked by pirates. They're regularly stopped too, along the length of the river, all too easy targets for random and intelligence-led searches by the federal police. It's not the easiest way to traffick cocaine!

'An alternative route is to fly through Venezuelan airspace, on through Guyana to Suriname and ship drugs from there. Jon believes the particular traffickers in my case took this route, but only so far. He thinks they landed instead on an airstrip near the border with Brazil, close to the Rio Jari. They could carry on from there by boat then— it's only fifty miles downstream into Amapá State—transfer to a lorry and take the dusty red-earth deserted highway to Santana. That way they avoid Brazilian airspace, the police-patrolled Amazon and Negro rivers.'

'Where is this leading, Ben?'

'To the extremely sensitive, difficult and dangerous activity your mother and I are now involved in. She insisted I had to do as Jon asked. She felt I had no option, whatever the risk. This is no tiddly little chicken-feed operation. I bit off

248

more than I'd bargained for, you see, when I took my problems to Jon. He kept his expression inscrutable then he asked for my help. That meant, I discovered, I had to carry on as though nothing had happened, business as before.'

'What are the implications of business as before? I need that spelled out.'

'The authorities are called upon to make very difficult moral judgements at times, Katie. Armed with my Finance Officer's inside information, MI6 and the police could make a selective strike, seize the contraband and round up a few criminals. But that leaves the seriously big guy, the mastermind, still at large, free to carry on flooding the market and doing incalculable harm by ever more cunning means. The alternative is to let through a few shipments and balance some of that harm, more drugs peddled on the high street, against the long-shot chance of landing the biggest fish in the pond. It is an agonisingly difficult call.

'Jon wanted the latter course of action. He trusted me, he felt I knew the ropes and could help, that they had to try for the whale-sized catch; it was too good a chance. He left the business of squaring Andy to me; someone had to keep us informed about shipments, you see, and the pattern, if any, of the movement of drugs. I had to keep my eyes and ears open, but Andy was key to this.'

'How could you trust him to play along?'

'He and I had another meeting—just the one, as meetings like that are fraught with risk. I told him that MI6 knew all about it now, so any ideas of turning turtle again, double-bluffing or having me silenced would do him no good at all. I said he would need an instant crash drama course, class

249

acting skills, since the second he was seen to look scared the game was up. And he wouldn't have me to protect him. That was pretty clear to him anyway, and that he stood to lose all round.

'Andy fell over himself, agreeing to help. He's a reasonably intelligent man. He'd been done over by some money-grubbing woman, an extra-marital affair, I think, and was in a financial bind. I'd worked out a simple code in advance of the meeting so that while carrying on dealing with Acai of Amapá Export, the plant out in Santana, he could send me perfectly normal inoffensive business emails, that wouldn't arouse a hair of suspicion, but contained the crucial information needed.'

Ben smiled, distressingly sadly, Kate thought, wondering why, bracing herself. 'So that's where we are,' he said. 'The reasons for absolute secrecy are obvious, but the most important one of all that I feel sick to my teeth to have to tell you, is that if we succeed—which is a big if—and I lead MI6 to their man, then it's more than likely your mother and I would have to disappear. That means, as I'm sure you know, living under an assumed name, probably abroad. It means no contact whatever with our families, not a phone call, nothing.

'Your mother would have walked away from me, much as we love each other, to be there for you and Sadie, but there's always the risk of someone using her to reach me. And we do desperately want to be together. So that's it, Katie, dear. What it means, the sad, harsh, terrible truth of it, is the real possibility that with no warning at all, your mother might simply not be there one day.'

CHAPTER 17

Kate had expected Ben to say things she didn't want to hear. To that extent she had been prepared. She had listened, hyper-alert, longing to feel able to trust in him with confidence. Wondering and doubting had left a vile soapy taste in her mouth and she'd wanted him to wash it clean away.

He hadn't entirely. She couldn't dissect his motives, whether he was telling the truth—or why he'd particularly wanted to have dinner alone with her. Her mother knew everything, after all; why couldn't she have been there too, giving support? Kate had a fear that Ben could have made subtle changes to the story, slanted it for her benefit in some way, slipped in differences from the facts as Rachel knew them. But that was a fuzzy, confused idea; her thoughts were blurred. The only thing that loomed up out of the shocking mire and truly mattered was the threat of losing her mother.

She stared at Ben, speechless and numb. The numbness took hold; she couldn't absorb the full extent of exactly what it all meant. Her brain wasn't like blotting paper, steadily soaking up the grim reality. The full significance was proving a stubborn lump, a solid block that wouldn't become assimilated. Her thoughts kept eddying round that lump and flowing to other places, channels and backwaters.

While her mind refused to handle losing her mother, it was active in other directions. She had lost Harry, lived through that pain. And in the last weeks, ever since falling so obsessively for Richard,

251

she had come to realise, however hard it was to admit to, that the guilt she had clung to over Harry was not for the reasons she'd believed. Her grief had been real enough, yet somewhere deep in the bowels of her subconscious she must have sensed that her feelings hadn't run as deep as she knew they should. They were bottomless for her mother. She couldn't imagine her not being there, she couldn't accept that what Ben had just said could conceivably happen. Life couldn't be that cruel. She longed not to have been childish about the past, putting her mother under still greater stress with her own pique. If only she'd been sweeter, more considerate, and not wasted precious time. She passionately wanted a future of cosy normality, lunches, chats, sharing the thrill of being in love, simply to bask in closeness.

Ben was giving her thinking time, but it was late and he'd been looking around, noticing the restaurant was emptying. They were almost the last there. Kate urgently wanted to rush home to Richard and lessen the shockwaves, pour out everything in a stream of disbelieving agony, but she couldn't tell him a word of it, not one syllable of what she'd just been told.

She thought about a future of loving and living for him. If only she had more than two thirds of his love it would help to see her through. Some women might be truly understanding, sincerely anxious and caring about an ex-wife's illness, but they were made of more virtuous stuff. Every minute he spent with Eleanor drove a stake deeper into her jealous heart. Ben talked about being strong and bearing the strain. Little did he know of her weaknesses.

He caught her eye. 'I know it's late, but shall we

have some more coffee? Talk it through a bit more?'

She stared at him a moment. His import company was being used for cocaine trafficking, Kate had no doubt about that—and of the accuracy of all the logistical detail. But . . . could she be sure he'd turned to a friend in MI6? Was he genuinely doing the right selfless thing? Or could Ben, just possibly, be planning an exit route with devilish cunning? Was he thinking ahead, covering all the bases in case of need?

'Yes thanks, I need coffee. It'll help,' she said, determined to stay calm and continue to press him for facts. She felt more in control, refocused and back in the booth again. 'It's almost impossible to believe all this, Ben. I feel shaken to the core. Can I ask a couple more questions? They're not easy ones.'

She could imagine a plan, an assumption that she'd explain it all to Sadie, and even if she later went to MI6 to try to check the story, it would have bought valuable time. Time to change names and live in a distant land with the woman he loved, money to burn ¿ . .

'Ask away.' Ben smiled. 'I'll try and help.'

'It's not that I don't believe you, but how can I be certain that everything you've said tonight is completely true? I mean, to be very far-fetched about it, you could actually be spinning some ingenious line and involved to a degree yourself. Telling me all about it like this is some sort of cleverly convoluted cover to explain away the situation, if you and Mum suddenly had to vanish without trace one day. This is all wildly off the top of my head, of course; I'm only going through the motions!'

Kate just stopped herself from voicing her worst-case fears; she'd almost said, 'If, just suppose, you were the man behind it all . . .' That might have been to test his reaction too far, too clear a warning signal that her suspicions were stronger than implied.

Ben was looking deeply concerned. 'I can understand how anxious you feel,' he said, 'and you're right to be wary, worried how to trust me, but I hope you don't seriously think I'm spinning a line? I'm distressed that that could even cross your mind.'

He paused for a moment, fingering his glass, then met her eyes. 'Look, Katie, I'll do my best. I'll talk to my friend in MI6 and explain that I've broken ranks and told you what's going on. There are rare times, I think, when meetings can be arranged with close family. Don't bank on it, though—and whatever else, don't talk to the police. It could be serious if they start making their own inquiries; you do see how that could implicate your mother? But if you can meet Jon, I'm sure it would put your mind at rest.'

'You've made me feel bad now,' Kate said, 'but thanks for not dismissing my worries entirely. I feel much better for clearing the air.'

'Jon may say no, I can't promise to succeed. And in that case, I'm afraid, it's down to keeping trust.'

It was all too much to cope with. Her eyes misted over and she fished in her handbag for a tissue, distressed and angry at showing such vulnerability. 'But what happens,' she asked, wiping her eyes, determined to carry on as though never really doubting him, 'if, despite all you're doing and the efforts of MI6, you never find your man? Is the search abandoned? Do customs simply seize the next shipment of drugs and you cut your losses? What would you do then—fold up your business and accept the shadow inevitably cast over your integrity? Or do you and MI6 carry on indefinitely?'

'Those are hard questions to answer. I don't know how long they'd keep the case open. They play things very close, never go into the fine detail. I was in an agony of indecision over whether to tell you at all, Katie; I felt like a doctor having to talk straight to a patient. But your mother said you had the strength of character to cope, that you'd manage to hold on, and I thought so too.'

The pressure brought Kate close to crumpling again. His analogy too, about breaking the news to a patient, only made her think of her father. She tried to imagine what Aidan would have done in such circumstances. He wouldn't have hesitated to respond to MI6's request, whatever the risk to himself, she felt sure. She longed to think Ben was as instinctively honourable a man.

'I can't help praying you never find the mastermind in all this,' she said, 'but supposing you do, is it certain you and Mum would have to disappear?'

'It's that or the fear of reprisals, your mother in constant danger and other people's lives on the line. I'm desperately sorry, Katie, but that's how it is. Do you have more questions, anything else on your mind? I hope I can allay any more fears, but you know there's no easy way.'

'I want to pass something by you that might sound almost as mad and off the wall as asking for proof. But I need a quid pro quo first—a promise

255

that you won't say a word to a soul, certainly not the person concerned, not even to Mum and categorically not to Richard. He'd be shocked as it's a confidence of his to me. It's about something he's investigating privately, and I know he'd feel extremely let down. It would be different if I could tell him anything you've told me tonight.'

'Let's get the coffee, first,' Ben said, catching a waiter's eye. A fresh pot came almost instantly and he settled back with an intent look on his face. 'Not a word to anyone,' he said.

'It's Spencer Morgan—whether you really trust him and whether you should.'

'Trust him over what? You're not suggesting, are you, Katie, that Spencer can possibly know anything about what's going on in my company?'

'No, no,' she said hurriedly. 'This is to do with his finances, certainly no connection with anything you've been talking about. It's just that Richard thinks too many of Spencer's dealings suggest financial sleights of hand.'

Had Ben's rather shocked and outraged reaction been a little too instant? Did that possibly tell her anything? She was no good at any of this, Kate felt. It had been a stupid confidence of hers; there was always a chance that Ben and Spencer were acting together, which would mean Ben tipping off Morgan now.

She sighed inwardly, impatient to meet the contact in MI6 and allay her depressing suspicions. Her mother believed Ben was a good man, astute, doing brave, difficult things. If he was on the level, Kate thought, he wouldn't have ruled out his billionaire-rich backer, either for business discrepancies, or even, however solid Morgan's reputation, as a possible suspect in this scam. An honest Ben would care about the integrity of his backer, he'd know the man's foibles and be well aware of his connection with the company in terms of the scam. All the same, Morgan's involvement was slight, Ben's business a pinhead in his vast financial portfolio.

Ben answered her question after deliberating a while. 'Spencer's colourful and needs supping with a longish spoon,' he said. 'I take him as I find him. He's a sharp operator, but he has a generous nature and he's been good to me. It was hard, at my age, to build up a new career and create a thriving, profitable company.'

'Richard's investigating is entirely off his own bat,' Kate said earnestly, imagining Ben having visions of stories slipped to the newspapers, tales of goings-on and hot gossip from the yacht. 'He minds people getting away with things, but this is purely for himself, not for any great exposé.'

Ben laughed out loud. 'You must be joking, Katie! Do you really think, much as you love him and have stars in your eyes, that if he finds any nasty financial skeletons in Spencer's diamond-studded cupboards, he wouldn't want to do a programme all about it and make it public? It would be a seriously big story, one that needed to be told.'

Kate felt acutely embarrassed. She was in a battered, vulnerable state. Of course Ben was right—what could be more blatantly obvious, after all? She felt hurt and furious with herself, too. Why hadn't she challenged Richard? He must have thought her painfully naive.

She sniffed and said tightly, 'I do see what you

257

mean, Ben. I guess I'm concerned that, considering Richard has his suspicions, coming on the yacht is kind of accepting hospitality on false pretences.'

'You can bet that thought won't have entered Richard's head! You needn't fret, Katie. Whatever else, Spencer is well able to look after himself. He's built up a monumental business empire and employs huge numbers of people, which is all to the good, and he has charitable foundations coming out of his ears. Quite a bit of his money reaches the places it should.'

'That doesn't mean he's law-abiding. Fraudsters do good works as well.'

'Sure. And so do the Gatess and Buffets of this world.'

'I remember Richard saying one of Spencer's many interests was in Colombia,' she said, feeling in so deep that it would seem more of a giveaway not to carry on.

'He has them the world over—I shouldn't read too much into that. I first met him out there, actually, way back. Anyway, you're about to meet him, too. And I'm sure he and Richard will talk finance, so you can keep a watchful eye.'

'Don't humour me, Ben.'

'I'm really not. It's often the way secrets slip out, the tiniest twitch or reaction. I certainly won't shut my mind to Richard's concerns about financial discrepancies. It affects me personally; Spencer invested in my business, helped me set it up. I'd hate to find that he wasn't basically straight in his financial affairs.'

Kate looked round the restaurant, feeling a discomforted fool. It was time to go, they were the last there. She had one final try over her pledge.

'Ben, please explain to me why I can't tell Richard even the most basic minimum of what you've told me tonight – to ease any off-shoot suspicions of his about you, at least.'

'Think about it, Katie. It might calm him down, but he wouldn't be human if he didn't want to try and help. And that would be a very serious problem indeed. We're dealing with a brilliant demon-mind here, a person who certainly wouldn't flinch from taking whatever brutal action was needed to shore up his personal safety. If Richard starts making discreet inquiries, the slightest cause for suspicion and both your lives could be at risk.

'I'm deadly serious about it,' Ben said, seeing her stubborn look of disbelief, 'and it's absolutely vital too, that you don't make any mention of the idea that seemed to cross your mind, however incredulous and dismissive I was myself about it, that Spencer has anything to do with drugs. Richard's thinking finances; keep it that way. I'm relying on you never to talk trafficking and drugs; we don't want you in the assumed-name territory, and having to disappear off the face of the earth as well. And one last point, Katie. Don't forget I'm breaking the rules telling you any of this at all. I'm going to have a tough job facing Jon about it and trying to arrange for you to be able to meet him.'

Kate sighed, thinking no job could be tougher than arriving home late and telling Richard she couldn't say a word about her evening. Perhaps they'd find a way through. After the inevitable explosions, which she would just have to suffer and endure, life might eventually settle down.

The tears pricked again; she bit on her lip and turned her head to stare fixedly at the small dark painting of the oysters.

'Don't cry, Katie. Go home to Richard and enjoy being in love. Spend some time with your mother. Think holidays.' He squeezed her hand, very tightly. 'I'm asking more of you than anyone should have to bear, putting a very great burden on your shoulders. You're going to have to break it to Sadie if it happens, it's you that will have all the responsibility. I'm desperately sorry, but I know you will be strong.'

Ben released her hand, giving a supportive, communicating smile. It was encouragement to trust him, Kate knew. 'Thanks for telling me, Ben,' she said, staring back at him with wet eyes, hopelessly unsure of what or how much to believe, 'and for being prepared to have this dinner. I would rather know than not. I'll hide my feelings. I won't cry when I'm with Richard—or with Mum.'

She gathered her bag and slid out of the booth, leaning against the tabletop for a second, to draw strength and steady her knees.

As they were leaving, her eye was caught by a large painting. It was of a haughty, heavily lipsticked woman of a certain age, and irresistibly witty. Kate suspected it was by Ruskin Spear. The woman was in profile, a heaped forkful of food poised, close to her mouth, and a look of such pure down-the-nose disdain on her face that it was impossible not to smile.

'Rather fun, isn't it?' the waiter said, leading his last customers firmly towards the door. 'It's a Ruskin Spear.'

Kate gave him a strained look, no longer managing to smile. She couldn't turn to Richard, share her new knowledge and cry. This was her agony alone. She believed the risk of Ben and Rachel's disappearance was live and genuine; it entirely explained the signs she'd seen of her mother's fear and stress.

She gave the Spear a last look and following after the waiter, spared a thought for the remarkable power of paintings. She'd been unable to part with some of her favourites from Harry's gallery; they'd carried her through guilt, misery, loneliness, but she knew now they could never be solace enough. Nothing could take the place of the warmth and nearness and love of her mother.

Part II

Part II

CHAPTER 18

'Those few days after New Year's Eve when I needed to get through to you,' Richard said, coming to stand by the draining board, 'I was out of my skin, eaten up, dreaming of you every minute.' Kate felt his eyes boring into her as she swilled coffee grounds down the sink. 'Then when you came here and I could make love to you, I had such a feeling of exultation. I carried it round with me, in the rainforest, filming, back home. I was a walking advertisement for happiness.'

He swung her round, gripping her by the arms. 'Can't you understand? I thought you trusted me, loved me. I felt as one with you, I could never imagine you being unyielding and cold, callously slamming a door in my face like this. I believed in you. God, do you think I'm so shallow that I'd tell your mother's secrets to my friends in the press? Or are they yours? Is that it?' Richard's grip tightened, as though resisting his urge to try and shake either of their secrets out of her. 'Can't you see the hurt I feel? You cut me up into a thousand pieces and don't seem to care a jot. What kind of a relationship is that?'

'One where I hoped you'd know that it's not for want of loving you; I'd tell you if I could, it simply isn't possible.' Kate had the wet glass body of the cafetière in her hands and felt a hapless captive; she couldn't escape the hurt in his demanding grey eyes.

'We've been through all this to destruction,' she said. 'Thursday night, Friday night, you've battled

265

at me till I've done my head in with misery and exhaustion.' She met his concentrated stare feeling drenched by his emotional overspill. 'And it's you who are so lacking in trust. Can't you simply accept my word? I can't repeat anything, please try to understand.'

Kate thought of Richard's firmly turned back the past couple of nights in bed; they might have had a Rottweiler between them, the way he had cleaved to his side.

She was worn out with all the bitter recriminations and even beginning to wonder whether he had professional reasons for persisting so obsessively with his need to know. He was taking it so personally, though. Breakfast that morning had been in complete silence, which on a Saturday, when they could have quality time together, seemed a criminal waste. He'd be driving her to her father's that afternoon and they were to stay the night. Would he still come? Would they leave for Rye after lunch as planned? Aidan was looking forward to it.

'Polly's here for lunch today, isn't she?' Kate said equably. 'And didn't you mention a family supper with your mother on Wednesday—before you went into orbit? You said she'll be up from Salisbury as it's half term and it's a good chance for me to meet her.'

No reaction. Her hesitant questions went unanswered, left to drift like feathers in the air. She sighed. Polly and Ed were on half term, they'd be around, staying overnight she was sure. Would Richard keep up this performance in front of them? The Caribbean trip was in six days; they had to reconnect and make plans.

266

She dreaded the thought of Polly hanging loose about the place, sharpening her verbal cat's claws. Kate longed to find a way to reach her. Richard had asked her to try for one thing, and they had to be able to communicate if they were going to be living under the same roof, however little hope there was of their being friends.

She met his soulful eyes that steadily willed her to relent and had a job to ward off tears. She felt bowed, lonely, creeping about in the shadows of her secret knowledge and useless without his support. 'Try to accept it,' she pleaded, battling on. 'I pray the reason I can't tell you never happens—which is the only way I could ever explain.'

'That's cryptic,' Richard muttered, still giving off waves of mortified hurt. She sensed a hint of closure and held her breath. 'It's been hateful,' he said at last, loosening his grip. 'How could you do it to me?'

Kate set down the coffee pot. As she turned to face him his mouth found hers with a force that overwhelmed her. All his pent-up frustration was suddenly over, resistance to reason wiped away; he kissed her till her lips throbbed and felt raw. It was a physical thrill, sensations of touch, searching tongues, mingled saliva, but it was more. The kiss was commitment, trust, a supportive shoulder to lean on, a sign of Richard's own need.

An hour later, lying in bed, she watched the slow movement of his half-drawn, cream cotton curtains and gazed out to the colourless daylight beyond. Heavy skies, the dreary redbrick backs of houses: she thought of Caribbean sun and making babies, of being a long way from her father in his dwindling days. He wanted her to go, the doctors said months

267

not weeks, he was coping. Her thoughts hesitated, moved closer, but she knew her mother and Ben were forbidden, boarded-up territory, a place it was dangerous to go.

*   *   *

Polly's arrival at lunchtime reminded Kate of her own pit-stop trips home in late teenage years, turning up with a couple of T-shirts in a carrier and wires attached to her ears. Polly chucked down a granny-style string bag with a hairbrush head sticking out of a hole, but unlike Kate who'd been full of smiles, Polly left in her earplugs and didn't so much as say hello.

She sat herself down at the kitchen table, kicking sideways at a chair leg with rhythmic thuds. She looked deathly white; her face with its dark under-eye shadows was a spectral mask and looked a shroud of misery. She had on a harsh, dark-brown lipstick and her eyelash extensions were crudely glued. Polly was all lips and puffy, unhappy black eyes. Her hair was unwashed, but the dangling Indian silver earrings she was wearing, the slouchy Noughties black sweater and denim mini seemed a token nod at making an effort. She was in platform ankle boots with fearsome knuckleduster fastenings that emphasised her skinniness, even in thick wool wintry leggings. She looked thin and unwell.

Kate got nowhere trying to chat. She gave up and busied herself slicing courgettes, onions and peppers to cheer up a microwavable lasagne, not turning, not keen to encourage a fresh broadside of vitriol. Polly's ashen face worried her far more than any sarkiness and sullen stares. Was she taking

268

drugs? Richard said she'd been shockingly late home the night he'd been looking for Eleanor and hysterically overwrought. Wouldn't he have sussed it, if she was spaced out or coming down from a high? Or had he been too blindly furious to notice?

'Do you want a drink, Polly? There's juice and water in the fridge, but no wine. We're not having any since your dad's driving after lunch. He's good about that.'

'You're implying he's bad about other things? I'll have a beer,' Polly said, scraping back her chair. 'Where's Dad gone?' she demanded, going to the fridge. 'Out deliberately, I expect, so we can have a nice little love-in, do some bonding or some such crap. God, what a joke. He's so transparent. Doesn't he *know*?'

He knew where they were at very well, Kate thought. 'He'll be back in a minute,' she said. 'He only went for some special cheese he wanted to take my father.'

'You wish he'd get back fast, don't you? He's protection, isn't he, a nice shield for you.' Polly was right about that. She carried on. 'You think you've won and he's all yours, now you've moved in, but don't you feel any guilt at all? Even if my mother wasn't ill Dad had no right to walk out. He's bound to her and he wants to be, deep down, if he only knew it. God, the way men treat women, talk about a bunch of dirt! It sucks, makes me sick. He made a contract with Mum—that clapped-out old thing called marriage. And then you have to come along and take him off the scene.'

'That's untrue and unfair, Polly. He'd left months before I met him, as you well know.'

'Not truly left, he was just like fucking around,

269

like he'd hit the mid-life crisis thing. It's gross, so typical. You won't catch me getting married.

'Don't you feel kind of *used*,' she carried on. 'Like it's degrading, being a trophy bird on his arm—like it's all macho self-gratification and men are such tools? No, I guess you don't. And now you've got Dad. No shit hang-ups, no problems . . .' Polly looked away as tears dribbled out and clung to her thick lashes. She sniffed and wiped her nose on her slouchy sleeve. 'No shit problems . . .'

'I have, Polly, plenty. My father's dying of cancer for one thing. But men have feelings, too; they can care, love and hurt just as much. It's wretched for your mother—bipolar is a serious illness, dreadful to live with—but she has her wonderful talent, she has you and Ed—'

'And you have Dad. Oh, fuck it, what's the point . . .' Polly banged down the bottle of beer, splashing some on the table and rushed upstairs in her clumping boots for somewhere to sob in privacy. She was strong-willed, intent on being tough. Kate imagined her soon dry-eyed, lying stretched out on her bed, gazing grimly at the cracks in the ceiling.

She must be really upset and worried to show such vulnerability. Probably boy trouble, as Richard thought, hormonal overreaction, but it could be anything, and serious. She was exhausted, drained by it too, given her deathly pale complexion, and in that bitter, sarcastic outburst she had implied that it was useless turning to her father, he'd never understand. Had it been some sort of coded cry for help? She had her mother, though; couldn't she confide in Eleanor who did have good times, some patches of normal life? Or did Polly fear that whatever it was might spark a fresh attack? What a burden for a sixteen year old.

Kate decided to go and talk quietly through Polly's door in the slim hope of leaving an open one. She went upstairs and paused, the door looked very shut. She had to try, though, and went close-up to the door. 'Please listen to me a moment, Polly. I wanted to say that if you ever needed any help . . . I know I'd probably be the last person you'd turn to, but sometimes it's better if it's not close family. You can always call me at work. I won't tell your dad any of this. I'm going to put my card in your coat pocket downstairs, just in case. Please hang onto it.'

She turned to go. 'Come down soon,' she called from the top of the stairs. 'A quick lunch before we go, your dad'll worry otherwise.'

She slipped her card in a pocket of Polly's coat that contained a near-empty cigarette packet and was in the kitchen when Richard returned. He gave her a peck and sniffed the air. The combination of onion and peppers was an inviting smell, but he looked anxious.

'Where's Polly?'

'She just went upstairs; I don't think she'll be long.'

'Ed will be here later to keep an eye on her, but can we leave Rye in time to have supper with them tomorrow night?' Richard touched her cheek. 'You don't mind? They'll be fine for eating late, we needn't hurry away.' He smiled and held her jaw in his hand, drawing her close for a kiss, although Kate could see Polly on the stairs.

'Can't get enough of her, can you, Dad?' she called out. 'But don't "hurry away" on our account, you needn't put yourself out.'

271

'Can't you cut the sarcasm, Polly, just for once in your life?'

'But you make it so tempting, Dad.'

'I'm looking forward to meeting your grandmother when she's up from Wiltshire for half term,' Kate said, in slight desperation, immediately wishing she'd kept quiet. It was a pointless remark, sure to provoke another acid riposte.

'Gran's nice,' Polly said unexpectedly. 'I like her.' Richard looked surprised.

He talked about plans while Kate dished up, including the midweek supper with his mother, Celia. She was coming up from Salisbury, taking Polly to lunch then on to hear Ed perform in a school concert. Richard was going from work, hoping not to be late. No mention of Kate possibly coming, too—but then Eleanor was bound to be there.

'I'll cook supper,' Richard said. 'We'll be back around six, I'll have time, but try to get off early from work so you can get to know Mum and keep her out of the kitchen.

'She'll need to stay over,' he eyed his daughter, 'probably in Ed's room, it's less messy. I'll have to take you and Ed back home for the night, Poll.'

'I'm cool for leaving early,' Kate said. 'The office is bliss with Dan away on his shoot. He's back Monday, though, and sure to have a fit about my holiday. I can imagine him hitching a ride out to Grenada on the *Sleepyhead* campaign's flying bed— anything to haul me back!' Richard looked blank. 'You know, the commercial with the girl's bed floating her off to her hunky man on a palm-fringed idyllic island.' Kate smiled. 'In her dreams, though—I'm luckier, actually going!'

'Suppose Mum has an attack while you're there, Dad?'

Polly's question, dropped not so innocently into the swill of their chat, acted like a pressed pause button. Kate and Richard were momentarily still, as static as paused actors on a television screen. Kate had had that same thought, but shut it out of her mind.

'It would be like one of those times when I'm away filming that I couldn't come and help,' Richard answered in measured tones. 'It takes a day to fly home, you see, too late for any immediate crisis. I'll let the doctors know as usual that I'm out of the country.'

'Your work trips are different,' Polly persisted. 'Mum sort of adjusts to those.' The implication that she might be less inclined to if he was having a glamorous week in the arms of his new live-in love wasn't far from anyone's mind.

Polly reverted to texting and looking bored. Kate caught glimpses of naked misery in her black-fringed eyes. Richard didn't seem especially anxious or aware of his daughter's accentuated pallor; perhaps he was too used to seeing her in rebelliously harsh make-up to notice.

Kate began clearing away food and Richard brought down their overnight bag. He gave his daughter a few repeatedly stressed instructions and kissed her cheek. 'No trashing the joint then, Poll, okay? We're back tomorrow, having supper together, remember.'

'See you,' Kate called, as they went to the door. 'Have a good time tonight.'

'I'm not in the mood,' Polly muttered coldly and went upstairs without a word of goodbye.

It was Wednesday already. Kate had slowed down with the worry of her father, after seeing his decline at the weekend. Richard hadn't said anything, but she was sure he'd noticed it, too. Aidan's eyes had seemed more sunken in the bony cavern of his face. His eyes were still lively and he'd had spirited chats, but the pinpoints of pink on his cheekbones had been giveaway signs of the strain. He would be in her thoughts the whole of her week away.

She had a mountain of work to do before the trip and was feeling nervous about meeting Richard's mother that night, anxious to make a good impression with one member of his family at least. He'd said his mother was only mildly eccentric and didn't bite, but after Polly with her sharp teeth . . .

Clearing her desk, trying to leave early as promised, Kate wondered about her clothes, a black skirt and plum sweater; officey and routine, but probably the safest bet. She got going, grabbing her bright coat that Richard was so keen on—more of a jacket, which wasn't ideal as it had begun to rain—and was about to make a quick getaway when her office phone rang.

It was Ben. 'I hoped you hadn't left yet, Katie. I had to call straight away and tell you, though, that I'm afraid to say that Jon, my friend at MI6, won't allow a meeting after all.'

'Oh. Why's that?' Kate said dully, feeling cold inside.

'It's for your own safety. Given the scale of criminality—the utterly ruthless brain we're dealing with who'll go to any lengths—Jon feels it would be grossly irresponsible of him to take chances and subject you to the slightest risk.'

'I don't quite see how it would, though.'

'Very sorry, Katie, I can't explain more. Keep the faith. Your mother believes, as I do, that we're doing what we have to and I had no option but to work with Jon. Must go—see you on the yacht at the weekend.' The line went dead and Kate returned the phone with a thudding heart.

She hurried off for the tube station feeling wretchedly subdued. Had the proposed meeting been a sham all along, simply to keep her happy at the time? Ben hadn't promised anything, he'd been cautious, but Kate had banked on it as her passport to being able to believe in him. Now she didn't know what to think. It was like taking ten steps backwards before ever going forward; her confidence in Ben was shattered.

She stopped to put up her umbrella and pull herself together, then walked on briskly, thinking things through. Her mother was the one who wasn't safe. Ben could be the nicest person on earth, as Rachel believed, or even, God forbid, a criminal mastermind. He could have cleverly seen the sense, when she suggested involving Kate, in going along with it. It was impossible to know what went on in the darkest corners of people's souls.

Kate didn't doubt that drugs were coming into the country in Ben's container loads. She knew too, that to go to the police or MI6—even to tell Richard, who might take dangerous action—was to put her mother's life at risk. Roger Grieve had been murdered.

She couldn't hope to nail a big-time drugs runner single-handed; all she could do was to have her wits

275

about her on the yacht and, with Ben, hope fervently for inspiration, and pray for a miraculous lead. The one thing crystal clear to her was that life had to go on as normal.

Her journey home was certainly normal, grindingly routine. It was more complicated since moving in with Richard in Chelsea and especially effortful in the thick of the rush hour—which it was now. Changing at Embankment station, Kate had to push and force her way onto a District Line train; the doors had a job to close behind her.

Her face was an inch from a tall man's ticklish coat-back, her arm captive against a jelly-like mass of matronly bosom, an umbrella dripping onto her black suede boots. With every jolt and swing the wet, weary train-load of passengers was flung even closer together. Kate was resigned, used to the damp, sweaty, germy fug, all the coughing, sneezing and uncovered yawns. But her heart was still pounding with anxiety over Ben's call and she hugged her bag tight to her chest, feeling weary with wretchedness.

Coming up from the underground at Sloane Square the air, even with the drizzle and in February darkness, was fresh on her skin and reviving. Kate hurried up King's Road's slippery pavements feeling better, less shattered and distressed.

Her cheeks were glowing when she walked in, or so Richard would have it as he shook the rain off her coat and harangued her for not taking a taxi.

'This is my mother, Celia,' he said, rather coyly, as she came up beside him—tall and straight-backed, holding out a ringed, veined hand. He was probably a bit on edge, too, Kate thought, smiling and taking his mother's hand.

Despite her daunting uprightness Celia had an original approach. 'It is good to meet you—aren't you a beautiful girl! Richard told me so, but I like seeing for myself.'

'I'm far from it, a complete wet rag! It's wonderful to meet you too. I hope you enjoyed the concert this afternoon. Richard said Ed played beautifully. Just give me a minute, then my job is to stop you even thinking of helping in the kitchen!'

'Those are my orders from Richard, too. Typical—he only wants to show off his cooking skills. We are rather in it already, though, aren't we, dear,' she said, turning to him, 'with all this open-plan living? No privacy at all. I can't say a thing to Katie I wouldn't want you to hear.'

She was in her seventies, a still-handsome woman who took obvious care of her looks. Her pure-white hair was piled high, held in place with silver-topped combs; she had the puckered lip-lines of a dry aging skin, a few crêpey neck folds, but high cheekbones too, that held up her face and gave it its dignity. A slightly imperious look came over it at times and Kate imagined her capable of haughty aloofness when she chose. Her love of bold jewellery was clear to see. Hefty rings, jade and zircon, adorned her fingers, thick silver bangles on her wrist, a chunky necklace of transparent, glittery pink stones. It looked very with-it and cheered up the chestnut jersey suit she was wearing no end.

Richard poured glasses of white wine for himself and Kate. 'Another whisky and soda, Mum?' He mixed it without waiting for an answer and accompanied them to the sofa end of the room. 'Polly and Ed stayed on after the concert,' he said

277

to Kate, who suspected they'd gone home with Eleanor. 'They'll be a while, I should think, but we'll eat straight away.'

They were back in good time after all. Richard produced a light, flavourful tomato tart, then plump roast chicken with roasted root vegetables. It was delicious. After fulsomely praising her son's cooking and Ed's guitar playing, Celia asked conventional grandmotherly questions about schoolwork and sport. Kate kept silent, feeling both out of it and, since she was there, effectively part of the family, more integral to Richard's life. She had a hopeful hunch his mother could become a friend and ally, a wishful thought with nothing to go on, but she felt easy in Celia's company and able to be herself. Ed was being as friendly as ever, Polly resisting any Arctic sourness with her grandmother around. Life felt surprisingly normal. If only she hadn't had the shock of Ben's call.

Celia rested a ringed, loose-skinned hand on top of her son's; determinedly, not so much out of maternal affection, more as a means of securing his concentrated attention.

'Now, darling,' she said, sitting upright as ever, 'I need some urgent advice and help. I've got a disaster on my hands; it's too awful for words! I'm subsiding in Salisbury and Ron, my lovely builder, says I'm going to have to move out for *months*.'

'You mean the house is subsiding, I take it, Mum. That is serious.' Richard looked pretty subsided himself. 'Your Ron's probably right.' He sighed. 'I don't suppose you've even checked up yet, but I do hope you're properly covered.'

'Darling, I'm not a horse! The policy is fine. I've read the small print and the nice broker man who

278

came to case it all out agreed the insurance didn't have any wriggle room. People are getting quotes. He said, just like Ron, that I'd have to move out and they'd pay for a hotel. But I'd be in misery! To think of months of swirly carpets and sauna-room smells, all those rowdy weddings and dances on Saturday nights . . .'

'What about the friends you play bridge with, Gran?' Polly asked. 'Can't one of them put you up?'

'They've all downsized into little matchboxes, my love, and anyway, they'd hardly still be friends, would they, if it's going to take months?'

'I have a suggestion,' Kate said tentatively. 'I can't easily let my flat in W11 because of the paintings and it's sitting there empty. You probably won't want to be in London, but possibly just for the weekdays if it's not too much of a wrench? Perhaps you can be home in Salisbury at weekends when the workmen knock off or stay with friends then.'

Celia stared at her, digesting it, then broke out into huge smiles. 'My dear, what a magnificently wonderful offer! Goodness, I'd be thrilled to bits to be in London. Think of all the things I could do. What joy! You must let me contribute, of course.'

'The whole point is you're not to do that,' Kate smiled.

'You could go to the Andrew Robson bridge place in Fulham, Mum,' Richard said, flashing Kate an amazed and certainly grateful look. 'It's just your thing. Plenty of like minds there, I'm sure.'

'I do have other interests, you know,' Celia said archly. 'I'm not a slave to my bridge.'

'Could have fooled me, Gran,' Polly said.

Her father grinned. 'Go on talking about it,' he

279

said, 'and I'll make the coffee.'

Ed started clearing plates, telling everyone not to move, then he rolled up his sleeves at the sink. Celia drank two cups of caffeinated coffee, she twiddled a heavy amber ring, looked at her polished pink nails and seemed oddly fidgety. She picked up her handbag suddenly and looked over to Polly. 'I need a little breath of air, Poll . . . Coming?'

'Cool, Gran! Out front's best.'

They slipped on coats and went out giggling like a pair of young shop girls. 'It's too bad of Gran,' Ed said primly, turning from the sink, 'encouraging Polly like that.'

Given the cigarette pack in his sister's pocket, Kate thought that was hardly the issue. A quick puff with her grandmother wasn't going to tip the scales—and anything to bring a spark into Polly's dull, unhappy eyes.

'My mother's impossible,' Richard said, siding with Ed, 'so subversive. She's cut right down now, and she does always go outside. She says her non-smoking friends, snotty old bats, she calls them, make her feel like a dog going out to pee, but I think she quite enjoys it. She sees people having a drag in doorways and thinks it's fashionable!'

'I should have discussed my offer about the flat with you first,' Kate said. 'I'm sorry, there could have been sensitivities, but the idea just came to me and I spoke first and thought later.'

'It was manna from heaven,' Richard said, 'a wonderful idea, fantastic of you. But do you still want to go ahead now you know about the smoking?'

'Yes—and you're sounding the most frightful old prude. You're not without vices, hardly one to preach. I bet I discover a few new ones too, when you've put away a few rum punches out in Grenada, like you're a closet nightclub limbo dancer or something.'

Ed giggled. 'Not likely, he's very stiff in the joints.'

'Are you two done?' Richard protested.

'Who knows what I'm about to discover when we hit the Grenadian nightspots, and you're let loose under the stars.'

CHAPTER 19

Kate stared at the ground flashing past. The immense surging power of a great jet taking off was an almost orgasmic thrill. She sighed, aching with anticipation as the plane lifted and soared into the clouds, then she turned from the window.

Richard was waiting for her to look his way. 'This is our week,' he said, 'no chance of another for a while. Try and relax.' She kissed his cheek, imagining the stress she would feel, being with her mother on the yacht, giving nothing away, no extra hugs, no clinging. Relaxing was impossible. She dreaded the prospect of Richard asking too many questions. Would Morgan be suspicious and regret having asked him, curse himself for inviting a sharp-minded member of the media on board?

Richard picked up her hand. 'You were miles away then. Where were you?' He kissed her fingers one by one, stroking them with his tongue. The sensation ran through her and concentrated her mind; she thought of the tinfoil strips of her contraceptive pill, left behind in the drawer of her bedside table.

'I was thinking,' she said untruthfully, 'of being photographed with you at Heathrow and not looking the part, how that excited couple after your autograph would have loved me to be a glamorous celebrity. And also,' she admitted more honestly before he could argue, 'worrying about all the nosy questions you'll start asking our generous host on the yacht.'

'I am house-trained, unlike my mother.' He looked injured and amused. His wonderful eyes could tease, josh, challenge, look sorry for themselves, all at the same time. 'But whatever Ben said or did to shut you up about him,' Richard said, 'I'm still convinced Spencer Morgan is a serial fraudster. And, just suppose I ever discovered any clinching proof . . .'

'You'd feel it was your journalistic duty to expose it to the world?'

'Well, yes.' He hardly looked rueful. 'But wouldn't you want me to? Wouldn't Ben?' That was provocative, Richard was still fishing for clues.

'We'll cross that bridge as and when,' Kate said firmly. 'Can we look for Mum's email? I want to mug up on all these people on the yacht.' She'd seen it had come through just as they were told to switch off mobiles and forwarded it to Richard's laptop as a way of reading it on the plane.

As soon as the seat-belt sign was switched off he stood up to reach for his briefcase. Kate thought whimsically about the fight they'd had over her ticket. She'd wanted to pay for her own and travel Economy. Richard had got steadily more enraged. 'What's wrong with you? Can't I even give you a

282

week's holiday? You're hardly a kept woman. Why must you always hold back?'

He sat down again. 'I hope you're enjoying my hard-won compromise! It is better, isn't it?' She had given in to his insistent demand to upgrade them, but only as far as World Traveller Plus. It still seemed a bit pointless, the seats only slightly roomier, but the third one in their row was vacant and Richard had a smile.

The drinks trolley was alongside. 'Mr Marshall, isn't it?' the steward inquired, seeing to Richard's request for champagne with a big beam; he obviously enjoyed recognising people. 'It's a pleasure to welcome you on the flight.' He smiled at Kate with interest and she sensed he'd stopped himself from adding automatically, 'And Mrs Marshall, too.'

Rachel's update had come through. She'd sent potted sketches of the other guests since she and Ben had been on the yacht for a couple of days.

Kate huddled close to see Richard's laptop. 'Here's the run-down,' Rachel's email began. 'Starting with Spencer's woman who's called Fleur: she's v glam and bosomy, but not, Ben thinks, about to be the next Mrs Morgan. Late forties, no ball of intellectual fire, but friendly, easy, talks a lot about all Spencer's lavish-sounding homes and "a fabulous moulding clinic" near one of them. Face-lifts to you and me . . .'

Kate looked up. 'There've been other Mrs Morgans then, if she says "next"?'

'Just one, I believe,' Richard answered. 'He's been divorced for years. His only son was killed, caught in the crossfire of some gangland shoot-out, aged about twenty. I read somewhere that it broke up the marriage.'

'What a ghastly thing,' Kate said. 'You'd think being hit by tragedy would keep couples close, like the McCann parents with their lost little girl, but more people do seem to split up than hold fast.'

They read on down the email. 'Henry and Tabatha Stevenson: he's Chief Exec of one of S's largest asset management companies; she's the pits! Henry, v old school and chortly, big round drum of a potbelly, swimmers always slipping below. Says things like "Capital" and "We must box on."! Drinks S's vintage Armagnac by the tumblerful, but vintage booze comes in tumblers round here. Wife, Tabatha, never without her pearls, desperate everyone should know which drawer she's out of, permanent smell under nose: you can sense her picking on the decor, food, staff (all terrific), the company . . . Faded blonde, thin pinched face: very au naturel, nothing lifted—no visits to moulding clinic! If anyone put on an adult film (vast viewing screen on board) I think she'd faint away.

'That ultra-smooth Labour guy, Paul Barber, is here—ex-minister, Culture, Media and Sport—and two models with impossibly long legs (not so great-looking close up!). Paul's hot for the American one, Kim, who's an ice-cream heiress quite apart from the modelling, but he makes off with the other girl too, her friend, Astrid, that famous German model. Astrid never smiles (probably to ward off the moulding clinic). Spencer thinks Paul scores with both, which would be impressive. He's known for it, of course (quantity) as well as all that witty, bitchy gossip. Jibes about unsuitably high living roll off his back; smile a touch cooler, maybe, but he can certainly turn on the charm. Nattily dressed, never a ruffled hair, even on a yacht!

'That's it, apart from the inscrutable Carl Simon who Ben says seems to run Spencer's entire business empire. He's a kind of adviser, organiser, mediator, PA, path-smoother, plonker. Doesn't enter in much; hard to say a thing about him. Younger than S—who's late fifties—by about ten years; bit stocky, sandy-haired, pale-blue eyes, that blank, neutral kind of face like he's been up all night. Probably has. Spends all day in the shade, mumbling into his phone or Spencer's ear while the rest of us sunbathe and idle our time away.'

The lunch trolley was approaching. Richard snapped shut his laptop and turned with a kiss. 'Your mother's great! Tabatha sounds painful and Carl a sinister yes-man, but I'm all for these long-legged top models. What a bonus.'

'Cocky with it, aren't you? You won't get a look in with Paul Barber on the scene, if Spencer and the newspapers are to be believed. Paul's sure to have them both sewn up and be into threesomes by now or some variation on the theme.'

'And what makes you think I'm not? Check them out, tell me which one you fancy and I'll work on it. This trip is really looking up.'

'Careful, you might end up with onesomes . . .' Kate was cut off by the arrival of lunch: chicken and rice with a pasta salad, which didn't seem a perfect balance.

'Can we talk a little about Polly?' Richard asked, as they tucked in. 'I do worry. If you're thinking drugs, I'm sure she's done a bundle, but not, I think, anything really bad. I'd know the signs of that.'

'She's very preoccupied. It may be nothing much,

285

but she seemed a little upset when she came for lunch at the start of half term.' Kate didn't feel able to say that whatever the cause of the misery, Polly was sour, cussed and bitchy with it. 'You'd popped out and she arrived looking dreadfully pale and drained. She seemed much better at supper with your mother, though,' Kate finished, wanting to sound more positive.

'It's so hard to tell where Poll's at,' Richard said. 'She's always fighting the system, authority, rules, but she does seem more spiky and brittle than usual. The washed-out look's nothing new; too many late nights and that hideous dried-blood lipstick doesn't help—drain a ruddy milkmaid. I've caved in over the make-up, lost that battle. Why can't she say what's bugging her, though, and open up? It's so frustrating. She's doing fuck-all work too. Polly's quick and bright, she knocked off all those GCSEs last year, at under sixteen with her August birthday, and got top grades. She thinks she has bags of time, the first year of As . . .'

'Couldn't you suggest having some quality time together and take her out to lunch?'

Richard sighed. 'It wouldn't work. She shuts me out and won't talk to me. That's what carves me up. I know it's her age and I should brush it off, but I mind the way she has to emphasize my every failing. She magnifies everything and really hates me for leaving. The most minor flaw is a criminal outrage, she always thinks the worst of me.'

'She doesn't at heart, I'm quite sure. I think it's far more to do with a load of feminist ideas in her head than any perceived sins of yours. She lumps all men together in the very few chats we've had, and pretty scathingly.'

It was hard to press her idea about lunch, but Kate felt that between father and daughter, communication lines were down and in need of repairing. Polly could be in some sort of real trouble and longing for a chance to talk. There seemed no other way to help, though, apart from the secret long-shot feeler she'd put out, her card slipped into Polly's coat pocket. The worry just had to be shelved.

After all the last-minute packing, the stresses and panics, wine at lunch, Kate's eyelids were drooping. Richard was reading the *Economist*. She leaned and rested her head on his shoulder and he absently fondled her hair. She thought about the call from Ben. Why had it been on her office phone? And why, assuming he was being truthful, was Jon in MI6 dealing with it, even as a friend? Wouldn't drugs and crime normally come under MI5? They were troubling questions that she yearned to share with Richard.

Kate was drifting, drowsy, very nearly asleep when he started talking. 'I'm not sure whether it's Ben or whatever he told you, but something is making you privately fearful and I want you to know there's no need. You're safe with me.'

She clung to the moment and fastened onto tropical Grenada, hot white beaches, crimson sunsets. She was enthralled with the sea, its roaring magnitude and the gentle lap of the calm. Richard was as powerful a force, as calming and beyond her control; he was her sea.

*   *   *

Spencer's driver, Grant, pulled up on the side of

the road. 'This is a great vantage point,' he said. 'Come and take a look.' Kate and Richard climbed out of the car. 'That's Port Louis Marina down there; you can't miss *Black Diamond,* she takes up at least two slips.' Grant was a big guy, basking in association and pride. Richard said he could imagine none to touch her, no rival to come near.

She was a magnificently beautiful yacht. Shining and black, tall, gracious, glinting like the priceless jewel of her name in the brilliant afternoon sun. She seemed almost to have the quality of shimmering weightlessness that had held Kate so unforgettably spellbound on her first sight of the Taj Mahal. It had been years ago in her backpacking days, a holiday with a university boyfriend.

Down on the quayside *Black Diamond* appeared more substantial. Kate went first up the gangway with Richard hard behind her, whispering in her ear. 'Don't get too hooked, it's hardly the manner I can keep you accustomed to, even not paying for your flights.'

Spencer helped her down onto the deck, greeted her and pumped Richard's hand. 'Welcome, welcome, you've made it, great!' He had a spreading grin that took up residence in his round face and didn't once budge. He looked on magnanimously as Kate hugged her mother like an uninhibited child. Flesh-and-blood contact felt very precious.

Ben gave her a light hug. It communicated a cautionary message, one that she understood, a warning to step back and steer clear of dangerous displays of emotion. No giveaways, no clues.

Rachel and Ben had come to the gangway deck

to see them and Spencer was trying to shepherd the group to a seating area on the deck. Richard was being dutifully well behaved, enthusing over *Black Diamond*'s magnificence and his host's generosity in inviting him along. Spencer, who radiated a natural impatience, beamed briefly then remembered the task in hand. 'Come along now, everyone, come and sit down, have some champagne. The bags are being seen to, you're here to relax!'

Taking Kate's arm he led her to the splendid glass table with sturdy director-style, plumply cushioned armchairs in spruce-green canvas. After a long flight she was only too glad to sink down. The table was spread with a scattering of little dishes of nibbles, almonds, cashews, olives, as well as a huge plate of sliced fruits, and an exotic flower arrangement with calla lilies and orchids. Two girl crew members in khaki shorts and logoed white shirts were on hand, smilingly anxious to jump to it.

'It's hard to believe we're actually here,' Kate said tritely, but with feeling. 'I mean the sun, the beauty of it all . . .'

'It gets better,' Rachel smiled. 'You wait.'

'I knew you'd have a beautiful daughter,' Spencer said, with well-practised charm. 'She's gorgeous, an absolute stunner—hot competition for our two models on board.'

Kate thought of the countless gossip-column photographs she'd seen of Spencer. Always chuckling, cheerful and hospitable, his rotund face never without an infectious grin; Spencer outdoors with his strands of wiry grey hair stuck down, dinner-jacketed in glossy magazines; she'd absorbed that he was burly and wide-shouldered and, had she thought about it, would have imagined him imposing and tall. But photographs did deceive. He was a short, stout man.

'Now,' he said, 'nobody has a drink—is it champagne all round?' One of the girls held a bottle ready.

'What I'd really love,' Kate confessed, despite Spencer's obvious need to ply his best vintage, 'is a nice cup of tea—builders' if possible, if you wouldn't mind?'

'Good idea, I'll have some, too.' It was soon tea all round. 'Fleur's up on top deck,' Spencer explained. 'Everyone's sunning or sleeping off lunch—not that those are mutually exclusive. I expect you'd like a proper rest, though, and meet everyone later over drinks. Say about eight and we'll eat at nine?'

'We'll enjoy the evening all the more,' Richard said, with a smarmy smile.

They were shown to a regally appointed cabin. Creamy orchids were sensitively placed; a bottle of champagne, naturally, awaited them, chilling in a bucket; a superb opalescent-blue Lalique glass bowl was piled with tropical fruits. Richard stared at it. 'That's a rare original,' he said, 'it has to be pre-war. See, "R. Lalique"? When he died, his son did away with the "R" for René and it's not on any factory pieces. Don't look so impressed, I wrote a piece about people's assets once, and looked him up.'

The cabin had an emperor-sized bed with a slithery, sexy cover of coffee-coloured silk. Richard flung himself down on it backwards and held out his arms. When Kate obediently fell into them he rolled her beside him and pointed upwards. 'Look up there. What do you reckon about that?'

The ceiling was mirrored, bronze-tinted and in large squares; the tinting was slightly misty and soft focus, which made them seem a lot more alluring and glamorous-looking than a travel-worn pair in denims and Tees.

'Just in case it's two-way,' Richard said, kneeling to pull off her jeans, 'I think we should put on a Saturday Spectacular . . .' Kate was nervous enough to believe anything.

'I'll do the sound effects,' she said. 'I'm good at those.'

They went up on deck for drinks, showered and much refreshed. They'd slept, they had a post-sex glow, and were feeling fit and ready to be sociable.

Henry Stevenson, the asset manager, and his wife, Tabatha, were the only ones to have surfaced. They were gazing out to sea, stiffly, as though in the aftermath of a row.

Rachel's potted histories had made introductions feel almost superfluous and the Stevensons seemed to know all about them as well. The early small talk was helped along by the sight of *Black Diamond* skilfully negotiating her way out of the marina. She was soon clear, carving a path through a tranquil ink-black sea; it was a wondrous night, milky-white with stars. 'We're pottering round a few islands tomorrow, apparently,' Henry said, 'making for one called Carriacou that has deserted bays and great swimming, that sort of thing.'

'They say it's a one-street town, a bit of a dump, stuck in a time warp,' Tabatha sniffed. 'Very hick with no good restaurants, but I suppose we'll eat on board.' She was in a neat, flowered cocktail dress, more Home Counties than tropics, and openly looked them up and down. Kate doubted her

291

lavender shoe-strap shift would pass muster, but Richard looked delicious in a white lawn shirt and brick linen trousers. 'Do you live in London?' Tabatha asked rather tediously, having exhausted the limitations of Carriacou.

'Yes, the rough end of Chelsea,' Richard said. 'I've dragged Katie right down.'

'Oh,' she replied, lost for words, clearly wondering what heights of residential grandeur Kate had been dragged from.

Spencer appeared on deck, spruce in nautical navy, snapping and clapping for canapés and refills of glasses. Fleur was with him, titian-haired and bulging out of a scoop neckline, but she was lean-hipped in the tight emerald cut-offs she was wearing.

'Hi guys,' she exclaimed cheerily, taking them in, 'welcome aboard!'

Her attention was turned by the models pitching up; Kim, pixie-faced with short dark hair and in an elongated boob-tube. Astrid was blonde, wearing a loose black tent, slit to the hip for her long tanned legs to feel the breeze. Paul Barber, the MP, was last to arrive, slim and elegant, smoothing back his fair hair.

He came over to say hello while Kate and Richard were still with the Stevensons. Henry chortled heartily. 'Must admit I was surprised to see a Labour MP on board. I thought you people would run a mile.'

Paul craned his long neck round in an exaggerated contortionist way. 'I can't say I can see any Russian oligarchs on board . . . Or am I missing something here?'

They went down to dinner on the deck below.

The table was exquisitely laid; fragrant, waxy frangipani blooms on each napkin, gleaming candelabra, contemporary glass, it was all in impeccable taste. Rachel whispered the name of a top interiors firm.

The first course was Beluga caviar, served with ice-cold vodka. Richard grinned across the table at Paul. 'I guess Parliament must be on its half-term break,' he said, unable to resist another small go. 'One little perk you guys managed to hang on to at least.'

Paul answered emolliently. 'Fascinating how you media people never give up. It's in your DNA. You're having a break too, with this lovely girl. Or are you doing some great exposé on mega-yachts or something and we're all about to be in your next documentary?'

'Good God, I hope not!' Tabatha looked ready to swoon.

'Nothing about yachts,' Richard said. 'I'd hate our wonderfully generous host—and Tabatha,' he smiled at her, 'to have any worries on that score. No, the programme I'm working on now is serious coalface stuff, a lot of grim statistics; I'm making the most of this fabulous holiday.'

'Can we know what it's about?' Spencer asked. With quite keen interest, Kate sensed, but then wouldn't anyone with his millions or billions always be on wary guard with the media anywhere around?

'Sure, it's on drugs,' Richard said, 'the cocaine story. Tracking the stuff from a growing leaf right through till it ends up as a line on someone's kitchen worktop—mashed and chopped up with a bank card, snorted through a rolled-up banknote. It's all about money!'

'Things have been hotting up in Colombia lately,' Henry remarked, flashing poor Tabatha an irritated glance, which was hard to understand. 'Might be a bit hairy if you need to go there, Richard. I did read, though, that they've knocked off a few key FARC terrorists recently, including a military commander called "Mono Jojoy"! They seized computer hard drives and memory sticks and it seems now that the FARC are into gold as well as kidnapping and drugs. They're running small gold mines, extorting "tax" payments from the miners, most of whom are unregulated. The mines release hideous levels of mercury into Colombia's rivers, apparently. Anyway the FARC's wings seem to have been clipped a bit with this haul!'

'They're ruthless operators,' Spencer said, 'they'll regroup for sure. I was out in Colombia years ago with one of my companies—it's actually where I first met Ben.'

'Since then I owe Spencer a lot,' Ben smiled. 'He had the idea for my business and was prepared to back me when I resigned from the Army and needed a job. I had local knowledge, was up in rainforest products and he thought I could trade out there.'

'I'm up in rainforest products too, now,' Richard laughed. 'We're more or less through in South America, but I'm just back from crashing about in the Peruvian rainforest, filming the paste stage of cocaine which took a lot of greasing bandits' palms!'

'So that's why you have a great tan already,' Kim said, giving him a slight eye.

She could take more of an interest in the documentary, Kate thought tartly.

'How will you tackle the trafficking side?' Paul asked, razoring in with his politically sharp mind. 'The cocaine coming in. Do you know something the border police don't?'

'Wish we did! Filming a sting would certainly put up the viewing figures. No, we'll talk to customs, film them doing their job, but we're concentrating more on the harm to health side, crime problems, the "toffs' drug" angle, interviews with doctors and ex-dealers, that sort of thing.'

Kate smiled round easily, still with her private fears, hoping in vain for a tiny clue. Ben had said himself that even a blink could be the snare. Could he and Spencer be working as a team? She felt she was getting paranoid, being extreme about Ben, and that even if Richard was right about Spencer, his crimes were purely financial. He was frowning at his staff, impatient for the plates to be cleared. Carl, his silent right-hand man, had kept looking down while Richard was talking; he'd glanced once, at Spencer, but not as though expecting to catch his eye.

Henry was watching the progress of the wine bottle. 'This Puligny-Montrachet is absolute nectar,' he said, showing delight as it reached him. 'Brilliant.'

'Just wait for the Lafite,' Spencer chuckled. 'It's 1989, you'll enjoy that.'

Kim and Astrid were talking across Paul, sharing lurid notes about a randy photographer. Tabatha was obviously fascinated while trying not to be seen to listen. She hadn't hidden her shocked disapproval of the cocaine story, although she'd shown no great interest in Henry's discussion about the FARC.

Rachel described the book she was translating: a searing account of a German soldier's love for a French woman during the war. Kim told of her grandmother's homemade ice-cream recipes that her father had grown into 'Martha's', the multi-million-dollar family business. 'I got to loathe ice cream as a child,' she complained. 'Yuk, yuk.'

'Not any more, though, surely?' Spencer queried. '"Martha's Coffee Bean Crunch" is to die for, and the "Pecan Brownie". We're having some of both of those tonight.'

The extraordinary wines flowed. Kate eventually gave up watching and worrying; she was sleepy from the flight and longed to sneak off with Richard to bed.

*   *   *

Pawpaws drenched in fresh lime juice, meltingly crisp croissants, good strong coffee, sleeping in . . . It was a film-set start to the day, Kate thought, as they joined Spencer, Ben and Rachel, who were still round the breakfast table. The others were already grilling themselves on the top deck. She and Richard soon went up to sunbathe too, Richard administering suncream while she lay back in an extremely expensive, new neon-orange bikini, soaking up compliments as well as the sun.

The Swedish captain came on deck to tell them about Carriacou. It was the most southerly island of the Grenadines, he said, in his clipped guttural accent, a place where turtles swam ashore at night to lay their eggs in sandy coves. It had a tiny town, a proper community, but was still very under-developed. That meant unspoilt, Kate felt, as

Carriacou's richly tropical coastline came into view.

They meandered along looking for a perfect bay. Rounding a corner they found it: sublime white sands, swaying palms, completely sheltered and deserted. *Black Diamond* slowed right down and with a series of shudders and rumbles, she dropped anchor. The breeze lessened and the sun scorched; the sea was incredibly still. Richard stood at the rail, gazing out; Kate was in her own world.

'Who's for a swim before lunch? Snorkelling? Jet skis?' Spencer's large round head appeared first as he climbed the steps, puffing and grinning, and came up on deck. He was in a loose flowery shirt and shorts, not about to launch into the water himself.

Paul, Kim and Astrid wanted to go ashore in the tender. The Stevensons were settled on loungers and chose to stay reading. Richard had a little work to do, calls and emails on his mobile. Kate thought she'd swim from the boat while he was busy. 'Then can you come with me to the beach? And not by tender, it's perfect swimming distance.'

'You might think so. If I peg out you'll have to tow me in.'

The ladder was down for the tender and she used it to slip into the indigo water, shivering a moment with the first shock then loving its dark sensual embrace. She swam breaststroke, quickly finding her rhythm and hardly stirring the silken sea.

Swimming was thinking time, like driving alone or having walks in the fields. Kate thought about her father's accelerating decline, so evident the weekend before leaving, and what a jolt it had been. She kept seeing those pink dots of strain on his cheeks. Even talking had taken it out of him. Millie hadn't yapped much either. She knew. No mauling of Richard; she'd given one subdued, token growl and stayed at her master's feet.

The house had smelled of illness, too. Not of ammonia and utility-catering like a hospital, but wet flannels and soapy basins, pills, over-worked radiators, overripe fruit in the bowl. Hannah's home cooking had helped, but there were none of the old outdoorsy smells Kate associated with home, like walked-in grass cuttings or pulled-out weeds in the rubbish bin. And Hannah had said— out of Aidan's hearing—that when Kate was back it might be the time to move his bed downstairs.

She swam on. Should she have come on this holiday? Was she going to lose her mother as well? Kate felt wretched, bitterly miserable at having to keep so much from Richard; if only she could share the burden. She wished too that he wasn't so dead-set on proving Spencer Morgan a grade-A fraudster. The man was very evidently nobody's fool, someone not to be crossed, but he was a warm host and even Richard had admitted to finding him entertaining. She longed to be able to have confidence in Ben who was so likeable and authoritative. The world seemed turned on its head.

It was easy to act starry-eyed and seem to love the luxury, but Kate actually felt wreathed in distaste for it all, almost guilty, in her present mood of dread anxiety and suspicion, to be accepting a single, solitary champagne bubble of Spencer's largesse. She couldn't wait to see the back of this beautiful yacht and be alone with Richard at the Blue Horizon, the hotel he'd booked for their last few days.

'It'll be quite a contrast,' he'd said, 'simple and

298

unfancy—the Calabash and Spice Island are Grenada's top hotels—but the rooms are dotted about in tropical gardens and have sea-view balconies, too. They're like little flatlets with a thundering fridge and a gas cooker. No one coming to check mini-bars every five minutes and turn down beds; we can do our own breakfast, potter and be completely private.' Richard grinned. 'And I did think that by the time we get there, you might be rather luxuried-out.'

Kate smiled to herself; he wasn't often given to understatement. There was no sign of him yet. She trod water looking for him then swam a bit more, thinking of the day ahead. They were returning to Grenada after lunch. Astrid was on a late flight, she had a modelling job the next day, an ad for a miracle self-tanning product, which everyone thought a bit of a cheat, considering her flawless Caribbean tan. Fleur even seemed to take it personally, saying behind her hand that Astrid had done nothing but sunbathe ever since coming on board.

Kate had become the object of Astrid and Kim's attentions; they'd been cosying up, since discovering she was in advertising, seeing her as a potential source of revenue. Kate told them her boss, Dan Green, would simply love to see their portfolios any time they were in London, which had caused Richard to have a small coughing fit into his vintage fizz.

He was taking ages. She decided to swim one full circuit round the yacht, then go back on board and chivvy him along.

She found herself in deep shadow swimming up the far side of *Black Diamond*, away from the tender ladder. The yacht towered above her, the sea was dark and silent and, with no other craft in sight to ripple the surface, almost eerily calm. It was like folds of lustrous jet-coloured silk, and cool against her skin, even under the burning sun, a great force tamed, a sea in benignly noble mood.

Black Diamond rose up, vast and high-sided as she swam in its shadow. Was she just being churlish and inverted, feeling such distaste for the excessive luxury? Spencer wasn't exactly her cup of builders' tea, but she was having a fabulous Caribbean holiday and with Richard all to herself, undiluted. Eleanor was a long way away.

Voices reached her, low murmurs. Kate glanced up, intensely curious, and tried not to make a sound. Spencer and Carl were leaning on the rail of the lower deck, directly above her and having a private talk, it would seem. They clearly had no idea she was there; if she kept as still and quiet and close in as possible . . . She prayed they would look out to sea, if anywhere, and not straight down the side of the boat.

Carl was speaking, sounding querulous. 'I was quite surprised at you having someone like that on board—what the hell was the point? You knew who he was, what he did.'

'Sure. But who cares? I'd asked the daughter, which seemed like a good idea at the time, and he came as part of the package. He's fucking media, but so what? It's fine.'

'You don't think it was all a bit too pointed, last night? Not worried?'

'Nah. Pure coincidence, unconnected with things in hand. Might as well check him out while he's here, I guess, if it makes you feel better, Carl—easy enough. Never hurts. But you concentrate on Trinidad. That meeting next Thursday is important, big. Plenty riding on that.'

They turned then and leaned with their backs to the rail. Kate swam away silently, keeping close to the hull, memorising every word. What did 'check him out while he's here' mean? Surely their cabin couldn't be bugged? She felt shaken and confused, relieved too, in a way, that Richard knew nothing of all Ben had said. A bug in the cabin, if one should conceivably exist, would pick up little more than lover's chat and a bit of Tabatha-teasing. Kate felt grateful to Ben for that at least; she was only too aware that any loose talk could increase the threat to her mother. Had she and Richard said anything incriminating about Spencer or Carl? She hoped not, swimming on, feeling chilled—more by her nerves than the cool of the sea.

Spencer's slightly chilling mutters about 'things in hand' must be to do with his mention of Trinidad, Kate thought, some dodgy financial deal or other, probably to do with banks or property. She decided to ask Richard what he knew about Spencer's Caribbean operations—once they were safely away from the yacht.

Richard was sitting on the ladder in his black Bermuda trunks when she rounded the yacht, looking agitated. 'Shit, Katie, don't do that to me,' he called. 'You were nowhere, I was about to send out a search party!' She clambered up beside him and he hugged her, shivering with the shock of her wetness. 'What about this swim to the bay then? But I warn you I'll want to come back by tender. Lunch is in an hour and it's lobster, crab and cold fillet of beef, according to those hard-working girls.

Think of the nice long siesta we'll need after that.'

*   *   *

Carriacou was close to Grenada and they were back and berthed in the marina by seven. Henry wanted to take everyone to dinner at the Calabash Hotel. 'And no arguing, Spencer,' he said, 'my treat. It's one of my favourite places, great food, and the restaurant is Gary Rhodes. It ticks all Tabatha's buttons too,' he joked bitchily. 'A messenger once delivered a parcel saying it was for the duchess. "Which one?" asked the attendant at the door. "We have three staying just now".'

Henry had too many digs at his wife, Kate thought, as she and Richard went down to the cabin to change. Tabatha's hurt was clear to see; Kate felt that with a little more warmth and affection the poor woman might start to lift her horizons and see beyond postcodes and pearls.

Kate felt revived. She'd had a sleepless siesta, lying still as a leaf, listening for Richard's steady breathing before letting rip with her fears. She'd gone over everything she'd overheard, trying to set it into context. Spencer and Carl's allusions to Richard had sounded menacing, but 'checking him out' could be done online; she was getting carried away. But then what had seemed 'all a bit too pointed'? The documentary on cocaine? Yet surely if that were the case, it would have been so glaringly obvious as to make Carl's edgy query superfluous.

It could have been anything. Richard protesting too much about his motives, Henry's talk of the FARC, nuances she was unaware of. It was all too easy to start reading in links, even if Spencer did seem to be up to something fishy. But financial jiggery, Kate told herself, not murder and the trafficking of cocaine on a grand scale. She wondered again about Spencer's relationship with Ben; he paid Ben warm attention, despite his business being barely a speck on the Morgan map. And Ben seemed very at home on the yacht.

It would have been so easy to trust in Ben, always warming to him, yet somehow something continued to hold Kate back. She sensed there were things he hadn't told her, vital missing pieces of information that might have helped her to see the light. The only course of action open to her, she felt, was to accept the facts of the situation as he'd explained them at their fateful dinner. She had to keep her wits as pin-sharp as possible and, back home again, see her mother and act normally. Kate couldn't let herself imagine life without Rachel there.

Perhaps asking Ben whether Spencer had interests in Trinidad might give a lead . . . But to figure out how to see Ben alone while imagining bugs in every sunbed and cranny of the yacht was as defeating as quantum mechanics. Kate had given up on her non-siesta, and tried instead, lying stiffly beside Richard, to relax herself back into the role of bright, appreciative admiring guest, sitting at the feet of Spencer.

The prospect of dinner out was a pick-me-up, a change of scene, a break from the intense feelings of claustrophobia she was experiencing on the yacht. She changed into a backless, gauzy lime-green dress for dinner, cooling to her sunburn. Richard called it a scrumptious wisp of nothing as they went up on deck to join the others and the party, less Astrid, piled into cars and left for the hotel restaurant.

The eating area was open to the garden and under a canopy of dangling vines that dropped pretty bell-shaped flowers onto the table at regular intervals. Kate was facing out to sea where she could see the dotted lights of little boats moored in the bay. She was seated between Carl and the MP, Paul, and since Paul, with his hand on Kim's thigh, was fully occupied on his other side, Kate was stuck with Carl. She talked art, asking his views about brilliant copies on the market, an old-chestnut issue, but currently in the news again.

'Art as an investment is one thing,' she said, 'but I don't see a beautiful copy as a sin.'

Carl looked shocked. 'You're not suggesting Spencer's paintings are fakes?'

Nothing was further from her mind, she assured him hurriedly. 'It's not fair to owners of originals,' he argued, showing a rare crumb of animation, 'and people can be fooled, ripped off—I think that it's a disgusting crime.'

'Of course it is, passing them off as the real thing, but I was only talking about copies. And the great paintings are so well known . . .' She'd lost Carl's attention. He had tuned in elsewhere and, from his body language, something was making him tense.

Was it Richard talking across the table, asking Spencer what exciting new ventures he had in train? That was a mild enough query.

Henry joined in, more in the know as CE of one of Spencer's larger financial outfits. 'Aren't you moving into Trinidad, Spencer? Opening that vast new casino complex any minute?'

'That's peanuts, hardly a venture,' he argued lightly. 'Don't know why I keep on with the casino business—old habits, I suppose! No, I'm pretty laid-back these days,' he said, answering Richard with an easy grin, 'branching into trendy foods, that's about all, pesto this and that; quite fun for a change. I have my Foundation of course, charitable ventures. And asset management is always profitably interesting . . .' They talked on.

Kate sat in silence. Her stomach had tightened at the mention of Trinidad, but she'd learned nothing new and now was being ignored on both sides. Ben looked over to her, smiling. 'Come for a stroll, Katie, just down the garden to the little beach. It's a beautiful sight, all those winking lights of the tiny yachts out there.'

The path was subtly lit, palms swishing softly, and she felt lucky to have the chance of a moment alone. Ben glanced backwards. 'Just wondered if your mother might be coming,' he said, feeling the need to explain. 'How are you coping? Anything you'd like to chat about? Do I sense Richard's anti-Spencer vibes might have turned into active dislike?'

'That would be hard, given all this largesse, but I don't think he's changed his views.'

'You're very tense, Katie.'

'Oh dear, is it that obvious?'

'Perhaps only to me. But Richard gives you besotted looks that are anxious as well.'

'I'm interested in Spencer's Trinidad venture, Ben. Does it involve you, too?'

'Why, Katie? That's an odd question. But no, not at all. I'm certainly not into casinos.'

She studied Ben's face in the moonlight, embarrassed when he met her eyes with quizzical concern. He was worried, she thought, bothered by her question, and on a rather spur-of-the-moment whim she started to tell him part of what she'd heard.

'I only ask because I overheard Spencer and Carl talking about a meeting in Trinidad on Thursday, which Spencer seemed to consider very big and important. And yet he played his new casino complex right down just now.'

'The yacht is going on to Trinidad, I know,' Ben said. 'Your mother and I are leaving on Wednesday, though.' He looked at Kate curiously. 'Spencer and Carl are always muttering, but very much to themselves. I'm surprised you could pick that up!'

'They were leaning on the deck-rail and I was in the water directly below.'

'I think perhaps,' Ben said, still staring at her, 'I should explain something about our host. My MI6 friend, Jon, wouldn't approve of my telling you this, but there's more going on with Spencer than you'd think. I happen to know he's in touch with MI6. He feeds in low-level stuff about Colombia; he does deals out there and picks up the occasional titbit of information. Any odd whispers would have been connected with that, I suspect.'

He looked over her shoulder towards the hotel. 'We should get back. But would you feel happier if we made a quick plan to meet in the future, Katie? You might have questions, things you want to ask.' She nodded, grateful, wondering if it was more about Ben wanting to keep tabs on her, in fact. He carried on. 'I know you can't help feeling desperately worried, but you absolutely mustn't talk to your mother about any of this—for all our safeties. She and I are going on to New York from here, so let's say we fix to meet three weeks this Thursday? It's a bit distant, I know, but we'll both be comfortably back by then, well in harness again. I'll accidentally bump into you in Charlotte Street at two-fifteen and suggest a quick coffee. Sorry, but we do have to take these silly little precautions.'

They wandered back. Henry was keying in his pin, paying the bill, Spencer was planning the next day. These were Kate and Richard's last hours on board and she couldn't wait to be through them and gone.

'We'll sail round the island tomorrow, and not venture far,' Spencer decided, 'since Paul needs to be back by early evening. You have drinks with the Grenadian Trade Minister, isn't that right, Paul?'

'Yes, just a little chat at a party,' Paul acknowledged smoothly. 'At a stunning villa, though, and the hosts, being American, have invited everyone on board along.'

'Mind if we give that the bye?' Richard said. 'I want to show Katie the hotel we're staying at, close to Grand Anse beach, when we're back tomorrow evening—bring her down slowly from all this luxury!'

'What a glorious glow she has and not all to do with a few days in the sun, I'm sure, you lucky man!' Spencer beamed his grin. 'We'll have a late dinner on board then. About nine-thirty? And some extra-special champagne as it's your last night.'

'Our whole stay has been extra special,' Kate said, 'beyond imagining. How can we begin to thank you for such incredible hospitality?'

'You were sounding as smooth as Paul Barber,' Richard muttered, on the way to the cars. 'Do I sense you've gone off our host a bit, the scales

307

fallen from your eyes?'

'Correct, but I was hardly his greatest fan in the first place. You'd seen to that.'

* * *

Only Paul, Kim and the Stevensons went to the drinks party in the end. Grant, the driver, dropped off Kate and Richard on the way. 'Can you stop here?' Richard called. 'We're right near the Blue Horizon and Grand Anse beach is just down the road.' He had a job to persuade Grant to let them make their own way back to the yacht.

Standing by the side of a hot dusty road they waved off the car and Richard squeezed Kate's hand. 'I wanted you to check out the hotel. I loved it, as you know, the time I was here interviewing some developer, but you might just have done a Tabatha and not approve.'

'You just wanted to get out of the drinks! I'd rather save seeing it for tomorrow and walk on the beach for now and watch the sunset.'

Kate felt superstitious, dreading the chance of any eleventh-hour dramas on their last night. Ben had put her in turmoil, suggesting Spencer was in contact with MI6. It was as though he'd led her into a dark tunnel and left her there, assuring her of an exit; she just had to have faith. She was sure it was overboard to imagine bugged cabins, but her mind kept coming back to Roger Grieve's fate. She had a slight sense too, of Ben gently trying to steer her away from having suspicious thoughts about Spencer. He'd done the same thing when they'd had dinner alone, she remembered, warning her off, telling her that Spencer was a sharp operator and nothing more. She wondered again about some sort of involvement between them.

A walk on the beach was just what she needed. Kate prayed Richard's mobile wouldn't ring and shatter the sweetness of this beautiful evening. It was a moment of freedom before having to psych herself up to be on form, shake a leg, laugh at Henry's jokes and genuflect. Arse-licking didn't come easily.

The setting sun cast a mauve-pink sheen on the rippling sea; it looked as though blood had spilled and mingled in with the silvery water. They sat on the sand, elbows on knees. Kate had a bikini on under her sundress; Richard had thought they might swim. It was almost dark, but others were; she could still see the black dots of swimmers in the water.

Grand Anse was a glorious beach. Local children were playing in groups, little girls with laughing smiles and pink bobble-bands in curly screws of hair, older boys playing ball games; there was just enough daylight. 'Let's walk a bit more,' Richard said. He stood up and held out his strong hands to pull her up. 'Still can't tell me anything? Even about the stroll with Ben? I want to be on the inside, darling, and find a way in.'

'I've never known you to have a problem there.' She smiled, they both did, and held hands as they ambled along the sand.

A Rasta guy shuffled up, dreadlocks piled into a coloured wool hat. He kept pace with them. 'Want ganja? Good ganja, very good—you want?'

'Good price too?' Richard queried, grinning. 'Have to be, if I want!'

The guy felt into a deep jacket pocket and

produced a crumpled paper bag. Richard peered inside. 'Sorry, no good,' he said, 'buds and stems no good. We want to smoke now. You chop it up first—no sale like that.'

The guy pointed to a few stalls further down the beach. 'You get knives, papers, tobacco, man.'

Richard eyed him. 'Okay, how much? God, what a sucker.' The pair of them went into a little huddle and Richard was soon shoving the spoils of the deal into a pocket of his shorts.

Kate was fascinated. 'We haven't even got any matches. You are a sucker!'

Half an hour later, after a few more coins had changed palms at a seedy little stall, they were kitted out with some fairly finely chopped cannabis—which Richard, squatting on the dark beach, proceeded to roll up with some tobacco in a large-size Rizla to make a spliff. 'The tobacco should help it to burn,' he said. 'I'll get you relaxed yet . . .'

It took a lot of matches, but with eventual success. They both puffed themselves silly. At the back of Kate's mind was the wishful thought that returning to the yacht stinking of weed, more than a bit high, might persuade Spencer and Carl away from any suspicions they had, either about her if she'd been seen by them in the water or of Richard as a typical investigative journalist on the prowl.

The third spliff wouldn't light. 'We're not very good, are we?' She giggled loudly. 'It went out! We need a big fat knife, chop, chop, chop. Try again, light it and get better.'

'Look how your arm glows!' Richard said, running a finger so, so slowly down her arm. 'You're a beach girl, a beautiful girl glow-worm . . .'

Kate couldn't keep pace, everything felt speeding, etched, distinct, brilliant. She held out her arms in front. Were they glowing? The sky was. It glittered. The sand was. It was fluorescent. 'The sand's fluorescent,' she said out loud. 'That's good, I can say it. Yes, I can.'

'Obama said that.' Richard trickled his fingers, raising the hairs on her arm. 'I think . . .'

She waited, pursing her lips for a kiss. He gave her one, eyes gleaming. 'I think, girl glow-worm,' he said very slowly, 'we should go in the sea and fuck.'

The sea floor was pure hard sand, the water lapping like cat's tongues. Kate looked back to their patch of beach. 'I can't see our clothes. Yes, I can!' She felt herself lifted and held, Richard settling her legs on his hips. 'They'll have us arrested!'

'And a few others out here.' He found a way round her bikini; she gripped hard with her thighs. She felt his tongue, high, right in the roof of her mouth; it excited her madly. The sea was carrying her; he was gripping her buttocks, his mouth pressing, fierce, hard, everything was hard, faster . . .

'I think heaven just fell into the sea,' Richard said, lifting her down.

'My feet are touching the ground now.' She stumbled into him and he held on, hugging her tightly as they splashed back to shore. 'Keep hugging me, I'm cold. But not inside, I'm not cold inside.' Kate felt the world was in its rightful place, their small pile of clothes was just where they'd left it. 'I'm warm inside, glow-worm warm.'

Richard rubbed her dry with his thick, khaki cargo shorts and she slipped her sundress over her wet bikini. 'Everything's still in my pockets,' he said, 'even what's left of the weed.'

'Didn't we smoke it all?'

'No, I kept a bit back. I thought we should save a little something for Tabatha.'

CHAPTER 20

Kate lifted her head from her hands. It was late, and moping in a heap at the kitchen table was achieving nothing at all. Dan had brought her tumbling down the minute they were home, almost three weeks ago now, and the sheer depressing ghastliness of it all seemed harder still to handle after being up in the stratosphere. It was tarnishing the memories.

She was ready for bed, in need of sleep, and looked over to Richard. He was tiredly flicking through the *Evening Standard*, although he had work to do, a transcript to go through. 'I've not known you as down as this,' he said, feeling her eyes on him and glancing up. 'It is just Dan getting to you, is it?'

'Yes. You wouldn't believe how awful it is at work; he hasn't let up once since we've been back.' Kate felt it wasn't the time for unloading, they should be going to bed, yet the urge to let off steam and earn some sympathy was building fast. 'Dan's a natural at shit-spreading and point-scoring, of course,' she said. 'He knows how to dish it on a good day. He was going to be bitter about the holiday, especially since it was the Caribbean. I expected some slagging off and my work being junked, but not this. It's in a different league. It's a

312

kind of systematic character assassination, intensifying if anything, and as if he's trying to ruin my whole career. I think of those peachy, heavenly few days we had in Grenada after the yacht, but it only compounds the misery.'

'Sounds like you're wondering if they were really worth having.'

Kate didn't bother to respond; Richard was only half listening to have made that tame little quip. The holiday sustained her. She loved to recall the tiny warbling house wren and the black Antillian bullfinch that had shared their balcony breakfasts. He was a red-throated fellow, definitely the boss-bird, yet the wren had stood her ground. The birds had come every morning, quite fearless. She thought of how she had strolled with Richard to the beach, past scented frangipani trees, their velvety blossoms creamy as the head on a pint of Guinness. Everyone had been full of Caribbean warmth, flashing welcoming smiles. It had been worth anything, even Dan's brutal campaign, to be alone with Richard in that serenely tropical paradise.

She felt that Dan's determination to do her down went beyond the holiday. She sensed that was somehow little connected and she said as much to Richard. 'It is all very odd, though. It must be entirely to do with being stood-up, the embarrassment and hefty knock to his pride. Talk about an eye for an eye, Dan wants a whole dead body and it's mine.'

'Don't waste all this energy on it,' Richard said, stifling a yawn. 'Stuff him.'

'The slander he's been spreading is grotesque,' Kate burst out, although Dan's particular mischief would infuriate Richard, she knew. Carrying on,

313

failing to hold back, she felt between a snakepit and a hard place. 'I mean he may be a desensitized, mud-slinging ad-man,' she complained, overtired and sorry for herself, 'but I thought he had an ounce of human decency in his bones.'

'Dan doesn't do decency, I did warn you.' Richard pushed away the newspaper looking irritatingly complacent as he rose, downing his coffee. 'I must look over this transcript in a minute, but let's have it, darling,' he said, his face breaking into a smile. 'Tell me what the fucker's been saying to have got you quite this uptight.'

Having brought it on herself Kate tried hard to row back. It was midnight and Richard had been up before five that morning. 'Forget it,' she urged. 'I'm whinging and it's been a long day. I'll start up to bed, I think.' She couldn't endure Dan's treatment, but to go into it all wasn't going to help. Richard would only tell her to jack in the job and look elsewhere. He had it in for Impetus; he'd once suggested a change of career, something less edgy and stressful, saying she could always sell a couple of paintings, earn a little less if need be and do something more relaxing and enjoyable—possibly connected with art. But she loved her job, the mad ad world, the creative buzz, and the independence was a bolster; it helped her to cope with the fear of Richard moving on one day.

He took his mug to the sink, put the milk in the fridge and lifted her into his arms. 'Tell me how I can help. Can't you aim a few darts back? Either that or simply ignore it? What is the problem exactly? What is Dan putting about?'

He leaned against the table, looking expectant, interested enough now to forget about the work he

314

had to do. Kate stared at him. She was in the warm haven of their kitchen, Richard on the edge of impatience, tired and frayed. He was only really being dutiful, she sensed, and she could imagine how easily his hostile questions could lead to a row.

She was keenly anxious to get to bed as well. She was sleeping badly and the meeting with Ben was the next day. Kate wasn't entirely sure that it was a good idea for them to meet. She had plenty of questions, but much as she wanted to trust him and ask them, she couldn't allow herself that freedom. What pressed most on her mind was the menacing tone of the mutterings between Spencer and Carl. Those chill words, icicles in the balmy air, had threatened like a raised axe. Would Spencer have spoken to Carl in those tones if it was about a planned meeting with criminals and he was doing useful work, garnering information for MI6?

Perhaps so, if the people they were in touch with were bad enough. That was as Ben would have it. He seemed convinced his backer was basically sound, but hadn't one or two people feeding titbits to MI5 or MI6 turned out rotten in the past? Kate's distaste for Spencer Morgan had grown steadily since being home. Carrying Ben's secret alone, being unable to breathe a word of it to Richard, was the hardest thing she'd ever had to do, heartbreaking. She sighed. There was little she could ask Ben when they met the next day. She wondered if he'd even remember the plan and the thought he mightn't put her in deeper despair.

'What was that sigh about?' Richard said, looking suspicious. ' Why are you hesitating, Katie? What *has* Dan been saying? I do want to know.'

'It's very long-winded to explain. I'll only hold

315

you up.'

'No, you won't. Go on then.'

She took a breath. 'It's all to do with my *Karess* client, Jack Clark—he's the nitpicky one out in Slough. You may not remember, but I told you once how kind and sensitive he'd been over Dad and that he'd asked me to spend a day with his family one Sunday.

'I'd taken Jack to lunch,' Kate continued. 'He was up in London for a meeting at the agency, to see some *Karess* animatics. He'd chosen to go to a restaurant near Victoria—which Dan had seemed to think meant Jack had afternoon plans over there, and was all about shagging some bird. I like Jack and didn't believe a word of it.'

'Where's this going, exactly?' Richard asked, with a set expression.

'Well, Dan's only managed to convince the entire office, top honchos down, that I'm the one Jack's shagging. It's so stupidly monstrous, it defies belief! But I get odd looks, lowered eyes on the stairs, arsehole males in the agency, Dan equivalents, touching their noses knowingly and pinging over email trash. It's incredible how he's made it stick.'

Kate knew she was swimming beyond the red flag, but she had to carry on. 'People I counted as friends have turned out lower than worms, gossiping, bitching, however well they know me. And I can just imagine the kind of thing being said behind my back. "Who'd have thought it?" "What a slag!" "It's always the quiet ones." It might surprise you, given your attitude to the ad world, but no one has sex with the client, it's a big sin in the advertising book. Dan knows exactly where to aim his lies.'

Richard's face was cloudy. 'He can't spread stuff like that around on nothing. He must have some basis, some germ to build on. I remember all about that lunch, as it happens. You'd said Jack was best handled alone—that you knew his foibles. Isn't it unusual, though, not to have backup, lunching a client? Did you add on time, go shopping or something? Have you had another long lunch with Jack that you haven't happened to mention— without a junior like that time? Been out to see him in Slough recently—without backup?'

'God, this is too much!' Kate exploded. 'Of course I see Jack. He's my principal client; fussy, neurotic, but a thoroughly decent man, I'm quite sure of that. I email him, text, talk on the phone, slog out to meetings in Slough on occasion, and have a canteen lunch. You think that means I'm bonking in a bedsit with him or shagging in a store-cupboard full of bottles of *Karess* shampoo?'

Richard looked slightly taken aback, obviously not expecting quite such an onslaught. 'Does the office know about me in your life?' he asked. 'Maybe you're acting a little differently these days—or so I'd like to think! And you look,' he smoothed back her hair with both of his hands, 'furious and beautiful! Your eyes are more green than gold tonight,' he said, kissing the lids in turn. 'What do you think, though? This stuff would stick if they didn't know about me, wouldn't you say?'

'Of course they do, stupid! From the very first day—the time you came to pick me up to go to Basingstoke. When I asked for a week's holiday, using the line about an invitation from one of Mum's friends, the woman in HR said whatever made her think *you* might be coming along! That's half the problem, I expect, they're all jealous!'

'I'm sure they're not, but Dan must have a strong case then, if they can genuinely believe it's Jack. It does make it easier to explain their attitude.'

Kate hadn't seen that coming; she felt in despair. 'Are you acting for the bloody prosecution or something? Are you seriously implying I spend my busy, fraught agency days taking off afternoons, being shagged by Jack Clark? That's what it sounds like. Don't you know me at all? What's the point of anything if you can't trust me?' She fought against tears.

'It's more your job I don't trust,' Richard muttered. Then he glared. 'I know what goes on, all the dirty tricks and doing down, the office shags, the whole amoral shit-bag. Dan's your stereoype ad man—a prick. And you were going to go out with him—and after we'd slept together. That really got to my gut, if you want to know. Still does.'

'You've made that clear enough,' Kate shot back, 'a real meal of it. You know I'd agreed to go to the opera before you came anywhere near me. It was a big deal to him and you could try and remember that I stood him up. The moment I knew you minded I didn't go. It's exactly the reason I'm having all this agro.'

'You only didn't go because I was back from the jungle a day early. You would have, with me out of the way.'

Kate ached with frustration and exhaustion. He didn't believe it, he was just picking a fight. No question that he'd never forgiven her over the opera, but how could he even pretend to think she could be having an affair with Jack Clark? He knew she loved him, whatever the problems, for all his

318

marital baggage.

'I thought I had to honour the date.' She was sobbing now. 'Dan never once pressed me all the time I was mourning Harry. I was only trying to be kind, not wanting him to turn nasty.'

'So even knowing what sort of a man he was, you weren't put off?'

'God, Richard! How can you be this distrustful and petty? You knew the scene, the whole goddamn business with the opera. It was pathetic of me, I know, and now I'm paying the price. Go on, be smug and nasty if you like. Silly of me to want to lean on you and expect a little sympathy and support.'

They made up. While not quite bringing himself to apologise, Richard said what she wanted to hear; she was his all, he couldn't bear to think of Dan coming anywhere near her, even being in the same building, let alone working closely with her every day.

His mobile rang as they were kissing and the force in him drained. His body went as limp as a cardboard cut-out left out in the rain. He separated slowly and answered the call with a bleak shrug of resignation. He seemed to lose height and look older, defeated, wearied by the anticipation of bad news.

Kate had felt the vibrations of his mobile as shudders of her own. She needed no telling, had instantly, instinctively, known it must be about Eleanor, and from Richard's reaction he'd obviously assumed the same. She hadn't, until that moment, been as conscious of how much he lived on his nerves. Now she saw it absolutely, the constant concern, the dread he must feel with every

319

call, fears of the degree and seriousness of the drama that was going to hit him and drag him to his other home.

Kate had to accept that Eleanor's actions were beyond her control, but she found it hard to suppress a sneaking feeling that the woman did seem to know exactly how to hijack Richard's freedom and keep him tightly reined. There was no denying the grimness of the illness, but why, she thought bitterly, just once, couldn't his wretched ex-wife find the strength of willpower and manage to leave him alone?

It wasn't Ed calling. It was a female voice. Kate listened without being able to hear much as Richard gave brief, mainly monosyllabic answers with the sort of unanimated neutrality of a football captain being interviewed after losing a game. She felt as separate as a stranger, on the outside of his life all over again.

'Yes, I understand,' Richard said, with polite formality. 'I'll come, see what I can do. Be with you in about twenty minutes.' He clicked off and stood motionless, looking down at his boots, distracted and drained. When he lifted up his head and met her eyes, the lines bracketing his mouth were deeper folds.

'That was the doctor—the psychiatrist. She's a good woman. She says Eleanor's been brandishing a knife and threatening to do herself in. The doctor can pump in the Lithium, Depakote or whatever, but she feels a little calming, steadying talk from me would be positive backup. She thinks I understand Eleanor, you see, that I know the triggers and how best to counter them. The trouble is, I probably am the one best placed to deal with this sort of

320

situation, and there's not much I can do except go.' He had a look of helpless apology.

'It's very late. Will you stay the night?'

'No, I'll be back; probably be almost morning at this rate, but my filming is in the afternoon, so it could be worse.' His eyes were soft as he slung on a jacket and pocketed his keys. 'Take a sleeping pill,' he said, kissing her lightly. 'You should, with the strain you're under, you need to sleep.' He kissed her again with a fierce urgency. 'I love you, Katie. Don't give up on me. Love me, too.'

Halfway out of the door he turned. 'And don't,' he said, with one of his more annoying grins on his face, 'let that bugger Dan get you down.'

Kate switched on the outside light and left one on in the hall. Her legs felt heavy, going upstairs; she felt weighted with emotion. Would Richard go on loving and staying loyal? What about the frumpy days, other temptations, scrappy moods like tonight? Did his feelings have a strong enough tap root to withstand the lures and storms?

She rejected the idea of a sleeping pill and lay in bed ticking off items on her lowness list and thinking about her mother. Richard was filming late the following Monday, interviewing a full-on crack-heroin addict who was struggling to stick at it in rehab. He had to time interviews around people's ability or inclination to fit him in and Kate planned to spend the evening with Rachel.

They'd had a couple of lunches in Soho bistros safe from any chance of bugged flats, but what she needed most of all and hadn't yet had the time, guts or even a suitable place for, was a seriously long heart-to-heart. Kate wanted to reach in deep and tell her mother everything: nuts, bolts, love of

321

Richard, dreams, whimsy, tell it all. And confess that she might be pregnant. She hadn't had a period for a while. But didn't contraceptive pills muck up the cycle a bit? It was only five or six weeks, nothing to get excited about. Her silly need not to tempt providence made her loath to take a test; she'd rather hang on, living on her nerves, than face the let-down—if it was to be one—right away.

Rachel wanted to open up as well, Kate felt sure. They both believed the risk was real, that there was every chance of the days and months they had together being finite—and the time for explaining was now. Rachel had admitted she hadn't been honest about the divorce and Kate longed to know the whole story. She felt it would seal the bonds of closeness between herself and her mother. Something more than Ivana had pulled her parents apart. If her father had died and her mother was lost to her, a complete understanding would, she believed, help with bearing the pain.

*　　　*　　　*

She worked hard all morning. Dan avoided looking at her directly except when he seemed to think she wasn't aware of it. She was conscious of him at all times, unavoidably aware of the heaviness of his mood. They discussed the various issues and challenges of the day with an ice-thin veneer of civility. It creaked dangerously in Kate's case. She felt anything she did or said could finally crack the surface, yet she didn't trust herself not to burst out into bitter protestations of her innocence.

She praised the progress of the *Sleepyhead* commercials that they'd worked on together and

322

she'd had her doubts about; they were genuinely looking good. The *Maximan Briefs* campaign, however, was entirely Dan's baby and proving a dismal failure. Sales were sluggish. Kate had criticized that vociferously, which he would certainly remember, and she tried not to appear to enjoy his discomfort. She had her own test to face. The *Karess* shampoo ads were about to roll and their success or otherwise could rescue or sink her career.

She and Dan came out of a meeting where the campaign's imminent launch had been discussed. 'Well, Kate,' he said, within everyone's hearing, 'amazing what little client agro we had with *Karess* in the end—you certainly know how to handle Jack Clark.'

'He's my client, Dan, I should do,' she replied coolly, masking her fury. 'I'll send him a list of the spot times and the various channels.' She was determined not to rise, but to keep the whole rotten show on the road and everything as normal as possible. 'Then I might pop out for a late lunch,' she added. 'Back about three.'

'No Eve of Launch-Day drinks with the client then?' Dan sneered, making sure his voice carried and anyone around could hear. Kate stared at him so hard and accusingly that he had to turn away. 'Don't be late for the three o'clock meeting,' he muttered, and swung off in the direction of his zone.

She breathed out slowly, starting to wind herself up about the meeting with Ben. Would it be easy to happen on each other 'accidentally' in Charlotte Street exactly as planned? Would he remember to turn up? He hadn't called, her mother hadn't mentioned it. Did she know? Kate thought she probably didn't.

She grabbed her coat and took the stairs, passing a colleague of hers, Mary, on the way. Mary was newly married, less obsessed with seamy office gossip than most, and she actually gave Kate a big smile. Kate seized the opportunity to have a word.

'Hi, Mary, can you spare a minute? All this stuff about me that's doing the rounds. I'm completely in the dark over it and feel really upset; it's a total fabrication, all lies. Can you bear to have a drink or coffee sometime, perhaps try and help me unravel what's going on? I'd be fantastically grateful.'

'Sure,' Mary said, slightly dubiously, looking cornered. 'You really don't get it then, what Dan's about?' Kate shook her head, feeling hopeful. That sounded like a straw, at least, to clutch. 'I don't know when, though, I'm on a shoot all tomorrow and dashing off on holiday almost straight from it.' Mary smiled again, forlornly, as if in apology for chickening out. 'We're skiing, although this late there's sure to be no snow!' She seemed to brighten then, whether from thoughts of the holiday or taking sudden pity, it was hard to tell. 'But I'm back a week Monday,' she said. 'Let's make a date for lunch then.'

Kate thanked her profusely and went on downstairs. She despaired at having to wait ten days. Once out of the building she walked swiftly, blinking in the intense sunlight and feeling more positive. The wind had dropped and the sun felt as warm and concentrated as if the rays were pouring through a window. It was early March. The daffodils in her father's garden, delicate old varieties remembered and loved from childhood,

324

would be just coming into flower, swathes of them in the lawn all round the ash tree. The bulbs she and Richard had planted so late in his garden were shooting up, too.

She was seeing her father at the weekend and Richard was coming with her. She worried about the strain on Aidan if they stayed too long. Richard hadn't yet met Donna either; it seemed an ideal time to call in. Romney Marsh was no distance from Rye and she needed a shot of her friend who saw the bigger picture—she painted it. It mattered to Kate that two people she loved should meet and get on.

Rounding a corner into Charlotte Street, still thinking about Donna, she jumped when Ben called out, 'Hey, Katie,' from the other side of the street. He came across to join her, nimbly dodging a car, and she felt sure it couldn't have looked like a planned meeting, which he seemed concerned that it shouldn't do. 'This is a surprise,' he said, looking delighted. 'I'd forgotten you work round here. Have you time for coffee? The man I had lunch with was in a rush and I do need some!'

'Me, too—but I'm tight on time,' Kate said, glancing at her watch. 'I've only got half an hour.' She smiled. 'I haven't even had lunch, actually. What about Salt Yard? It's just round the corner and I could have a pudding or something.' It was where she'd had supper with Richard and Ed and she was always in need of connection. 'They've one or two tables outside too, with this lovely sun . . .' Stupid, saying that: how could they have a private conversation? She looked wryly at Ben, trying to convey that thought.

'It's a bit noisy outdoors,' he said with a smile,

'with all the traffic.'

The only free table inside was conveniently right at the back of the bar. Kate ordered peach cake with crème fraiche ice cream and Ben kept her company with pannacotta and roast figs. 'You're a bad influence,' he said. 'Don't tell your mother!'

The coffee came instantly. Kate took a fortifying sip and stared at Ben. She longed to talk openly. She felt herself back in the silky Caribbean sea again, sheltering in the shadow of the Black Diamond's elegant hull, and felt a shaft of naked fear. 'Remember I mentioned swimming round the yacht,' she murmured, 'and overhearing a private chat?'

Ben nodded. 'Sure. Have you thought of other things that were said?'

'They were talking about "checking out" Richard. Not naming him, but I was in no doubt. I began to think of bugged cabins, Ben! I really don't trust Spencer—I didn't from that moment on. I'd felt a sense of almost physical menace; their words carried very clearly.' Kate didn't know why she'd told him. Ben just had that effect. Was she risking speeding him into a decision to make a quick exit, taking Rachel with him? Kate ached for a clue, something, anything, to make Ben show his hand—for better or worse.

'I wish I could tell you more, Katie. But I should point out that nothing you've heard was in fact especially incriminating. The very rich do "check people out". What you heard was a raw, unpleasant confirmation of the greyer, murkier side of Spencer's life, dealings that give him access to information of possible use to MI6.'

That had got her nowhere. It was twenty-five to

326

three, Kate had little time, but the nattering girls at the next-door table had left and the puddings were on their way.

'Do you like Spencer?' she asked, feeling a sudden intensity of frustration, the moment the waiter had left.

Her question seemed to catch Ben unawares; he hadn't a ready answer. 'You'd better eat this in a hurry,' he said, his smile an acknowledgement that the food was a timely interruption. 'That's a difficult question,' he carried on. 'I suppose the honest answer is that I'm used to him. I've known him a very long time—ever since I was a young man, out in Colombia. I was grateful too, as you know, for his idea. I would never, for instance, have thought of maximising my South American experiences to build up a business. Spencer put money up too, of course, and had faith in me. But really like him? I can't honestly say I positively do!'

Kate was glad. Ben's cautious answer had sounded truthful. It still troubled her, though, the amount of time that he and her mother spent with Spencer, however popular he was, and full of largesse. Women who went in for dinner parties fell over themselves to invite Spencer Morgan. He sent them fabulous flowers, made eye-watering donations to their pet charities, to go by a profile article Kate had read. Having seen it in action on the yacht, she resented his short-lived attention span, yet he helped people in trouble, dreamed up ingenious solutions to their problems, gave generous loans that went unheralded—according to quotes in the press.

'You need to go in a minute,' Ben said, cutting into her thoughts, 'but you must eat, you'll waste away. Have you got a problem at work, Katie? I sensed your anxiety when you talked about having to be back on time.'

His astuteness surprised her. 'Yes, and it's a lousy one,' she said, wishing she could stay longer and ask his advice. 'There's someone I work with who seems really out to do me down. I'll tell Mum about it on Monday then perhaps you'd give me a view as well.' Suppressing a sigh Kate took two mouthfuls of cake and looked at her watch. She had a question she wanted to ask.

'One last thing,' she said, with slight embarrassment. 'Richard wondered about the name of your company and I didn't like to bring it up with Mum. He's still poring over Spencer's impenetrable thicket of businesses and thinks knowing how Spencer's shareholding is registered in your company might be a lead into discovering his involvement in others. It's impossible to know what he owns and what he doesn't, apparently, among all the big and little fishes and sharks in Spencer's net. Talk about opaque, Richard says. He's very frustrated.'

'He does seem to have his blood up,' Ben said. 'It would certainly be an achievement to nab Spencer. Endless ferreting financial sleuths must have been over his books for years. We're called "Ocean Shipping Company" rather unimaginatively— although Spencer's shareholding is only registered as Lloyds Bank Nominees.'

'Oh,' Kate said. 'Pity, that won't please Richard, I'm sure.' She stood up to go. 'Must run, I'm very late.' Ben came too, catching the barman's eye and handing over the bill and a couple of twenties on the way.

Out in the street he seemed to want a last few words. 'I'm glad you're having the evening with your mother on Monday; it means a lot to her, the chance of a proper chat. I know you want her to tell you about the past,' he said, his face anxious, which was unexpected. 'It's been difficult for her to be honest about it before.' Ben hesitated, looking awkward, searching for the right words. 'But now, I think, she really does want to try and explain.'

He would feel uncomfortable, Kate thought, talking about Rachel's marital problems, but why should he be anyway, when it was all long before his time?

'I know it's asking a lot,' Ben continued, 'and on top of everything else, but I hope you'll try to make allowances and understand.'

'Of course I will, no question,' she assured him, feeling bemused. The beseeching look in his eyes, his careful, diffident words . . . she longed to know what was going on in his head. 'And now I really have to race!'

She was three minutes late for the meeting. Dan wore a pinched, pained expression, but she had no interest in that, couldn't have cared less. Her thoughts were entirely with Ben. He had spoken with heartfelt pleading. It was mystifying; she could never have imagined him showing such emotional vulnerability. It wiped out thoughts of Spencer, and of Dan too, sitting opposite, carefully avoiding her eyes. Suddenly it was all about Ben and everything else was pushed to the back of her overloaded mind.

CHAPTER 21

Kate had all evening to think about her mother and Ben. Richard had called to say he'd be late, they'd just finished filming and he was going to a pub with the crew. He'd been in the East End, in a charity's offices, sitting in on a moving session between a young girl on heroin and her counsellor. She was wretchedly thin, he said, all bone and needle scars. She'd had her back to camera, anonymity preserved, and her long fair hair had been in such a lank, greasy, filthy condition that it had hung down in strips like a plastic partitioning curtain.

His emotional feelings about the girl had made Kate think of Polly. She hoped Richard was right to believe his daughter wasn't into serious drugs. Polly could be mixed up with people who were, though, being used by dealers; she certainly had a problem. Richard's car was drawing up. Kate knew the sound of the engine intimately and she stood up from her chair, heart thudding; with the thought of seeing him a tight knot of anticipation formed in her gut every time.

He came in bringing in a gust of chilly air and quickly closed the door. The evenings still had a wintry bite. He looked shattered, which wasn't surprising; he'd hardly returned from Barnes that early morning before Kate had had to be up and off to work. They'd had a sleepy coming together, which had left her with time only for anticipating the alarm; she'd wanted to pounce on it and stop him from waking. She'd succeeded with the alarm, but he'd still struggled out of bed to say goodbye.

His face was cold from the outside evening air and Kate cupped it in her hands, feeling motherly. 'You need an early night! Coffee? More whisky?' He smiled. He'd had one or two already, she could smell it on his breath, along with the faint reek of a beery fug from the pub that clung to his hair and clothes. He did look exhausted.

The phone rang and answering it, easing out of his leather jacket, one arm at a time, he mouthed it was Polly. 'That's fine, Poll, we're here tomorrow night; out for dinner, but be great to see you either end. We're in Rye most of the weekend. Any parties, any plans?' He listened, frowning. 'Okay, fair enough. See you, then.

'She wants to stay tomorrow night,' he said, returning the phone. 'Not for a party, just a change of scene, I think. I wish she'd sounded a bit more cheerful.'

'Yes,' Kate said, wishing it too. 'Pity we're out tonight really, she might have hoped for a chance to talk to you. I'll try and make myself scarce later.'

They were seeing friends of Richard's, old mates from his undergraduate days at the LSE: Rod Lewis who was the founder of a punchy think tank and his economist wife, Sophie. They saw more of Richard's friends than hers, but that was the way it went. Kate's friends were much younger, too— apart from Donna.

He touched her cheek. 'You're very good about Polly. And I like this idea of an early night. But I had better catch the news, haven't heard it all day. Come and watch it with me on the sofa.'

She lifted his feet up onto the coffee table and sat beside him, festering slightly, wondering about Eleanor and the awful drama with the knife.

Richard had called, but on a busy day, said no more than that the panic was over—'That particular one at least!' Richard never elaborated, Kate always had to ask after her, and she minded his inwardness.

'How bad was it last night?' she asked now. 'You managed to calm Eleanor all right?'

Kate saw the immense strain and weariness in his face, how drained he was, and she felt powerless—ineffectual and inhibited. 'Talk to me,' she said. 'Can't you share the load?'

Richard sighed. 'I hate to involve you, it's so debilitating. Anyway, I did what I could. I praised her work. She needs that. I said her violin playing was up with the gods. She's in a bad way, though, in a heavy phase. It'll pass, she'll change, it goes like that.' He gave a little shake of the head and touched Kate's lips. 'Did you have a better day? How was your friend Dan?'

'He's hell on a stick, but I'm trying to let it wash over.' She wasn't inclined to open up; if Richard needed closure on Eleanor she wanted it with Dan as well. 'Oh, I bumped into Ben in Charlotte Street,' she said carefully, 'which was a bit of luck. We had a quick coffee and I was able to find out the name of his company. But he said Spencer's shareholding is simply registered as "Lloyds Bank Nominees".'

'Fuck. I suppose that was blatantly obvious. He hardly offers clarity on a plate.'

'You'll get there.' Kate turned and smiled encouragingly. 'Somebody has to nail him after all, and I know in my bones your instincts about Spencer are right.'

She had a sudden, adrenaline-fuelled, burning

need for Richard to deliver Spencer Morgan, and clarity, on a plate. She had to know if Morgan was guilty of deeds that matched the menace she'd heard in his voice. He seemed inextricably linked to Ben, though, and just suppose—which was her worst nightmare—that either or both of them was behind the scam? Did she really want Richard to get anywhere? Ben had warned that snooping could lead to waking up one day and finding her mother gone.

And if Spencer had a black side, as she now believed, Ben seemed many-faceted. He confused her at every turn; strong, worldly, authoritative, on the outside, but always playing things close—and now she'd had a perplexing glimpse of emotional vulnerability. It was as if he wore protective gear like bulletproof vests, beekeepers' hoods, and hadn't had them on that day. Ben was a mystery and he was her mother's lover.

Kate stared at the television. Richard had switched over to *Newsnight* whose latest report on global warming, she noticed, was sending him to sleep.

He opened his eyes and looked sheepish. 'Just dozing. Don't write me off as an old man.'

'I'd love you even if you snored like thunder, well, probably! But if you're awake and alert, I've just had a thought about Spencer.' It had slipped into her head almost as she spoke and was bringing a rush. 'You'll shout this down, it's hardly worth telling.'

'Anything is. Try me.'

'Since "Lloyds Bank Nominees" is such a nice neutral undiscoverable way of registering shareholdings, wouldn't Spencer—if he's as

333

obsessed as you say he is with being opaque—use it everywhere? Certainly with all the companies where he wants no visible connection. I mean, might he never bother to try and vary it?'

'Sure, very likely,' Richard said, 'but with the greatest respect, I don't quite see where that gets us. It's used by everyone in the business world after all, that's the whole point; it's such a convenient smokescreen.'

'But you're as convinced as can be about what he's up to: Ponzi schemes, fictional trades, fiddles in the hospitality business, all his hotels and stuff. You have your hunches about the companies he chooses to keep dark, so if you found mammoth shareholdings in all those, all consistently listed as "Lloyds Bank Nominees", mightn't that establish a pattern? I mean, couldn't it be a way of proving that Spencer was involved?'

'Sorry, love, nice idea. It might bring some slight private satisfaction, but it would prove nothing at all, certainly nothing that would stand up.'

'Let me try this on you then,' Kate persisted, her mind already jumping ahead to an obscure acai processing plant in Santana, Brazil. 'Suppose you take a bunch of companies in say, South America, since we know Spencer has interests out there, and just concentrated on those for starters: businesses dealing in rainforest products, overseeing nightclubs and casinos, off-shore banks, investment funds. He's into small investors and charities, you said, mass-market investment. Couldn't his Ponzi scheme perhaps operate, not from some hideout upper-floor London office, but well away from prying, post credit-crunch snoopers, maybe even in a country in South America?'

Richard eyed her. 'Okay, so suppose I actually establish this pattern—what then?'

'You choose a very remote little financial outfit, call up on some pretext like the ace investigative journalist you are, and take a punt.'

'You want me to chat about Spencer as though he's a bosom mate, my cousin or whatever and talk openly and knowingly—in my best Spanish or Portuguese—as if he's their boss? If he's not they'd tell me so, but if he is it might be a start?'

'Exactly!' Richard still looked dubious. 'Isn't that what you're all about,' she urged, feeling a spark, 'professionally speaking—pulling the wool over unsuspecting eyes?'

'I'm not sure I like your tone there, madam. Okay, you're on. Let's see what I can come up with, even though I do have enormous doubts we'll even make first base.'

Kate suddenly lost all her excitement and buzz. She couldn't share the complicated thoughts in her head, she was sworn to secrecy; she had a hidden agenda. Any modest success of Richard's, nailing Spencer over shady business dealings, wasn't going to help unravel criminal goings-on in Ben's company. How could it prove any links? She vaguely remembered Ben talking about early investors in rainforest products being onto a good thing. Spencer invested all over the world; he could easily be a shareholder in a consortium that included Acai of Amapá Export, Ben's packaging company, without even knowing it. He wouldn't know half the myriad off-shoot businesses in his vast empire. It proved nothing.

What about Carl? He might deal more directly with the nitty-gritty of any dirty dealing. But that

335

was an extreme long-shot and needn't in fact nail his boss; the whole idea was fizzling out like a wet firework. Kate felt defeated and struggled to hide it.

* * *

She struggled through Friday as well. She was late leaving work and finally, turning into Thornby Terrace next evening, she remembered that Polly was around. Madge and Justin, the friendly guys upstairs, were taking out their rubbish and their white cat, whose activity in the garden Kate could do without, was patrolling the low wall that fronted onto the pavement. She gave it a few dutiful strokes and the cat purred and arched her back in pleasure. 'Delilah won't let you go now,' Madge said. 'She's a sucker for loving.'

'Aren't we all?' Kate said, which caused a roll of the eyes between the two young men and neighbourly harmony all round.

She slotted in her key and went indoors, wishing Richard was home; she didn't feel up to any spiked mortars being lobbed at her by his recalcitrant, bloody-minded daughter.

'You're first back,' Polly called out lazily from her seat at the kitchen table as Kate hung up her coat and shook out her hair. 'Do you ever wonder what Dad's doing?'

'I know, pretty much,' she answered, coming to the table and dumping her work bag onto a chair. 'How are you, Polly? It's good to see you.'

'Is it?' She certainly knew how to stare. Her eyes in that chalk-pale face were puffy and raw from crying, though, and she looked lonely and desolate as well as defiant.

'Yes, it is, actually. I'm glad you could come.' Kate contained her urge to ask what was making the girl so desperately unhappy; it would only be met with a brick wall. Polly had to make the first move. She wore a baggy black sweater and jeans; her school had a policy of no uniform, it believed in encouraging individuality. She had a mug of tea in front of her and her laptop out on the table. Kate asked equably, 'Have you been here long? Have you come straight from school? And how is your mother?' she added cautiously. 'Is she better now?'

Kate knew it wasn't a cool thing to say and would probably lead to a barrage. Eleanor was so much on her mind, though, and she often wondered about Polly's relationship with her.

'No, she's fat,' Polly answered crisply, taking Kate by surprise. 'She's gone huge, never stops eating—and no prizes for guessing why she's on a downer . . .' Her eyes accused, but the look in them lacked any real triumph.

Kate understood more what Richard had meant by 'in a heavy phase'. She met his daughter's belligerent eyes, briefly lost for words, relieved, if ashamed of it, to think of Eleanor blown-up and unappealing. It was pathetic, his ex-wife probably looked curvily magnificent.

'You can't have liked Dad being with her all the other night,' Polly sneered, 'home where he belongs. He really does love her underneath, whatever he says to you.'

That was too close, cruel. Kate tried not to let it show. 'Of course he cares about her, he wants her to be well. But he is divorced from her, Polly. And while your mother has sick phases, she's there for you, always ready to share problems and be close, I'm sure.'

'It's not like that,' Polly mumbled, pushing furiously at a cuticle with her head bent low. She looked up. 'It was better with Dad there, more of a home. He, he stopped me doing things . . .' There was a tiny silence. 'Oh, fuck it, what do you care?' She turned her head, avoiding Kate's eyes, and pushed her chair free of the table, scrambling up from it and running upstairs.

Polly would rather choke on the words than appeal for help, but she had been trying to communicate, allowing a chink in her armour. It was tiny progress, the first steps of a marathon, something to go on. And just for once she hadn't remembered to say, with lip-smacking satisfaction, that Kate was sure to go the way of the others, the blondes and the redheads, and never last.

*   *   *

On Saturday morning Richard went to pick up his Mercedes. He'd taken it in for a service the day before and been too late to collect it on the way home. Kate put a few things together for Rye, keen to be off as soon as he was back. She'd felt slightly nauseous at breakfast and was glad Polly was sleeping in. The sensation hadn't lasted and Kate was suppressing any hopes, but coping with Polly would have been draining.

She wished Richard would make time for his daughter. She'd suggested he didn't come to Rye, but he'd brushed that idea aside. He seemed almost to avoid being alone with Polly, disheartened by her attitude and defeatist about talking to her. Perhaps

338

he would on Sunday night; he was planning to go to Barnes and catch up with his children then. Kate didn't hold out much hope. It was often the way with close family, she thought, failing to reach in for fear of rebuff.

The doorbell rang and she tensed, stomach tightening; it was inevitable, she could never forget the policeman on her doorstep, calling with his terrible news.

She opened the door to an unsmiling woman holding a sports bag; Kate thought she must have come to sell something.

'I've brought Polly some clothes,' the woman said. 'She came straight from school and can't have any.'

'Oh, I see. It's Eleanor, isn't it?' Kate smiled brightly, feeling concave inside. 'Come on in—will you have some coffee? I'll call up to Polly. She's still asleep. Richard's gone for his car, I'm afraid. It was having a service,' Kate tailed off, well aware she was gabbling. Eleanor was giving nothing, no hint of a reaction; her expression was blank. They stood staring at each other, Kate keeping up her smile, Eleanor coldly impassive.

She was certainly overweight, bulging over the waistband of her fawn trousers, but not obese; the pale-green sweater she was wearing was low enough to reveal fleshy, milk-white shoulders and a heavy cleavage. The most arresting, shocking thing about her was her puffy, blotchy face. Eleanor had strong, impressive features, though, that overrode the ravages: a full mouth; long, prominent nose; her eyes were sepia-coloured, her eyebrows plucked in a high arch. She was blonde, unexpectedly, her hair fluffy and out of condition. Kate was unnerved, compelled to stare; she could see past the mess Eleanor was in, see that she was a striking, complex woman.

'You must come in,' she pressed, feeling weak-kneed as she faced Eleanor's remorseless gaze. 'It's very kind to have brought Polly's clothes. Sorry Richard isn't here.'

'I knew that. I watched him go. Are you taking my daughter now, as well as my husband, I want to know? Well? Are you? Will it be my son next?' Eleanor came in through the door, with Kate backing away, and she filled the small confined space before the hall opened up into the room beyond.

Kate felt a fresh wave of nausea and put out a steadying hand to the wall. A swell of defiant anger took over then and she met the cold eyes in that alcohol-ravaged face, feeling more in control. She wasn't having it, being treated that way. Eleanor might be ill, ten years older, a bitter, unbalanced prima donna, but she had no right to come making trouble.

'He's not your husband,' she snapped. 'You're divorced—as I believe you chose to be . . .' She heard the sound of footfall and swung round to see Polly at the bottom of the stairs.

The girl pushed past her without a glance. She was barefoot, still in the man's T-shirt she slept in, looking frail and thin-legged, like a street-child off the set of *Oliver*. She went straight up to her misshapen mother and kissed her cheek. 'Barging in, making a stupid fuss, she's not *taking* me, Mum, nobody is. I don't know what you're doing,' she said soothingly, prising away the bag, dumping it and smoothing her mother's hand. 'She's not even

340

around this weekend, they're going to Rye. I just wanted a bit of peace and quiet, fuck it, and to be alone. You need to practise, Ed's a drag with his revision and that endless bloody strumming—it does my head in.'

Kate had taken a few steps backwards and was holding onto a chair. She felt overcome, dumbfounded. Polly in the role of saviour wasn't in the script.

'You go on home, Mum,' Polly was urging. 'You've had a look at her now. She's just the usual. And Grandma will flap. Lemme get my shoes on and I'll come.'

Polly squeezed her mother's arm and took off upstairs without giving Kate a passing glance. 'You go on out to the car, Mum,' she called. 'I'll only be a mo.'

Eleanor showed no sign of going anywhere and Kate found her voice again. 'How can I possibly "take" your daughter?' she protested angrily, releasing her hold on the chair. 'You can see how much your children love you, how deeply they care.' She'd just had a moving example of Polly's care herself.

No word, no reaction. Eleanor stayed firmly rooted, grossly out of condition, sullen and proud. She made a move, half turned to go, and Kate let out a slow breath—only to draw it in again when Eleanor threw back a venomous glare.

'Bitch,' she hissed, as though not wanting Polly to hear. But then she began to shout it out loud. 'Bitch. Bitch. Bitch!' she yelled, going out of the door.

She went on shouting it out in the street, laughing harshly. More like cackling, it seemed to

341

Kate, who shrank with horror to think of the neighbours, home on a Saturday, the American couple, the family with small children, who couldn't fail to hear. Madge and Justin would enjoy a scene, she suspected, clutching at any strand of comfort as well as the chair behind her again.

Polly came clumping downstairs, boots trailing laces, jeans pulled on under the T-shirt, and made for the door. 'Mum only wanted to take a look,' she tossed out, giving Kate a sharp, frosty glance. 'And now you've had one, too. Make you any happier?'

She banged the door behind her, which didn't latch, and Kate flinched, quivering with the noise, the anger she felt, the agony of it all. Did the girl have to be so hostile? But Polly had been crying, and half the night too, by the look of it. Her eyes were red and raw. Edging round to the front of the chair, never letting go her hold, Kate sank down onto it unsteadily. Her thighs and knees had set up an involuntary tremble. Would Eleanor keep coming now, finding ever more inventive means of making trouble?

It seemed like hours, but Richard was back minutes later. Kate kept her lips tightly pressed, hearing his car; she was determined not to show her misery.

He came in with Polly, who'd obviously filled him in 'You okay?' he whispered, gathering her to him, then he separated and briskly collected coats and the bag Kate had packed, as though determined to press a normality button and move on. 'Ready to roll?' he said. 'Shall we go? You'll be okay, Poll? Be sure you're home in time for supper with Mum. See you Sunday then—see you behave!'

The drive out of South London was slow. The shoppers were out on a bright Saturday morning, Lewisham was teeming. Cars were cutting in, horns hooting; youths tearing out into the street from nowhere. Richard shook his fist at them.

'I'd skip the road rage,' Kate said, 'you'll come off worst.'

She looked out of the window. Richard had assured her—just as Polly had, in her way—that Eleanor had only wanted to take a look and was unlikely to make more trouble. He seemed anxious to draw a line, which Kate knew was the only sensible thing to do. She continued to stare out. Signs of neglect were everywhere in that run-down part of London. Georgian terraces set back from the busy main road had broken windows, shops looked dingy and houses down side-streets were in a shoddy state of repair.

'Didn't you once say that Spencer started out round here?' she asked. 'Wasn't he a barman in a club off the Old Kent Road or something? Beats me how you get from that, though, to being a sought-after socialite billionaire. How do you even make the leap from employee to owner? Were banks much freer with loans in those days?'

'Not much, I'd say, not for ease of buying out the boss. I'd hazard a guess, perhaps uncharitably, that Morgan raised the money, doing a bit of dealing. Drugs are sold freely in nightclubs after all. It's a dead simple way for the dealers or a non-squeamish barman to make a fast buck. Fifty pounds a gram of cocaine, twenty pounds a couple of ecstasy tablets, ketamine at twenty pounds a gram—probably more

343

like half a gram since who's to know in a dark club—that's plenty of illegal profit.'

'I suppose it's hard to police the clubs; do they just let it go half the time?'

'Pretty much. And, of course, selling the stuff in clubs makes for an easy life with the money-laundering as well.'

'Tell me how that works?' Kate touched his still-tanned hand on the steering wheel, feeling glad of his look of connection when he glanced over. She was still shaky from the confrontation with Eleanor. 'I thought money-laundering was a tricky business.' She withdrew her hand, anxious to hold on to her cool.

'Not in nightclubs and casinos. Owners simply inflate the head count, the number of customers through the door, and they're away! I'll give you a for instance. Say, with an entry fee of twenty pounds you have two thousand people through in a week and make forty grand. All you have to do is claim that it was four thousand people, which doubles the take and you bank twice as much. That's a hefty slice of drugs takings laundered in a single week. You can do fiddles with flyers that give cheaper entries—claiming people paid full price— double up on cloakroom charges, one pound becomes two pounds, that's another few k. You count people on the guest list as having paid . . . Get the picture?'

Kate was fascinated, although nervous about Richard linking Spencer to drugs and extending the scope of his sleuthing. She lived with Ben's forcible warning about the risks to her mother . However far-fetched, Spencer could just conceivably be involved in the criminal goings-on in Ben's

344

business. He was the major backer, after all.

'To go back to Spencer,' she said lightly, 'even supposing he was able to buy out the owner of a rubbish little club, how does he scale his next heights, Snowdon if not Everest?'

'Slowly but surely, I'd think, building up a canny knowledge of the hospitality business for starters. He changed his name, you know. It was Gary Flack. I guess Spencer Morgan does set the tone more. Anyway, he carried on in nightlife, bought bigger and better clubs, branched into casinos, hotels and resorts, invested in allied businesses. Then eventually he used his wealth—considerable by that stage—to launch his first investment fund. It was for ordinary people, small investors, and I'm as certain as can be,' Richard continued, 'that Morgan's into Ponzi schemes.

'I suspect he saw the sense of going for the small guys rather than the serious investors who'd be wiser to the sort of cheating schemes likely to yield unnaturally consistent profits. The last credit crunch took its toll; the people in the know, happy as they were to take the cash beforehand, are a little more cautious these days!'

Kate was only partly listening, distracted by thoughts of Eleanor and concern about Spencer's early life. Richard's educated guess at his progression from barman to big-timer did seem to suggest an intimacy with the underworld. It sounded almost a blueprint pathway to drugs baron, but surely it would have to the authorities as well? Wouldn't anyone with Spencer's background and meteoric rise to riches have come under constant scrutiny?

'So assuming Morgan's into Ponzi schemes with

345

small investors,' she remarked, tuning back in, 'must that mean he's risking the life savings of doctors, dentists and hard-working little charities?'

'Sure does. And that's money made here at home, quite apart from the vast revenues I'm convinced he's siphoning off from his businesses in places like South America, not to mention all his other interests, resort hotels and casinos.'

'That sounds like unfettered capitalism taken to its ultimate ruthless extremes.'

Richard laughed. 'That's a bit hard on capitalism. Sounds more like hard-nosed crookery to me. Anyway, I'm convinced Morgan's involved in a shocking, stupendous fraud right across the board. I think he'd cheat at anything. I read Bernard Madoff was suspected of understating his handicap at a golf tournament once, to win a piddly little prize, and I'm sure Morgan would cheat at tiddlywinks with his grandmother.

'I've followed a paper trail, picked over all his claimed assets minutely and it's clear that they account for less than a quarter of his Group's stated wealth. I've thought of using the media, but there's not a cat's chance of getting the authorities interested in any unproven exposé. They're never going to take on a giant like Spencer Morgan's Group on allegations alone. Some hope!' Richard glanced at her with a frustrated grin. 'All his good works, the funding of academies and sports centres, that's his membership fee, an entrée into being trusted and liked. And of course he wants a gong.'

'Shouldn't he have had one by now?'

'The Government's tight about giving them out, scared of being thought in the pockets of the rich. They're wearing hair shirts, driving smaller cars, tightening up all round. Where do we turn off, Katie? We're just coming up to Ashford.'

'Next exit, fourth turning off the roundabout, and I'll tell you soon where to turn onto Romney Marsh. It's a maze of winding lanes—people often end up where they started from. It's so remote with the dykes and ditches and tall reeds. The Marsh has a kind of windswept thrill about it that I love. Donna paints it and she has some of that wildness herself.'

The wind certainly buffeted them, but the sun burned bright. Kate thought about the relationship between Polly and her mother. The roles had seemed reversed: Polly, with her sharp tongue, her sly, hurtful remarks, had been the one in charge, like a gentle, mindful nurse. Kate could see why the poor girl couldn't turn to her mother with her troubles, whatever they were. And it was clear that she herself couldn't help with them either. She felt the forces were stacked against her.

'I've been thinking about Polly,' she said, cutting into the silence, 'wondering if she could be feeling neglected. It's inevitable that you're caring and worrying more about Eleanor whenever you're home, concentrating on her exclusively. Polly might mind, however unreasonably, and imagine she's out of your thoughts. She is at an age for feeling oversensitive.' Kate gave him a quick glance. 'And then I'm a further distraction that she could definitely do without!'

Richard spun round, swerving dangerously on a bend. 'What's she been saying now? Don't *you* be oversensitive, Katie. I'm truly sorry about this morning—all I can say is that it could have been a whole lot worse! Polly resents me leaving and I've no defence to that, but for God's sake, don't start believing every little smart-Alec jibe of hers. She is a liability, that girl. I won't have her putting ideas in your head and making you upset,' he said angrily, swinging into another bend.

'Careful. Don't go into a ditch.'

'Have some faith in me. You should know how much I love you by now, it's you I care and think and worry about constantly. Sure, I agonize like hell about Eleanor, she's suicidal half the time—and just imagine having to live with the guilt if she ever copped it. She either feels like a queen or hasn't a shred of confidence; she doesn't want me around, hates me to have a life of my own. It's why . . . Oh, forget it, now's not the time. Are we nearly there?'

'Just one more bend, there, the open gate. It never is the time,' Kate muttered, more or less to herself. 'I hate unfinished sentences.'

Richard didn't respond. He was turning in, trying not to run over the squawking hens and crowding over-excited dogs. He parked without loss of life and squeezed Kate's hand. 'Have some trust,' he repeated, before his words were drowned out by the violent screeching of the peacocks. Donna was approaching the car.

She sorted out the animals and eyed Richard with interest, shaking his hand firmly as they were introduced. She was wearing a paint-encrusted man's shirt over a forest-green roll-neck and jeans tucked into stylish, if scuffed, leather boots; her thick leonine hair was escaping as ever from tortoiseshell combs. She looked terrific, Kate thought, her handsome best.

'I thought we'd have sangria and cheese straws outside in the sun. But the question is,' Donna said,

348

walking just ahead with Richard, leading him into the cool of her hall to deposit his offering of wine, 'whether you can live up to Katie's phenomenal build-up.'

'I couldn't possibly make first brick,' Richard said, 'but you've had a skyscraper build-up too! I like this idea of sangria in sunny Kent in March. Who needs Spain or the Caribbean?'

Kate caught up and gave him a punch. 'I do. Grenada did us proud. I wish you'd go out there and paint it, Donna; the long white sands and silver-flecked sea, all the shades of green and roadside hibiscus, the sun's suffusing brilliance. You'd capture the pulse of the place more than anyone.'

They had lunch. Dover sole, bought locally that morning in Dungeness, followed by apple tart, Cheddar with homemade oat and honey biscuits and quince cheese. Donna told of the Doctor Syn novels, smuggling stories based on local eighteenth-century life, and Richard had them laughing over his anecdotes, mainly at the expense of politicians, about whoopsies picked up on the grey furry sound mike, the 416, as it was affectionately known in the trade. It was the make that had been going for decades.

After lunch and with some persuading, Donna took them to her impossibly messy studio. Kate could see Richard adjusting, being lifted by the evocative canvases and lured by the remote landscape they portrayed, shutting out the world, concentrating on the paintings and the effect they had on him.

'Think of all the writers who've lived on Romney Marsh,' he said, 'from Conrad and Henry James to

349

Nöel Coward. And wasn't it Ford Madox Ford who called it The Sixth Continent?' He smiled at Donna. 'Well, this is it! You've captured the whole continent on canvas and I can understand what impelled those writers to come. How can we persuade you to part with one of your paintings? I know it'll be hard!'

'I gave Katie a painting the other day,' Donna said, raising an eyebrow in her direction. 'What did you do with it in the end? Stamp on it or give it away?'

'You really think I'd do either?' Kate muttered, embarrassed. 'It's with Dad. I was going on to Rye so I left it with him for safekeeping.'

'What's this all about?' Richard said, looking from one to the other.

'It was a painting meant for Harry,' Kate said, deciding to tell it straight. 'Donna had promised him one and she was holding out, having a bit of a tease, making him wait, so it's mine by default, you see. She gave it to me just before New Year's Eve.'

'I didn't want it hanging round, reminding me,' Donna said, 'but Katie didn't want it for the same reason so I told her to do with it whatever. Complicated, isn't it?'

Kate wished Harry hadn't had to come into the equation. She felt upset, cornered, covered in confusion.

But Donna had been Harry's friend originally, they'd been as close as paint on canvas; she'd loved him almost as a son. Was it some sort of test, Kate wondered, a way of making sure she hadn't forgotten all about him? And for all Donna's offhand chat, she cared passionately about her paintings. She would have wanted to check up on

350

this one's fate, as well as feeling that a little homage was due to Harry.

Kate couldn't help a sudden onslaught of tears, a steady rise, unpreventable and building up to a flood. Harry was suddenly, piercingly, vivid again and she covered her face. She could see him walking towards her in his old baggy cords, waving both arms across exhibition halls, leaping athletically into his little plane . . . She could see him pushing on his glasses, arguing heatedly with Donna about painters he thought of as mere colourists, sharing insights and inspiration for hours.

Poor Harry, dear forgotten Harry, the tears were streaming. Shit, shit, it was a disaster, painful in the extreme for Richard and she hadn't thought of Harry in weeks.

'It's the most powerful, beautiful painting imaginable,' she said, desperate to recover and make up ground. 'It haunts me. At least Dad has the joy of it for now.'

Richard managed the situation with sensible calm. 'It never hurts to cry,' he said. 'Memories are only dormant; they're going to break out and they should have an airing now and then, it's the debt we owe. It was bound to hit you, thinking and talking of Harry—and of your father too.'

Kate turned and buried her face in his chest. He gave her an awkward pat on the back. 'Buck up, you'll need to be tougher than this for Aidan, he won't want to see you giving into tears.'

'I know,' she said, straightening up and sniffing. 'God, I'm sorry, Donna! What a performance! I wish I was made of your mettle.' Kate felt suffused, suddenly, with an immense envy; her friend had enormous strengths, such compassion, her capacity to contain her feelings and blank out any personal pain was extraordinary.

She vividly remembered the time she had asked Donna if she'd ever been married. 'I know about loving a man,' she answered, showing a flash of such searing emotion that Kate had had to cast her eyes down. Had he been married at the time? Walked out on her? Made her abort a baby? Donna had quickly shrouded her feelings again, muttering that keeping things secret was a way of preserving her dignity.

'We really must go,' Kate said, worried she'd been stretching Richard's patience beyond its limits with her collapse. 'Dad's expecting us for tea. But thanks—and for sticking with me.'

That sounded futile, inadequate at best, but she found it hard how to transmit how much she depended on Donna for strength and support. Kate just had to hope it was self-evident.

Gazing round the cold studio she was fortified by a last look at the canvas on the easel. It showed a haze of early light over spring fields, a luminous pink glow, and with that quality of 'somewhere else', unique to Romney Marsh. Donna could see it, feel it, express it in oils. Perhaps that was the particular power of painting; its ability to speak for the heart. Kate thought that the hearts of great artists were well served; they had a medium, a voice that could communicate beautiful truths and strong emotions, a whole spectrum of feelings that normal hearts could only spill out in tears.

* * *

352

Driving to Rye, Kate wondered if perhaps Donna had been testing Richard more than her, by turning an arc light onto Harry. After hearing from Kate all about his ridiculous nonsense over Dan and Jack, Donna might have wanted to explore Richard's character and reassure herself.

Richard was sensitive about Harry and Kate's feelings for him. He imagined she saw Harry only in the unsullied light of newly married love. It was far from the truth. She remembered Ben saying on Boxing Day how guilty Harry would have felt if she hadn't found future happiness, but would he, she wondered, had he known that in Richard she'd found a greater, more consuming love, love beyond her imaginings? It was an impossible thought ever to share.

Reaching the main road, which was near deserted, they drove on in silence. It didn't seem the time to talk about Donna's generous offer, her suggestion, just as they were leaving, that Richard might like to stay with her at the time of Aidan's dying. He could be near at hand then, she said, while giving Kate space to grieve.

Kate didn't want to talk much at all. The acute ache over Harry wouldn't leave her. It coated her heart. No sin felt greater than to feel only fondness for him. It sharpened the pain of loving Richard, but where was the pain she should feel for a lost husband? His death had freed her to love with an intensity that in turn had brought a fresh concentration of guilt. But perhaps that was only just.

'Katie,' Richard said, 'tell me if you'd rather see your father alone. I want to be with you, but not to get in the way.'

'When Hannah says it's a matter of days, I think then that'll be a time to sit with him on my own. I need you now, though, desperately. And he does too. Sadie came with the children the weekend we were away. It's hard for her, though, I expect she'll only manage it one more time before the end. Dad loves your company. And Hannah was glad to hear you were coming; she wants us to help move his bed downstairs.'

They were almost there, in the lane. Richard slowed and parked on the verge, right by the Millie-inspired post box attached to the gate.

Kate felt fearful of going in. Her heart was leaden as a cannonball, her breath coming unevenly. Her father would be frighteningly hollowed and gaunt. It was worse every week. He was unable to walk unaided, in bed or in his chair all day. And now she had to face the symbolic moving of the bed. It was his wish, though. He had decided he'd rather not die in his bedroom, which—as Hannah had said with less than her usual restraint—had many memories.

The tears were too close. Kate felt as weak as a child, choking them back and saying pathetically, 'It's Dad's birthday next month. He'll be sixty-one. He's still young, it's not right, he can't die.'

'He's going to,' Richard said calmly, kissing her. 'Think practically and try to be happy and positive with him; talk about books and films, us, my mother staying at your flat, anything but his illness. Cry now and when you're ready, keep hold of my hand as we go in.'

354

CHAPTER 22

Kate had set aside Sunday night to check over her flat and see what needed to be done in advance of Richard's mother moving in. Celia had to be out of her Salisbury house at the beginning of May, which was in six weeks' time. Kate imagined being three months' pregnant by then. She was trying not to build false hopes while fighting a strong hunch about it, a feeling of quiet confidence that wouldn't go away.

She had to do a test and know for sure, childish to keep thinking it was tempting providence. Better to see off her phantom hopes, if that's what they were, and struggle through the pain of the letdown. Kate sighed, aching to be pregnant and able to give her father the news.

He would have died by the beginning of May. Kate leaned back against a worktop in the flat's narrow kitchen, feeling a wave of despair. She was alone in the silent flat; she and Richard had driven there straight from Rye. Richard had dropped her off and gone on to Barnes to see Ed and Polly. He'd rejected Kate's idea of bringing them for supper at her flat, which would have been little trouble since Hannah had given them a pannier of food, parsnip soup, winter salad leaves and an amazing chocolate torte.

'Don't make work for yourself,' Richard said. 'We'd be eating late and have to clear up before leaving; the kids have school in the morning, unfinished homework for sure.'

'Will you eat there?' Kate asked rigidly.

'Hannah's supper will keep till tomorrow.'

'Oh, I'll be back, I can't wait for the parsnip soup! It's just a chance to be with them a bit and try to keep tabs on Polly.'

Kate knew the problems, starkly enough, but she bitterly resented him being with them in Barnes. Other divorced fathers saw their children well away from the family home. Kate's fear of dramas and disruption had moved up a notch; now, like an animal anticipating intruders, she felt the threat in her bones. Eleanor had invaded her space as well as her peace of mind, stepped right inside her door. 'Bitch, bitch, bitch,' that harsh, crazed laughter; it rang on in Kate's ears. She couldn't relax for a second while Richard was in Barnes.

And, on top of the agony of her father, it made everything feel ephemeral and about to fall apart. She thought of the heartache and torment of the day in Rye, Aidan's hollowed face with its jutting cheekbones, the unnatural black brightness of his eyes in their sunken sockets. He couldn't weigh more than five stone.

They'd had a few moments alone together before having to say goodbye. Her father had seen straight though her efforts to hide her wretchedness. 'I wish you'd tell me your troubles, Katie, I hate to see you down. Don't feel you can't bother me because I'm ill. Is it something Richard can't help with? He isn't to blame, I'm sure. He loves you and that makes me happy at least.'

'It's only a boring work problem, Dad, a jealous slighted colleague. And Mum and I are having supper tomorrow, a proper old heart-to-heart; I may be a wee bit wound up about that. I think she's going to tell me what you said had to come from

356

her!'

Kate couldn't tell him her overriding fears about Ben, the drugs trafficking, that her mother was in serious trouble, and possibly about to disappear.

Aidan hadn't commented on her work problems, but the mention of a heart-to-heart with her mother had him gripping her arm with a bony strength that had surprised and unnerved her. 'What makes you so certain, suddenly, that Mum's going into our past history when she hasn't been prepared to before?'

'I just thought she might,' Kate said cautiously, 'but we'll see tomorrow tonight.'

Despite his understandable tension and scepticism, he'd seemed oddly relieved to think Rachel would—as though deep down he wanted her to bring the secrets of their relationship out into the open and say what had caused the rift. Kate imagined that to shine a light into the dark corners of the past would be cathartic and help him to find emotional peace.

She set about the dull job of sorting bed-linen, boxing up letters and mementoes, still thinking about it. She'd been pressurizing her mother to tell her side of the story, but she wondered now whether Rachel's keenness to tie up emotional ends and put her house in order was more to do with the trafficking and Ben. Did that explain Ben's anxiety when they'd contrived to meet and have coffee? Kate had thought then that he'd simply been feeling for Rachel and pressing her case in advance. Were the authorities, MI6 or whatever, closing in on their man now, though? Kate shivered. That and Aidan's tense, bony grasp would keep her awake long into the night.

Hannah was on her mind, too. She had given

Kate, and Richard, plenty to think about, coming out of the house as they were leaving with a veneer of calm that had soon lost its sheen.

'Dr Jones says your father could fade any day now,' she said, speaking in the level, dispassionate tones of a nurse. Such control, she loved Aidan, had shared his home for years. 'He might linger on,' she continued, 'but probably in a semi-coma. He won't be able to communicate as he does now.'

Her cool composure was vital. Aidan had to be nursed, yet Kate felt sure it was a tiny tip, all Hannah could manage, and she was forcing back a vast iceberg of intense desolation just below the surface. 'Call me at the first sign,' Kate said. 'I'll want to come and sit with him however bad he is, whatever his condition.'

Richard had made himself scarce, put their bags in the car and started hurling sticks down the lane for Millie.

During those vital moments of privacy Kate had broached what needed to be raised. 'You and I do need to talk, Hannah. Dad asked me to help, to find you somewhere to live, somewhere quiet and out of the way, and he made clear it was to be strictly between us alone. I have had a thought about it, but you'll need to trust me completely just as you've trusted Dad. I will have to know what's going on,' she said firmly, feeling the oddness and mystery of it all acutely.

Hannah might have inclined her head, given a small nod of acquiescence, it was hard to tell. Her eyes had glazed over and her face become so white and stricken that Kate had been moved almost to tears.

'You've given Dad years of happiness,' she said,

gentling her tone, 'as well as nursing him selflessly now. I hope you know how very much we owe you.'

Hannah said nothing. Her misted, deep-brown eyes kept on gazing impenetrably at Kate. Her fears and secrets, whatever they were, seemed to give her a formidable resilience.

'Guess we'd better be off.' Richard smiled, rejoining them.

'Look after Dad,' Kate said, feeling in pieces.

Turning to glance back as they started off, she saw that Hannah hadn't moved. She was still standing rooted to the same spot, staring after the car.

'Want to know what I think?' Richard said, waiting till Kate had settled back again.

'About Hannah, you mean?' It was no surprise he should have been speculating, he was always wise to every nuance, every flicker of an eye.

'Yes. For what it's worth, since you seem to be involving yourself with Hannah and something's obviously up, I'd say that woman was on the run.'

Kate felt fresh nerves as she cleared a few more drawers, piling everything into the small second bedroom. Who or what was Hannah hiding from? She felt terrified that Richard might mention it to some newspaper journalist friend who'd see a potential story in Hannah and check it out. Surely Richard wouldn't do that? He'd know how much it would upset her.

The best thing, Kate decided, was to involve him after all, tell him what her father wanted her to do and how he'd begged her to keep it secret. Richard was picking up clues about it anyway and she longed to share one confidence with him at least, as well as her idea of a possible discreet new home for

Hannah.

She put the soup on to warm. Richard hadn't called yet to say he was leaving. Her mobile rang then and her depression flew out of the window; Richard's voice did it for her every time, he made the blood flow.

*   *   *

The next morning was a typical Monday, steady rain. With another long week of Dan to face at work the last thing Kate felt like doing was fighting her way onto a steamy tube train and struggling into work. She was on a high wire of tension about seeing her mother that evening, trying to shut her mind to the chance of her disappearance being real and imminent. God, it was going to be a long day.

They had yet to decide on a restaurant; Rachel hadn't wanted to meet in either home. Kate expected a call, but was surprised that she rang on the office line.

'Why this phone, Mum?' she asked, remembering Ben had called on it too.

'Ben says you can't trust mobiles.' Rachel laughed, which sounded like a thin attempt at lightness. 'Where's it to be, tonight?' she said. 'Somewhere quiet and unfussy. You know places, love, you choose.'

Kate rejected her regular haunts, then, seeing Dan in the distance, she remembered the restaurant in Victoria that Jack had chosen for lunch. It was close to her mother in Pimlico.

'I was at one of your locals the other day, Gran Paradiso. I took a client there.'

'That sounds fine. Will you book? Say eight

o'clock? See you, darling, I can't wait.'

Kate settled down to work. Sales of *Sleepyhead,* the bedtime drink, were soaring. The older-age traditional drinkers seemed to love the ad's soppy fantasy and a new younger group had taken to *Sleepyhead Slimma,* the calorie-light range, with a sort of retro-based zeal. And *Karess,* too, was walking off the shelves. Puce bottle or not, it was a good product and from the sales figures, every other swinging head of hair down Oxford Street owed its shine to a dose of *Karess*. Having worked on both campaigns, Kate felt due a share of the accolades, but no dice. She was below the salt at Impetus; few people wanted to be seen talking to her.

At least her one friend, Mary, was back, that was something. They were due to have lunch that Wednesday, although Kate had her doubts as to whether a newly married, little-involved colleague, just back from holiday, could really provide useful intelligence. Dan's relentless vendetta was incomprehensible. He'd had every right to feel angry, slighted, antagonistic; keeping it up was probably in his nature, but his feuding was lethal. He was doing everything possible to undermine her, making it clear he wanted her out of her job.

Kate watched time pass. She had decided to go to the restaurant straight from work since Richard wasn't at home. He had his interview with a crack-cocaine addict that evening, a guy who'd been left for dead in a doorway, but found a seed of inner strength and changed the course of his destiny. The programme needed a scene of hope as well as laying on the harm, Richard said. He'd sounded low, though, in need of some hope himself after a row about nothing with Polly the night before. She'd refused even to say goodbye to him through the bedroom door.

Richard called then, while he was in her thoughts, to wish Kate luck with her mother.

'I need unwinding,' she said.

'Difficult, down the line. Shall I nip over?'

She sat back with a silly grin, feeling loved in her loveless office. She was about to go into a meeting to discuss the next batch of *Karess* ads. Her client, Jack, was in London for it, just to add to the day's strains, and Richard's call was the lift to carry her through. Jack had wanted an afternoon meeting, which was a significant mercy since it avoided the finger-pointing minefield of having to take him out to lunch—and possibly two trips to the same restaurant in a day.

The meeting involved much crowing about the first campaign's great success, followed by typical client haggles about the next one planned. Jack's perfectly normal warmth towards her caused knowing looks to shoot round faster than greyhounds on the track, yet the hands on the clock dragged. Kate wished she could tell Jack how little he was helping her cause.

Going out through the revolving doors of the office, Kate missed a call on her mobile; whoever it was clicked off after two rings. It was a number she didn't recognize, but some telepathic sense, a whisper on the late March wind, or perhaps straight curiosity and time to spare, made her stop on the pavement and return the call.

It rang a few times. She almost clicked off when finally it was answered.

'Why bother calling back? Snooping cow, what's

it to you? Leave me alone for fuck's sake, can't you?' The sour, carping voice, easily recognisable and dripping with suspicion, put Kate instantly on high alert.

'You rang me, Polly. It can't have been for no reason, you must need to talk. I'm in the street as you can probably hear, no one about. Wait, nothing's ever easy on the phone, much better if we can fix to meet. Anywhere you say—tomorrow evening after school?' Had she kept her on the line long enough? She prayed Polly would hold onto her courage and agree.

'Is Dad there with you?'

'No. He's filming—and again tomorrow evening, somewhere near Heathrow. Suppose I come to Hammersmith, say, seven-thirty tomorrow and we find a local cafe.'

'Not anywhere near here. You can't come here.'

'What about Earl's Court then?' Polly didn't answer and, taking silence as a positive sign, Kate carried on. 'We'll settle on that then. I'll come out of the tube, the Earl's Court Road exit, and be waiting by the ticket stiles at half-past seven—that do?'

'I may not show,' Polly muttered. 'You take your chances.'

'Lay off, Polly. We've made a date. Your dad will be busy and in his car anyway. No chance you'll see him at Earl's Court.'

*   *   *

Kate sat in the restaurant waiting for her mother, watching the door and jittery. She'd requested a particular table in a back corner of the restaurant, which from memory was secluded, but it was still possible to see the door. She thought, given her mother's extreme precautions over the use of mobiles, she might want to check on any comings or goings.

The need for such care and secrecy had shaken her. She had to accept that her mother could be forced, through love of Ben, to take a false identity and disappear. Kate felt in turmoil; would she be given any warning at all? She had a sense of clinging on with her fingertips and expecting, at any moment, some advancing henchman would come and trample away her grasp.

Ben seemed determined that she shouldn't think Spencer was involved, let alone the string-puller, but why was he so convinced of it? Even assuming it was true that Spencer had been feeding titbits to MI6 for years, he could still be the brains behind the trafficking, couldn't he?

Kate tried to think about it in reverse. Eavesdropping out in the Caribbean, Spencer's words with Carl had seemed laced with naked menace, yet had she been embellishing that exchange in her mind? It had sounded threatening, but only really the bit about Richard. And to imagine that Spencer Morgan, socialite, philanthropist, was masterminding a mammoth drugs operation? Yet she still couldn't shake off her strong sense that he wasn't to be trusted. Richard certainly thought so.

But where did that leave Ben? He was generous, he lived well, always seemed to have money, only the best was good enough. Kate's instincts led her to believe he was working with MI6 and his friend, Jon. She was sure, too, that what he'd told her had been factually true and his company was being used to smuggle in cocaine. And given the strain her mother was under, he must be in some serious trouble.

Had he been sucked into something with Spencer? Richard had mentioned the chance he was being blackmailed, but it was hard to imagine Ben as a candidate for past indiscretions. Or was he an incredibly brilliant operator, biding his time, playing everyone like chess pieces, Spencer included? It had to be possible, didn't it, that the whole story, as he'd told it to her over dinner, was simply insurance in case he needed a smokescreen to buy time to get away?

Surely that couldn't be? Perhaps Richard, going down his financial avenue, would hit on a killer revelation that would nail Spencer and make everything startlingly clear. Kate thought of doing some quiet investigating of her own. If she could just link Spencer or Carl to the acai packaging plant in Santana port, Amapá . . . prove a close involvement . . . But it wouldn't prove they knew about quantities of cocaine being frozen along with the fruit puree. It wouldn't be conclusive evidence and nor would it absolve Ben. Still a telling connection, though.

*   *   *

Kate felt a flush of love and pride as her mother walked in. Heads turned, eyes glanced; Rachel was in a light-blue sweater-dress, simple and elegant with a chic silver chain necklace, yet it was her grace, her poise that attracted the looks. She was conscious of making an impact, yet somehow hung

365

onto an aura of humility as well. Her smiles for the greeting waiter were open and genuine; she had time for everyone, whoever they were.

She came straight over with more smiles. 'Hi, love! I'm not late, am I? I've been with Sadie all afternoon,' she kissed Kate, pulling out the chair beside her, 'buying Joseph's first school uniform! He starts in the summer term at that little pre-school place. We had to buy it at least two sizes too big, but he did look so cute. And you, darling, I love seeing you still with that glow of yours, you look blooming. I like the burgundy top; the black stripe makes it.'

'It's a tunic, Mum, and it has the stripe at the bottom, too. I must give Sadie a call, she's on my conscience, but I've been all over the place lately with problems at work, Dad every weekend . . .'

'She more than understands.'

'Shall we order? I'll have the herby cod; it was good and fresh last time I was here.'

Rachel chose veal; they ordered a salad between them and a glass each of Sauvignon. The restaurant was quiet, but not empty, just as it had been with Jack. Kate was reminded of Dan's unfair sneers about Jack having a woman somewhere nearby— before he'd started putting it about that that woman was her.

She began telling her mother all about it. She started with Jack, his neuroses and nitpicks, his invitation to his home in Slough, then went on to explain about Dan's obsessive campaign against her. She went into her own pickle over the invitation to the opera, Richard's extreme reaction. 'He's never going to let me forget it, Mum, never misses a chance to have a go. Men can be so . . . .

naively, obtusely idiotic!'

'You must see how hard Richard would find it to understand that you only really accepted Dan's opera date out of guilt. Have you ever thought about a change of job, darling? You work long hours, give it your all, but is it really worth it? What about a completely new direction, some public-interest job? You're clever, you'd be good at researching policy, perhaps working in a think tank, a future-forecasting company, somewhere with more hospitable hours.'

'I'm single, Mum, I need a full-time job—if only I can hold onto it. And I love the thrust and buzz of advertising, that's why this Dan business is so cruel. What do I do about him?'

'See what this girl, Mary, says, but my advice is, prepare to be the loser in this battle. Don't demean yourself. Change jobs, call it a day. Dan clearly doesn't want you around. He sounds an unhappy man.'

Kate had expected to be told to take her complaints to the CEO, to fight, take action; her mother's words were unexpected and unappealing.

She sneaked a sideways look. Rachel was toying with a salad spinach leaf and it seemed the moment to ask what she most feared and needed to know.

'Mum, is it about to happen? Can you say anything at all?'

Rachel laughed lightly. It took Kate a second or two to realize that it was a form of cover, even though no one was near enough to hear them. Her mother kept up a broad smile and leaned to whisper confidentially in her ear, 'I don't trust that couple over by the window. Act like I'm having a bitch.'

Kate managed a wide-eyed 'you don't say!' sort of look. 'Go on,' she said out loud, 'tell me more!'

Rachel leaned close again and murmured in a gossipy way, 'Don't ask a thing, love, and don't, whatever else, involve yourself. Stay in one piece for all our sakes. Sadie will need you. And since Ben's only told you, you'd have to be the one to tell her if I'm "away". Chat some more now, can you? Let's keep this up.'

'She had it coming, that woman,' Kate remarked, with a complaisant pressed-lip grimace, noticing a thin, bald man wander past their table and peer in through the service door. 'Such a cow!' she added, as he passed them again and returned to his seat at the window table. Her heart was beating fast. Did Rachel think she was being followed? Had that couple been here earlier? Kate racked her brains, she couldn't remember.

'Mum,' she said, thinking it was time to ask, 'you are going to explain why you left Dad? He told me about Ivana; was it all just too much for you to bear?'

'No, Katie, that was more of a consequence than a cause. I was entirely to blame.'

'But he was the one who strayed . . .'

'Loving less can be worse and cause even greater pain.'

'I don't understand. Dad told me that woman had clung like a gold-digger, and he said how his one weak moment had put you under the most terrible strain. She'd followed him home to England, plagued you both. By any stretch that must have caused a crack in your relationship. But you divorced long afterwards, though, and you'd always had such laughs and seemed so close.'

'Oh, we were, we adored each other, but for my part it became a sham.'

'Why?' Kate entirely forgot about the couple at the table in the window, the bald man and his over-made-up woman companion whose distemper-coloured foundation was laid on thick enough to grout in tiles. 'Why, Mum? Why "for your part"?'

'Dad met someone else in Bosnia as well as Ivana. He came back from his first stint out there, full of someone he'd met whom he'd really liked. He said he was an unusually impressive colonel, doing tricky intelligence work and about to return for a spell at the Ministry of Defence. Dad wanted to catch up with him again, meet his wife, for us all to have dinner in London—much as he knew I wasn't into formality and uniforms, he said.'

'And the colonel was called Ben Townsend?'

'That's right. I was happy to go along with it, quite curious since your father was a choosy picker of friends. Dad took us all to Soho House, which had just opened that year and had a good buzz, and introduced Ben to the television world. I became obsessed after meeting him and knew I should never see him again.'

'But you did?'

'We were asked to a party and Ben had been invited to it too, by someone he'd met on the evening we'd had out together. His wife hadn't come with him; he said she wasn't well when Dad asked after her. I think your father knew even then the strength of the pull between Ben and myself. We had a dance, I couldn't have refused, and Ben said as we danced, "We can't meet." He knew, I knew, the consequences if we did.'

'Go on, Mum.' Kate was seeing the jigsaw pieces

falling into the shape of her own obsessive love. 'When did you see him next?'

'He asked me to call him at work. "We can't meet, but can we talk?" he said. I put it off for weeks, Katie. When I finally did he told me about his wife's recently diagnosed tumour and that, above all else, she mustn't be hurt.'

Had Harry lived, had they still been married, Kate thought, she could never have understood what her mother was saying as she did now. She tried to imagine meeting Richard while Harry was alive . . .

Their food arrived and they picked at it. Kate barely touched her wine. It tasted sour. She asked for another bottle of water.

'Will you forgive me, Katie—and Ben? I tried so hard to make Dad happy. He knew he'd lost me, though. I think he even guessed we'd resisted falling into an affair. But I do believe, given Ben's sense of honour and loyalty, his wife, Helen, never knew.'

'And life just went on for you, Mum—all through the Ivana business?'

'Yes. Ben and I had a few long calls. We did meet once too, a quick lunch, before he went to Iraq. You're smiling, Katie, why?'

'It just seems quite old-fashioned, the abstinence bit, hard to credit!'

'That was Ben. I would have been weaker, incapable of resisting had he pressed. We felt a little purer, perhaps, but infidelity of thought and word is virtually as bad.'

'There's nothing to forgive, of course. I couldn't have a more acute understanding—as well as enormous heartache for Dad.'

'It was all the more poignant because I did, do, love your father very much. We would have gone on being just as happy and that's the aching piquancy of it, what he must feel. It is a strange quirk of chance, the millions of people, scattered, different, contentedly muddling along in life, and yet a storm of attraction can lift two hearts into a separate realm and cause chaos. Keep the happy memories of Harry, darling, for all the force of the love you feel now.'

Kate stayed silent, unable to admit how hard that was. 'I think I might be pregnant, Mum. But it is only one missed period. I'm going to do a test this week.'

'I did wonder. You're hardly drinking! I know how much it means to you, of course, and it would be the greatest joy, but I assume it wasn't planned and Richard doesn't know yet.'

'It was half planned and actually his idea in the first place. He said it was obvious how much I wanted a baby and he would leave it to me whether I went ahead. I haven't told him I did. He sprang it on me very soon after we'd met and I worried then how neutral about it he seemed, as though it was something for me, almost like a present instead of something wonderful to be shared.'

Kate looked at her mother, desperate for some small reassurance.

'I should think,' Rachel said slowly, breaking off then to smile at a waiter coming to clear the plates. Kate tried not to stare at the couple in the window, suddenly struck by the thought that, had they been there, they would have had to know her mother's movements in advance. They must have arrived at much the same time.

Rachel ordered coffee, Kate asked for fresh mint tea and, eventually left in peace again, her mother carried on. 'I should think it possible Richard is trying to steer a course and prepare the ground; he has to balance his wife's needs along with yours and your life together. She must have been on his mind.'

'*She* is his *ex*-wife, Mum—and even if that was the case it's not as though she was there to overhear. Why couldn't he have been more positive and spontaneous?'

'I don't know, love. But the main thing for you now is to do that test and make sure. And you never know, Richard might surprise you with how he reacts to the news.'

Kate couldn't handle it; she was feeling raw with jealous resentment. Eleanor was even encroaching on her maternal dreams. And Rachel wasn't the only one to say 'his wife'; Aidan had made that infuriating slip too, not to mention Eleanor herself.

'Buck up, love,' Rachel said. 'Richard has just been through a divorce; he wouldn't choose to bring fatherhood upon himself without giving it a deal of thought. He knows what he's doing, he's nothing if not responsible.'

'But he acts so much on impulse. He wanted me to move in almost in the first week!'

'He knew what he wanted—didn't you?'

Kate had a sudden distraught flare-up of self-pitying need. Watchful eyes, keeping up the pretence of banter and normality, feeling their old intimacy, but at one remove—the evening was taking its toll. She wanted to be able to rely on her mother, to feel she was always there. On the phone to ask about colic, on email to send snapshots of the first smile, someone to run to if the baby was a phantom after all. Rachel had said Sadie would need her, but, Kate thought, she would need Sadie equally as much—as never before.

She had to probe further. 'More confidences, Mum,' she said, smiling archly as a signal. 'You avoided using your mobile this morning,' she whispered, 'so did that couple across the room follow you here? Why do you suspect them?'

'Ah, here's our coffee and tea.' Rachel beamed at the waiter, obviously thinking he had good timing. 'I walked here, actually, Katie,' she said casually, 'and saw the people hanging around in Warwick Square. The gardens are so pretty at this time of year.' She smiled again at the waiter. 'And perhaps we could have our bill?'

Did that mean Ben's flat was being watched? It must do. And that people had become suspicious and were keeping tabs on Ben. Kate looked ahead of her distantly, out into the restaurant. Her attention was caught suddenly and she stared.

Her mother, sitting beside her, gave an anxious glance. 'Something wrong, Katie? You're not feeling ill?'

'Not ill, just shocked, gobsmacked by what I've seen.'

'Is it something to do with that couple waiting for coats? Do you know them?'

Rachel had cottoned on quick enough. Not difficult since Kate couldn't take her eyes off the pair. She had seen them come through from the smaller L of the restaurant; they were standing in a central space, touching lips with the man's fingering hand suggestively placed on the woman's rear. A raincoat and jacket were forthcoming and they left the restaurant.

'Well?' Rachel asked, fascinated. 'What's up with them, what was the problem?'

'That bum-cradling male only happens to be my supposedly clean-living client, Jack Clark, and that woman in her eight-inch heels and plunge-bra'd stretch leopard print, is definitely not his wife. Nor is that woman a daughter, cousin, aunt . . . God, it pisses me off. I really thought Jack was a decent soul and he turns out to be just another run-of-the-mill fucker, same as them all.'

'Darling, language . . .'

'Accurate in this instance—and I'm not thirteen,' Kate snapped, hoping Jack hadn't seen she was there. 'I'll be thirty-four in a couple of weeks.'

Her mother looked irritatingly amused. 'Why are you quite so heated about it, though? He's one more husband out for kicks and sex, but so what, really? What's it to you?'

'It's not so much Jack being one of the lousy rest, it's more about Dan. You see Dan assured me, in that sneering, put-down nasal drawl of his, that Jack's choice of this restaurant, far from the agency, was because he was seeing a bird round here. It bugs me like mad that Dan was a hundred per cent right.'

'We have to be going,' Rachel said, dealing with the bill. 'I can't help feeling there's more to Dan than would seem. Bitter as he clearly is, it could be for all sorts of complicated, emotional reasons. He might not be quite as bad as you're determined to believe. People seldom are.'

'You wouldn't say that,' Kate muttered sardonically, as they rose from the table, 'if you'd lived through the hell of my last month.'

On the way out they avoided any casual glance at

the suspect couple at the window table, the bald man and his stage-paint companion. 'What thrilling news it would be,' Rachel said carefully, within their hearing. 'I knew you must want supper for a good reason! Call me the very minute you know.'

Outside, Kate flagged down a taxi. 'Let me drop you off, Mum. I want to ask something very big of you. It's important to me, I need you to do it.' Her words were met with a nervous-eyed look, but her mother climbed into the cab without question.

Ben's flat was minutes away, so Kate had to be quick. 'Will you go and see Dad—like tomorrow? He's in his last two or three weeks, Mum. Just for a few hours; sit with him a little and love him like you did. I do believe it would give him some peace and a sort of closure. Will you do it?'

Rachel blinked her eyes. 'I need closure, too,' she said, wiping at them with the back of her hand. 'I'll go tomorrow. But can you call him and say I'm coming? And try to prepare Hannah for it too. She'll find it an ordeal.'

Kate promised she would pave the way. The taxi drew up in Warwick Square and she stepped out for a moment to hug her mother goodnight. She had never clung more tightly nor kept her cheek more closely pressed; she needed the feel and shape of her, to drink in the delicate texture of her skin, its particular fragrant honeyed smell, to hear her mother's heartbeat and be warmed by her breath. It was a quick goodnight hug, but it might be all she had to sustain and fortify her and keep her mother close. Her senses were alive to the approaching menace, the forces of the unknown and looming heartache and loss.

'Night, Mum,' she said.

CHAPTER 23

Kate was home before Richard. She made a cup of tea and sat at the white table feeling a surprising calm, as though she was so overrun with emotion that numbness had set in. It was what she'd believed must happen with terrible injuries; people could stare at a separated limb feeling remote from it, in a numb state of suspended pain.

She totted up all she was keeping from Richard, this man she loved to distraction. He knew all too well that she had secrets and he minded intensely. She shuddered to remember living through her refusal to tell him a word of the life-changing dinner with Ben. It would be less of a problem tonight, though. The same overwhelming secret had to be kept, but she had plenty to talk about; her mother and Ben, how they first met and the immense force of the attraction, Ben's physical loyalty to his wife, Aidan's pain. Kate couldn't apportion blame, it had happened, it was life. And if any of her own tense emotion seeped through, she didn't believe Richard would think it unnatural.

She considered the downside of mentioning seeing Jack, but it gave her more to chat about and with her sore sense of injustice and letdown, it would be hard to keep it bottled.

Richard was late. Where was he? Losing all proportion was part of loving someone to distraction, but she couldn't start worrying like this. He wasn't Jack, he wasn't cheating and shallow, that was the whole point. She lived with a man who could be trusted, who was prepared to saddle himself with fatherhood, who cared—and his key was just turning in the door.

Whenever he walked in Kate had an image of a stage curtain giving way to sudden brightness, an unfolding scene. He was open-armed, looking glad to be home and she felt quite light-headed.

'I hoped you wouldn't still be with your mother,' he said. 'How was she? Did you cover a lot of ground?'

'Yes. She didn't hold back, thank goodness, and it's a help to know.'

'As I can imagine,' Richard muttered dryly. He glanced at her mug on the table. 'Is that coffee? I need a shot of caffeine or something stronger; I thought I knew it all, but it was harrowing stuff tonight.'

'It's tea. I'll do some coffee,' Kate offered, not really wanting the smell of it.

'No, I will. You talk to me.'

Kate relayed all her mother had told her: the meeting between Ben and Aidan in Bosnia, the friendship formed with its eventful consequences, all that had flowed. Richard listened with interest.

'I can understand your father's agony,' he said, 'but what a powerful story. I guess I owe you an apology over Ben.'

'Why? What do you mean exactly?' Kate had stiffened.

'Well, I've been in a state ever since you had that dinner with him. I was convinced he'd managed to con you in some way, despite all your suspicions. But I must admit it's harder to see Ben as a confidence trickster now; he sounds like a helluva guy.'

'You think so?' she said, longing to agree. 'It

377

would be a relief to feel complete trust . . .' Richard gave her a sharp look and she said, smiling, 'Obviously, for Mum's sake—sad as I am for Dad.'

Richard let it drop. He'd skipped the coffee and poured himself whisky. Fondling her hair, he took a sip. 'It is extraordinary, the turnabouts people have to handle in their lives. This ex-crackhead I've been with tonight, he's been through it all right, and it's astonishing what he's achieved.'

'Tell me,' Kate said, enjoying the way Richard loved to fill her in.

'His childhood was a psychiatrist's casebook for starters. His father beat him with straps, he was sexually abused by older boys, in trouble for fighting back. Then the cycle of peer pressure, prison, spiralling addiction, more prison. He was rattling on heroin, high on crack, chemically impelled to commit crime after crime; pranged, paranoid, and living with rats, as he put it, making a packet and sleeping on the floor in public toilets. He's written a book about it, but hearing him tell it was amazing.'

'Quite something to come back from that and write it up.'

'He's a tall, fit taxpayer now, a young-achiever award winner, a contract gardener and employing guys out of rehab. But God, how low can you get? Living on the streets, almost killing for a hit, snowballs in the toilets—that's crack and heroin, the heroin blurs the crack climb-down. This guy described how bone-thin he was, and scabby, shoes stuck to the sores on his feet, the constant threat of police and prison. He had to lose the stuff fast, not to get caught—up his arse, in his foreskin, down his throat. Heroin puts the brakes on shitting, so when

378

it came to swallowing it he had to rattle for a bit to get at that little packet.'

'God, how bad can it get?'

'Worse! These guys get body lice and think of it as protection. Nobody wants to search them then. If the police tried to move him on, he said, they'd radio each other calling out, "AB-D,"—airborne disease—and leave him to fester in his doorway. I remember how we used to chant in the playground, "It's no good standing on the seat/ the crabs in here jump fifteen feet".' Richard grinned. 'His toughest test seems to have been surviving rehab, but he did it and thinks himself one of the lucky ones.'

'It must have taken some guts, kicking that habit—real grit.'

'Anyway, next time you fall over a scabby dropout in a doorway, remember he could find a dose of that human spirit and end up landscaping our future garden.' Kate liked his use of the plural.

He eyed her over his glass. 'What else did you and Rachel talk about? Did you tell her about the bad scene with Dan? Did she have any views, any advice?'

'Nothing very helpful really,' Kate muttered, knowing Richard would take her mother's side. 'But after I'd gone on about it, by the weirdest coincidence, who do you think I should see in the restaurant, but Jack! He was just leaving. I don't think he saw me, which could have been embarrassing. He was with a woman—not his wife.'

'That must have shaken you a bit! You seemed blindly determined that he was purer than pure, a saint in white satin from Slough. I could have told you he wasn't if only you'd listened. Asking you out to his home was just a means of getting close; he

379

couldn't chat you up, with you still mourning Harry, but you can bet he had the hots for you all through that lunch, the turd. It was obvious.'

'I don't see why you have to be so extreme about it. I was quite shocked. I'm beginning to think Polly's take on men is a lot closer to the mark than mine.'

'Now who's being extreme? Men do have their uses. And if I had my way, as I seldom do, I'd say it was past our bedtime and I want to make myself useful there.'

*   *   *

Kate stared across the carriage above the row of tired, bent heads opposite, studying the map of the District and Circle Line stations. She had no need to, she knew them backwards. Two stops to go before Earl's Court; she was fine for time, ten minutes or so early. She had checked out the nearest Starbucks, which was just fifteen seconds from the station. The best course of action, she felt, was to present Polly with a firm decision and avoid any scowling discussion of where to go.

She thought how desperate Polly must have been to make that call to her. She was in an obvious panic about her father, or anyone else, knowing, but depending on the seriousness of the problem it was inevitable that Richard would have to be told. Kate shuddered at the prospect of having to give him some difficult, stressful news. She hoped he wouldn't feel too gutted that his daughter hadn't been able to turn to him. It all depended on the nature of the trouble she was in.

Was it too dark and deep a problem even to

share with a friend? Kate couldn't shut her mind to the spectre of drugs, despite Richard's conviction that it wasn't that; he thought pot was routine, inevitable, and he knew all about the hyperactive highs and dilated pupils of cocaine. But what else could it be?

She stood on the right on the escalator, not hurrying up as she often did, suddenly feeling shattered, frozen with nerves. It was an empty hope to expect a spark of warmth from Polly, but it would be as comforting as a blanket, as heartening as an embrace of gratitude; it would make all the difference.

Touching-out into the small station ticket-office area, Kate saw Polly was already there. She affected not to notice Kate's arrival and hid herself, sidling behind a group of youths. Kate wandered past the talkative young men thinking two could play that game; she stopped dead just beyond them, turning abruptly with a look of pleased surprise. At least contact had been established with little stress.

'Hi Polly, good to see you! Shall we go for a cuppa? Starbucks is almost next door. Let's hope we can find a quiet table.'

Polly had no sharp combative comeback, she didn't say a word. Kate thought how young, vulnerable and waif-like she looked, very different without her kohl eye-liner and spiked hair. Her hair was clean, short, shining, and it looked more the chestnut colour of her father's. It must have been tinted as well as gelled. Polly hadn't armoured herself with defiant make-up and, having been braced for sarcasm and rebellious sneers, Kate was quite taken aback to see her so subdued.

Her face was as sheet-white as ever. It was as if

381

Polly's need for help was so great that she was trying to shed all her previous resentment and even scrub her face in a forlorn attempt to atone for past nastiness.

Kate felt a weight of responsibility. As they left the grimy station entrance she had to stop herself putting an arm round the thin, young shoulders, sure that it would have been pushing her luck. It was early days. They made a sombre couple, she thought; she in a black trouser suit and cream shirt, Polly in black jeans, sloppy black sweater and the predictable clumping black boots, the retro Doc Martens she always wore, with the laces half undone.

'Can we go to a back table?' she asked, finding her voice. Kate had been scanning round, anxious about being overheard, they both had. She couldn't imagine anyone there would take any interest; a man in a cheap suit was peering at charts on his laptop, two loud Australian girls were gassing, a bling-covered chancer was holding hands with a chic black girl, and a squat elderly woman in pebble glasses was reading *The Times*. She and Polly would be private enough at the back, remote from the outer world.

She paid for two cups of tea, which they took to the tiny table, sitting down opposite and lifting their cups for a student waiter to wipe it down. He gave it a single swipe.

'I was glad you called,' Kate said. 'I hope you'll let me try and help. It's easier at times to talk to someone who isn't close family and I do know a few ropes.' She smiled. 'I've got no hang-ups, Polly, I'm not in the business of judging. You can say anything you like.' Was she pitching it right? It was hard to

382

know.

'You can't help. No one can.' Polly stared coldly, more typically, finding a bit of fight. She angled her head stiffly sideways and fixed on the counter where people were waiting to be served.

'Maybe not, but I can listen. Just sharing things might help.'

Polly laughed brusquely. 'Some hope.'

Kate held her eyes. 'You can't know if you don't even try and talk it through with me.' Polly looked cornered, as supremely terrified as a captive facing a gun. The strain proved too much and her eyes filled with tears.

'I'm pregnant,' she mumbled. 'You can't share that.'

Kate felt winded. Why hadn't she thought of that before? Her head spun as she tried to take in all the ramifications. Polly was sixteen, first year A-levels. Did she want help with having an abortion—without her parents knowing?

Two huge tears trailed down the frightened teenage face opposite; Polly was too proud to wipe them away. Kate felt overwhelmed with sudden fondness. 'You'll have to give me a second to think it all through.' She smiled. 'But it's not such a terrible thing,' she said, anxiously trying to lift the girl out of her misery. 'We'll find a way.'

'I'm not having an abortion. They'll try and make me. They'll throw school in my face, Dad will yell and rant, but he can't make me. I'm not going to kill my baby, not for anyone.'

There was steel in Polly's tone, no sign of hysteria; Kate felt convinced that her mind was really made up and it wasn't just a defiant testing of the water. It must have contributed to her dread of telling her father, her fear of being pressurized not to keep it. Polly had guts as well as strong passions and beliefs—and obduracy. She was going to have the baby, unquestionably determined to see it through.

'How many months are you? Do you know?'

'Three and a half.'

'Are you feeling okay, not sick?' Kate felt slight nausea herself, as she spoke, it was the pervading smell of coffee, the stuffiness, and the uncomfortable stools needed for the high little table.

'I was sick a few mornings,' Polly said. 'I'm fine now.'

Richard would be in despair. He would demand to know how his bright, quick daughter could have been so *stupidly* irresponsible—and how she could carry on at school. Kate thought he would blame himself. Would he try anything to persuade Polly to have an abortion? He'd certainly have a string of furious, uncontrolled questions about the prospective father.

'Are you in a proper relationship, Polly?' she asked. 'Does whoever it is know? Do you think he'll take some responsibility and want to help?'

The terrified look was back in her large waif's eyes. 'I don't know who it is. I'll never be able to tell my child who its dad is, that's what's so awful. There'll come a time, children ask, they want to know . . .' Her tears streamed, but she cried silently, her head bowed low.

'Polly, you must say how it happened. You're having a baby, which is wonderful—not in ideal circumstances, but we'll all help. I will, certainly, and,' Kate thought of Richard's mother, how well

384

Polly got on with her, 'perhaps your grandmother, Celia, will, too. I'm in touch with her over the flat. We can talk it through; we have time on our side. You can lean on me and trust me, I promise. But you must have some idea who it was. Or was it against your will?'

'Sort of, not really rape or anything like that. I had been going with a boy at school. We'd done it a few times, I was no virgin. He was into condoms and he was always boringly careful, like everything had to be clean, clinical; it did bug me a bit, how fastidious and *systematic* he was. But I quite liked him. Then at the start of the Christmas holidays it was a bit wild. We went to this party and people were high, like I've never seen. I was drunk, high, the joints were going round, people doing shit, some cocaine—crap stuff, someone said, all glucose—and even crack, I think. A guy was pushing E and I bought one; it was only seven pounds, you have to try it once . . .'

'Go on,' Kate said. 'Did the ecstasy have a bad effect?'

'I felt really disorientated on top of being drunk; kind of euphoric, but a bit nauseous and off balance. Anyway, this boy, my friend Si, wanted to fuck,' Polly mumbled, trying not to be heard. Kate had to strain to catch it all. 'So we found a corner and did it. He used a condom, so it wasn't him, you see. When he pulled out, though, I saw these two guys were staring, slack-mouthed. And my mood was swinging from good to bad; you're kind of hyper-aware of your feelings on E and I was all shitted-up about Christmas.'

'How do you mean?'

'I hated that Dad had a girl sometimes; it was

385

just sex, but he was going to be home for Christmas and I thought he'd only half want to be there. I felt so bitter. No halves about it when you turned up, I knew where he wanted to be.'

'But what happened? Had these boys, or were they men, got turned on watching?'

'They were wanking their fingers off by then. "Move over," they said to Si. He could have told them to get stuffed and looked after me better, but all the tool could do was say did I really want that? I mean, what did he think? I was spaced out, down on the floor. I felt full of energy, though, and floaty on the E. Nothing seemed to matter, and I said to them, kind of in defiance of Si, "Go on. Have your fill. Who cares?"'

'Do you know their names? Would you recognize them again?'

'I don't know who the hell they were. It was like a warehouse kind of place; not a club, but people paid. I got out from under eventually, really sore, and wandered about till I found Si again. I was so sick at him, felt like spitting in his face, but I just told him it was over. He did find me a taxi, I think he wanted a tidy end . . .' Polly looked wry and Kate had to smile, although there was little to smile about.

Polly said she'd felt so filthy and degraded later, after what had happened, that she'd gone clubbing and drinking trying to lose herself, but it hadn't been any fun without a boyfriend. She missed her father, she said, didn't see friends, who were mostly away for Christmas anyway. She'd done a pregnancy test when Kate and Richard were in the Caribbean and lived with the knowledge ever since.

Kate looked at her watch. They'd been in the

386

cafe half an hour, they were on a second cup of tea. 'You didn't turn to Ed?' she asked, thinking how sensible Polly's brother was.

'He's all work and his guitar. And he can be such a prude—he'd have fainted!'

'And you didn't feel able to tell your mother?' Kate asked tightly, staring, knowing the answer for herself. She'd seen the reversal of roles, Polly's mature, gentle attempts to handle her mother. Kate felt she'd lost ground with that question, but it was beyond her not to show tension where Eleanor was concerned.

Polly knew vulnerability when she saw it, she couldn't resist a dig. 'You can't hack it, can you? But bad luck. You have to let Dad help out with her, you can't have him all. He knows how to play the rope, give her slack, row her in. He's needed. Anyway, how could I have told her I was pregnant? You've seen it, you know. She'd go to pieces, feel a bad, useless parent, scream and break her fiddle or something—and she'd think I was blaming her. She'd take all the wrong pills and want to die. We can't do much to help. She probably will do it one day; meanwhile we live on our nerves.'

'It's hard on the family, the demands of the illness,' Kate said lamely. 'But at some stage, Polly, she is going to have to know about the baby.'

'Dad has to know first; he can prepare her best, get her used to it.' Polly looked ashen, suddenly, desperate. 'But he can't make me have an abortion,' she hissed. 'I won't. He can do what he likes, I won't have one. And you're not telling him any of what I've told you, you couldn't do that to me.'

Her head was in her hands again, shoulders shaking. But her father had to know about it—and

387

it couldn't wait, Kate thought, with another glance at her watch. He'd be on his way home soon, calling her to say so. He would want to know where she'd been. She hoped the whisky was in good supply with all she had to tell him.

'We have to go, Polly, it's late. But this is what I think is the best plan. I'll tell your dad and prepare the ground for you, if you agree. He can have his first reactions with me. I'll explain you're fourteen weeks' pregnant and want to have the baby. And I will tell him the minimum, just a skeleton outline of what happened. He has to know that he's not going to be marching you up the aisle!

'He loves you,' Kate urged. 'He's been so worried. Please believe how much you mean to him and what a proud grandfather I'm sure he'll be. And don't fret about the years down the line when any questions might come up. Things will come right, you'll find someone who'll love you, who'll give this baby a wonderfully happy two-parent home.'

'The fuck I will,' Polly muttered. 'Why are you doing this, Kate?'

'I care, I want to love and be a friend to you if you'll let me. I love your father, but try not to see me as competition; nothing can change his feelings for you.'

She stood up, edgy about time and impatient suddenly. 'Can you come round, Friday or Sunday night? You'll have a lot to talk through with your dad. I'll have tried my best, tried to programme him into your thinking. He'll know the score. And shall I talk to your grandmother Celia? Your other grandmother has your mum to look after, it would be difficult for her to help much. But I won't do a thing without telling you first, Polly. This is your show.'

'Granny won't understand.'

'She might. She might surprise you.'

Outside, the air was chilly and refreshing; Kate had felt a touch of queasiness in the fuggy cafe. People were pushing past, flat-dwellers on their way home, but she stopped a moment, swallowing back the slight metallic taste in her mouth.

She smiled at Polly and cleared her throat.

'Um, just before we go, can I tell you some news of my own?' Kate couldn't help herself, it was the high emotion of the moment—terrible to tell Polly before Richard, but she couldn't stop it bursting out. 'It's kind of relevant,' she said. 'I hope you won't be too upset about this, I've worried so much that you'd resent it if it happened, but, you see, I'm actually pregnant, too. I did that pee-test in my lunch hour today. I'm about six weeks behind you. Yours comes first. I'm sorry, Polly, springing that on top of everything, but Dad won't love you any less, not one jot, and we can, after all, share notes and baby buggies.'

She almost lost her balance, had to take a step backwards when Polly flung her arms round her and gave her a breath-stifling bear hug. 'Oh, that's wonderful, amazing. I'm so glad! I won't have to do it alone.' She pulled back suddenly then and fixed Kate with a very Polly-like laser-inquisition stare. 'But if you've only just done the test at lunch . . . does that mean Dad doesn't know yet?'

'No, he doesn't,' Kate said, feeling relieved that she was going straight home to tell him. 'I guess I can lump us together, give him a left and a right. He might need to sit down and have a stiff drink.'

389

They stared at each other in the grimy, cafe-lit street until Polly suddenly spluttered into laughter.

'Rather you than me,' she said, and, with another hug and bursting squeeze, she ran ahead into the station before Kate could offer to put her in a taxi home.

CHAPTER 24

Richard called. 'Sorry, darling, I'm still stuck out here. The security procedures took ages and the guy we're interviewing—he's a colourful character and knows what went on here—has only just been prised out of the pub.'

'What did go on?' Kate was trying to calm her breathing, having just rushed in through the front door.

'Manufacturing and supplying massive quantities of crack-cocaine; bucketloads of the stuff were shovelled onto the markets—the police landed a real haul. It was a while back. When it came to trying the guy who'd set it up, who was a tango dancer before he moved here from Buenos Aires, they thought him so dangerous he was taken to court in a helicopter and cross-examined through a bulletproof screen.'

So she wouldn't be breaking the news about Polly that night—nor her own piece of equally far-reaching news. It was a hefty anticlimax after being so psyched up, but in some ways a relief. Pitching it right was so important and a day's reflection might be no bad thing.

'What about food?' she asked. 'Have you eaten?'

'We sent out for sandwiches. And you have something proper yourself, darling, not just an egg. Did you notice I've done some shopping and cooking? Have some of the chicken tagine.'

'I've never seen such a stuffed fridge.' Kate said, shouldering the phone to open it and peer inside. 'We should have the tagine tomorrow night, it'll be good to catch up over supper. Plenty to talk about one way and another—and I'll have just seen Mary, my friend in the office, so I might even be a bit further on about Dan.'

'Forget Dan, forget the office. What does it matter? When I was messing about cooking this morning, I thought how terrific it would have been, both of us home, being boringly domestic together. I wanted you with me.'

'Gardening in the afternoon as well, I suppose?'

'You bet!' To hear the warmth in his voice and have a sense of his need lifted Kate's heart, it gave her a feeling of quiet pride. And hope. The baby was going to bring about a great upheaval.

'Home as soon as I can,' Richard said. 'About a couple of hours, I should think.'

'Drive carefully.'

The strains of the evening were beginning to tell, the emotion, the responsibility. The postponement had taken its toll, too. But all the while Kate had the thought of a living growing speck inside her, no bigger than a broad bean; it was unbelievable. Nothing could dim the thrill. It would grow steadily larger and so would she. Would Richard still love her and want mornings of togetherness when she was bulky, when the baby was crying, smelling, puking up over his clean shirt? Was he going to regret the ball he'd tossed in the air so casually at that early stage? Kate had taken it and run with it, never once asking if he'd changed his mind.

The sense of anticlimax was hard to lose. She'd been rehearsing her words, feeling flushed with nerves and indecision. Which baby to tell him about first had obsessed her most, but it had to be Polly's. It was a life-changing event and so much had to be made clear to him; it had to be tackled first.

School, Kate felt, could be handled; the timing wasn't too bad. Polly could carry on as normal through the summer term then, after the long holidays, either—if she was brave enough to take her bump into class—have a last month at school or stay away and prepare for an October birth. She needn't miss much more than a term, she was bright and could cope, she must carry on with her exams.

The biggest worry Kate could see was having the newborn baby at home in Barnes. Eleanor wasn't stable, she could have attacks. Even with full-time help it mightn't be safe. Her own pregnancy, she thought, would concentrate Richard's mind on the need to move; Thornby Terrace was stretched to its limits and her flat couldn't stay fallow forever. Perhaps they could sell both flats and pool resources.

How would Eleanor react if Polly came to live with them? It would make sense to have the two babies under one roof; Polly could have her own set-up, they could share help. Kate smiled to herself thinking of screams in unison, or alternately. Would Ed mind deeply, being left to hold the fort? He'd be off to university soon. They had time enough to plan and thrash things out, there was no rush.

Kate put on the water to boil an egg, thinking

back to her mother. After the pregnancy test she had sent her a one-word text, 'Positive!' and her mother had sent one back, 'Best news ever!'

She longed to pick up the phone to Rachel now and have a good old natter about it all, even to tell her about Polly, but it wasn't an ideal time; Ben and her mother were probably having a meal. And Kate suddenly knew, with an overflowing sense of urgency, what she wanted to do in the hours before Richard came home—a little investigation of her own.

Ben had warned her against getting involved; it was flying in the face of her mother's agitated pleading. The evidence would be in her laptop. Too bad. Even if she had to throw the thing in a lake, feed it to the Loch Ness monster, Kate thought, she was going to try and see what she could find.

She gave up on the egg, made herself some toast and tea, and brought her laptop to the table. She'd come to detest Spencer Morgan, she was bristling with suspicion about him, determined to pursue her few fuzzy little ideas, however hopeless they proved to be. At least she'd feel she had tried.

The first step was to find out about setting up a business in Brazil. After a few wrong turns she arrived at the Sao Paulo Chamber of Commerce whose guide was usefully informative. Any company in Brazil had to have two or more partners. They could be individuals or legal entities and needn't be resident in Brazil. The country's Central Bank had responsibility for registering and monitoring foreign activity, and an investor based abroad had to have an attorney in Brazil, someone with the powers to represent it as a partner in the company being set up.

It shouldn't be too difficult, Kate believed, to find out the name of Spencer's Brazilian lawyers. However opaque and tenuous, his business links and interests in South America were strong and she knew from Richard that a couple in Brazil were declared and on the level.

Richard had made a list of every company he could find that he believed to be under Spencer's ownership. Almost all were loosely affiliated or privately held; hard-fact public data wasn't exactly free-flowing in the Morgan Empire, and it had taken him hours of diligent snooping. Kate had the list. Richard had sent it to her laptop after she'd had the sudden idea about Lloyds Bank Nominees. And he'd pointed up the few companies in Spencer's panoply of financial services that were definitely bona fide, two of which were in Brazil.

Kate thought that for a start she had to find out the name of the lawyers who acted for Spencer in those two companies. The time difference was on her side. The telephone numbers were easily obtainable from Overseas Directories. She had a friendly telephone voice and a good way with her after a lot of client practice. Kate was about to pick up the phone when her mother's extreme concern about bugs and tapped phones flew into her mind. How far did she have to take such precautions? If she went to her flat, surely that couldn't be bugged? She wasn't living there after all.

She texted Richard to say that she was nipping over to her flat for some clothes, then grabbed her laptop and jumped into her car. Twenty minutes later she had let herself into the silent flat feeling she was acting crazily, irresponsibly, even dangerously, and set herself up beside the phone.

The first of Spencer's legitimately owned Brazilian companies she tried were happy to tell her that the name of their firm of lawyers was Santos & Oliveira Ltda., and yes, they could certainly recommend them. Being armed with a name made it easier next time and she was able to discover, very satisfyingly, that the same firm acted for Spencer's other declared company as well.

Kate wondered ruefully whether Richard might have known Spencer Morgan's lawyers in Brazil. It would have been difficult to ask him, though, and have led to unanswerable questions. She looked at her watch, must get on . . .

The name of the acai packaging company in Santana was Acai of Amapá Export. Ben had mentioned it over dinner at Wiltons'. It seemed a good sign, Kate thought hopefully. Would Ben have named the company if he wasn't to be trusted?

With a little more searching she learned that it was possible to find out the ownership of a company in Brazil, either from the Central Bank or from the Federal Revenue Office. She felt more comfortable ringing the bank and got through.

Her English slowed things a bit, but they sorted it. 'Ah, *Acai do Amapá Exportacao Limitada!* One moment, madam.' The enlightened male voice was replaced with canned classical music, but her helpful contact was soon back—and with information that caused Kate's pulse to beat a little faster. She seemed to be getting somewhere.

Both partners in the company that owned Acai of Amapá Export were registered at a legal firm in the Cayman Islands, the tax haven used by Spencer Morgan. And one of the partners in Amapá Export itself was a member of Spencer's firm of lawyers in

395

Brazil, Santos & Oliveira, whose head office was in Sao Paulo, a great distance from a small packaging plant in the remote rainforest state of Amapá. It was inconclusive, proved nothing, but it was progress. It felt, Kate thought, like stitching a patchwork bedcover; plenty of the multi-sided, differently patterned pieces were in place, but they had yet to be sewn together.

She sat back. She had just seen her mother who was desperate to preserve a facade of normality, but Kate needed to see Ben. She urgently wanted to pass on all discovered information. She believed she could trust him now and you never knew, it could be useful, even a vital missing link.

Supper with her mother the previous night had been wonderfully intimate and illuminating, but neither of them had been able to relax for a second. Coded warnings wrapped up in glossy gossip, not being able to ask questions, Rachel's conviction she was being watched, followed—and that strange couple had certainly looked the part; it had been hard to bear.

And later that night, unable to sleep, Kate had felt in panic, imagining MI6 were closing in on their man and the witches of fate were about to clothe Rachel in a new identity and spirit her away beyond reach. Kate had thought about Roger Grieve, the dinner with Ben. She'd worried too, about feeling trust in Ben. Just suppose he had kept Rachel waiting all those years, not from a noble sense of duty to a sick wife, but because of some ongoing criminal activity. The most unexpected people of all could have hidden, terrible fault lines in their characters.

Then in the bright light of day, after a sunny

exchange of texts about pregnancy, a sense of orderliness had overtaken her and optimism returned. It was surely alarmist to believe that time was really running out.

Kate didn't feel optimistic now. Alone in her silent, empty flat, she felt in anguish; fired up by her discoveries about Spencer Morgan, yet desperately frightened and confused. She felt in need of certainties; more dependant on her mother than ever, she felt in deep despair.

She eyed her watch. It was after eleven. Richard would be home soon, possibly already there. Her mind was weary, her body limp with exhaustion. She collected a few summery clothes, remembering her reason for coming to the flat, locked up and left.

*   *   *

At work the next morning the push was on for a new pitch. It was a chain of health-based, fast-food outlets selling smoothies, salads, fruit pots, cereal bars, and made a feature of its fine Brazilian coffee. Kate felt nauseous and struggled to contribute, but others were fizzing with witty ideas. She couldn't forget the dinner in Grenada at the Calabash Hotel, Spencer Morgan saying in a joking, dismissive way that his only new business interest was a little dabble in a trendy health foods business. Acai was a key ingredient in smoothies . . . It gave her a moment of sourly ironic amusement to think she might be working on an account to promote the latest of Morgan's little business ventures.

It didn't help to lessen the stomach-turning feeling that she was being not-so-subtly eased out

397

of a job. In meetings no one asked her views. If she chipped in she was listened to coldly, with rude, drumming-finger impatience. Lunch with Mary would have to be rushed too, because of extended sessions to discuss the new pitch. It couldn't come quick enough.

Polly called. 'Well? What did he say?' She sounded on such desperate tenterhooks that Kate could almost hear the poor girl's heart banging against those thin ribs.

'Hold your horses,' she said, relieved that she only had to explain about the delay. She felt inadequate and self-obsessed, incapable of wise words. 'It'll be all right, Polly,' she promised rashly, 'you'll see.'

It was almost two o'clock before she and Mary could nip out for a bite. Mary suggested the tapas bar and Kate thought of meeting Ed there, seeing a new side of Ben; was this to be another such sensitive encounter? She longed to spill out the news of her pregnancy, but that was for another day—always assuming she was still employed at Impetus.

They ordered plates of charcuterie and cheese to pick at, water and a glass of wine for Mary. Kate asked if she'd had a good time skiing and good snow.

'I hope the holiday does its stuff,' Mary said, 'as we've just decided to try for a baby! It was amazing sun, going this late. And hot—we were skiing in Courchevel and all the men's eyes were on swivel sticks, ogling the French girls sunbathing in their ski-pants and bras at the cafe up the top!'

Mary laughed, a tinkly little sound; she was an elf, tiny, with wishbone-thin wrists, a pointy chin and a gamine cut of dark hair that hugged her face.

'You caught some sun too,' Kate said. 'You look great—so it's watch this space for a baby?'

'Sure is! Shouldn't talk about it, I know, but I've never been superstitious. Well, Kate, what can I do for you? You hardly need telling about Dan's feelings, and the rest, to be honest, is a bit shocking and embarrassing to explain.'

Kate did need telling. Dan had spite and vengeance scored right through him, but *feelings* . . . And whatever did she mean by 'the rest'?

'I know Dan's bitter,' Kate said. 'I felt terrible about standing him up when I fell for Richard, but that was months ago now. And why put it about that I'm in a scene with a client? No one can seriously think I'm having it off with Jack Clark. It's a joke. The usual suspects snigger right to my face. And one or two people cold-shoulder me almost like I've been caught shoplifting in a charity shop.' Her lip began trembling as she stared miserably across the table.

'People think you led Dan on and then dumped him, Kate. They forget you were mourning your husband and did no such thing.' Mary smiled. 'Also you do look madly in love; it always shows—can't you understand what that does to Dan?'

'No, I really can't, particularly given his attitude. I don't know what you mean.'

'Kate, you must know he's in love with you! He's eaten up with it. He's been a lovesick hound ever since he set eyes on you—however many years ago that was—hardly accepting you were married, thinking, I expect, when your husband died that it was meant to be. It makes all those sex-mad PA's all the keener, and a couple of account managers I

399

could name, too. It's his soulful donkey eyes. They feel sorry for him and really have it in for you.'

Mary gave her elf's tinkle of a laugh. 'I can't believe it! It's staring you in the face, the whole agency's clocking it and you really didn't know. What did you think? But can you see it now? He's a sensitive individual somewhere inside, as well as convinced of his chances once you were through your grief. And then along comes Richard.

'Try to understand what this involvement of yours is doing to him; it's a red-hot poker to his heart. He's jealous of Jack too, because you work closely with him so I suppose it was inevitable he'd put that story about. Of course no one really believes you're bonking a client.'

Kate couldn't bring herself to accept it; nothing fitted. She was dumbfounded. It was hardly a picture of Dan she recognized, about as far from it as a gigolo from a monk. She felt Mary must be conning her out of misguided kindness, fobbing her off. No one even having a tease could call Dan, with all his bad-taste jokes and off-key crudeness, *sensitive*. He was being evilly foul to her, gross and ruthless. She wasn't having that.

'That's not the Dan I know, Mary. A few girls may drool, but he's a full-time creep as far as I'm concerned with those awful quips and mannerisms, and he's putting me through hell backwards. I knew he was keen—and patient. But he made it clear enough, when I scrubbed a great date at the opera he'd planned, that it had been with the usual endgame in sight.

'You can't call that very sensitive,' she finished with another apologetic smile, hoping to encourage Mary to explain.

400

'Perhaps thin-skinned would be a better word,' she said. 'Dan's not the most intuitive thing on two legs, I'll admit.'

'He's undermining me and out to get me, winning just the way he planned. I work with him, after all—I know. He's spreading straight lies, slagging off my work in front of people who matter—and you say that's all because he fancies himself in love!'

Kate flushed, she'd been talking in mutters, but heatedly, and Mary was only trying to help. 'Sorry, getting a bit carried away there,' she said sheepishly. 'It's good of you to tell it all, I shouldn't be this wound-up. But you said something about the rest of it being a bit shocking and embarrassing—what do you mean?' She picked up her glass and sipped water; she couldn't imagine what was coming.

Mary sighed. 'Don't be mad at me for saying this, it's just that he can't stand you around now, it's killing him and he wants you out. It's either you or him, Kate. People think one of you has to go. They think it gets in the way of business when the atmosphere's so heavy that even clients kick up. That *Maximan* jerk has whinged about rudeness and internal strife apparently, the fucker. The head honchos rate Dan, however unfair and misguided that is. They think he's solid, no high-flyer, but a workhorse who can smooth client feathers. I know you do a great job, but in the cold, hard ad-world light of day he's more useful to the bosses than you.'

She looked agonised, a tiny slip of a bearer of bad news in her honey wool shift, and she concentrated on sipping cappuccino. 'Sorry, Kate, but that's the way it goes. You're a rung below, you had lots of time off over your tragedy, you're in love with a celeb and everyone knows it—and they assume you're probably less focussed. And the rest of the agency layabouts do think of their own skins, I'm afraid . . .'

'You're a real friend,' Kate said, worrying about Mary's motives, but deciding she was sorted, happy, trying for a baby and could afford to tell it straight. 'I still find it hard to see Dan in that light, though, I mean having feelings—he's always seemed as shallow as a plate.'

'No, he's really not that. His mum's got MS, as you know. He does a lot for her. He just has this great unhealthy obsession for you and needs you out of his sight.' She stood up, a dainty little twinkletoes, having insisted on paying the bill. 'What'll you do? Stick it out? Try and face them down? Try for constructive dismissal?'

Kate thought of her mother's advice, Richard's feelings about the agency. She could imagine circumstances where she might have wanted to do battle, but not now. 'I've been thinking of leaving for some time now, actually,' she said. 'And to be honest I can do without a stand-up fight with Dan. Maybe it'll look like being a loser at work, but I can handle that, I think—I'd just hate to be a loser in love!'

'But it's going okay with Richard?' Mary asked, as they wandered back to the agency.

'I think so, hope so. But I've got to tell him something extremely difficult about his daughter tonight and all bets are off on how he'll react.'

CHAPTER 25

Kate went to a wine merchant's on her way home and asked for a suitable choice of wine to drink with a chicken tagine. The man behind the counter was middle-aged, bearded and wearing a yellow bow tie. 'Either of these,' he said, hunting out a couple of bottles, 'would do excellently. This is a 2001 Château Dalmeran from Provence and this Yarden Cabernet Sauvignon 2006 is very smooth. You don't want anything too peppery with Moroccan food.'

'I'll take both,' Kate said, not up in the concept of peppery wines, 'and let my partner choose.'

The right wine, she thought, since Richard had done all the cooking, might be an alternative way to his heart. She hopped on a bus up the King's Road, her nerves on fire, yet with a feeling of imminent freedom from making lonely, stressful decisions. Richard was about to have a considerable shock, but Polly's baby was a fact, a problem to be shared and he must see the need for calm thought and rational discussion. And better, Kate felt, if he was over the immediate distress, with his more impetuous paternal instincts contained, before he talked to Polly himself, face to face.

She was later leaving the office than hoped. It was almost eight; he was home, waiting on supper. Kate's long agency day, all the sessions on the new pitch for the food-outlet chain, had held her up. As well as calls to Jack, which were more effortful since seeing him in the restaurant; it was hard to convey her usual warmth. It had been a day, too,

403

with no time to ring her mother and find out how soon they could meet. She needed contact, the reassurance of seeing her, and she wanted to speak to Ben urgently, a message that Rachel was best placed to pass on. Kate felt sure that Spencer Morgan's link with the acai plant at the heart of the scam, even if only through his lawyers, had to have some significance. It was a hot coal, burning her fingers. A processing plant in Santana Port, a tiny outpost in a remote, rainforested corner of Brazil—wasn't that just too improbable a coincidence? Rachel was being so hyper-careful, though, taking such immense precautions, might she not worry about listeners-in? Possibly, and with justification; anyone hacking into a call might wonder at arrangements being made, carefully crafted, for another meeting in a public place.

Hopping off her bus, she sent her mother a text. 'Rushing now but must chat! Call tomorrow. So excited!!!' She would call from work and bubble over on the phone, saying how hard it was to talk in a frantic office. Her mother couldn't refuse to meet.

She hurried up the street, walked in the door and was greeted by the spicy aroma of Moroccan cooking. Hunger gnawed, she'd hardly eaten a bite at lunch. Richard kissed her. 'I'm heating up the supper, but no rush. You tired? You should be! You've had almost a twelve-hour day at that place and it's too much. They treat you like a skivvy. What's this?' he said, taking the bag with its clinking bottles from her hands. 'Freebees from work?'

'No, they're not! I stopped at that wine shop off Sidney Street. It's just a small present.'

'I was about to open a very routine bottle. Give me a hug. What have I done to deserve you—or even a present? Anyone would think you were buttering me up!' His hug became a long slow kiss. 'Want to go upstairs?' he said, nuzzling her hair, pressing against her.

'Later, later! I just need to unwind a little right now.'

Richard searched in the kitchen drawer for the corkscrew. 'Let's try the Dalmeran, shall we? What a difficult choice!' Kate wished the problems she was about to tell him were as simple as deciding between two wines. He put the bottle on the table and went to the stove; he tossed chopped greens into a waiting pan. Kate came beside him, loving the look of him in his worn jeans and dark-grey sweatshirt. She kissed his cheek and squatted to take the plates out of the warmer drawer. She imagined being less mobile, feeling the baby kick. Would Richard rest his hand on her taut, rounded belly and love feeling the jerks of its tiny feet?

'I'm starving,' she said, as they sat down. 'Thanks for doing this. It's been a shattering day at work, frantic, and I didn't have much at lunch.'

'But didn't you have it with Mary? Tell me what's going on. I would like to know.'

Kate stared at him. 'Not now.' She paused. 'I saw Polly last night. She'd called me at work, but wouldn't say what it was about, so I suggested we meet. She would only agree to it if I didn't say a word about it to you. Whatever her problem was, she was terrified how you'd react.'

Richard looked drained. 'So you know the reason now,' he said tightly, 'why Polly's been so pent-up and miserable? I've hated seeing her puffy

405

eyes.' His face looked older, without its animation and warmth, sagging under the strain. 'She doesn't terrify easily,' he said. 'Tell me what she's done. It's not dealing, is it? Has she stolen things? I can imagine her shoplifting for kicks.'

'Nothing like that. She's pregnant.'

Richard didn't speak. He picked up his glass, took a few sips. Kate would almost rather an instant outburst. She could only wait while he sat in silence.

'The thing I mind most,' he said eventually, 'is why she couldn't have come and told me herself. Am I Elizabeth Barrett's tyrannical father of Wimpole Street, for fuck's sake?' he demanded, becoming more heated. 'Have I so lost touch with my daughter that she doesn't know instinctively I'd only want to help? That really hurts. What have I done wrong, Katie? Tell me. Set me straight.'

His wretchedness was clear, but he looked aggrieved as well and while she admired and felt grateful for his lack of unreasonable anger, Kate felt he was seeing it only from his point of view. She found herself speaking up for Polly; it seemed only right to plead her case.

'Think how hard it was for her. You and Polly have been having rows; you felt guilty about leaving and thought she was blaming you, but you never did any straight talking and asked her how she truly felt. You kept up a pretence. She doesn't blame you for going, she just feels insecure and in need of feeling loved.'

'You try talking to a stroppy, rebellious teenager,' Richard retaliated, clearly touched on the raw. 'Hell, Katie, I've done all I can . . .' He sighed, heaving his shoulders. 'Anyway, that's all hardly the point. Did she talk about having an

406

abortion? Is she keen on the boy? How much has she told you? I'd better hear it all!' He made an effort to smile.

Kate rose and went to lean over his chair and kiss him. She had a sudden vision of how hard she might find it herself, seventeen years down the line, facing a perverse, recalcitrant teenager, and at an older age than Richard was now. It made her understand more, how easily impasses could happen; anxious protective parents wanting to set guidelines, children fighting to find their own identities. Both trying to live up to an image they believed to be right and always expecting so much.

Richard took hold of her arm and leaned his head to it. 'It's always easier,' she said, 'when it's not blood family and Polly, I'm afraid, had plenty of reasons to feel scared about turning to you. Far from being keen on the boy, she doesn't know who it was.'

Richard went rigid. 'Christ, Katie! What do you mean? She must know.' He turned and looked up at her in grey-faced disbelief.

Kate pulled out the chair beside him, sat down and carefully explained about the warehouse party and the ecstasy tablet. She told him about the boyfriend with his condoms and the watching, salivating, unknown men. She didn't lie, but tried to make it sound as if only one of them had taken advantage; she felt the spelled-out truth might be particularly hard for a father to bear.

Richard put his head in his hands. 'She'll have to have an abortion,' he said heavily, 'much as I hate the thought. It's not too late, is it? God, it's a mess . . . And it never even crossed my mind to think she might be pregnant, I can't think why not.'

'She wants to have this baby. She seems adamant, absolutely determined, and I really do believe it's a genuine gut need and not just a case of protesting too much.'

'How's she going to cope, Katie? How are we? How can we make her see the need for an abortion, the full enormity of what it would all mean? How can she take on all that responsibility so young?' Richard stared ahead, looking incredibly drawn and defeated then he gave a long slow sigh. 'It's hopeless, dreaming of charmed lives for one's children. She'll be so dragged down. And what about school and her exams, I'd like to know? She would have had every chance of top grades.'

'Why "would have"? I'm sure she can stay at school and do fine. She'll probably even work that little bit harder. We'll sort it, you'll see. And one small upside, especially from my point of view, is that now, having braved turning to me, Polly sees me as a friend. I'm just sorry about what it took to do it, though . . .' Richard gave a briefly uncomprehending look then smiled and squeezed Kate's hand.

'I was dreading telling you,' she said, feeling intense relief to have it behind her. 'I was braced for you to have stormed and raged! I'm very glad that you didn't.'

'What would have been the point? It's happened, we just have to do our best and help her all we can. She's lost a whole slice of carefree fun living, though, which is criminally sad—and we've only just scratched the surface of all the problems.'

His eyes were distant suddenly; he was elsewhere, no doubt thinking of Eleanor. Kate could usually tell when he was. She couldn't talk about selling her flat and buying a house together, the possibility of Polly moving in, talk future plans and sound positive, without telling him she was pregnant, too. It would be the most double of double whammies. Was now the moment? She held off.

Richard pulled himself together. He cleared their plates and told her she must have some of the apple tart—made with the wonderful Bramleys from Aidan's garden, he said. Hannah had piled them up with her home cooking and half the garden produce on their recent visits.

He cut slices of tart, standing at the worktop with his back to Kate. She came beside him and he took her hands and looked her straight in the eye. 'You've got to understand something,' he said. 'This can't be allowed to affect our life. You shouldn't have to suffer or feel Polly's going to come before everything else. You do. You should know that. And your work problems, don't feel you can't talk about them, just because of all this. I don't know how to thank you for tonight, Katie, for all you've done. I love you so very much.'

'I'm having a baby, too,' she blurted out, looking down at her nails, frozen with the suspense before glancing up from beneath her lashes. She needed to feel it was a wanted baby and longed for his support.

Richard grinned. 'I've been waiting for you to tell me that. Why has it taken you so long? You must have known at least two or three weeks ago if I did. I was beginning to think I'd got it wrong and you were on some hormone course or other to be swelling in all the right places.'

'You thought I was pregnant and kept quiet?

You could have asked!'

'And you could have said.'

'Is it a great shock to you, now you know for sure? We couldn't easily manage to stay here, it would mean a huge upheaval. But it's my responsibility,' Kate said desperately. 'I wanted it and you must be able to have your children around. Of course, I have had some ideas about what to do . . .'

Richard burst out laughing. 'And so have I! I've been thinking of nothing else, distracted for the last few minutes, of course, with what you've just dropped in my lap. You've had a head start, twenty-four hours to be able to factor in Polly, so I hope you're going to give me the benefit of your far better ideas.' He put his arm round her, gathering her close. 'Come and sit down and let's deal with everything else first. What did you discover about Dan and the office? What happened?'

That was too much. Kate broke away and exploded. 'Fuck Dan and the office—can't you tell me how you feel about the baby? Doesn't it mean anything to you? I'm beginning to think it was just a little present, that offer to get me pregnant, something to keep me sweet.'

Richard stopped dead. 'That's a most terrible thing to say. You can't seriously think such a thing?'

Kate glared into his hurt, angry eyes. 'Yes, I do think it. You've never given the slightest indication that you really wanted this baby, or even thought much at all about becoming a father again. But you needn't be involved if you don't want to. You're not tied, you can walk away.'

'Stop this, Katie, this madness, and let me talk. I shouldn't have assumed anything, I can see now

410

how wrong that was, but surely my feelings were blazingly evident. I'd told you how I hoped you'd surprise me one day and hadn't wanted to push it when you were feeling your way—explain to me what was half-hearted about that?'

'But it is going to affect our life together,' Kate pressed, feeling exhausted, weak with emotion. 'Also you said just now that Polly's baby mustn't be allowed to do that, but it will, just as much as ours will, and I want it to—she's an extension of you. And though I do understand now that you want this baby of ours and it's not a complete shock, I still don't know what it really means to you, deep inside.'

Richard hugged her tight. 'Everything! You're making me feel terrible.' He took her hand, led her to the sofa. 'Out in the Caribbean I thought about little else than making babies. It was the worry of Eleanor, the same inevitable wretched problem, blinding me to the most fundamentally important thing, your sensitivities in all this! I've been so stressed out, worrying how Eleanor would react to you being pregnant, trying to think of ways to minimize how much it meant to me, planning how to let her know casually, imply it was just an embarrassing slip, one that I'm stuck with that's making me feel duty bound.

'Try to understand, darling, it would take so little to tip her over. And God knows what Polly's news is going to do. I suspect Eleanor's first thought will be about the disruption to her routine, how badly it will affect her chance to practise and perform. In Eleanor's eyes her music, her violin, is like God: it speaks to her and she has to obey. If she feels thwarted in doing its bidding she loses confidence,

411

which is at the heart of her entire bipolar lifetime, and so another manic depressive cycle begins. Doctors place sufferers on the "bipolar spectrum" according to the severity and intensity of their mood swings and she's diagnosed as Bipolar 1, which means the most full-blown.'

Kate wondered if she'd ever truly understand; her jealousy of a sick woman was terrible, but it was live and raw. Would Richard, too, ever really appreciate that he couldn't assume things and that she was in constant need of reassurance? She wanted to talk about the advantages of Polly moving in with them, his mother, Celia, possibly becoming involved in some way and her ideas for a housing shake-up. But she sensed that they'd exhausted their emotional quota, their two minds could only assimilate so much in one night without a dangerous overload, and now wasn't the time.

Richard asked again about Dan and the office. Since no mention of Dan ever turned out to be an easy ride, it felt best to play it down. Kate debated implying that any decision to leave Impetus would be of her own choosing; she didn't much fancy having to admit that it was being more or less forced upon her.

As it was she weakened and told Richard everything. It was some small satisfaction being able to explain about Dan's feelings for her. He was hardly the most glamorous conquest, no fast bowler or football star, but she liked being able to say that, according to Mary, he'd been obsessively in love with her for years.

That didn't wash with Richard. 'I'm sure Dan's been burning up for years, as frustrated as hell at not succeeding with you, but don't tell me he isn't

412

shagging every other female in the building. He's far too shallow for this great depth of love! Sounds more like Mary was doing someone's bidding, acting for whoever has an eye on your job. Probably Mary herself—is she a rung below you?'

'Not exactly. Need we talk any more about all this?' Kate said impatiently, quite put out. 'I've taken the decision, I'm going to leave. Although I can't think what job I'll do. Mum's talked about think tanks, working on policies, but I'm not sure about that. It would be a very different path.'

'What about something to do with art? Writing a book, having a newspaper or magazine column of your own? I've got the contacts, I could help with that. Just don't,' Richard said, 'get another job in advertising.'

'Depends on the offer—and the prospective boss . . .' She kissed him. 'Anyway, my job's the least of it. And all this telling has done me in; I'm a shattered wreck, ready for bed.'

'Do you think it's too late for me to ring Polly? She must be chewing her nails to the quick, worrying how you're doing, taming the ogre. I did take to heart what you said earlier about communicating better.'

'I'd say you were pretty safe,' Kate said, thinking that the last thing Polly would be was asleep at eleven-fifteen. 'I wondered about her coming to supper,' she added cautiously, 'as soon as possible really, if you agree, like this Friday. You could suggest it, perhaps. Or would you rather see her alone?'

Richard looked horrified. 'No, I can't do this thing without you, Katie. I need you there, desperately. You must see that?'

413

'Um, before you call you should just know that I mentioned my news to Polly. It was kind of accidental, it slipped out, but I was so worried she'd mind about it and resent me even more. She actually seemed delighted, though, for whatever reason, safety in numbers or something, in fact she seemed quite over the moon.'

'You told her before me? That makes me feel a bit jealous.'

'Sorry, but it helped to bring us together in a way, Polly and me. And I was dead scared of telling you, after all. You have that effect!'

Richard practically had to carry Kate to bed. To be through the evening, the ordeal of uncertainty, to be feeling exultant, she thought her legs would give way.

'I'm glad you're not going to cut off your daughter and cast her out into the snows,' she said sleepily, 'and cast me out as well.'

'Better see you play your cards right, then. Oh, and before you drop off—thanks!'

Kate woke in the small hours, once more. She must get a message to Ben about Spencer's lawyers; it could be crucially important. She stifled a sigh and gently eased her position, but sensed Richard was awake too. They put out exploratory hands and made contact.

'I feel awful, I never asked how you're feeling. Is it going okay? I know you're off coffee and wine,' Richard said.

'My boobs are a bit sore, but I don't know if that's your fault or the baby's.'

'Am I allowed to know now, in my new father-to-be role, what happened the night you had dinner with Ben?'

414

'That was on my mind too; thinking about it must have woken me up. But sorry, no, I can't tell you. You can't know now and I hope never at all.'

* * *

Kate did an hour's work at her desk the next morning, cleared her emails, then decided to act on her decision. No point in hanging about. She went to see the woman in HR and said she wanted to leave. The woman didn't look entirely surprised and they discussed a few practicalities quite civilly.

'Is there any particular reason?' she asked, which Kate presumed was the sort of thing she was trained to say.

She couldn't hold it in. 'Well, yes, actually,' she said. 'I'm having a baby and thinking ahead. I'll want to work at a different pace and do fewer hours.' It was the first time of saying it publicly; it made her pregnancy a glorious reality, a dream realized, and Kate felt herself blush to the roots of her hair. She hoped the woman wouldn't put it down to prudish embarrassment about being newly in a relationship and unmarried.

Richard had convinced her of his feelings. He wanted the baby, he'd looked smugly happy last night, she thought—quite something after hearing his daughter had landed him with another child to house, clothe and feed. But he didn't want marriage, nothing could be clearer than that.

Back at her desk she checked her mobile. No message from her mother, but she'd made plain in her own text that she'd be the one to call. Not the time to do it now, she was already late for a meeting.

415

Kate put her phone on silent, steeled herself to struggle through the meeting and prepared to concentrate. She glanced nervously at the phone once or twice. Putting it away she saw that Dan had been watching, sourly disapproving.

'Problems?' he asked. 'Lover let you down?' Kate looked at him coldly, not deigning to reply. He was ghastly. How had she let Mary con her into softening her view?

At midday she was back at her desk with a few moments' privacy and free to make calls. She clicked on her mother's number, drumming her fingers with tense impatience. No warm, responsive voice greeted her, only an automated female drone: 'This number is not taking calls.' She remembered Rachel was being super-careful about mobiles; could she be keeping it off? She might have popped to the shops for something, Kate thought dubiously, and left it behind. But then why—in either case really—should the phone be switched off?

She immediately tried the house phone. The phone rang and rang; she left it ringing so long it eventually made a continuous jarring sound as if the line had been disconnected. What had happened to the voicemail? The phone couldn't be off the hook, it would have had a busy tone. No panicking. It would ring on like that, Kate told herself, thinking back to her flat-sharing days, if the bill hadn't been paid. She felt sure, though, that Ben, with his army career, his air of capable authority, would have paid the bills. Could he have whisked Rachel away on a surprise mini-holiday? But wouldn't she have called or texted even so?

Kate stood up from her desk too abruptly and felt dizzy. She held on to the table. Think calmly.

Suppose it had really happened? What would her mother want her to do? Wouldn't she want her to act a part, to fluster and panic? Probably, but not right away, Kate thought, since she wasn't supposed to know a thing about what was going on.

She tried her mother's phone again. She remembered that Ben's mobile number was in her contacts and rang that. It was switched off. She called Directories for the number of Ocean Shipping Company. 'Sorry,' his assistant said, 'Mr Townsend isn't at his desk. I'm not sure if he was coming in today . . .'

Kate's hands were shaking, she gripped the table. If her mother and Ben really had disappeared, it must mean that MI6 had their man. Were they rounding him in right now, along with his chief henchmen, like so many head of violent cattle? They must know who he was. Or had the authorities failed, foundered, let her mother down? Kate thought of pleasant, decent Roger Grieve who'd raised a few questions about financial discrepancies and had his face brutally smashed into his glass desk for his troubles. Was her mother even still alive?

Kate caved in. She buried her head in her hands, shoulders heaving. One of the PAs came running over. 'Kate, whatever's wrong?'

Strength came to her and she sat up and wiped her eyes. 'Sorry, I'll be fine in a minute; it's family, something troubling.' The girl was hesitating, about to offer help. Kate stood up. 'I need to go right now,' she said, her voice tight as she tried to stay in control. 'I'll call in later and explain.'

Just then her mobile whirred and buzzed on her desk. She fell on it with a quivering hand as the girl

417

left. It was Sadie.

'Hi, I'm just a bit worried; I've been trying to raise Mum. Her mobile's off and the phone's not answering. Was she going anywhere? Do you know anything about it?'

'I've been calling her, too. I'm about to go round to the flat and see if she's there. I pray nothing's wrong. But we mustn't panic. There's probably a simple explanation, usually is. If I think anything's up or find any real problem, I'll call right away, Sadie, obviously. And if we need to meet, I'll drive down, soon as I can. Try not to worry. I'm trying not to as well.'

CHAPTER 26

Kate knew what she had to do. She took a taxi to Warwick Square, sitting stiffly upright, thinking of all the things she passionately wanted to have said to her mother: the promises she would have made, the last-minute questions, pleas for advice—along with all the greedy clinging hugs. To think it might have happened, her mother's disappearance, it felt an emotional catastrophe, a different pain from the awful finality of a death like Harry's, yet an acuteness of misery such as she couldn't have believed. Loss was abject grief, but this, the aching, harrowing strain of knowing her mother and Ben might be somewhere, living, breathing, watchful, wearing another skin, signing in another name, was unique.

Would MI6 follow through and protect them properly? Had everything gone according to plan?

418

Was MI6 involved at all? Kate prayed there really was a simple explanation; she was overwrought, pregnant, being pushed out of a job—she might easily have forgotten about some function or commitment of her mother's. Rachel could be on a plane and about to call on landing. But it didn't feel like that. She remembered the hug they'd had, saying goodnight in Warwick Square, how precious it had felt and full of significance.

Her taxi was drawing up in the Square. Kate felt drenched in fear. She shivered, entering the building and taking the carpeted stairs, hearing the silence. No one was about, it was a working day. She had the key to Ben's flat on her ring, a precaution for emergencies that she hadn't expected to use. She rang the bell, stood waiting, then fumbled with the key that undid both locks and went inside.

'Mum? Ben? Anyone here?' Not a sound. It was a fine day, sunshine streaming in, dust particles in the air. Wandering about, Kate found nothing untoward. The fridge was full of food, the bed was made, not slept in. Her mother's favourite deep-red tulips, spilling out of a round glass vase, hadn't even begun to droop.

She wondered what to do. Go home to another empty house—sit and cry? Drive to Basingstoke that afternoon and talk it over with Sadie? That would mean explaining everything, all that Ben had said, and about the need for secrecy. It felt a bit soon, she wasn't supposed to know anything after all, and there was always a chance it could be a false alarm. Perhaps it was best to call Sadie now, from the flat, and float the idea of Ben springing a surprise holiday, that they could be on a plane,

Rachel's mobile off for a reason. She could report that all was well at the flat and suggest they postpone any decision about calling the police till the evening or the following day. Then, if neither she nor Sadie heard anything in the next twenty-four hours, break her heavy secret to her sister.

The house phone wasn't cut off or out of order so she called Sadie on it. Punching in the number, the stillness and quiet was unnerving, but she had a hard job shouting out all she needed to say over the combined screams of Amelia and Rose.

'They want their lunch,' Sadie said, with an affection that, just at that moment, Kate found hard to share. She felt that what she was doing, postponing the agony, was probably right, but she longed to lean on her sister and share the wretchedness.

'I can't see Ben really going in for surprise holidays,' Sadie said, 'and it's hard to believe Mum wouldn't have called from the airport. I do feel worried.'

'Me too, but we must hang on.'

She wouldn't go home, Kate thought. Better to go back to work, having taken little more than a lunch break, and stick it out for the day. She could tell the PA, if necessary, that she'd been alarmist and was fine. Deciding on a path of action should have been calming, but Kate felt a storm of sobs rushing to the surface as she had a last look round the silent, sunny, warmly decorated flat and left. Rational thought had taken so much out of her she felt in danger of collapse. She forced back the tears.

Turning the corner out of the Square she had to tangle with five excitable, ill-behaved dogs on leads. The walker failing to control them made no apology and Kate strode up Belgrave Road towards Victoria station, cursing under her breath all the way. It released a tension valve and strengthened her spine.

An afternoon session on the new pitch for the health-foods chain dragged on painfully; she dug her nails into her palms and stifled exhausted yawns. It was indeed Spencer's food-outlet chain, Richard had confirmed that, so she could think of no better time to be leaving Impetus. Was Spencer Morgan the mastermind? Kate couldn't imagine him being involved in anything without running the show and she had just managed to link him to Acai of Amapá Export. Did MI6 have the wrong man? Did they know anything about it?

By five o'clock hunger set in, she'd had little breakfast and no lunch; she went down to the pink-lit cafe and bought a chicken-salad wrap and took it back upstairs, grateful to snatch a few minutes at her desk. She had the little speck of a bean inside her, it had to grow.

Her mobile rang.

'Is that Kate Nichols? We haven't met, but you'll understand the reason for the call if I tell you my name is Jon and that I'm a friend of Ben Townsend. I wish we could have met earlier, but it simply wasn't possible, I'm afraid.'

Kate gripped the phone. 'Can you tell me anything?' she asked, flooded with a combined sense of panic and relief. He was being slightly circumspect, speaking cautiously, and she continued in the same vein. 'Is there any chance that you're less busy now and we might be able to meet after all? I do have a lot of questions.' Her voice was tremulous, catching in her throat, and she couldn't go on.

'That's actually why I was ringing. I have to be in Covent Garden tomorrow and thought it might be helpful if we met. Could you manage a cup of coffee, say around ten o'clock tomorrow morning? Forgive me if I'm a little late, though, don't despair!' He gave directions and Kate confirmed calmly that she would be there.

She packed up her desk, held over unfinished work and left without any goodbyes. She couldn't stay at work after that call. Jon existed, MI6 were involved, Ben wasn't the man of her worst nightmares; but it meant too that her mother was gone and there was no doubt, no more clinging to slim chance and happenstance.

Jon's call had come without warning, she hadn't been prepared. The full significance of how fundamentally her life was about to change, with no parent to run to, no guiding hand, was only just sinking in. Her father might not live more than another week.

It was peak rush-hour so she took a taxi straight home. Richard had to be told, he'd see the state she was in. He would be home about seven. Best leave her suspicions about Spencer Morgan out of it, she felt, since she had faith in Ben and MI6 now, and thought they must know what they were doing and the identity of the mastermind. They wouldn't want any whisper of this, certainly not his name, to reach the press, she was sure.

She called Sadie the moment she was home. It was agonisingly painful, being able to tell her so little. She said their mother, she believed, was safe, before going on to explain guardedly about seeing someone in the morning, after which they might have a great deal to talk about. She felt dreadful to be still stringing out her sister, but the children were screaming, distracting her, and Kate knew she had to keep her painful secret close until after the meeting with Jon.

Could she face cooking supper? She was alone, staring into the fridge, not knowing where to begin. How could she get on with normal life and cook a meal? Suppose Jon, with his pleasant, educated voice that had reminded her of Roger Grieve, never showed? Suppose he had some terrible news that he hadn't wanted to tell her on the phone? The house was so quiet. She wanted her mother.

* * *

Kate found the coffee shop, which was decorated in an old-fashioned style with blue-check tablecloths, a large, cream-painted dresser and rush-seated chairs. It was a warm, fine day; she was wearing a pearl-grey, sleeveless linen dress, a cardigan over her shoulders, and had walked from work, thinking it would help to ease the tension. She felt quite hot as she went in and chose a table where she could take in the sweep of the room. Kate ordered a pot of tea from a yawning waitress. The cafe was almost empty, the breakfasters gone and the shoppers and lunch trade yet to arrive.

It was five minutes to ten. She was subdued, numb with the strain and beyond practical thought about the right questions to ask. Waiting, fingering the strap of her bag in her lap and feeling overwhelmingly fearful, her mind was on Richard and the night before.

He'd come home to find her curled on the sofa

423

in tears.

'Is it your father?' he'd asked urgently, lifting her up, kissing her face, desperate in his need to comfort her.

'No, not that, not yet, it's Mum . . .' Kate had buried her head in his leather jacket, masculine-smelling like his car, then steeled herself and told him everything. The cocaine-trafficking scam piggy-backing on Ben's business, the dangerous mission he'd undertaken, carrying on as normal while keeping his friend in MI6 informed, the risk to both his and Rachel's lives. Richard had heard her out— her heavy secret shared at last—before taking her by surprise and pouring out his own heart.

Kate felt a shadow and looked up to see a man with receding ginger hair and mild blue eyes coming up to her table. She gave a cautious smile. He was in a dark suit with a discreet maroon tie, not a man to draw attention, but she was quickly aware of an alert, assessing intelligence behind his gaze.

'It's Kate isn't it, if I may call you that? I hope you haven't been waiting long. May I join you?'

'I hope this table's all right,' Kate said, as he chose a chair at right angles to hers, so that he too, was looking out into the room. 'It's a nice, quiet time of day . . .'

'It's good you could make it,' he said, setting his briefcase down at his feet. 'Can I order you a coffee?'

'I've got a pot of tea on the way.' She saw the waitress was about to bring it over.

Jon ordered a latte, chatting about the spring sun and the flocking tourists. Once he had his coffee and they were alone, he looked at her gravely. 'You know we owe you a very great deal,' he said, causing her to stare in amazement. 'You'll soon see why.' He leaned forward, his elbows on the table to bring him closer. 'First, though, I have to mention that the man we've been tracking for so long is about to be exposed; he'll be making headlines any day now, but until that happens this must be for your ears alone.'

Kate glanced around. The serving counter was out of earshot, a couple at the window table who looked like dancers—the only other customers there at that hour of the morning—were also too distant to hear. She was burning to ask a question before he carried on. 'My mother and Ben—just reassure me, they are safe and where they need to be?'

'They are, and the risks they took were exceptionally courageous and selfless. But you've shown that same courage, too. I did have my worries when Ben wanted you to be put in the picture, but I realize they were unfounded!'

'You really do have your man now?' Kate asked, kneading her hands together, rubbing at the wedding ring she still wore. She felt cold suddenly, through and through. 'Ben explained the scale of the trafficking, the ruthlessness. He seemed to think that nailing this man would be no easy task.'

'He was right. You gave Ben quite a few problems, you know,' Jon smiled. 'He worried constantly too, that you didn't truly trust him—which he understood; he had, after all, of necessity, been a bit furtive and not always entirely straight with you.'

'Why wasn't he—since he'd already told me so much?'

'Your questions about our man, your recent holiday host, were on the right track, you see, and Ben had to keep diverting you and steering you off. He was rightly terrified for your safety. He feared he hadn't succeeded and joked to me that it would be even more costly to the taxpayer if you'd had to be given a new identity too.'

She was slowly beginning to understand—and if anything could have lessened the pain she was feeling it was that her suspicions about Ben had been unfounded. He was brave and honourable; her mother had called him exceptional.

Her father was exceptional too. Kate thought of his deep, enduring love for Rachel and what he must have been through, losing her, living with the knowledge that he'd brought Ben into her life himself. What agony.

Kate had so many queries. She looked at Jon anxiously. 'But Ben once told me—which surely he wasn't making up—that this man, the elusive mastermind, was actually feeding you information?'

'It took a long time, many years, for us to be certain of his guilt, if not able to prove it. We were pleased to have him on board at first, the information was useful. He had contacts in the terrorist organisation, the FARC, with the drugs barons who were all-powerful at the time, and the two are intertwined. We don't shout about it, but we do provide specific assistance to Colombia and run counter-narcotics activities out there. Our man was brilliantly clever, but slowly, slowly, while his financial empire scaled loftier heights, certain things didn't add up.

'Ben, in fact, smelled something rotten in the woodshed many years ago. Having been in the

426

Intelligence Corps in Colombia and secretly in touch with our unit out there, he knew more about our man's criminal links and contacts than could have been expected. Seeing Ben as a straight-up army guy was our man's one big mistake; he obviously thought he was on to a good thing, encouraging Ben to start an import business, offering to back him. He would be a guiding force, he said, with his superb business acumen, and help Ben make the most of his South American knowledge.

'But he'd misread the quality of his underling. Ben came to us for advice and it was our view that he should set up the company and get stuck in. He ended up with a thriving business, but couldn't find out anything conclusive, certainly no hard proof. The man is devilishly devious.'

'Is he connected with the FARC then, as well as all his trafficking of cocaine?'

Jon smiled. 'He sure is. It goes like this. The FARC take care of the local coca production, our man ships the stuff—in Ben's containers among others—which he then floods onto the British market to devastating effect. He garners in the money, launders it through his clubs and casinos, takes truckloads of cash out to Dubai where he does business, or somewhere else very lightly regulated like that. He changes the dirty money into bonds that he sends electronically, through Central and South American banks, back to the FARC. But only after slicing himself a tidy cut. It's a nice little earner, you could say.'

'But,' she said, 'if this man makes all those billions in his financial dealings, which, incidentally, my friend Richard thinks stink pretty potently too,

427

why does he actually need to take such enormous risks and dirty his hands with drugs?'

'For the thrill of it? Possibly the FARC have some kind of hold on him. He wasn't where he is now, you see, when he was dealing with rough trade out in Colombia all those years ago. He would be easy enough to eliminate if they decided to get rougher still. He's out in the open, an accessible public figure, however many hidden bodyguards he employs. The FARC are a formidable body who can lose themselves very effortlessly in that impenetrable Colombian jungle. But who knows what drives a man like that. It's impossible to tell.'

'Can I know what finally tripped him up?'

'You did! You gave us a crucial clue.'

Kate couldn't believe she had done, couldn't see how; she hadn't even unloaded her discovery about Spencer's Brazilian lawyer, which she was keen to do.

'I did a tiny little bit of research the other day,' she said. 'I know I was under instructions not to get involved, but I'd started feeling such loathing for the man in question that I was desperate to find out what I could.' She explained about Morgan's Brazilian lawyer being a partner in the acai processing plant. 'Do I have to throw away my laptop or anything now?' she asked.

Jon smiled politely. 'That won't be necessary. If we thought this man and his henchmen believed you knew the slightest thing, you'd be travelling under an assumed name as we speak.'

'I wanted to reach Ben and tell him about the lawyer,' she said, 'but you've closed off any chance of that.' Her eyes filmed and she fished for a tissue with an embarrassed smile. 'I can't, seriously, have

428

been any real help,' she continued, back in control, 'but what was the clue you think I gave you?'

'When you swam round the yacht and picked up on a private conversation—a unique achievement, given the particular parties concerned—you heard a date mentioned. You told it to Ben that evening, after dinner. It was a vital clue.'

Jon could see she was confused, trying to remember, and he carried on. 'It was about the meeting in Trinidad, planned for that coming Thursday—you'd overheard the two men talking about it and passed the information on to Ben. Our man had stressed the importance of the meeting, you said, and sounded menacing.'

He gave his dry spook's smile. 'And I can't stress strongly enough how important that clue was to *us*. We have our ways of doing things and we were able to establish that a senior figure from the FARC was expected to arrive in Trinidad that Thursday, travelling via Venezuela on a scheduled flight. His trip was thought to concern an important finance meeting. One of the mastermind's drivers met the flight from Caracas, which was a good start and, since we have our ways and cameras, we acquired some valuable footage of our man himself, meeting that key figure.

'We'd had almost enough on him, the trail had been hotting up, but proof of that vital connection had always eluded us. He was never at the scene of the crime. We knew, thanks to the whistle-blower in Ben's company, the route the drugs took from Colombia—how they were smuggled into Brazil, buried in frozen fruit pouches, carried by sea-container and finally unleashed onto our streets. That meeting with the FARC was crucial, though, the final link in the chain.'

Kate's mind was suddenly filled with a picture of the billionaire philanthropist Spencer Morgan, that thought-to-be pillar of society, finally in the dock.

Jon, she sensed, sitting beside her on one of the cafe's rush-seat chairs, was allowing her time to absorb his news. Her thoughts were wrapped up with Richard, though, as she remembered how restorative his support had been the evening before; consoling, carrying her through the long night hours, a taut net to break her fall. Yet he'd been the one to suffer, in many ways, having to cope and keep faith while she bottled up all her secrets and suspicions.

To hear him speak of his innermost feelings had shaken her.

Richard had talked while her head was buried in his jacket, his fingers playing with her hair.

'Ben wasn't exactly my favourite person for quite a while,' Richard had said. 'What I've wanted to do to him at times! I'd thought of every conceivable situation, anything you could ever have needed to keep secret from me, you see, and got nowhere. I love you, I could live with it, but, God, I minded the lack of trust. It really stung. Now I understand. I know I shouldn't be talking about me like this, but I can't tell you the relief I feel!

'Try and remember that your mother is out of harm and being protected. She's somewhere, sensing your needs—and I'm here for you. Sadie's the baby guru, she'll be the fount of all practical help, and I know my way round the back end of a baby, too. You're not alone.'

Kate sighed, a deep sigh, and focused on Jon again. He wasn't looking at his watch, he was being patient, waiting, as if he hadn't quite finished what he wanted to say.

She nipped in first. 'Can I ask one or two last questions?'

'Ask anything. I'll tell you if I can.'

'I know Richard is in the media world, but is it all right to tell him who I now know it is?'

'Would you wait till late tonight? The story will be breaking news tomorrow. And it would be best, can you explain, not to talk about your mother and Ben. It's precautionary, but we'd prefer the least attention drawn possible.'

Kate assured him of all that. 'So I can tell my sister everything now, too?'

'Of course, you must. Perhaps,' Jon hesitated, 'since she might be upset to think of Ben involving you and how much you'd known, it might be best just to say your mother only explained what could be about to happen when you met up at supper two nights ago. It would help to avoid your sister feeling you hadn't been straight with her.'

That sounded wise advice. Kate smiled gratefully while planning in her head to call the office, talk of a family crisis, rush to Thornby Terrace for her car and drive immediately to Basingstoke.

Jon's light eyes were warm, but watchful too, as though assessing how she was bearing up. 'Shall I just tie up one or more ends before you rush away?'

'Everything you can,' she said. 'I'd be grateful.'

'You know about Roger Grieve?'

'Yes. I'd met him once, actually, at a New Year's Eve party with my mother and Ben. It distresses me to think that was only three weeks before he died.'

'It was shocking that he got caught up in this, but we think we know now who might have murdered him, which should be possible to prove with the help of DNA. We suspect that Grieve innocently took his concerns about discrepancies and inflated living standards to the boss. He advised on pensions in a number of his companies and wouldn't have considered the man at the top himself was involved. That man, we think, would have acted horrified and arranged to meet Grieve, possibly when he had more time, to discuss it further—a private meeting after hours in his office, explained away by a late arrival back on a plane. We know the time our man's plane landed, it does all fit.'

Kate stared at Jon in disbelief. 'You mean Grieve could have opened the door unsuspectingly and it was the boss himself who battered the back of his head and smashed his face down repeatedly onto his glass-topped desk?'

Her pulse had quickened, thinking about being a guest on the yacht of a murderer. 'I can't imagine it,' she went on. 'I mean, his society lifestyle, the luminaries he mixes with . . . surely he'd have employed a hit man or had his sidekick do it at the very least? And wouldn't there have been other people in the building?'

'Only night staff a few floors down. No one would have heard.'

'And what with—what suitable object could he have had in his hands?'

'He could have slipped out a heavy gun, been carrying a lead-lined briefcase . . .'

Jon had a dry grimace on his face. 'You can take the boy out of the East End, but you'll never take the East End out of the boy. He wouldn't have had kind thoughts about an intelligent person like Grieve cottoning on and meddling, edging a little

432

too close. His every instinct would have been to get Grieve and bash him hard, which he did.'

Kate was reminded of hearing Spencer tell Carl to 'check out' Richard, and the hairs on her arm stood on end. She could believe it quite easily after all. No wonder Ben had been so anxious to steer her away from any dangerous speculation.

'What about Andy, Ben's CFO?' she asked. 'What happens to him?'

'He's important to us, we'll need him to give evidence. You needn't worry, we'll come to some sort of accommodation.'

She felt it was time to go. Jon had given her his unhurried and full attention, but he must have a busy day ahead of him and she had to get to Basingstoke. She gathered her bag, made to stand up, only to pause and stay seated. Jon was the last link. Walking out of the coffee shop, she would be cut adrift for ever.

She looked at him, feeling a tight soreness in her chest. 'But my mother . . . Is there any chance . . . any way I can just have a last quick goodbye?'

'No, Kate. None, I'm sorry. But she wanted me to explain something that she thought might bring a small smile. It's about the couple in the restaurant. Your mother was right to think they were following her, but they were ours, you see, we were just keeping an eye. We will look after her, you can rest assured.'

It was kindly put and her cue to leave. Kate stood up wondering if that was the end of all contact or whether Jon or a colleague would call sometime, in years to come, with an address, a number, or she would pick up the phone to her mother. She shut out those thoughts and thanked him with all her heart.

He rose and shook her hand. 'Please don't thank me,' he said. 'The thanks should all come from me to you.'

*　　　*　　　*

Sadie was out, collecting Joseph from his playgroup. Kate hung about chatting to Hayley, the mother's help, in a desultory way, watching her spoon avocado mush into Rose's unaccommodating mouth while Amelia banged her plastic mug on the kitchen table ceaselessly. Kate sensed Hayley's curiosity about what was going on.

Sadie arrived back looking ashen. Her hair was greasy, she was in an ill-chosen pink sweater and tan trousers and her face was tinged green with tiredness. 'I didn't sleep a wink last night,' she muttered over Joseph's head as Kate hugged him. 'I couldn't stand the strain. Go and have a pee, Joseph, will you? It's time for lunch.'

He sensed his mother meant business and dutifully ran off. 'Put me out of my agony, Katie. What have you found out? Is Mum all right? Rupert keeps ringing, demanding to know if you've been onto the police.'

'Mum is all right,' Kate assured her, 'but we do have to have a very long, private talk, Sadie. Stay calm, see to the children, and after lunch we'll have a walk round the garden and I'll tell you the whole thing.'

Over lunch Kate tried to keep everything bright and cheerful in front of the children; Hayley was being a brick, too. She was uncomplaining when Kate murmured about needing Sadie for an hour or so, and looked sympathetic when told she might be needed later to lend support.

It took a long time to make Sadie accept the hard reality. She fought against it, but in the end dropped her head into Kate's lap as they sat together on the garden seat, and cried bitter, heart-rending tears. She lifted her face up eventually, wet and blotchy, and started all over again. 'It can't be true, Katie, tell me it's not true, I can't bear it. And Dad's very close to the end. Mum won't even know when it happens . . . I've been hoping she'd come to the funeral—I can't bear it.'

Eventually the emotion became just too much. 'Rupert will say it's all fantasy, he's very mistrustful of spooks. He might be right, Katie—have you thought of that? We can't lose our mother, we can't be that careless. We've got to find her, send out search parties . . .'

'She isn't lost, Sadie. She's safe with Ben who loves her; they could be in New York, Vancouver, somewhere like Vienna or Berlin where she can use her languages—who knows? And we must think of what's been achieved, a huge criminal network destroyed, trafficking on a vast scale, fewer killer drugs; the public better protected . . .'

'Who fucking cares?' Sadie screamed. 'How can I manage without Mum?'

'And how can I?' Kate demanded fiercely, which caused a look. 'I'm having a baby.'

That stopped Sadie in her tracks. She stared a moment then lit up. 'But that's great, fantastic news, hon—not what I was expecting to hear. Heartening in all this misery! Does Richard know? Will he mind? Will you get married?'

'He knows and he's pleased—but I won't have

435

Mum, won't be able to share the thrill . . .' Kate wondered suddenly if Sadie might have been a little jealous, had their mother's attention been diverted. She'd always been able to ask favours, to call on Rachel and expect her to drop everything and nip to Basingstoke. 'I'm going to need help and advice, Sadie, someone to turn to,' Kate carried on. 'And no, we're not getting married. I think Richard genuinely loves me, but I'm still scared stiff of the future. If he left me it would be the end, I'd want to die.'

'I'm quite sure he won't,' Sadie said, with brisk authority. 'What rubbish, pathetic talk. And you know it too. And I know all about babies. I'm here for you, Katie, we do still have each other.'

CHAPTER 27

Kate struggled to come round. Richard had just woken her up from a deep sleep.

'I'm going for the papers—I've been glued to the news! I suppose you knew?' He sounded accusing.

'Only since yesterday,' she said soothingly. 'Jon asked me to hold off for a day.' She couldn't help an enormous yawn, but Richard was out of the door.

It was early on Friday morning. She'd seen her mother on Monday, met Polly on Tuesday, told Richard their joint news on Wednesday, had her meeting with Jon on Thursday and faced telling her sister, the same afternoon. It was hardly surprising, she thought, that she'd slept for a solid eight hours.

The arrest of Spencer Morgan was a huge story.

436

Every newspaper had page after page on the appalling scandal. The night desks must have had a frenzied time. Photographs of Morgan escorting Royals, partying, cutting the ribbon on one of his philanthropic new hostels for the homeless; his yacht was featured prominently. The papers had hit it rich. Morgan would never have riches again, Kate hoped. He only had the rigours of prison life to look forward to: confinement, indignities and interminable, grinding boredom.

She wasn't going into work. Richard had called in and cheerfully lied on her behalf, saying that she was feverish and he'd ordered her to stay home. He had to rush, having changed his schedule for Polly, and he stood up from the table, tidying the newspapers absentmindedly, as though about to voice a thought.

'What about tonight?' he said. 'I think I should put Polly off coming. I can explain, and tell her she can relax, that I'm not going to lock her in a back bedroom or cut her off for life. It makes sense, darling; you've been through so much. And since Sadie's in Rye this weekend, and we're here, we can see Polly tomorrow or Sunday.'

Kate wondered whether it had a bit more to do with his nerves about facing his daughter than solicitousness for her. It wasn't going to be an easy evening. She thought he was anticipating a failure to win through. And the consequences of that were enormous, a terrible strain for him to think of and wearing him down.

Richard had been home when she got back from Basingstoke, supportive, listening intently while she told him all the details of the meeting with Jon, sympathetic as she went into how Sadie had taken

437

it. To be able to talk freely was a joy, as reviving and unwinding as a warm bath and a reminder of trust and intimacy. But Richard hadn't mentioned postponing Polly then, which would have been the more natural time.

'No,' Kate said, with a firmness that seemed to quite spook him, 'Polly must come tonight. You couldn't do that to her. She needs to get past this hurdle—think of how it's been for her, feeling nauseous, sick with worry, and the loneliness of it too. I'm fine, that's the least of it. I'm going to shop, get my hair cut, cook, have a meal ready—meat and two veg . . .'

Her day would be a dry-run, she thought, being home on a Friday; she'd be out of a job in weeks.

* * *

Polly arrived early with a bunch of deep-violet irises for Kate and nervous smiles. Her head was bent low over a cup of tea when Kate heard Richard's car drawing up. The double doors to the small back garden were open and it seemed a good moment to go out and pick some mint. Kate came in again to see Richard and his daughter smiling cautiously at each other, keeping their distance, before Polly launched herself into her father's arms and he gave her an awkward hug.

'It's okay, Pol, I wouldn't have eaten you,' he mumbled, patting her back with an embarrassed look on his face, a strained smile over her head at Kate. As she came up, he separated from Polly and looked at her squarely. 'But we do need to talk,' he said.

'Food first,' Kate said, 'and do I get a hug and a

438

kiss, too?'

She had spent half the afternoon cooking a salmon coulibiac, layering mushrooms, herbs, grated ginger, a few tiny currants, cooked rice; placing the large piece of salmon, sealing it all up in a pastry case. It would be useful to have cold over the weekend, she thought, bringing it out of the oven with a certain pride. Richard and Polly, who'd been awkwardly laying the table, leaped to it and brought over the vegetables.

'I'm sorry, Dad,' Polly said, as she took delivery of a slice of salmon and helped herself to spinach. 'Truly. I know how hard it must be for you, the strain.'

'The thing that really hurts, Pol, is that you didn't feel able to come and tell me in the first place. Surely you know you could bring me any problem at all. I mean, even if I'd reacted strongly for a moment, I'd have calmed down and we could have talked it through sanely; you must have known that I'd understand and only want to help.'

'No, Dad, not with this problem. You'd have had your preconceptions, you wouldn't have tried to see it from my point of view or even really listened properly. And you weren't reaching out to me, giving me any openings, anyway. I wasn't top of the list.'

Polly wasn't making it easy for him, but Kate felt the worst thing she could do was to chip in. She watched as his daughter tucked into the food with gusto, as though she hadn't eaten for weeks. 'Fab, this, Katie,' she said, shovelling in mouthfuls and avoiding her father's eye.

Richard looked doubly injured, as though it was a slur on his cooking on top of slights to his

439

character. He glanced helplessly at Kate. 'Sorry, darling, I should have said. It is delicious.' He gave a weary sigh and stared at Polly's bent head.

'Okay Pol, you've had a good go, I dare say I deserved it, but I want to say my piece now. And don't, please, start protesting, hon, until you've heard me out.' She looked at him without answering or even nodding in acquiescence. Her face was closed, her mind set on its course.

Richard was used to that blank look on her face; he ignored it and carried on. 'I know from Kate that you want to keep the baby, but think, love—just for a moment, will you? Can you really try to? It's not school and your exams, you'll manage that— handing in coursework with baby-sick stains. It's not how you'll live. You're lucky; you've got me, Mum . . . between us you'll have a home for the baby, people to pay the bills. But think about being eighteen, nineteen, in your young twenties, all the challenges, travel, sport, parties, that you'd miss. You'd be lucky to get to university; you could, possibly, in London, but you'd have no chance of a year off. You'd miss those adventures, bumming round India, Australia . . .'

Polly scowled. 'I don't see why. People take babies abroad. I can take mine in a papoose and feed it myself in the early days . . .'

'And travel with bagfuls of Pampers, kettles, tins of mushed peas? Babies soon need a routine, Pol, after the first few months, a regular bedtime, familiar surroundings, afternoons socializing in the park. And don't leave out of account the hen weekends you'll want to go to, the clubbing. I know you want to keep this baby for the best of motives, but . . . is it fair? Children thrive better with two

440

parents and any child would ask about its father soon enough. What are you going to say?'

'Is it *fair* to deny it life?' Polly looked close to tears, but she held off. She was an amazing girl, so much character. 'I'll tell it the truth—in time, when it's old enough. And I'll find a form of words until then. I've thought more about that than anything else.'

'Don't you agree with me, Katie?' Richard turned, pleading for help with his eyes. 'Could you have managed with a growing baby, starting in a new, exciting job? Wouldn't you have felt impossibly tied—and hard done by, too, missing out on all the fun?'

Kate couldn't come to his rescue, and she privately hoped that had she been in the same situation, she would have had some of his daughter's strength.

'It has to be Polly's decision,' she said. 'But I think she's given it more serious thought than you realize. You're right, of course, to underline all the downsides, and there's no getting away from them, but shouldn't you perhaps give her a chance to speak and hear more of it from her side now?'

'All right, then, Pol—and don't think I'm not listening.'

'I'm fifteen weeks' pregnant, Dad. I have this being inside me, growing fast, moving soon and able to feel pain. I've no right to deny it a living future. Sure I might lighten my load, but I'd wake up with horrible thoughts in my head every morning, and hate myself to death.'

'Have you thought about adoption?' Richard muttered hopelessly.

Polly flashed him a withering look. 'And would I

441

feel any better, passing on my baby like it's second-hand? I can be a responsible person, you know, its needs will come first. I'll work, get qualifications. Think of all the high-flying women around, doctors, publishers, barristers, City whizzes, who have three, four, five children . . .'

'They have husbands mostly, support structures in the background.'

'And you've just offered to give me that support. I'll work hard, I promise, and get to be self-sufficient. Pay you back—everything you'd have put in and done for me. I can do it. I want an exciting life, but with my child. We'll have all the adventures together.'

'Have you seen a doctor?' Richard said, gazing despairingly at his daughter, possibly in awe as well. Kate thought he should be proud of her spirit at least.

'I haven't seen or told anyone but Katie.' Polly's pale, drained face suddenly broke out in a smile. 'I'm not being stubborn just for the hell of it, Dad—though on past history you might think so. I don't feel sort of like cornered and not wanting to lose face. I've given it endless thought. Perhaps I'm just growing up a bit.'

She had warmth in her eyes, gazing at her father across the table. Richard stared back. His expression was opaque. 'Well then,' he said, glancing at Kate as if to include her, 'that seems to be that. Two pregnant women on my hands. But, I suppose, thinking about it, if I'm going to be a grandfather and a father again in one go, maybe I've got some growing up to do as well—if I'm going to live up to both roles.'

'A very young grandfather, Dad.'

'Flattery, my girl, will get you nowhere.'

*   *   *

Kate felt like a sloth, having slept heavily for two more nights in a row. She thought her mind had shut-up shop and taken a break or her hormones were working overtime. She dressed in stretch denims and a navy Tee, while she still could, and went downstairs to see to breakfast. Richard was out buying the Sunday papers, keen to have another fix of Spencer Morgan being hung out to dry. Billboards had been trailing a Sunday exposé, a minor actress's well-paid revelations, 'My nights of passion with Spencer Morgan: Blue Movies aboard *Black Diamond*.'

She cut up a grapefruit and set out a couple of plates, but left the bacon and eggs to Richard. He liked cooking breakfast on weekends. It felt strange, being in London on a Sunday. Kate thought about her sister in Rye. Rupert and the children were there too; Sadie had wanted Joseph and Amelia to see their grandfather, to have a memory of him, however dimly in their subconscious it would be. They wouldn't see him alive again, she'd said without sentiment. Being practical about it was probably the way she coped best.

Richard came in and dumped down his bundle. 'They weigh a ton, these papers.' He gave the headlines a quick glance then concentrated on filling the house with the irresistible smell of sizzling bacon. He was a bit sore and sensitive about Spencer Morgan. Kate knew the long hours of work he'd put in, trying to nail Morgan, poring over the smallest financial detail, trying to catch him out and find gold-plated proof; to have come up with zilch was frustrating, if not mortifying, a blow to his professional pride.

Richard turned from the cooker, plates in hand, egg, bacon and tomato, and came to sit down. 'I'm thinking of doing a documentary on Morgan,' he said. '"The Making and Breaking of a Billionaire". Sound okay to you?'

'Great,' she said, crunching into a crispy sliver of bacon. 'People love how-the-mighty-have-fallen stories and you might just have your heart in it. Perfect accuracy too, on the subject of his yacht.'

'I want to add a Morgan bit into my cocaine story as well—trafficking the stuff from Colombia to Amapá and Santana Port, which is certainly not one of the tried and tested routes. It's near impossible to fathom out how they did it, Brazilian airspace and the Amazon and Negro Rivers are so well patrolled.'

'I know from Ben the route the spooks think was taken, if that's any help,' Kate said mildly. 'By plane through Venezuelan airspace and into Guyana; land on an airstrip near the border with Brazil, down the Rio Jari; by lorry from there, using the Amapá highway, which is red-earth, deserted and virtually not policed, so I'm told . . .' Richard was staring. 'Don't let your eggs get cold,' she smiled. 'Anything else I can help with?'

It was a companionable day: the newspapers, a walk, a chat with Madge and Justin who were ecstatic about the baby, an evening stroll down the King's Road to see a film.

*　　　*　　　*

Monday morning at the office was different, depressing. Kate apologised for a family crisis, reminded people her father was dying, but she was leaving, nobody cared.

Sadie called to report on Aidan. 'He wafts, Katie. He's fine one minute, quite sharp, then he goes sort of woozy and half there. I had to psych myself up to handle it; he told me to remember to be a mum, not a daughter when he fades. Hannah looked a complete wreck. She's doing her stuff, but, God, what a gloom-box. She gets on my nerves, padding about like she's in mourning before he's even gone. I've never understood the thing with Dad, how he can like having her around. She's weird.'

'You could be a bit more sympathetic, Sadie. She loves him and we owe her a lot.' Kate hoped Hannah wouldn't go over the edge, driven by fear and loneliness.

The morning wore on. When her mobile went again and she saw it was Hannah, she shrank inside. The call was like ice on her stomach, surely not yet, not this soon. Coming just after the call from Sadie it had an awful prophetic inevitability about it.

'You asked me to call at the first sign,' Hannah said. 'Doctor Jones was just here. He says your father could slip any day now, he thinks it will be this week.'

'Oh. Oh dear. Thanks for calling—I'll come. I'll stay through the week. You must let me help you however I can.'

Kate's tears stayed where they were, ready to stream, but she held off, conceding the need to be as practical as her sister. Richard, when she called, said she was doing the right thing. He knew now

445

about her promise to her father to find Hannah a discreet new home, and urged her to sort it out fast, in advance of Aidan's last hours. She saw the wisdom of that. Neither of them would be able to cope in the wake of his loss; Kate mourning a beloved father and Hannah a man who seemed, for her, to have been life itself.

*   *   *

'He's slept most of the afternoon,' Hannah said, when Kate arrived at six o'clock that evening. 'He's rested, he'll talk to you for a bit. The morphine helps. Sit with him a while and I'll make something for supper.'

Kate went to his bedside. He looked much as he had done the weekend before. His eyes were focused on her as she approached and with a commanding clarity, like eyes peering in through a letterbox, as though the rest of him was so frail as to be invisible. 'Hi, Dad,' she said, bending to put her lips to his cool head. 'I really missed seeing you this weekend, but it was nice you could see Sadie and the children.'

'Joseph's a good little chap. He's got his maternal grandmother's eyes.' Aidan sighed. 'Don't give me that look, Katie,' he said. 'Mum was here, as I think you know, but I'm all right. She said she'd just told you all about Ben. It was good she came and we saw each other. I feel more ready to die, more natural about it. We held hands.'

Kate's tears were out of line, unbidden. 'Can I hold your hand too?' she said, with an uncontrollably trembling lip. 'I need to hold onto something and you're nearest—and dearest. Oh,

446

Dad, I love you so much.'

He laid his other hand on top of hers and closed his eyes. Kate sat still, willing him to open them again, to give her a little more time. His hands felt so chilled. She couldn't swallow, fought back the lump; this was the last of his life, his adventurous, big-hearted, brave, heart-torn, all too eventful life.

'Lovely Kate,' he said, before slowly opening his eyes again. 'Tell me, how's Richard? Looking after you, I hope. He said he would.'

'He cooks well, that's a good start. I'm having a baby, Dad. He's happy about it, he wanted me to, but he's never talked about marriage.'

'A baby, Katie, that's wonderful. I like hearing that. Sometimes marriage is too tidy. He's stuck with responsibilities, don't let it bug you so much.'

But it did. Kate longed to say how insecure she felt, how unsettled; loving Richard obsessively, wanting too much in return. She saw Aidan's eyes were flickering and tried to shut out thoughts about commitment and focus on keeping him close.

'I do like knowing about the baby,' he murmured hazily. 'It's your birthday this week, isn't it? Richard's present to you—I want you to celebrate.'

'And yours next week, too!' She wished she hadn't said that and hurtled on. 'If it's a boy, Dad, it's definitely going to be Aidan. I don't know about girls' names, but I just have a hunch it's a boy.'

'Aidan's old-fangled, an out-of-date name, you'd hardly be thanked. Make it his middle name if you like, I wouldn't mind that, up on my little cloud,' he mumbled, slightly slurring the words.

His eyes rolled inwards then, as with a faint, and slowly closed. He was very still. Kate ran to the kitchen for Hannah. 'Can you come, his hands are

447

so cold—he is breathing, isn't he?'

'It's the morphine,' Hannah said efficiently. 'He slips off for a bit. We'll have our supper in here, on trays. I've been doing that, never leaving him for long.'

Kate was tense and it felt too soon after arriving to raise difficult issues of the future with her. They had the meal then she spoke to Richard and called Donna as well. She had a reason to drive over and see Donna, and Hannah suggested early in the morning would be best. 'Your father's very in and out and you can sit with him for the rest of the day. I'll call you back if need be.'

Kate asked about keeping an eye in the night and suspected, when Hannah inclined her head towards the sofa, that she'd been snatching no more than short naps for weeks. She was physically, mentally, emotionally, drained and exhausted. Hannah needed help, Kate thought, if she was ever going to pick up the pieces and hang on to life.

*   *   *

Donna was a good listener and Kate tested her skills of absorption to the limit. She told her about Rachel's long relationship with Ben, gave the inside gen, most of it, on the Spencer saga raging on; said she was pregnant and Richard's daughter was too. 'Christ, what a basinful,' Donna said eventually, when Kate drew breath. 'You lost Harry, you're over that. Your mother's gone missing, no father, no wedding bells; you're in charge of your life now, you're going to have to make it work. How d'you think you'll handle it? What's first on the list?'

'Ask my one true friend for a particular piece of

448

help.'

'Already? Don't I get a break?'

'The opposite: this is a seriously big ask. I want you to take in Hannah who's lived with Dad and who Richard thinks is on the run. I've yet to find out what she's running from, but I promised Dad . . . She needs a safe home.'

'Go on.'

Kate explained as much as she could. 'She's wonderful with animals, a great cook, a dedicated nurse, unobtrusive . . . And you could have an exhibition at last, Donna. Hannah would hold the fort. I'd even loan you back Harry's painting for it.'

'It sounds to me, if she's loved and looked after Aidan all this time, she could do with a man to mother. I might try and find her a nice sheep farmer in time—one or two going spare on Romney Marsh. She can hole up here for a while. We'll see how it goes. It does depend a bit on what her problem is. You'd better find out what it's all about first. I might change my mind yet.'

'Can I help with the exhibition that I'm going to make you have? I'm out of a job, after all, good at publicity and Harry taught me well, I know my stuff.'

'No quid pro quos for Hannah, but I'll bear it in mind. You get back now, I don't need thanks.'

Kate sat with her father all day. The doctor came. After he'd left, Aidan raised a limp hand and pointed to his desk that was close to his bed in the sitting room. She saw two large manila envelopes resting on the blotter. 'Hannah got those out for me,' he mumbled faintly. 'The thick one has the memoir I've been writing; it might make a book, I don't know . . . if you can knock it into shape . . .'

His eyes closed. Kate wished he'd told her what to do with the other envelope. She sat on, hoping he'd manage a few more words before he slept.

She saw his lids flicker upwards a moment and she leaned down close. 'What about the other envelope, Dad?'

'That one's . . . for Mum . . . I know she's gone, she told me about it when she was here, but . . . one day . . . she'll be back. It's poems, stories of our happy times . . .'

Kate sat on by his bedside and by evening sensed a change; less flickering of his eyes.

'He's all right for tonight,' Hannah said, coming in with scrambled eggs. 'He'll sleep.' She handed Kate a plate of food and sat down. She ate little, she was chalk-white.

'I'm afraid, Hannah,' Kate said, looking at her, 'this is the moment you're really going to have to tell me everything.'

She didn't prevaricate. She rested her plate, stared straight at Kate and began. 'I was living in Lebanon. A nursing job had come up. I was young, late twenties, having a good time then I started seeing a Lebanese businessman. He was in his forties, free, rich and quite glamorous. I fell pregnant and he asked me to marry him. My parents refused to come to the wedding, they thought I was a disgrace. I'm an only child and they had me late. I don't think they ever felt much love, I was in the way of their library books and a quiet life.'

'Did he treat you badly?'

'I was a virtual prisoner in his house. It was a big high-walled house with servants and gardens, out in the leafy suburbs. He had my passport and he refused to let me work. He was cruel in clever ways, he never left bruises. Things like twisting arms and bending fingers back, near suffocation, threats— plain old cruelty. He'd lock me in the bedroom, call me a filthy little British whore and come in later to debase and abuse me.'

'And the baby,' Kate asked, staring at the pallid, exhausted woman, sitting stiffly in an armchair with her supper-tray, 'do you have a child?'

'I'd deliberately fallen down a marble staircase, hoping for some bruises, thinking it might help. No one believed much was wrong, you see. I don't know what he'd felt about the baby, but he was worse, if anything, after the miscarriage. I didn't care, hating him as much as I did. And the hatred grew. One night after he'd turned the key to lock me in I thought of that old trick of pushing out the key onto a piece of paper and drawing it back in underneath the door. It worked. It didn't even make much noise falling on the paper and I could unlock the door from the inside. He was in his study across the hall.'

Kate dreaded to think of Hannah's state of mind and what she was about to hear.

'I can move very quietly,' Hannah said, 'and the television was on, he hadn't heard me. He was at his safe and to see him standing in front of it, notes in neat piles, even my passport—I could see my British passport—was too much. I picked up a heavy brass ball from a tray on a hall table and threw it at the back of his head.'

'Did you kill him?'

'I almost wish I had. It would have needed a bit more force. I'm a nurse, I knew he was knocked out, unconscious, but not dead. He'd fallen on a thick rug and hadn't made much sound and it was eleven at night. No servants came running. I took my passport, feeling very calm, and went round the garden to the servants' entrance and found to my great good luck, the chauffeur was up, outside, smoking in the garden. I'd stolen money out of the safe and flashed notes in his face, telling him I needed an all-night chemist and that everyone was sleeping. Once we were out through the locked main gates I won him over and he took me to the airport.'

'Your husband didn't come round in time to chase after you?'

'No. Planes leave around midnight from that part of the world and I had my other bit of luck, the last available seat on a flight just leaving. It was a time of political convulsions in the country, one of many, and the airport was chaos. Who knows? Maybe he was glad to be shot of me, maybe he'd had a heart attack, but he didn't turn up. I thought I'd be picked up when I arrived in England. Six years on, though, I'm still waiting for the police to find me.

'My stolen money had covered the ticket, but I had barely forty pounds. Your father was at the airport. He asked if I was lost and he was friendly. I opened up and asked his advice on where in the country, not London, I might find work. I had some notion that the police might track me down more easily in London and I knew living costs would be high. I didn't see how I could nurse without giving personal details and being easily traced. Your father said he was off abroad, but only overnight, and he'd help me find a job on his return.

'That's how I came to be in Rye. I took a coach, slept in a bus station and he was true to his word,

452

he met me at the time and place he'd mentioned. Kindness like that,' she said, 'after living through months of cruelty, was a strange and mystical land.'

Hannah cried then. The tears rolled silently down her blanched cheeks while Kate told her about Donna, her house and animals and her generosity. It was obviously an extraordinary relief to Hannah, but her wet eyes were trained on the skeletal sleeping face of her dying patient whom they both loved.

'Millie's pining already,' she said suddenly. 'Can I bring her with me? Your father wanted it.' Kate looked over to his wretched little dog, lying head on outstretched paws at his feet. She lifted her snout, eyed her master and gave an audible canine sigh.

Millie's fate had been miles from Kate's radar. 'I'll call Donna and ask,' she said. 'She has all those animals, she can't mind one more, even monstrous little Millie.'

She had to hold the phone away from her ear. 'That appalling Jack Russell? No and no! I'm not having a beastly, snappy short-legged bitch chasing my peacocks and baby lambs. Think again, Katie, remember I've been to meet your father—and that squitty little monster. Tough titty on that one.'

Hannah had heard the explosion. 'Millie would hate the competition,' she said seriously, 'she's a sensitive little dog.'

'I'd never have guessed!' Kate snorted. She called Sadie in desperation; her sister was more apologetic but no dice. Ru would *hate* it and it would upset her horse. Richard said Millie was too free with her fangs; he wouldn't trust her with the baby, she'd wolf it down in two jealous bites.

Kate cursed. But Hannah loved Millie by

association and she felt softer-hearted, looking at the little dog, prostrate, pining, and tried to summon up inspiration. It was nine o'clock, not too late, she thought, to call whiskery old Mrs Brooks. She was widowed, free of her pint-sized husband Sidney Brooks, the vile runt, and living alone in her cottage by the sea. Kate wanted to tie up ends; she looked up her phone number and called.

'My father's dying, Mrs Brooks,' she said, 'and Millie, his dog, is pining. Have you room in your heart to give her a home? She's a small dog, not a big eater . . .'

Mrs Brooks's heart was as stout as she herself used to be. 'Aw, your poor dear father—and the poor luvvie, too. I love dogs, she'll be company. She can race along the beach; it's right out the back, and chase Mrs Rabin's Siamese. I hate that woman—and her cat.'

*　　　*　　　*

Aidan didn't wake up. It was crushingly unexpected, for all her knowledge of its nearness. Kate had been feeling life was tidying itself, finding drawers and compartments, and now suddenly all her emotions were scattered again like clothes on the floor. The shock of his coma was immense. An ache of panic clawed at her gut and reached right into her heart. He couldn't just go without giving her a last chance, a look, a smile; he couldn't do that to her . . .

She sat by his bedside watching his chest, for breathing, for any faint signs of life. She talked to him, urgently, 'Dad, Dad, I love you, open your eyes, say a last word, whisper you can hear me. They say hearing is the last thing to go . . .' She kept

454

it up, whispering in his ear, touching his face, saying she would give him a wonderful grandchild. She said she'd look for the baby tawny owl he'd been hoping for; she would always try and make him proud; lead an adventurous life as he had done, not be set in her ways.

She was staring into his still-closed face when he suddenly opened his eyes. They locked into hers, wide, staring; she thought he was still comatose, but his lips moved. She strained to hear, stroking his hand, saying she loved him. 'Going now,' she fancied he said. And then he was gone.

Kate laid her head on his chest and let out a long slow sigh. Then she called to Hannah.

*   *   *

The weeks slipped by. Kate mourned her father with a yearning heart. She woke up in the early hours a few times and shed silent tears in the cloak of darkness. She felt a soaring sadness at the cruelty of an illness that could eat into a previously fit strong man, yet his death had strengthened her in its way; she felt a new maturity. The knocks of his life were, in a way, the joys of her mother's, twists of fate that all went into the mix; she felt she'd learned more compassion and, in a deeper way, what love was all about.

Her baby began to show. Kate spent time with Richard's mother, moving her into the flat, warming her up to helping and supporting Polly; they found an easy wavelength and she knew a good friendship had been formed.

She had her last day at the office, and, shortly afterwards, a fit of nerves about the future. They were irrational. Donna was interested in having an exhibition, and the editor of a weekly news magazine seemed in the market for a column on the London art scene. Kate had worked on Aidan's memoir and just taken it to a publisher; she was on tenterhooks to hear what they thought. She had plenty to plan and talk about and keep her occupied.

Her wobbly mood must have shown. Richard suggested they went out to dinner; he had things to say, future plans. And as well as seeing the back of Dan, which, he thought, was cause for cheer, they had never celebrated her birthday, he said, which he'd been waiting to do for some time.

They went to a tucked-away Italian restaurant off King's Road, a regular of theirs where they had a warm welcome from the elderly, chubby owner. So much was in walking distance from where they lived, but change was about to happen, the business of finding buyers, selling their two properties and moving. The agent they were in touch with, a spruce young man, always in a snappy suit and tie, said both properties were 'highly desirable' and it should be no problem at all.

'I went to see a couple of houses in Shepherds Bush this afternoon,' Richard said, once they'd settled in and ordered scallops and pasta. 'I want you to come and look at them tomorrow. Good gardens and great potential for opening up and modernizing. It's not a bad corner of London, the right side for Sadie, handy for work. It'll knock off a few traffic jams, and be great for Polly, too. She can almost walk to school. Ed can be in and out much more easily as well, living in two homes, being with us more.'

456

Kate thought, by the same token, how much closer they'd be to Eleanor and that Richard could be in and out more easily too. She said, carefully, 'It's the right side of London for your mother as well, while she's living in my flat.'

'She wants to buy it,' Richard said. 'She loves London and wants to be near us all.'

It was early July, still light when they finished the meal and wandered home, Richard with one hand in his pocket, the other reaching for Kate's. They walked down quiet residential backstreets where richly-stocked gardens threw arching branches over their high protective walls. The scent of rose blooms was intoxicating. Scents mingled. The air was mellow, hung with silence, privacy, the confidence of belonging.

Richard heaved a sigh. He tugged on Kate's hand, slowing then stopping under the foliage of an over-flowing mulberry tree. 'I can't marry you, Katie,' he said, turning with a grave, warm smile. 'You know the problems with Eleanor. It would be a risk, it might push her over. I can't believe my luck in having you and our child on the way, and for that very reason I feel I owe Eleanor all the more.'

Kate looked into his eyes feeling fearfulness and uncertainty, an unreadable sense of premonition.

'But will you do something for me?' Richard said. 'Will you stop wearing Harry's wedding ring?' He reached back into his pocket, standing facing her on the pavement, and brought out a small box. 'This ring,' he said, opening the box, 'is in place of the one I want you to stop wearing. It's an eternity ring, which is quite a long time, after all. It should see us through.'

Kate felt a wash of calm, a peaceful feeling of

457

rightness. 'In the early days,' she said, 'when you moved so fast, I found myself saying, "one small step at a time". Well now,' she paused to lick and moisten her finger to make it easier to slip off Harry's ring, 'you seem to think we have all the time in the world!' She managed to pull off the ring and handed it to Richard. 'Can you keep charge of this one? Put it away in a drawer or something?'

He took it with a smile and swapped over the rings, slipping the box with her old wedding ring in it back into his pocket. She held out her finger. 'I hope it fits,' he said, taking hold of her hand and sliding on the circle of tiny diamonds.

'And I hope you'll always get things this right,' Kate said. 'It fits perfectly.'